Searching For The Evergreen Man

A Tall Tale told by
Dean Barton

Llumina Press

ISBN: 1-932047-23-9
Printed in the United States of America

Dedicated to Darrell, my brother, whose trail through the woods has been steep and rocky with many sharp switchbacks. An old timbertramp once said that those are the trails that break out into the clear high places.

Gratitude

The following people *asked* me for the unfinished manuscript. They were willing to work their way through a work in progress and give me their feedback in return. Definitely a good trade – for me. I can never thank them enough. But I'll try. Much thanks to: Elena Barton, my wife, for her honest and pointed criticism. Jack DeVore, the first reader, whose positive comments and insight gave me encouragement and direction when I most needed it. I owe him more than I can say. Bob Collins, fellow lover of the written thought, for his keen interest and intense scrutiny. I owe him a big Cuban cigar. Darcy, our grown-up kid and my energetic cheerleader, for her feedback and loving support. Janice Cornelius, my cousin, for her interest, her love, and for being here for me. Ed Barton, my father, for his reading and encouragement. Manuel Robledo, my hay-bucking buddy, for his expression of disappointment because he couldn't finish reading it. At the time, Book Two was hopelessly lost deep in ethereal cyberspace. A year or two later, to the rescue came Dana Bishop, old friend and mouse magician. A click and then another click and then another, and presto . . .

To Elizabeth Lyon, author, teacher, editor, and my guide early on in the work, for her professional criticism.

To these great old woodsmen, some still here and some headed off to other necks of the big woods: my father, Ed Barton, logging contractor; cousin, Wayne Kennedy, gyppo logger extraordinaire; uncle, Harris Kennedy, long-time logger and fellow tall tale teller; grandfather and timberjack, Newton Barton; Bill Abbey, great timberjack and my dad's partner at the saw; Whitey, the side boss; Milo, the cat skinner; Blackie, another side boss; Shorty, good all-round logger; Orville, top-notch diesel mechanic; Ken Blatchley, head mechanic and truck boss -- and to those bull whackers turned log truckers: brother Glenn Barton; uncle Houston Barton; cousin Gerald Barton; cousin Tide Cartwright; old-time mentor Bob Gosser -- all double clutchers par excellence. Thanks for your examples and the evergreen memories in my soul, and to some of you, for the use of your names in my fiction. I must admit that the heroes in the tale are composites of you all.

To a certain old apple tree: We've both sprouted and cast away a million leaves or more since that sunny day in spring when I took a seat beneath your limbs and scribbled down those first timid words of the outline for this novel. I'm finished with mine; I hope you're still sprouting yours.

To that loveable couple -- those two timbertramps, Ed and Jane: Special thanks and all my love for bearing me in the woods and rearing me there.

To Mike Bush, long-time camping companion, for the photograph on the back cover.

To the Eugene Library and Llumina Press.

Acknowledgements

The forest grows up out of its humus. In much the same way, this tale could not have grown to anywhere near as tall as it is without those tellers, both tall and literal, who preceded it. To a tall degree, this work grew out of the fertile leavings of the following:

Glory Days of Logging by Ralph W. Andrews

Timberbeast by William N Roy

Deadfall by James Lemonds

This was Logging by Ralph W Andrews.

Grisdale, Last of the Logging Camps by Dave Jones

Stories of Western Loggers by Ted Goodwin

Big Timber; Big Men by Carol J. Lind

An Oregon Logging Pioneer by Joyce Hall

Timber! The Bygone Life of the Northwoods Lumberjack by Lucy F. Miele

The Loggers by Richard L. Williams

When Timber Stood Tall by Joseph H. Pierre

Epitaph for the Giants; the story of the Tillamook Burn by J. Larry Kemp

Searching for the Evergreen Man is about the logger culture, not logging techniques. The listed works are well written, descriptive, and if a picture truly says a thousand words, most are voluminous. For the person hungry to pursue the techniques, culture, and history of the timberjack world right up to and including the modern logger, these books and others like them are sure to satisfy the largest appetite.

Author's Note

Searching for the Evergreen Man is a tall tale; all events and characters in the novel are imaginary fiction, except for one: the spirit of the place is imaginary, but not what I'd call fiction. She's called by many names; in this tale she's "the forest queen." The camp at Lava Lake was real and appeared pretty much as described. The red wolf was real and still is. His colorful name was dropped when the tall tale masters finally died off and the literalists took over. The big woods were also real, but beyond description.

My apologies to the timberjack culture if I took too many liberties with its actual history. My excuse is that I only wanted to tell it taller. If the tale falls short, then all shortcomings are entirely my own.

Contents

Lil' ladies, laddies 'n gents, there be some shrouded shores
Where the whistle punk whistles an' the donkey roars.
So let's spread our wings an' stretch 'em now that we can,
An' like birds of a feather we'll fly off together
To a far-distant land, and go t':
SEARCHING FOR THE EVERGREEN MAN

BOOK ONE
Abe's Tale

Along the northern coast,
Just back from the rock-bound shore and caves,
In the saline air from the sea in the Mendocino country,
With the surge for base and accompaniment low and hoarse,
I heard the mighty tree Its death-chant chanting;
The choppers heard not, the camp shanties echoed not,
The quick ear'd teamsters and chain and jack-screw men heard not,
As the wood spirits came from their haunts of a thousand years to join the refrain,
But in my soul I plainly heard.

- Walt Whitman

So our human life but dies down to its root, and still puts forth its green blade to
eternity.

- Henry David Thoreau

Abe's tale honors those men and women who have fallen fighting the red wolf.
Fire warriors one and all, they forever remain
the great knights of the forest queen.

Chapter 1 The Days Of Woody Leather

April 1923, somewhere west of the Rockies and east of the Cascades . . .

The rails clicked and rattled, and the car trembled. Mountains rose up and fell away again like thoughts. Endless snow fields were shrinking, slipping down the steep slopes, gathering age blotches, giving up ground to a warm youthful rain. Meandering rain-filled rivers streaked the window, merged, spread into deltas, and then flowed off the edge of the glass into some unseen ocean. The sun had set into that ocean and the glass was growing dark. All those rocky gorges, sagebrush, and stunted junipers passing by outside the window could be downright disconcerting to an incipient timberjack looking for trees—big trees. But he wasn't looking. What Henry was seeing as he peered out the window was his own reflection staring back at himself, as if he were peering at this endless vacant land through his own vague image. The image peered back, caught him eye to eye . . . dim reflections.

Henry stared into the window, studying the image in the glass. Those eyes in there were weary, or disappointed, maybe. He wasn't certain. Stubble on the chin and cheeks reminded him of the Rockies: steep slopes covered with pale-headed stumps but not much else, any more. *Jesus sake, there's endless miles of sagebrush out there. Traded stumps for sage. Just look at it, not a tree in sight, nothing but brush, brush everywhere. Should've headed due north, I suppose . . . Montana, or Alberta—maybe the Ketchikan country.*

He saw one other thing through the window: his hair, unnoticed by him until now, had turned from the color of butter to the color of buttermilk. But how could he have known? He hadn't looked into a mirror since Peppa died. Used to primp back then. But he had forgotten the shape of his own face and didn't much give a damn. Still, twenty-three years old seemed too young to have white hair. At least it was still thick.

The face in the window contorted itself into a grimace and seemed to say: *"Here you go again. You're running away from home just like when you left the farm in Oklahoma, just skedaddled, didn't even say goodbye. Who'll tend the graves? Peppa loved flowers, you know."*

Yeah, she always wore one in her hair . . . Christamighty it hurt when I lost her.

"You deserved to lose her. You should have married Peppa, shouldn't have let the Professor talk you out of it. If you'd married her, you could've taken her away from that riffraff-infested hellhole. She'd be alive now and right here warming you up, not laying back there in that cold grave with a hole in her heart."

But I thought the Professor would be pleased. I thought he loved Peppa, too.

"He probably did, but not the same way you loved her. Remember what he said when you came bearing the happy news?"

I had mostly forgotten. That was a while back.

"Then, let me keep your memory fresh. He said to you: 'Do what? Marry Peppa? Bloody Jesus, my boy! You have gone bonkers! She's a whore and you're a swamper. What kind of life can you make out of that? You do not own enough substance between the two of you to cohere and bond you together. It will make a breeder out of you, Henry, and god knows the world has enough of those. Just look at them, lad. Most live like a couple of screwed-out dogs, stuck and tangled up and looking one another in the eye and each blaming the other for their predicament. Both are dreading the sharp pain of the separation that's soon to occur and they will most likely snap at each other when it happens. All this work for nothing . . . no . . . absolutely not! I shall hear no more of it.'

"You started to protest, to tell of mutual love and make a play upon his sympathy, but you were always meek in the face of the Professor. Remember? So, there you stood, dumb-tongued and squirming. Then, the old boy put his foot down. He said: 'Well, it's going to be her or me, and I'm not done with you, yet. You're far from being finished and your very words concerning this marriage nonsense prove it. Obviously, our work together is not complete, and I have my obligations, you know. You might say I have one more job to do, and I'm no shirker. As for you: you have your agreement with me, and like me, you're no shirker. I have taught you that much, I hope.'

"And that was that; the Professor held you in his will like a cur in a leg trap— as if you don't remember."

How could I forget? I couldn't take a stand against the Professor. I was sorta indentured to him, you know.

"Well, by god, this time you should've stood up for yourself, because if you had, Peppa would still be alive. She'd have been with you when it happened and not alone and vulnerable."

Henry wanted to ignore this dialogue. He tried to look through the image into the darkness beyond the window. Seemed he and his image couldn't get along. But everything he was saying, everything Henry heard, was true. Damned ironic: now it was the Professor and Peppa who were together, lying together, back there in that graveyard. Those graves were the only things in his entire life he'd hated to leave behind.

The image was persistent. He was back, slowly shaking his head, sad-eyed, clicking his tongue, and saying: *"Damn it all, Henry, she was so all alone, must have died so lonely. You should've been together. The people you loved needed you. The Professor, he died all alone, too, remember? It was a thick, muggy day—hot as hell. Air's thin at seven thousand feet; a hard working man has to gulp for a breath. An old man can't gulp so deep. There was more water there to breathe than air. You knew he was ailing. You should've taken that turn, skidded in that string of logs, should've made that last round for him. An old man like that needs someone to . . ."*

"Shoo! Shoo! Go away, you silly bloke! Glass for brains, a man can't take a turn for another man. Round and round goes a man, spinning like a top—never stops. Nasty, nasty, out the window with ye! Go away now, and leave Henry alone!"

Henry jerked back his head and looked around for the source of these words that shattered his melancholy.

"There, that's better. Pesky damned doppelganger, bloody-good riddance to him."

Henry knew the speaker—knew him well. Last he knew he was in his grave. But evidently he was on the loose again. The Professor was a sly old fox—take more than death to keep him down.

"Hello there, Henry, didn't mean to startle you that way. That other chap's who I was after. Don't let that bloke in the glass influence you so much, Henry. For Christ's sake cheer up, lad! Kick your ghosts; boot them with your calks. You're shoveling out your own grave one morbid thought at a time. It's a deeper colder grave than the one I lay in, believe me. Always remember what I told you? If I said it once I said it a dozen times: the man who does not believe in magic is not a realist and neither is the man who does. Magic's a *fact* that's as real as your ass."

It was that unmistakable British clip of the Professor's—felt good to hear that clip, once again.

"Thought you left me back there in my grave, didn't you? Nothing there but worms and those worms are poor company, Henry, compared to you. I'm still not finished with you, not quite yet. And like I like to say: I have my obligations, you know. So I thought I'd tag along, if you don't mind. The past clings to the shirttails of the present, you know."

The words Henry was hearing seemed to condense into a mist of tiny particles, and the particles congealed into the man, and there sat the Professor, in the seat right across from Henry. Next to him, double chin resting against his breast, snoring the miles away, sat a blabber-mouthed lumber salesman, on his way back to Eugene from a business trip to Albuquerque. He'd drawn one too many sips from a flask he carried in his pocket and so he wasn't listening in, couldn't, even if he had his wits about him; the Professor's words weren't for meant for him. Henry wasn't even surprised that he wasn't surprised to see his old mentor sitting there. He'd learned over six years before not to be caught off guard by any thing the Professor did or said. Reality is magical, after all—surprising too.

Well, a man can't have better company than the Professor, even if he is a crazy old coot, and dead to boot.

"Mind your thoughts, Henry. I am not so old, and I'm getting younger all the time. And I'm considerably more than just a coot. But I'm not here to discuss me; there's nothing left to say about me. But just look at you, some magician you are. You're peering blank-eyed into your black hat, Henry. Besides gloomy, it's empty as holy hell in there. Put a perky little cottontail in it then reach in and pull him out. Have you ever wondered why a magician pulls a rabbit out of his hat and not a lion or a dodo bird? The rabbit's a nibbler, nibbles when and where he can, loves greens, puts nary a thought into his belly, but he's food for almost everything that eats. He's humble and he listens. He's one of the best listeners there is, that's why his ears are so big. That fluffy tail of his is his heart. He flaunts it, holds it tall, and waves it at the hawks. The rabbit knows the hawk can't eat his tail. It's too light; it would ball up in the craw.

"Turn your rabbit loose. He'll poke his tail up, give it a wiggle or two, and then look to see where it points. And off he'll hop, straight into the tall timber. His tail will lead him there. You'll see. Keep your eye on that tail and follow the rabbit in. But, be sure to take a double-headed axe along. Put an edge to it. You'll need it in there, if you're going to learn what the big woods have to teach you."

The Professor made a short forward gesture of his hand, following the motion of a running rabbit. He said: "Maybe he'll even lead you all the way to the evergreen man." Saying this, he breathed out a heavy sigh, as though burdened, or weary. But the Professor was never burdened for long. As though to lighten up the moment, he said: "Well, I'm getting bloody well gone out of here before this chap next to me comes to his senses and talks me into buying a bloody damn board. As usual, I haven't a pence to pay for it with. These times, I carry only dirt in my pockets—so, you take care till later. See you when we get to where we're going. Remember: two-headed."

Henry started to ask where it was they were going. But before he could speak the Professor shrugged and said: "Hell if I know where. If I knew that, I'd already be there. Right now, I'm following you." As he faded off he chuckled and said: "By the way, as always, Peppa offers her love. She said that's all she ever had to give you and so it's all that she left behind for you. And so I say nothing has changed, except now days you can't go introduce Sir Peter to 'er." And the Professor threw back his head and laughed like a crazy man. Then he was gone. The laughter lingered on.

Henry was alone again and preferred to stay that way. Hopefully, that salesman would keep right on sleeping and not wake up and start in jabbering about lumber grades and the "board market" again. Worms would be better company than him. In the distance, somewhere up the tracks, around a curve or two, Henry heard the train whistle, hooting, hooting like a crazy man, laughing.

The miles rolled away with the darkness. The eastern sky was blushing pink, as the train rolled over the sage flats toward the Cascades. The flats ended where a river valley began; then the train commenced to pull a long grade. The sun was rising, making the air glow, when the sage left off and the stands of Ponderosa Pine suddenly appeared. They stood as regular as colonnades. Their scaly red bark absorbed the glow and appeared to be on fire. Henry had never imagined pines as fine as these. And the royalty of trees, the Douglas fir, lie just over the crest—or so he'd heard.

The train strained its way through curves of the pass, up the shallow slopes, and the sun rose, and the light changed from red to orange and finally to bright silver at the summit of the pass. Then the summit peaked and dropped off, and the straining ceased, and the train entered the realm where the cold Pacific is king of creation. The light turned musky blue, tinged with silver. And Henry saw that he didn't look through this light so much as he peered into it. It didn't glare like the light in the Rockies. It was a heavy light, and deep. Henry got the feeling that he was being lowered into this light, as though into water, and the deeper he went the silver was filtered out in favor of a strange greenish-blue hue, growing, glowing, slowly losing the blue. And there were shadows moving through, fleeting shadows. It seemed a man could drown in this cold light.

Enraptured, Henry was holding his breath. His lungs were straining. He breathed deeply and resurfaced.

Yet, deeper, down deeper, into the realm of the sylvan queen, where Henry didn't go, where the glow is as green as the leaves of spring, winged shadows, more numerous than summer's seeds, the dryads and the hammas, gather together around the man down there, like fish around Neptune, excited! Some whispering, some humming, some singing a little song: "He's come; he's here at last; time to sum the rings; our course completes its cycle; we see the ceaseless circles cease. No time to feel the windy blasts against our mossy backs or the breeze through our wings or snow lying upon our limbs and leaves. No more time for such things. No time to wander through windy waves, the breaths of Earth, to freely fly, for the *witness* arrives to see us die, to return to dirt and sky—to return. He comes alone, as one searching for home."

Slowly, the train descended the western slopes, hugging the banks of a stream. Fed by snowmelt, small creeks tumbled down the canyon sides and merged into the stream. Higher up than the train could go, up there where these little creeks get their start for the downhill run, sparse stands of weathered alpine fir give way to delicate stands of silver fir on the way down the mountain. And the silver fir soon give way to the looming Dougfir, huge in volume and girth and stature and whiskered with moss. It drinks in the light and fills the land with shadow. The stream was now a raging river. He could hear it even through the rumble of steel wheels.

Here, at last, were the trees he'd heard all the tales about. Tall tales, told by men given to exaggeration. *Tall tales . . .?* At first, he'd considered them little more than that, but the stories persisted and many had even come from sober men. Well, he'd come a long way since then just to test those tales and now here they stood, trees taller than the tallest tale. Those men weren't exaggerators; they were tall tale tellers too short for their tales, talking over their heads. There were no words for what he saw from his coach window—only feelings. Feelings of the tree country: country fed by the sun and Pacific rains. And the country feeds the trees in return, and the trees feed the soil and the air in return—reciprocal country. Rich country that gives more than it takes. Country that could only be experienced—and felt.

Suddenly the car closed in on him and seemed to squeeze from all sides. Henry rose, left his seat, walked to the caboose platform and stood in the cool air. He spread his nostrils and sucked in the heavy redolence of firs, mosses, and ferns.

The town was all a-bustle. Broad streets were alive with big black automobiles coming and going and lining the boardwalks. Stretched out and over the busiest intersection in town strung a banner that proclaimed:

←Chamber of Commerce - **WELCOME TO MEDFORD** - Crater Lake →

Henry was looking for information and a good axe, not lakes, so he followed the arrow that pointed west. As luck would have it, he didn't need to search out the Chamber of Commerce office, because he found just what he needed along the boardwalk. Halfway down the block, a sign protruding over the walk read: *Leatherwood's Logger Supply.* He stopped and tried to peer inside, but the glaring window was backed by a dark room, and he saw only himself reflected, along with the busy street behind. The door was wide open, so he left the bright street and entered in through a glowing beam of light. The room was all abuzz with flies. They darted to and fro making gossamer flashes through the light beam, disappearing into the gloominess on either side. The atmosphere waxed dingy and heavy in the scent of canvas and wool. Henry squinted and looked around. Double-headed axes with long handles hanging down like stiff tails lined the bare-wood walls. Above the axes, near the ceiling, hung several old-time oxen yokes. But where was the proprietor?

His given name was John Leatherwood, but now everyone called him Woody. This was a corruption from the old days when the other timberjacks called him as he appeared and named him Woody Leather. In those days he was stronger than wood and tougher than leather, and so Woody Leather fit the bill. He was once a bull puncher who could out punch the meanest bull punchers, and he'd punched out more than a few of those in his time. Yes, those were the days: working the light away, snoring away the night, and brawling all weekend.

In those days, he could spend all day on the end of an axe handle, peeling away bark from a felled redwood or Dougfir, readying them up for the ox team one stroke at a time, stripping them down to the naked wet skin, making them easier to slide down the skid road—that road built over the bones of stumblebums. Then he could out rise the sun and the noseeums on the morning of the next day and do it all again, and the next, and the next, until a string of logs were all slicked and sniped and ready for the skid to the river where the riverhogs waited. He was a tall buck, but those logs were bigger around than he was tall.

Using his strongest four bulls, he'd line the logs up in a row of three, four, or even five, then, like Thor with his hammer, he'd make the forest thunder when he pounded in the fangs of the dogs. He could heft more chain than any other jack, chaining metal dogs to logs, linking up the train for the skid. Then he'd thread the long steel lines through the metal blind eyes, yoking up all the bulls side by side, two by two, nose to tail into two long rows. Those bulls were the strongest animals on Earth and he was the strongest bull whacker. Their hair was slick as satin and shiny in the sun, sheeny in the rain. With muscles bulging, they'd lower their heads and dig in their iron-clad cloven hooves and heave against the pressure of their chained-up yokes, until they sank in up to their hocks. He'd sight down the backs of a dozen or more brutes, thirty thousand pounds of raw surging power, grunting and groaning in long low rumbles, like growling demons from hell. But he was stronger than them, and he growled his curses louder than them. They were like giant puppy dogs in his hands, responsive to his slightest command or sharp prod, and he'd skid those log trains through mud or snow, over rocks, up hill, down hill, and along the greased skid roads that led to the riverbanks. He could put out more and be in better shape at the end of the day than them, and they respected him for it, too.

He wasn't near as big as the trees, but he could whittle 'em down to his size. He could fall 'em, buck 'em, peel 'em, snip 'em, hook 'em, and teamster 'em. Weather was either too wet or too dry, too hot or too cold, not one bit fit for a man, but the incessant bugs thrived in it—the air came alive with 'em. If the noseeums didn't eat you early the mosquitos'd eat you later, and the lice ate the long johns right off a man's ass. Agile-footed as a cat, he never tangled his calks with the brush and stumbled, unless it was in his own black brushy beard.

He was a bull himself, in those days, and he lived with bull-like men. There were plenty of tough ol' bulls of the woods, men so big and mean they'd hang a man by his balls from a high limb and skin the poor bastard alive, so's to listen to him squeal and to show off in front of the crew. In those days everything was out in the open, just like the trees—out there for a man to see and to know and to measure himself against. It was raw close-to-the-bone living.

He could out fight 'em, out eat 'em, out drink 'em, out spit 'em, out work 'em, out snore 'em, out cuss 'em, out womanize 'em, and his tall tales were taller than the tallest, and so they called him Woody Leather.

Oh, those were the days, along the skid roads down in the redwoods or in the big Dougfirs, timberjack days, before the jacks started taking over. Those were the days when there was a relationship between a man and a tree. When a redwood or Dougfir was a challenge to a man's will and moving their sections tested his endurance, his intent, his body, and his life. In those days, the man met the tree one on one. The tree stood its ground and gave way to nothing, except to time—or to a determined man. The man who met the tree one on one became as one with the tree and stood his ground and refused to give way to forces that would uproot him

In those days, men fell many trees and the trees fell many men, and the man who lived to be thirty-five was rare and the tree that lived to be a thousand or more was common. And the man who came to know the tree became humble like the tree. And the man who survived the woods had skin like bark and muscles like knots and a disposition that was as alive and as pliable as wood and his heart ran his length. He grew quiet in wisdom. It rained in spring; it snowed in winter; the shade was cool in summer. *His* company was the man he talked to or drank with or the woman he laid down with. When it was his day to die, he gave his spirit up to the damp Chinook wind and covered his body with a blanket of humus, and he dozed off to sleep in peace. That man was the timberjack, and in those days there were many timberjacks. Those were the days of innocence, when a man didn't want anything, because a man can only want what he doesn't have. A timberjack doesn't need to want anything. A timberjack owns his double-headed axe, a good pair of well-greased cork boots, and the shirt on his back. What else is not his to want?

Oh yes, those were the days, but they were over for him. They were long gone, and they ended all too soon and all too painfully quick, and they didn't last nearly long enough.

Now, for a name, just plain old Woody would have to do. He was once a giant, but muscle gave way to fat, timberjack to shopkeeper, vitality to pain, gusto to dreamless nights where there was no way to lie that didn't hurt. Now, some of his old oxen yoke hung from the wall of his shop as mementos of those bygone days—the days of Woody Leather

Those were the times: times alive. Now he sensed some sort of finality—and not his own either; he could feel that. This was something smelled in the wind of the times: time's ending, or perhaps the ending of a time, because time consists of the great things in it, that fill it, consume it. They leave time behind. These days, timberjacks were as rare as the Sequoia and there were few left to tell the old tales. Those old tales helped to keep a man grounded and there was a whole lot more truth in them than they sounded. A man only needed to listen, keep his heart light and not be so damned serious about life or death or a single doomed thing in between. These days, there was a hidden thing, furtive and lurking, sucking on the woods like a sapsucker, growing, getting fatter, eating every last thing it can digest. It can digest men. Heavy hearts are its tidbits. A particular kind of evil was moving into the woods, coming, coming on, gathering force, yoking men like ox, goading them with its greed stick, while it waited for its overseer to arrive and crack the whip. It's a big-bellied-glutton-of-a-thing that herds men up, fattens them on insecurity, and then eats them alive. Why, it would hang its head in utter defeat if people weren't so damned serious and ignored its lies and poked a little fun at it every now and then. But these days, nobody even wanted to talk about it, much less poke fun at it. Who would listen? These new fellas weren't timberjacks, didn't have the grit or the guts for it. For the most part they were pretty damned sappy-hearted. Hell, there wasn't a tall tale teller among the lot worth his salt.

Timberjacks didn't use machines; timberjacks used the raw muscle God gave them to use. These newcomers needed their machines, and the woods were the worse off for it, too. And for sure, so were the men. A machine comes and goes and leaves with no time to claim. A machine doesn't know time. A machine can't tell time, because a machine doesn't live for a single moment. A machine never has its day. Never creates a single memory it can call its own. Unlike a man, on the day that it's done a machine will be less than it was on the day that it began. But the machine men say: "It's good for production." But then, who the hell listens to machine men? Certainly not a timberjack. A timberjack listens to the tellings that fill his days with tall tales about lies and life and Truth. And so a timberjack becomes his own production.

Woody loved his inventory: the wool coats, cotton shirts, wide suspenders for broad shoulders, calk boots for sure feet, wool socks, canvas pants, rubber rain gear, felt hats, canvas hats, watch caps, tin pants, axes, crosscut saws, sledge hammers, peaveys, wooden mallets for driving in the dogs (though few of these were sold any more), and all the rest of the paraphernalia. But more than any of this, he loved the young men who came in to buy all the stuff, because they told him what he longed to hear. From them he heard all about the logging shows: who was where and who wasn't anywhere any more. And to those who cared to listen he told his old stories in return. So, he knew the top gyppos: which ones paid the best and those who didn't pay at all, where to get the best grub and where to get poisoned. But now, he was just a big fat shopkeeper, dispenser of clothes and equipment, and dispenser of information about the big woods to anyone who inquired, and he was this because it was as close as he could come to being what he had once been—a timberjack.

Chapter 2   The Last Timberjack

Today, on this unseasonably hot day, Woody ignored his pain and bent over some unopened boxes in the storage room of the shop. He'd procrastinated long enough, and now there was some heavy work to do, although this was about as heavy as it got any more. The wedges, axes, and peaveys hauled in the day before were packed in wooden crates. As he worked the top slats loose with a crowbar, copious streams of sweat ran down his face into his thick salt-and-pepper beard and off the tip of his nose to splatter against the box tops. His beard and hair were wet with it, and his shirt stuck to his back. This was nothing new—it didn't have to be hot or sultry to make him sweat; he sweat on cold dry days as well. Long ago pain had robbed him of his vitality and muscle and turned him into fat and fat sweats.

Woody peered at the sweat. He watched it fall and break apart in the thin dust of one of the crates and sink into stains, which, similar to his moments, began to fast fade away. "Damn it all anyhow," he muttered as he reached for the rag hanging from his hip pocket, pulled it free, and wiped his face and neck. "Someday I'll just up and sweat myself into a big puddle."

Footsteps against the wood floor of the store caught Woody's attention. He was glad of it, too; he'd rather talk than work any old day. He pulled his can out of his back pocket, pinched out a wad, and used his thumb to stuff it in good and tight, way back in there where the jaw ties in to the cheek bone. He patted it a couple of times with his tongue, taking the rough edge off. Still holding the crowbar, he entered the store and squinted against the glare at the shadowy form that blocked the doorway. "Can I help ya," he said, savoring the first sweet runny drops from his fresh wad of Copenhagen, greasing up his talker.

"Maybe," came the reply. "I'm after some information. Figured I might find it in a logger's supply. I'm looking for work. And I need the necessary equipment. I especially need an axe."

Though he still faced a black form against the glare, the voice Woody heard was mellow but firm and spoke with the finesse of an educated man, even sounded sorta foreign. The words rolled out slowly but clipped their ends a little bit. Beads of sweat trickled into the corners of Woody's eyes, causing them to burn. He wiped his face with his rag.

"Hell-blasted heat," he said. "Shouldn't be this hot this time of the year. Next week it'll prob'ly ice over. Step out of the light so's I can see ya. Like to see the man I'm talkin' to."

Henry did as told and stepped toward a wall on which were suspended an assortment of axes. "I need a good axe. Have any worth a man's money over here?"

Now Woody could see the man, and he *knew* him in an instant. There used to be a lot of them like him in this part of the big woods, but now they were as scarce as white robins. All he needed was a team of bulls; everything else fit the mold perfectly. Over a shoulder was slung a canvass duffel bag. A pair of well-used corkies, tied together by their rawhide laces, hung around his neck like a necklace made up of two huge black pearls. Black suspenders crisscrossed a gray cotton shirt and held up denim pants. He carried the trademark of a woodsman: though young, his hands were thick and hard, permanently work-swollen from gripping saws and axe handles and pulling on cable and chain. Those hands could crush rocks. But it was the eyes . . . pale blue and deep . . . but more . . . a certain look to the eyes . . . those eyes . . . unmistakable . . . deep, and lonely eyes . . . a tad bit sad . . . only a timberjack can know. And for a moment, so brief and fleeting, it was as though Woody peered into his own eyes, when his eyes were the eyes of a timberjack.

In that moment, an owl was hooting the night away. The sky was turning steel-gray. Overcast was coming down, creeping through, filling all the empty spaces with thick drizzle. Woody felt the bite of pre-dawn air, and the hairs on his back stiffened. He smelled pitch, and he heard the grunts of the brutes. His calks were soaked and gripped his legs like bear traps. Rain beat upon his shoulders, but he didn't care. He saw the giant wave splashes the logs heaved up when they rolled into the river.

There's a certain sense, an inside sense, a knowing sense when a man simply knows and the knowing is enough. Everyone has it right along with the sense of taste or of fear or of love, but only a few know about it and can see it and recognize it when it kicks in. Very few can kick *it* in. It's fleeting and hard to catch, easier to ignore. It kicked in with such powerful presence right now that Woody couldn't have ignored it if he wanted to. In a moment's knowing, he saw that here stood his kin and that nothing short of time stood between them, and he looked into the mirror of his own longings. Right here, into his store had entered the man who was destined to become the last timberjack. He knew that for a fact because he himself was closing the page on those times. So here he stood, looking for information and a good axe. Boy, had he come to the right place! He knew exactly *who* and *what* the man was looking for. And just in the nick of time, too—funny how that works—downright magical . . .

By gawd, if this wasn't an invitation to join a shindy then there was no such thing. Just goes to show that the angel of fate is merciful as well as timely and will smile on an old man, if he prays long enough. Right now, the unseasonable heat didn't matter; the sweat didn't even matter, nor the pain. Suddenly, he felt light-hearted and carefree, as though he'd just tossed a burden and was free to begin an adventure. A single moment can contain a grand adventure, when time is precious.

"What kind of axe ya got in mind?" said Woody.

"A good one," came the reply.

"Only kind I got. Good for what, choppin' kindlin'?"

"Well, yes, that and a few redwoods to boot."

"Oh, a few redwoods, you say now . . . Ever took an axe to one o' them reddies before?"

"Can't say yes."

Henry lifted a hefty, long-handled, double-headed axe off the wall and examined it. He ran his hand along the handle and tested the blade with a light touch of his fingers. He liked its feel and balance.

It was perfectly obvious to Woody, by the casual way that Henry held the axe, how his fingers stroked the smooth handle, how he flexed his wrists to feel the heft, and how he eyed its razor-sharp lips, that this man knew axes. In the hands of a man such as this an axe such as this one comes to life and blossoms like a flower. He watched the axe bloom under the spell of those hands that held it and those steel-gray eyes that massaged it as though it were a pretty woman ready for stroking. Yes, only a timberjack holds an axe this way, and only a timberjack knows a timberjack. This one was top rate, no doubt about it.

Henry said: "How much money is it?"

Woody said: "Three bucks."

Henry gave the axe another look-over and was just about to buy it, when Woody said: "I see you got a good eye for quality. That's a mighty good axe, an' it'll serve ya long an' well. But you look to me like a man who can appreciate the best an' can use it right." Woody didn't wait for a reply. He turned on his heels and entered the storeroom, leaving Henry to wait out front. He opened a dusty old trunk and lifted out a long narrow oaken box. Then he returned to the store and handed the box to Henry. "Step over into the light an' take a gander at what's in here. Ain't she a dandy?"

Henry opened the box and in it reclined a double-lipped western-style axe upon a bed of folded linen. He gently lifted the axe out. Its heads were ruby-red and its lips glittered like polished silver. The handle caught the light and absorbed it. It resembled tight-grained oak with a pinkish cast and was etched with dark meandering lines and swirls, as though fashioned from the flowing heart of a knot. This wood contained depth. It was obviously as stout as steel, but there was a give to the touch and it felt slightly moist. The waist was long and slender with a subtle flair. Thick shoulders supported the heads. No matter which way he held it, the axe held its balance.

He examined the axe for a long while, spellbound. Woody stood off his shoulder and a little behind, as a good shopkeeper should while the customer browses. He slowly shook his head in amazement as he silently listened to the *knowing* voice in there, saying: *Wouldn't ya just know it, he don't even know what the hell he is, where in hell he is, or where in the hell he's goin'. He's standing as close to a timberjack as a jack can stand an' he ain't figgerd it out. But he will. Oh yes, he most certainly will 'cause he ain't on his way into the big woods for nothin'; the woods are gonna show 'im whatever it is they expect from 'im.*

Searching for words to say, Henry could only think of one: *"Beautiful."* Hearing that, Woody smiled broadly. Henry shook off the spell and looked directly at Woody, caught his smile, smiled back, and their eyes locked, and that moment forever clinched their friendship.

Woody spoke: "That's the last of a kind ya got there. She's a beauty, awright. An' she'll be faithful to hands that hold her right. She was handmade by an ol' timberjack I knew, who got banged up like me so went to makin' axes. Said he made them out of special wood an' alloys. Only he himself knew where he got the makin's from an' how he put 'em together, an' he kept it a big secret right down into the grave. Only thing I know about 'em is, that handle came out of a myrtle wood knot harder'n steel, and you never have to oil 'er. She sweats her own oils, and sips in the oil from yer hands; that's all she needs to live. It took the ol' boy a long while to make one, so he only made twenty or so of 'em before he died a few years back. He was as particular about who he sold one to as if he was sellin' his soul. Couldn't of showed you a better axe for what ya say ya need one for. See that head?" Henry eyed the head. "That head ain't painted; I mean that steel *is* red. Rumor had it the maker of 'em poured his own blood into 'em and if you chip one of these she'll bleed. Now turn her edgewise an' eye her straight on."

Henry split his eyeball with one of the blades and studied the axe, wondering exactly what it was he should be looking for.

Woody studied Henry studying the axe. He knew Henry had never eyed such an axe as this. Very few men ever had. He said: "Flairs out real nice an' pretty, don't she? She's powerful through her middle. Now eye down the other edge." Henry obeyed and cut his sight with the opposite blade. "Perfect ain't she? Lots o' swing in them hips. Ya get *two* hefty broads in *one* with that double-header. You keep them blades honed an' out o' the dirt an' they'll never chip, an' she'll keep her edge longer than you or me ever will." Woody paused, slowly shaking his head. "Funny thing," he said, "I was plannin' to keep that one all to m'self, then changed my mind. Figgerd somethin' as fine as that shouldn't go unused. Her place is in the big woods, right up to the end." Woody eyed the axe in silence for a long moment, and then he smiled and said: "Look at 'er. Funny how words can miss the mark. 'Double-headed' they say . . . . My eyes tell me she's one-headed with two lips. She can take a quick lick, comin' or goin'."

"She's mighty fine," said Henry, knowing full well that he couldn't afford her.

Said Woody: "What'll she set you back yer a wonderin', ain't ya? It's a tough one: how to price somethin' ya don't really own – owns itself. I'm gonna make it easy on m'self. You can have 'er for what I got 'er for when she didn't have no place else to go. Gimme a buck an' she goes with you to where she belongs.

"One dollar?" Henry couldn't believe the price. The axe was worth many times a dollar. Surely the man misquoted. "That sounds a might low," he said.

"Yep. One buck. Take 'er, or leave 'er. I ain't a gonna raise that price no matter how hard you try to jew me up."

"Sold."

"She comes with a lifetime guarantee, an' that information you said ya needed. What's been yer experience?"

"Well, I've done some farming, fell corn with a broad axe," kidded Henry, not knowing quite yet that he had entered the rare presence of a foremost kidder in the world.

"What did ya yell when they fell—comber?" said Woody, grinning real big. "If farmin's what yer after, you done come about a hundred miles or so out o' yer way. Plenty of that down in California. You can go down there an' go to pickin' cotton."

"I don't have a cotton sack, anyway, and it's obvious you don't sell them, so it looks as though I'll have to stick to cutting. I've certainly cut my share, and that's what I'm here to do now."

"Cuttin', huh?" Woody rubbed his chin and scratched himself through his beard, as though thinking down deep in his attempt to pull out the information he had promised. "So yer a cutter, are ya? Think I can help you out." He grinned and walked over to a dusty old roll-top desk in the corner, opened a drawer, and pulled out a pair of scissors. "Here," he said, "trade ya these for the axe. I hear they might be hirin' down at Lulu's Beauty Parlor. I'd be dyein' them corkies pink before I applied if I was you. But I hear the good pay for that sorta thing is down in San Francisco."

Woody acted as serious as if he were reciting gospel, but Henry could see the faint beginnings of a grin through all that beard. Woody was telling him something that he already knew well: that to fit in with any group or culture it's best to study the nomenclature and how to apply its syntax, to study it well and learn it fast. While you're at it, spare your words and choose *those* carefully— and keep your ears wide open. He smiled and held out the axe to Woody. "Okay, you got yourself a trade," he said, "but I'm going to bypass Lulu's place and use those scissors to cut down redwoods."

"Gonna fall the reddies, eh?" Woody handed him the scissors and took the axe. "These scissors won't do too good for them," he said. "Them things are too big an' tough for these. Lookin' atcha, though, I'd guess you could fall yer share of Dougfir with em, an' the loggers up in the gyppo camps are in bad need for experienced fallers. They might giggle a little bit though when they see you acomin' with yer scissors." Saying this he handed Henry back the axe and made a show of looking him over. "Don't tell me now, lemme guess. Yer from the Rockies, because what we call fallers they call cutters, an' from the width of yer suspenders an' the color of the dirt between them calks, I'd say Colorada."

"Nope. You're way off; New Mexico."

"New Mexico, is it? Well, I never woulda guessed. You look like a Colorada man to me. Came through Colorada m'self some time in the last century, lost track of when. We all come here from somewhere else, ya know."

Henry admired the old man's keen wit and perception. There he stood in the beam of light, sweating like an old war horse, slouchy and unkempt in big baggy pants that scuffed the floor behind his heels, and shoes worn out before their time by heavy limping weight. Still, he held his back straight, squared his shoulders, and thrust up his chin to look Henry in the eye.

Then Woody commenced to laugh. It started in his eyes and traveled down his cheeks, causing his beard to toss. Then some of it flowed out his mouth in rumbling guffaws and the rest traveled on down his chest and into his stomach, causing the fat to roll and his baggy pants to quiver and shake.

Amused, Henry could only stand and smile. As something big that gets to going and builds inertia, it took Woody a while to stop. Then he looked at Henry and in all seriousness said: "Well what's it gonna be? Looks to me like ya can't decide 'tween cuttin' hair at Lulu's or fallin' trees in the woods."

Now Henry realized what it was that tickled Woody's funny bone so much, because here he stood with his hefty new axe in one hand and the pair of scissors in the other. He looked down first at the axe, then the scissors, then the axe, then the scissors again, mocking indecisiveness, and Woody started to laugh again. It came on the same way as before, and Woody held his side as though to keep from bursting. But the fact was that Woody didn't have a rib that wasn't broken in several places and the expression, *it only hurts when I laugh*, was a literal one.

Woody's laughter turned out to be infectious, and now Henry caught the tickle bug. It made his sides heave and poured out his mouth in guffaws to rival those of Woody himself. It turned his face pink and came out his eyes and dribbled down his cheeks. God, it felt good to laugh like this! He wondered when it was that he had last laughed right out loud. It had been some time back, long before Peppa died, for sure, but he couldn't remember when. It occurred to him that laughter wasn't something that grows on rock farms and it wasn't a thing that the Professor taught, and that somewhere, a long time ago, he'd forgotten it, if he'd ever known it at all. Somehow, he got the impression that now he stood in the company of the ultimate practitioner of the art of laughing.

He handed Woody the scissors. "Don't want to dye my corkies pink," he said, through his laughter.

Woody introduced himself. "Name's John Leatherwood, but call me Woody. That's what my friends call me. Now for that information yer after:"

According to Woody the best money was to be made in the Coast Range down toward Crescent City or up in the area of Marshfield, because that was where the year-round work was to be had. There was too much snow in the Cascades, and a man would go hungry trying to eat snow all winter when he was snowed out of work. All that high Cascade snow came down as lots of mighty wet rain in the Coast Range. This meant year-round but miserable work in those low-lying but steep and tangled coastal hills. Those mountains were crawling with gyppo logging camps, full of old-timers as well as late-arrivals, and the gyppos were all begging like hungry pups for experienced loggers. In fact, Henry didn't have to purchase a thing, except possibly clothing, because the gyppo would have all the tools of the trade needed to do the job. What they wanted was muscle and stamina—and will.

Henry bought the clothing Woody recommended. Woody said that the clothes he already owned would do fine for summer work but were intended for a dryer climate than he was headed for and that some stiff canvass pants, a wool shirt, a wool coat, a light canvass coat, heavy wool socks, and, of course, sturdy calks such as Henry already owned, were a must.

"The wool'l keep you warm even when yer wet, an' the tin pants are to cover the cotton ones when it rains. Here, hold them up with these purty red s'penders; the s'penders are on the house."

Woody handed him some red extra-wide suspenders, made heavy and stout. Now Henry was ready and set to dress the part because, here again, they both had learned a social truth: right up there with verbalizing the right nomenclature, a man had better know how to dress for the role. It's best to go in as unobtrusively as possible.

"Which way should a man set out, Woody, and who should he ask for?"

"If a man ain't never seen them redwoods, he should, so I'd say to head off down that way. Lots of fellas to ask fer, but I'd look up one Slim Hoskings who's the best damned gyppo in these parts. Last I heard he was down towards Crescent City aloggin' along the Smith."

"Then I'm Crescent City bound, Woody my friend, and I sure do thank you for the information."

Henry was set to go. Crescent City had a good ring to it, and he knew it sat on the rim of the Pacific. He made to toss his sack over his shoulder, but Woody had no intentions of letting him get away this easy.

"Got a way to get down there? Train ends here, ya know."

"I've done a good deal of walking in my day, Woody, and I'm not too good for it now."

"Yes, I'm sure you have. But why walk when a man can ride? Besides that, you got a lot more to carry now, what with all the junk ya just bought here," said Woody with a chuckle. "My cousin Hack is headin' down that way. He's in town awhorin'. Do ya good to wait around and catch a ride with him."

"Well, I don't know . . . don't want to impose. I mean, he might not like the idea. May need his rest after a hard time whorin' and all."

Woody laughed. "Rest, ya say? You're right about the hard time. Hell, ol' Hack's famous for his hard timer. He's got a *big* reputation, if you know what I mean. That Hack's a real pistol. When these gals hear word he's hit town they all come arunnin' an' Hack takes 'em on all at once. Out lasts 'em all, I hear. I once asked him what that was like bein' all tangled up with a bunch o' gals like that. He said there was lots of twistin', turnin', legs awrapin', and wet and oozy slitherin' for position. 'Prob'ly a whole lot like crawlin' into a can of night crawlers,' he said."

Still, Henry was hesitant. "He might not be in the mood for more company, having just had so much of it."

But Woody assured him: "Oh he'll like the idea of havin' you fer company alright, because I'll tell him to. An' besides, when he lays eyes on ya he'll be too chicken to turn ya down anyhow. Way I figger it, you'll need a place to stay till ol' Hack shows up, an' the place he'll show up is my house. He always drops by to fill his big belly before he heads out o' town.

Woody looked at Henry to see if he approved of the idea of laying over a few days at his house. He tried to read his expression and was encouraged by what he saw when Henry smiled.

How could Henry say no? The last time he'd been approached by a total stranger, an old man, offering him hospitality was when he met the Professor. So he said the obvious: "I'd appreciate that." He watched Woody's eyes light up as though someone just lit his wick.

"What say I close this place up an' buy my only customer of the day a beer?"

"You're on," said Henry, "but I buy."

"No, I buy, 'cause I said it first," argued Woody

"Then I buy next, because I said it second," countered Henry.

So, in the little tavern in the middle of the next block, just down from Leatherwood's Logger Supply, they both took turns buying beers and had a gala of a time.

Woody was the hit of the bar. He was obviously one of the town celebrities, if not in worth of office then in the status and stature of his nature. Everyone present made it a point to spend at least a few moments in his company. It was outright competition for his attention. It was also obvious that he relished the affection. But, still, there was something missing. It was as though a certain spark in Woody dulled just a tiny bit when he talked to the others, but when he addressed Henry he sparked up. Henry felt that Woody was a very lonely man, in spite of his popularity. He suspected he was the first person that Woody had found to talk with in a long while.

"Worked in the woods m'self," said Woody over a beer. "Log rolled on me an' broke my bones long time ago. She was a big one. It took them two days an' three nights to git her off me. Couldn't just roll her off, ya know; had to jerry rig a hoist an' lift her up just 'nuff to get the weight off, an' then dig under me. Ever'one thought I was gonna be dead fer sure—includin' me. 'Boy's,' I said, 'I'll give ya my ox, my axe, an' my ass can belong to the devil if'n ya untangle me from this here fix.' They removed their hats an' shook their heads. 'Thanks for the ox,' said one. 'Been needin' a good axe,' I heard somebody say. They roused a preacher outa the nearest whorehouse who said some prayers over me, an' then told me to go to hell contented, assuring me that he himself'd take special good care of my lady friends." Woody paused and dropped his eyes and quietly said: "But they got me out. So, that day I gave up my ox an' my axe, but got to keep my ass, 'cause it weren't worth a blowed-over pecker pole afterwards, not to the devil, not to nobody. Had to leave the big woods. Been livin' in the jack pines ever since."

"Living in the jack pines?" said Henry, not getting Woody's drift.

Woody set his jaw and looked at Henry for a long moment. A serious expression covered his face; he seemed close to being angry. "Yeah, you know—

them poor little pines in those thickets? Those pines ain't very big to begin with, and then they go and make things harder on themselves by growin' all bunched up an' crowded together, competin' like crazy for their little bit o' dirt an' sunlight. You know what I mean—company men. This company, that company, don't matter which company or what they name it, it's all the same damned company and the same damned mill. Same thing. An' that thing'll strip yer soul from you like it was dry bark and heave it into the slash pile. But that's not the worries of it, 'cause a man can cover his ass and he can even hide his soul from the cursed devil if he uses the brain he was given. If he don't, who the hell cares about him? But this country here can't hide. These trees are bare-ass naked with nothin' fer cover. An' these damnable companies just don't give a frigger's hoot about nothin' except the bottom line on the balance sheet." Woody stretched his neck, pursed his lips, turned his head, and: "Ptuu!" let fly a big wad over into the brass spittoon—as though making a point. "They're gettin' richer an' richer an' bigger an' bigger, an' the richer they get the bigger they want to be—so's they can get richer."

Woody gulped his beer and emptied the glass. "All this talk's dryin' out my whistle," he said. "Tell ya this, forest's gonna run out. It can't take the pressure forever. I've lived longer than you, an' I know this neck of the woods an' it sure ain't what it used to be. I can see it goin'—goin' faster all the time. Them companies are gonna hightail it outa here when it's all used up, an' when they do they're gonna leave a lot of nameless jacks scattered behind, along with some smolderin' mills—them mills have a way of burnin' down, ya know, when the bottom line don't show good."

Woody dropped his eyes to his empty mug. "Little jacks, they're all just little jacks. Poor buggers." Then he perked up again, smiled, and said: "But a man can't go gettin' despondent, can he? Go out there into the big woods and do what you have to do, Henry, but keep yer ass covered and guard yer soul. I envy you. Miss the woods somethin' terrible, I do. Go back this very minute if I could. Do okay with that store, but gets real borin'. Can't get no exercise, so I just turn t' fat." He looked at Henry with a grin and a twinkle in his eye. "O' course all this beer don't help none, but what the hell, eh? Way I see it, we gotta be close to heaven right now, 'cause they say there ain't no beer in hell." He ordered two more.

Henry related his horse-logging experience in the Rockies, and Woody was keenly interested. "Percherons," said Woody, as though playing with the word on his tongue. "Never seen any of 'em. Heard stories about 'em, though. Heard they be fine horses, mighty fine . . ."

"Hup, boys. Step 'em up and get along. Hup, hup, step 'em up." Oh, the time of the mind; it flows like a river, blows like the wind. Like a microbe on a particle, a man is here and then he's gone again. A familiar little song floats in and fills the room. Woody's words fall away like an echo, and then even Woody's gone, and the table, and the beer mugs. There's only Henry—and the

time of the mind. Henry leans against his axe, pulls his bandanna from his back pocket, removes his hat, and wipes the perspiration from his brow. The Professor is clicking his tongue, shaking the reins. He speaks softly, sings: *"Hup, Cleo; hup, hup, Dapple; you too, Greylemantle. Come along, boys. Last turn of the day—last half of the last round to do. Don't be lazy, you."* It's a muggy day in the high Rockies. Sun's been beating down relentlessly. A thunderstorm just passed through, but its rain didn't cool things off a bit, just watered down the air – thick heavy air—like breathing goo. *"Come along, boys. Step lively."* The horses become one horse. They lower their heads in perfect unison and strain against the drag. Muscles gather and bulge. There's not a lazy one in the bunch. The train of logs gathers slack, skids across the floorboards of the saloon, maneuvers through the tables like a slinky snake through a field of stumps.

The Professor glances at Henry, grins, winks, and gives the come-on-along sign with his head. Henry follows. Once again, he's traipsing along behind the Professor, stretching his legs to step in his footsteps, watching him handle the high-spirited horses as delicately as if they were plucked flowers tied together at the stems with strings of yarn—don't disturb a petal; let them show their colors. They're all lathered up—smell as sweet as flowers. His fingers are light on the reins, his wrists relaxed. The horses feel his will, and they give without knowing—they're one. And the Professor sings: *"Hup, boys, hup, hup. Last turn. Hay at the end of the day. Hup, hup, hay for ye, one and all."*

Henry follows, ready to lend a hand, if needed. More than anything he wants to be a teamster, just like the Professor.

But for the Professor this is the last turn of a lifetime—the end of this round. But Henry was out of step. He wasn't there, wasn't following, when it happened, when it ended. *Damn! Damn! Never even got a chance to say goodbye. I'll forever regret that. I'll always wish . . .*

"Give us two more, an' fill 'em full."

Time of the clock: Woody was back, ordering another round. The Professor was gone; horses filled with spirit were mugs full of beer. Henry lifted a mug, looked into the beer and took a long deep sip. Then he said: "That they are, Woody, sure-footed, sure-minded. Fine horses, they truly are. They're faithful and they'll work their hearts out for the man who treats them right." *Hell, the Professor treated them like equals.*

"Know whatcha mean. Mostly used bulls out here when I was in it. Horses came later. But some mule-headed fellers got it in their heads to try mules. That's what dragged the log over me, was a team of damned ol' stubborn mules. Dang it all, anyhow. I was a bull-whacker not a blasted muleskinner. Them mules wouldn't pull when a man wanted 'em to an' they'd pull when he didn't want. Then one day they pulled when I didn't want, an' I weren't ready . . . well, what the hell, never could communicate with damned stupid mules. Loved m' bulls."

Woody quickly tipped his mug and took another big gulp of beer. He wiped the foam away from his mouth with his cuff, dropped his eyes to his mug, and stared into his beer for a long moment. He said: "My own damned fault, gettin' downhill from them that a way. Knew better, too, an' that's the thing, Henry: these are powerful big trees, these big ol' redwoods an' Dougfirs. When they fall, they sound like thunder. An' these here slopes are as steep as a cow's face. If one of them logs gets to rollin' an' a man stands in its way it sure won't stop for 'im. Flatten him out like a cow turd is what it'll do. You be careful out there so's not to end up like ya see sittin' right here. Believe it or not, I'm one of the lucky ones. Lots of mighty good fellers are a turnin' up moss under them trees." Woody paused and looked off. "Way too many," he whispered. Then he looked Henry in the eye and said: "Somethin' else I should warn you about. There's a certain breed o' man who comes to these woods to hide out, hidin' from unspeakable doin's. There's not a lot of 'em but a few's far more'n enough. The son of a bitch'll chop off your balls and feed 'em to his bull, and you won't even know he plans to do it till after he's taken his axe to ya. If one of these trees don't getcha some gawddamned maverick bull of the woods just might. Keep yer eyes open on both sides. Be ready to jump and be ready to duck. But whatever you do, don't turn yer tail on him; don't expose your balls. Lose sight of him and he's gotcha by the tail, like yer a downside-up possum. Then all you can do is grin an' squeal.

And so here, once again, some old man in a brand new place singled Henry out for special attention. Henry wondered what it was about him that warranted this consideration. And so, his second education began several beers into the evening and continued on for many more before the frothy-lipped night was over. The first teacher had taught the letters of learning, the thoughts of the poets, and the arts of being; but this teacher taught the big woods and made it seem as if the big woods had a unique being of their own, separate and inseparable from their inhabitants. Woody's way of teaching was an art in itself.

Woody started his endless stories about muscle and brawn, love and hate, babies born, and men killed in the old timberjack camps that he had known so well. He was a master of the tall tale and laced his stories with comic wit and subtle rhymes, like the one about the last time anybody saw Tall Paul.:

"Let me tell ya how it was. It weren't always like it is now in this here neck of the big woods. Was a time when it was a whole lot different: trees were bigger, mountains were higher, and snow fell deeper. It all changed back in ninety-two. A blizzard was blowin' snow through the air, so soft an' fine, pilin' it up high as a bull's behind. Some say it was the same damned snow that turned ol' Babe bright blue. Then it rained in the night, but the sun rose cold as ice. It froze that snow stiff as a dead man's pecker. It was real timberjack weather—good ground for skiddin' 'em in. They turned the bulls outa their pens an' hoisted 'em up in the air, hung 'em up there, an' filed the cleats on the shoes as sharp as pins. An' they turned up their collars and pulled down their hats and greased up their calks, 'cause these men were timberjacks.

"Two crews an' two teams set out that day to earn their pay and to earn their hay the only way they knew how: bringin' in the timber. They had a big one fell. They'd worked like men in hell to lay that giant on the ground. They lost count of the days it took to saw her down. Many a time the clock'd made its round.

"Mid mornin' it started to snow again, quiet as a sleepin' baby's breath, no wind.

"They lined up the bulls and drove in the dogs and went to pullin'—but the tree wouldn't go to skiddin'. The only things that did skid were the bulls and the men, and they slid under one another's feet and fell on their asses. Cleats tangled with spikes, sliced though skin and cut the meat on the legs of bulls and men. Bulls bellerd, men hollered, and the blood ran as thick as red molasses on the snow an' down the skid road. But that ol' tree had skid not an inch, an' the men yelled and bitched, and they prodded the bulls, and the bulls heaved and grunted, an' the day passed, an' the night, an' another day, an' another night, an' try as they may, an' try as they might, they just couldn't get that ol' dead tree to go. An' another day an' another night went by. Filled with woe, they cursed hell and they cursed heaven and they cursed their births an' were ready to die sooner than give up the try. They were on the verge of cursing their god and even Earth when in the distance they heard: 'Hellooo . . . !' They cocked their ears and listened. Again: 'Helloo, up the way.'

"'Helloooo, up the way,' they answered back. And then they waited. Soon, to their surprise and total dismay, here came the other crew, that same crew that they'd set out with on that first cold day, in the snow—seemed like so long ago. Seems they'd lost the way down from the way up in all that heavy weather, an' each crew had gone to opposite ends of the tree an' had been pullin' again' one another an' not together. At first they all got riled an' curled their fingers into fists an' them two crews were agonna come to blows. But somebody, a curious feller, put down a tape to see if they had managed to skid that timber. 'One inch!' yelled he and pointed down the skid road in the direction of the river. And so the crew pullin' down thata way let out a hoot an' tossed their hats an' declared themselves the winner." Woody winked as he said: "An' that, my young feller, is how the tug o' war contests began."

Woody tossed back his head and laughed and bottomed-up his mug, and so did Henry. Woody ordered two more. Henry thought the tale was over. But a good tall tale never ends; it only begins. The better ones go on forever.

The laughter faded clean away. The glint in Woody's eye was gone now, his voice was lower, the tone subdued. The tiny froth bubbles in his beard silently popped away one by one as he continued his tale.

"Well, them timberjacks got it into their heads that all that hard work would some day leave 'em as dead as skinned polecats. 'For us this tree is way too big,' they said. So here's what they did: they sawed that mighty timber up into short little sections all strung out in a line so's to haul 'em in one at a time an' then deck 'em up into a cold-dead cold deck. Said they: 'We know it ain't our way, but it be easy pay, an' what the heck, ever'body knows that time's money.' An then they danced a little jig, singin': 'Oh yes, money, gotta get my money, money for my honey who's awaitin' for me down in the town away from these trees.'

"But, right then, out of the woods stepped an' old timberjack who was as tall as the tallest timber, carryin' his fallin' axe, as sharp as its blades could bear. The jig stopped on the spot and frose right there. The singin' hushed. Somebody said: 'Take a look, each an' all, I think it be ol' Tall Paul.' Another said: 'Naa, I think he be dead. Ain't him a'tall.' Said yet another, a crusty ol' jack: 'Hell's fire, boys, ol' Paul never *was* an' he ain't *now*, neither. That man's an apparition, nothin' but an ambition of yer imagination.'

"Whoever he was—or whatever—he made 'em all shiver and he made 'em each quiver, when he said: 'I see yer all ashakin' in yer boots. That's 'cause yer all in cahoots.' He looked 'round about, seemed in a dither, and said: 'You galoots'll be in hell next.' An' then he sadly shook his head, as he said: 'See, ya went an' made it easy on yerselves, by Jesus. Ya bucked that timber up into itty bitty pieces. Ya made it easy on yer backs. *Easy* just ain't in the timberjack syntax. It appears ya can't be called timberjacks no longer. So from here on out yer gonna be called loggers. I ain't agonna claim ya as being my kin, 'cause ya ain't much more than green-chain men. Next thing ya know ya'll employ a machine to yard 'em in. She'll sure go out fast then. Ya'll fill yer nose with smoke and deafen yer ears; ya'll all go broke an' shorten yer years; ya'll look around ya at no livin' wet lover to 'rouse ya, but at only dead dry lumber to house ya. Yer agonna lose the good cool shade that the good Lord made. Yer alettin' other men tell ya what to do, so way too soon ya'll be all through, 'cause yer a doin' it fer *them* an' not fer you.

"And then that timberjack, that ol' prophet, stepped down offa that stump. He said not another word. He walked off into the timber. The last thing them fellers saw of him was his rump. An' though some few jacks still listen fer him, he's never again been seen nor heard."

Woody sighed and slowly shook his head, as though to signal that he was done with his tale.

But there's more than a rhyme in a tall tale teller's tale; there's a moral flowing through it, down deep in it, like a subterranean creek. It's there for the thirsty man who's willing to probe. A good ear is like a divining rod. A great tall tale teller eyes his listener and he knows a good witcher when he sees one—the ears are twitching.

Woody watched Henry's ears twitch and bend in his direction, and so he welled his moral and capped his tale.

Said Woody: "As they watched the old timberjack go, one of them loggers said to his partner: 'Gawdamn, it's hard to see the times end. I'd as soon die on the spot as to give up what's lost. But hell, I wouldn't trade one single sliver of my imagination for all the ruminations of the past. So let's just remember, good ol' friend, this here time we're astandin' in. As fer all the rest, I suspect that it meets its end right here where we begin.'"

The sparkle returned to Woody's eyes, and he said: "Buck yer timber, Henry. Buck it as clean ya can, because they buck it, these days, an' probably they always have."

This tale was but one of many. Each story led into another as easy as water flows downhill—as easy as a tree turns green in the springtime. Old characters took on new, if exaggerated, life. At first, Henry thought the stories would never end; then he was afraid they would. However, to his delight, they went on and on through the night, till the saloon disgorged its flow of beer-soused clients and turned out its lights. Then Woody and Henry piled into Woody's old jalopy and headed out of town. Woody told his tales while he shifted gears. Henry was hard pressed to determine if Woody made all those stories up on the spot or if he held them in his head. Reality and fiction lost their distinctions in his little myths. This simple man was a foremost master of hyperbole. A careless person might take them for fact or as an outright lie. When Woody said that the old-time timberjacks threw their long johns on ant hills so the ants would clean out the lice, Henry didn't know whether he spoke true or tall. Either way, he figured, it was all mighty remarkable.

It was a fair distance from town to Woody's shack. Too far, it seemed, over the rough roads, bouncing along with a tight bladder and a gut full of frothy beer. Obviously, Woody would condescend to work in town, but not live there. It was also obvious that Woody enjoyed playing the role of host. The next morning, Henry ate the best breakfast of pancakes and bacon he had savored in a long while. The pancakes were heavier, the syrup was thicker, the butter was sweeter, and the bacon was fatter. So went the weekend: eating like a timberjack and listening to Woody's never-ending tales. Woody didn't even bother to open his store on Saturday. "If they want me, they know where to find me. Hack should show up on Sunday, so what's another day or two of being lazy," he said.

That evening, feeling loose from home-brewed ale, Woody demonstrated some of the old timberjack jigs that he had danced in his youth, way back in another century. For Woody, it was a rare painless evening of mirth and song. Time-logged memories grew lighter, lifted, and floated off and out across the tossing sea of time and then rose up like mist through the draws and the canyons and the convolutions of his brain, and settled into a rivulet of his mind and gathered in an eddy and swirled around a partially submerged stump. Again he was young, and firm with muscle, and only weighed two hundred and forty-five pounds. The trees were tall and uncrowded and uncountable. They covered the sky. He wore his corkies and cut a rug twenty feet high on a fresh-cut stump, lost somewhere deep in the redwoods, dancing like a long-legged limber-kneed bog bird. He held two mugs full of ale over his head, jigged his feet to the triple-time beat, and twirled around to an old fiddle tune, playing:

Welll, nowww, grab up yer axe 'n go t' choppin'.
Then, head fer the hall 'n go t' rompin'.

An', kick up yer calks 'n go t' stompin'.
Yes'n, dance the night away, lad.

And Woody threw back his head and laughed at the irony of it all, and his laughter mingled with the music, filling up the hall of his mind—standing room only and not much of that. Won'tcha just listen, Woody . . . Gawdamighty, how that fiddle can sing! Yes, listen while you can:

Yes'n, play yer life away, lad.
Play yer life awayyy . . .

Henry sat wide-eyed and grinning with amazement at the huge, decrepit, happy, old timberjack. A feather would outweigh the man's heart.

"Here, you do it now," said Woody, breathing hard and sweating and all wore out but wanting more.

"Naa," answered Henry, feeling ungainly, "I'll just watch you."

Woody sat down, guzzled the two mugs of ale, and started in again on his instructive myths.

Sunday came and went along with Monday morning with no Hack. "Shoulda been here by now," said Woody, seeming a bit concerned. "Maybe Slim gave him Monday off or the lunkhead's just being irresponsible. He'll do that when he thinks he can get away with it. But he can buckle down when he needs to; he has his serious side. Ain't very many people know that about 'im 'cause he never shows it. But what the hell, it's Hack's ass if Slim cans 'im."

Now, even Henry was concerned. "Do you really think he'll get fired," he said.

"Naaa," replied Woody. Serve 'im right if he did. As fer me, I'm self-employed, so I'm gonna skip work fer another day. Only reason I keep that store is for the social. Can't beat the company I got right here right now."

The feeling was completely mutual. "I could grow real lazy here," said Henry, sitting down deeper into his cushioned chair, a cup of coffee in his hand

"Good. Seems to me a man should work hard when he has to, play hard whenever he gets to, an' go to being real lazy all the rest of the time," said Woody.

Around noon, Hack finally showed up. "Runnin' late as usual," according to Woody. Woody and Henry were sitting at the table, bent over plates of pork chops, brown gravy, and sourdough biscuits, when they heard the sound of Hack's automobile pulling the hill and then the sharp slam of a car door.

"Just as I figger'd, right in time for grub an' hungry as a damned mule." Woody got up and went to fetch another plate.

The door suddenly opened and a flash of light flooded through and just as suddenly the light was blocked again. The form of a man filled the door opening. He wore a cotton shirt tucked into heavy black cotton pants that were held up by green suspenders. On his feet were moccasin slippers. A felt hat, similar to a fedora, with the brim pulled down and the crown pushed up into a cone to expedite the shedding of rain, was perched on his head. The family resemblance was remarkable, both in mannerisms and appearance. Hack wasn't just big; he was huge, with the neck of a bull ox, and he had to turn his shoulders slightly to get through the doorway. His face was rounded, and his cheeks were plump and rosy. A ready smile dominated his face, and right now he was sporting an ear-to-ear grin. He carried a little more fat than muscle. He was much younger than Woody, being closer to Henry's age. Henry's first impression was of a giant cherub.

"Howdy, cousin. Bring on the eatins?" bellowed Hack.

Woody was busy at the stove, heaping Hack's plate. "It's all been et up," he said, without even looking over his shoulder. Then, turning: "But we saved ya some scraps." And handing the plate to Hack: "Well, how was the shenanigans?"

Hack took the plate, grinned, and said: "Sorta like crawlin' into a can o' night crawlers."

"Didn't I tell ya," said Woody to Henry.

It was plain to see that these two men loved to poke fun at each other. "You actually ate this poison?" were Hack's first words to Henry, after being introduced.

"You mooch enough of it," Woody interjected

"Yeah, but I done built up an immunity. Poor ol' Henry here'll prob'ly be dead 'afore nightfall."

"Only thing you built up any immunity to is the clap."

"Wish that were the case."

And so went the one-upmanship for a few moments, but Hack was in a hurry and couldn't stay much longer than it took to wolf down three or four plates of pork chops and several ladles of gravy over biscuits.

"Henry's a logger lookin' fer work," said Woody.

"The hell you say. Why'd a man wanna go do a fool thing like look for work? Nuff of that comes along natural." Hack peered up from his plate, looked Henry over, and grinned. "Kinda puny, ain't he? Ain't an ol' slow-footed Okie is he? And ya better not tell me he's a dumb ol' Tarheel."

"Naa, he's a New Mexican."

"Ya don't say," said Hack, feigning surprise. "I'm real glad to hear that, because I always wondered about somethin' an' now I can find out." Then he looked directly at Henry and said: "Henry, does bein' a New Mexican mean that yer a young Mexican, or that you just recently became one of them Mexican fellers?"

Henry was taken in by the question and the serious expression on Hack's face. As he searched his brain for some words, it occurred to him that the man might be something of a block-headed simpleton. Hack chomped away on his mouthful of pork chop and waited for a reply.

Woody came to his rescue. "Either he's joshin' ya, Henry, or the big dummy ain't never heard of New Mexico before, an' I suspect he ain't heard."

"Oh, Woody, you old tattletale! You killjoy, won't even let a man have no fun! An' hell yes, I know all there is to know 'bout the great state of New Mexico. A little whore I met this very weekend told me ever'thing there is to know about it," said Hack with a wink at Henry.

When Hack said this, it flashed through Henry's mind that maybe, by some wild chance, Hack was referring to one the women he'd known back in New Mexico. He heard that most of them headed off west after the mill town got respectable and shut the whorehouse down. "Really?" he blurted. "What's her name?"

Hack grinned, and said: ""Wilma Lei."

It's a big country. The absurdity of thinking he might know a prostitute from out of his past now plying her trade way out here in this little place dawned on Henry. He craved a fresh-old face because it's hard to leave. "Oh . . . I guess I don't know her," he said, feeling sheepish.

Hack steadied his gaze on Henry for a long moment, and then he slowly shook his head. "That's a real shame," he said. Then he grinned and his eyes lit up.

That devil-may-care glint sparking up Hack's eyes told Henry that those weren't the eyes of a simpleton.

Said Hack: "Trouble with whoring is it don't put money in a man's pocket, cleans it all out. Done much loggin'?"

"Yeah, lots of horse logging in the Rockies.

"Well, ain't much of that goin' on in these parts no more. But if you done that you can do this, 'specially if ya can swing an axe an' play a lively harp."

"Thought he might get on with Slim's outfit," said Woody. "Whatcha think?"

"I think no doubt about it," said Hack, rubbing his chin with his thumb and index finger and looking hard at Henry, as though measuring him up, taking inventory. "Why hell, ol' Slim'll kiss me if I show up with this guy."

"Yuuuuk!" exclaimed Woody, as he contorted his face in disgust and wiped his mouth with his sleeve.

"Yeah. Know whatcha mean. It almost makes me sick just to think about gettin' kissed by someone ugly as that."

"No, I meant who'd want to go an' kiss the likes of you? Sooner kiss a waterdog," replied Woody.

Hearing this, Hack put down his empty plate and darted over to Woody with a free-flowing ease that was incredible for a man of his size. The two began to play-jab each other in the ribs while giggling like young schoolmates, all giddy in the pleasure of one another's company. Hack, being the spry one, went to hopping about, making exaggerated moves as if he were a hot-shot boxer, saying: "C'mon, c'mon, c'mon, put 'em up, put 'em up."

After just a little of this, Woody, showing some fatigue, dropped his guard, hung his hands limply at his sides, and let Hack gently punch on him a few times. "Jack Dempsey you ain't never gonna be, so why waste my time on ya? If yer done moochin' grub, I got dishes t' tend to," he said.

"Looks like I'm too tough for ya, so we're off 'n runnin'. Time to get my ass down the track. Got some road to cover." Hack looked at Henry. "Got yer balloon all blowed up?" he said.

Henry nodded.

"Pile 'er in an' we're on our way up the hill."

"My ass or my sack?" Henry said, jokingly. As was the laughter, this humor was catching.

Hack pretended to consider the question then cocked his head and grinned.

"Oh, what the hell, both I guess. Stuff in yer sack probably wouldn't fit me nohow."

"Wouldn't go aroun' yer big ol' butt," said Woody.

Henry tossed his boots and bag into the rumble seat of Hack's shiny-black roadster, then he turned to face Woody. "I can't thank you enough," he said.

"Don't need to thank me, Henry. Just take care an' come by an' see me when yer in these parts."

"I'll be back as soon as I can make it," said Henry. "Then I get to buy *all* the beer."

"That a promise?" said Woody, holding out his hand.

"I'll shake on it," said Henry.

Hack, more serious now, walked over and gave Woody a big but easy bear hug. "Thanks for the chow, cousin," he said.

Woody, returning the hug, said: "Any time, any time, Haskell. But next time, you leave them gals be an' come stay here with me."

"It's a promise."

Woody rolled his eyes. "Sure it is. Sure it is," he said, exaggerating a tone of exasperation. Then he looked at Henry and said: "Henry, I'm old an' yer young, an' old men have got the whiskers. So they get to tell the young ones a thing or two, if'n they think their words might take the steep outa their trail an' level it out some. Fer what it be worth, ya oughta remember them jigs an' practice 'em a lot. Lots o' worse things than knowin' how to cut a timberjack rug, ya know. Seems to me yer a bit heavy-footed. You need to wiggle yer toes ever so often an' limber 'em up some, so ya won't never become no stumble bum. An' this too: I think that if ya slipped in a bit of rhyme ever here an' there it would serve ya well. It'll limber up yer tongue an' ya might even start to have some fun. I'm not tryin' to tell ya how to talk to other men but I suspect that, just like beer, there ain't no rhymin' in hell."

A moment in time flashes by quick as a photon; it's here and gone again before a man can open the shutter of his mind's eye. But, fortunately, often he clicks and captures some of the better ones and stores them in his album of memories. It seems the brightest ones burn their way in whether he knows it or not, shutter closed or shutter open. This moment's image, the expression in Woody's face, his big smile and the shine in his eyes, imprinted itself in Henry's mind as indelibly as if it were a high resolution photograph, taken in the shadowless evening light with the most perfect of lenses and light-sensitive plates.

"Now you two mossy butts go t' gettin', or ol' Slim'll can ya both." Then

Woody handed Hack a pie and said: "Half of this is Henry's."

Hack piled into his seat and surprised Henry with a big loud cowboy: "Yaaahoooo!" That all let out, he said: "Git in an' hang on Henry; we're on our way." Then he looked back at Woody, and said: "Kiss me on the ass, Woody, 'cause that's all yer gonna see of me. I'm a headed down the road to find me a tall tree."

They pulled away. Henry looked back over his shoulder at Woody who was standing in the doorway of his shack, watching them go. Hack's eyes were on the rearview mirror. The mood abruptly changed.

"Poor ol' goat. Gawd, he hates to stay behind. Hard for 'im," said Hack.

"Yeah, I can see that."

"Time was, Henry, when it would o' took me on one an' you on the other jus' to keep his corks greased up."

"I can see that, too."

As it turned out, Henry didn't get to keep his parting promise to Woody, even though he shook on it. It wasn't long after this, when Woody went to dreaming sweet dreams at last, in his painless sleep. His departure came as no surprise to anyone, though it saddened everyone in the big woods. Henry's heart was burdened with that sadness. He'd needed more of Woody; their time together had been cut too short. But the sorrow was soon replaced with a certain kind of gratitude and memorable joy. It was as if Woody had known his days were at their end and replanted his fertile seed in the richness of Henry's heart. Though their time together had been brief, it doesn't take long to plant a seed. Thereafter, it seemed to Henry that Woody's presence was strong within him and growing as sure and as stout as a redwood. He never passed through another day without warm thoughts of the worn-out old timberjack; and often, when he gazed upon a giant Dougfir or sniffed the breeze or heard the sounds of owls or woodpeckers, it would be as though an eerie sensation settled over him, and Woody Leather was present, too, looking at that tree and sniffing the evergreens and listening to those birds.

Chapter 3 Somewhere, the Other Side of Remote

Hack had been quiet, too quiet, seemed to have something on his mind. He turned his head and spit a wad of used-up snuff out the window. Then he looked over at Henry, grinned, eyed him over, grinned again, then looked back down the road and said: "Ol' Slim pays five fifty a day, which is about as good as she gets 'round here. Gotta say the food's good, an' Slim *will* pay ya. That's a lot more than most of these ol' boys will do."

"Sounds okay to me, as long as you're certain I can hire on," said Henry.

"I'm certain," Hack said, nodding his head.

Henry was impressed with the gentle majesty of the country. He was riding through a wide valley, laying north-south, grass greened up by spring rains and flowers in the pastures. Low mountains rolled in from two sides. Off to the east stood snowy solitary peaks. It was the kind of beauty that could make a man forget his cares if not his loneliness; it's easy to feel lonely in bigness.

"These mountains are a lot different from the Rockies," said Henry.

"Oh yeah, how's that?"

"Well, from a distance, the Rockies look more like a crosscut saw turned tooth-edge up. They're jagged and sharp. These roll along nice and easy-like and then make a giant leap, sorta like wolf fangs.

"Oh," said Hack with a distant gaze, as he worked on the mental picture. "Boy, I'd sure like to see them Rockies. I hear they're really somethin' to look at."

"That, they certainly are." Saying this, Henry's mind drifted for a moment to far away east of this place, to a time when he lay in his bed and dreamed about going to the Rockies, which were somewhere way out west from there. He suddenly realized that those same Rockies were a long way back behind him now, and a sense of vast distance stirred his heart, and he felt a slight blush of nostalgia and loss. He'd left a lot of himself between here and there. "But they don't have trees like these have," he added.

"Oh yeah. What kinda trees they got?"

"Smaller."

Both men settled back and watched the miles roll by for a while. Finally Hack broke the silence: "What job you got in mind doin', Henry?"

"Don't know. Any suggestions?

"Well, I got me a purdy good idea what you'll get put to doin'." Saying this, he threw Henry a quick glance along with a sly smile.

"What's that?" Henry could see that Hack was leading up to something, and he was curious about what it was

"You done much fallin'?"

"Plenty."

"Are ya good at it?"

"If I must say so myself."

"I take that fer a yes, an' that's good because I've a feelin' that ya better be."

There was that silly grin again, like a goad stick, prodding a slow bull. Hack was egging him on. "You don't say," said Henry. "Can you say what it was that caused that feeling to come over you all of a sudden?"

"Oh, you'll see, maybe. Can't say fer sure, but I've got me a feelin' that yer a gonna be meetin' up with a feller called Abe, real soon-like—yessir, soon."

No doubt about it, he was being goaded. He said: "Oh, is that a fact? And just who is this Abe?"

"Abe's just Abe. Last name's Biddle, or some such. No one pays much attention to last names around here. Ever'body in these parts knows Abe or knows about him. Tell all kind of stories about him. Told a few m'self. More'n a few bulls have tried to take him on—take him apart. Know what I mean?

"Yeah, I've got a pretty good idea what you're saying. You one of them?

Hack threw back his head and belly laughed. Then he said: "Me take on Abe? No way! I wanna live to see another day. Collect my pay an' go an' play." And he laughed again real loud, while shaking his head. Then he looked back down the road, and said: "Among other things, he's one hell of a logger, tell ya that."

Hack settled back down and was quiet, apparently concentrating on his driving. But Henry saw that same sly grin, creeping in again. "So what are you getting at, Hack?"

"Not gettin', speculatin'. Just by lookin' atcha, I'd speculate that yer headed to be a faller. Hope you're handy with a harp."

"Well, like I said, I have no qualms about that. Played more than one."

"Oh, we'll *see* purdy soon. Yessir, we'll see." Now Hack added a chuckle to his grin.

This furtive speech of Hack's was meant to tease him and pique his curiosity, and it was succeeding, but thanks to the Professor, he'd learned to welcome a sense of mystery into his life. He turned his attention away and stared out the window for a few moments. Mountains were falling away behind them. Everything falls away: trees, mountains, men, women, moments, memories, even stars they say—all ticked away by the relentless ticking of the clock during *clock time*. Leave the clock behind with time for a few ticks, Henry, and let it tick without you; it's time for mind time again. Let memories tick by. There's the Professor. He's leaning back in that old rocker of his, right next to the potbellied stove, sucking on his pipe, blowing smoke rings, and playing with his thoughts. He liked to speak his thoughts out loud; that's how he played with them. He talked with his thoughts as if it were somebody else, talking back. Often he'd fuss with them. People thought he was nuts. He enjoyed speaking his thoughts out loud for others to hear so he could observe their echo. That's what he was doing tonight: talking to himself through Henry.

A memory remembered is the past in the present and so memories have a future. Like good well water one can be drawn up, but it can't be held very long and remain fresh. The Professor rocked forward. The floorboards creaked. He looked Henry right in the eye so that Henry'd know that he was the one being talked to, and said: "We people like to think we be *important*. Thinking's all it is. We're not one bloody bit more important than these trees we fall. Do you think a man can't learn from a tree? If so consider again, because a tree is the supreme practitioner of patience. That's why a tree lives so long. Practice the ways of a tree. Patience is in love with mystery, and patience is indifferent. For the sense of mystery, she waits through all the comings and goings of the revolving storms— indifferently. We human beings agitate ourselves into early graves because we're so bloody impatient, and that's because we lack indifference. Time is indifferent, too, and Earth and animals, but not men. We like to believe that we have to be very different so we can be some important *somebody*."

Henry remembered the evening well. A storm was blowing through, exhausting itself against the bare-logged sides of the little cabin which made it seem all the more cozy. Feeling a bit smart-alecky he'd said: "Well, I saw a big ol' dog turd along side the road today that seemed to be mighty indifferent."

"You don't say . . . I take it you didn't step in it; if you didn't you were just lucky. Here's a lesson for you: tomorrow you can go and step right in the middle of that turd and see if you feel indifferent afterwards. Indifferent things make you feel indifferent if you practice paying attention and this takes patience. I think patience is paying attention to your workings and not always anticipating some desire or another. It's a discipline and it will lead you to indifference – I think."

This little lesson took place several years in the past but the scene in his mind was as new to him right now as the scene outside the window. During their time together, Henry'd had a problem figuring out if the Professor was a stodgy old Englishman or a free-wheeling spirit, if he was completely crazy or the wisest man on Earth. This minute, he didn't know if he was real or a phantom. If the Professor was real, then what was Hack?

Hack snickered.

The Professor smiled, tilted back his head and blew a smoke ring, and then vanished.

Hack snickered again. But Henry didn't respond to this prod. The Professor had spoken, and so this sort of talk Hack was putting out, along with these silly snickers and grins, couldn't goad Henry, because off in another time he'd just now learned to practice the ways of Patience—or maybe he'd known all along, having learned that lesson a long time ago, and just now remembered. Or the Professor was playing games with his mind again . . . What the hell—didn't matter. He knew this: Hack could either come out with it or drop this Abe thing. He'd simply be indifferent and enjoy his new surroundings. It's not every day when everything's new.

Obviously Hack had expected to make Henry fidget. Disappointed, his grin vanished. He spit a wad out the window again then went silent.

Suddenly, it occurred to Henry that things were not as they should be. The sun was setting off to their left, and to his right shadows were creeping up the mountain; they should be headed for the sun. If he didn't know better, he'd say they were going in the wrong direction. "I see we're still headed due north, and I thought Crescent City was southwest," he said.

"That's right, it is. But we ain't goin' to Crescent City. We're goin' to the other side of Remote."

"Remote? Where's Remote?" Henry was surprised, because Woody had mentioned Crescent City and the redwoods as the place to go.

"Northwest from here, right out in the middle of nowhere."

Henry's expression reflected his disappointment.

Looking concerned, Hack said: "Somethin' wrong?"

"Well sort of. It's just that Woody said something about going into the redwood country."

Hack bumped his forehead with the ham of his hand. "Now I get it! Woody led you to think we're headed down around the Smith. That explains it. Ol' Woody, he's a little bit behind the times. Slim finished his contract down that way three months ago an' moved lock, stock 'n barrel up to out of Remote. Guess I plumb forgot t' tell the ol' boy. Damn it all anyhow! He likes to know what's goin' on out in the woods an' he don't know less'n people like me tell 'im. I gotta pay more attention to 'im next time and a lot less to all them gals. It's the least I can do, considerin' all he's done fer me."

Henry didn't know what to say about this sudden change in circumstances; his heart was set on the redwoods.

"Still want to go?" Hack asked. "If not, I can drop ya off up here at Grants Pass, an' you can hitch yer way down there. Plenty work down that way, no problem."

"What's it like around Remote?"

"It's real nice, Henry. Lots o' big firs an' cedars an' a real purdy little river we're camped alongside. Good crew, too."

Henry looked over at Hack who was looking off down the road, minus his jolly mood from a few moments before. He liked this man a great deal, and though he seemed a little crazy, his judgment could probably be trusted. Besides, a man is always where he wants to be anyway, if he practices the ways of Patience. "Well, what the hell, looks like I'm bound for the middle of nowhere, which is somewhere the other side of Remote," he said with a chuckle.

Hack was instantly relieved. "Yahoooo!" he whooped. "Hang on, Henry!" And off they went, twisting, turning, and bouncing their way along the narrow roads on their way to somewhere, the other side of Remote.

Well into the night, Hack braked to a stop. "Ain't no need goin' in an' wakin' ever'body up tonight," he said. "Grab yer soogans an' we'll bag it here."

"My what?"

Henry had heard him right. "Soogans," came the reply.

Hack killed the motor, reached behind him, and grabbed some thick wool blankets. Now Henry reached for his own "soogans.

They ate Woody's pie and slept alongside the dusty roadster, under the trees. Henry lay on his back for a long while and looked up through the thick branches at the few stars that managed to twinkle through, while Hack snored and owls *hoo-hooo-hooted* in crescendo.

The short night's sleep was behind them, though the night was far from over, when they threw their soogans into the car and headed off. Though he didn't want to show it, Hack was in a rush. He seemed mighty anxious.

They were outrunning the sun, traveling through an inky darkness. If Henry thought the roads they left behind when they turned off the main road yesterday were bad, these last miles were beyond belief. He couldn't say if they'd traveled thirty miles or three hundred. On some of the curves, if it were daylight enough, he'd swear that he'd be able to look off his shoulder and see the back bumper, going by in the opposite direction. He couldn't understand how Hack could maneuver the car on such roads. But it wasn't his to doubt, considering this trip with Hack was his second automobile trip ever, the ride with Woody being the first. The car's lights only showed him the thin slice of road immediately ahead, but for some reason he suspected that the darkness off to the side, in many places, dropped off into abysmal canyons. Hack, however, wasn't nervous in the least. He just sat there, sometimes talking, sometimes silent, other times singing to himself, or spitting out the window, while his beloved automobile bumped, twisted, gyrated, and hummed along.

Before daybreak, they dropped off a high ridge and descended along a series of switchbacks into a steep river valley. Soon the headlights lit up some shabby brown shacks. From what Henry could see in the limited light, there were outhouses, several storage sheds, and a long low-slung building, which was the only one with windows.

"There's the bunkhouse," said Hack. "That's where we eat, tell big lies, an' sleep—except for a few of the fellers who sleep out in the woods."

"Where's the logging operation?" asked Henry. The camp was set among the trees and he saw no signs of logging activity.

"Right now, we're workin' about an hour's walk from here, up the other side of the canyon."

Dim yellow light glowed out through the windows of the bunkhouse and men were moving about. Three or four could be seen walking to and from the outhouses.

Hack pulled to a stop near the bunkhouse and parked beside a beat-up old truck. He killed the motor but left the lights on. "We're home!" he said, through a happy grin.

Before he could open his door someone opened it from the outside. A jovial voice said: "Hay ya ol' knothole, glad ya made it back. Thought maybe ya weren't gonna."

"Hell yes, I made it back; I always do." Hack was obviously happy to see this man

"Jus' barely. You sobered up, yet?"

"Hell yes, I'm sober. Whatcha talkin' about?"

"Hungover?"

"Hell no, I ain't hungover, an' I got me a witness right here." Hack looked at Henry and winked.

"Got the clap?"

"Hell, I don't know. More'n likely." Hack climbed out of the car and called to Henry: "C'mon, Henry, someone I wantcha to meet."

Henry got out and walked around the front of the car, passing through the glaring headlight beams. His shadow silently moved in and merged with the forest

"Henry, this here's m' best pal, ol' Zimm Zimmermann. Zimm, this here's Henry.

"Howdy, Henry." Holding out a huge hand was a man about six feet tall, built like a bull, and sporting the biggest handlebar mustache Henry'd ever seen. The mustache roofed a wide smile, and his eyes sparkled in backwash from the headlights.

"He's a special friend of Woody's," said Hack to Zimm.

"Ya don't say. A friend o' Woody's is a special thing to be awright. Here to hire on, Henry?"

"Hope so."

"Well if you'd showed up one day later, you could'a had ol' Hack's job."

"Bullshit!" interjected Hack. "I ain't givin' up that donkey punchin' job to Jesus hisself."

"Well, I'm here to tell ya, Haskell my boy, that Slim's mighty pissed atcha. He was lookin' for ya to be back an' ready to go Monday mornin'. Operated the donkey hisself because Swede was the only one he could break loose, but Swede can't hear the whistle punk good enough."

Hack suddenly dropped his carefree facade and expressed a concerned look, then began to fidget. "Gawdamn, ya say . . . How pissed is he?"

"Plumb full o' it, t' where pressure's buildin' up – sorta like a hot piss boiler fixin t' blow pee steam! That's why I met you here. I been watchin' fer ya. Wanted t' get to ya before he did so's I could warn ya an' ya could figger out some way t' cover yer over-growed ass."

"Is he gonna tie the can to m' ass."

"Prob'ly, but he needs ya so damned bad he'll likely hire ya right back. But then ya won't have whiskers no more an' ya'll have to go t' choker settin'." Zimm grinned and flashed Henry a quick wink.

Hack looked at Henry. "Ever punched a donkey?" he said.

"Can't say that I have. They didn't use them where I came from."

"Oh yeah, that's right, sorta forgot. Used horses didn'tcha?" said Hack, obviously relieved.

Zimm chuckled and said: "Got lucky again didn'tcha, Hack? Purdy near brought along yer own replacement, ya lunkhead." He turned his head to the side and spit out a mouthful of snoose.

Hack took a deep breath. "Welll, hell, let's go get it over with," he drawled to no one in particular. "Grab yer bag, Henry, an' stay right beside me, 'cause I'm afraid I'm gonna need ya."

Zimm reached in the car, turned off the lights, and Henry followed Hack down alongside the bunkhouse to its far end, where they entered a door that opened into the mess room and kitchen area. About a dozen men sat on rough-hewn benches at a long wooden table. Constructed from Dougfir timbers, the table was massive enough for Vikings. Its legs were as thick as pillars. It was as though it had grown there through centuries, waiting for hungry men to come so it could perform its duty, and these loggers had finally come along and built a chow house around it. The place was aglow with lantern light and the scents from pancakes, bacon, coffee, warm damp wool, and raw wood perfumed the air. Henry felt like an awkward stepchild but liked the feel and smell of the place.

When they entered, every man bent his neck and looked up and all the faces widened into big wide grins—all but one, and this one was far from grinning. It was a clean-shaven face, long and lean, with prominent cheekbones and a high balding forehead backed with light brown hair. Its eyes were sky-blue, deep set, and serious. Its owner stood up. He was a tall lanky man with large hands and feet, and skin as coarse and tough as fir bark. His long neck rooted by fibrous ridges into his shoulders like the trunk of a swamp cedar. He was older than most of the others, being well into his fifties, and he was obviously no one to get on the bad side of. Judging from the expression on that face, it was just as obvious that this was the side Hack was on at the moment.

"Howdy ever'body!" Hack hollered out, happily waving both his arms, feigning unconcern. Some of the men waved back, along with a cheerful "howdy;" others just grinned and gawked—all but that one. He was already standing and moving toward them. Heavy corks were thudding against the floor planks, spiked teeth biting into bare wood. In between each step, Henry could've heard a pine needle drop. Hack's rosy cheeks paled. Henry watched him draw in and slump his shoulders. He wasn't afraid of losing his job; a job was the last thing on his mind. At this moment, he was as scared of this tall man as if he faced-off with the devil.

Before the man could speak, Hack blurted out: "Hey, Slim, look what I broughtcha. Slowed me down a little bit, because we had to outfit him up at Woody's, but he's here now an' ready n' rarin' to go afallin'."

"Clever, Hack, very clever," Henry mumbled under his breath. He had a feeling that he had just been well used. Hack was a quick-witted bugger, no doubt about that. He didn't need Zimm to tell him he'd better cover his ass. He'd brought Henry along to cover it with. Now Henry watched as Slim's expression softened.

"You come with me," said Slim to Hack. "I want to talk to you alone." He looked at Henry, extended his hand, and smiled. "Name's Slim Hoskings."

"Mine's Henry Olsen."

"Wait here for me, if you will. I'll be back in a few moments. Got me some gawddamned serious business to tend to outside right now." He looked Hack square in the eye. "An' I don't mean goin' to no shit house," he said. Then, still glaring at Hack, he yelled back over his shoulder: "Cookie, hash Henry here up some grub, but not Hack." Then, in a long slow tone drawled through clenched teeth: "Hack, you come with me." He strode on long steps out the door into the dark, with poor Hack tagging along on his heels like a worried puppy.

A small man with a severe limp walked over to Henry. In spite of his limp, he balanced a plate, heaped with pancakes smothered in maple syrup and topped with strips of bacon, in one hand and a full cup of coffee in the other. He was unsmiling and carried an indifferent air and seemed to be the only one in the room who was unconcerned with Hack's predicament. "Eat up. Want more, go get it," he said. He handed the plate to Henry then turned and walked back to his pots, pans, and ladles.

Still feeling awkward, Henry stood there, holding his cup and plate. "Hey there, Whitey," someone yelled out, "come on over here an' plop yer ass. Gotcha a clean fork. Wiped it with my shirttail."

Henry didn't know who had called out but knew they addressed him, so he followed the sound of the voice to a card table off to the side of the room, where sat a man and a boy. Evidently the crew was growing and had outgrown the chow table, so this card table caught the overflow.

Everyone began to chat and joke around about the goings on outside: "Gawddamn, ol' Hack's gonna wear teeth marks on his ass for the rest of his miserable life," he heard someone say.

"Tell ya this, he won't be asittin' down for a long while, lessen he carries his pillow around to plop his sore behind down on," said a second.

"Betcha Slim ties the can to his rear-end," said a third.

"Nope. Slim won't can him, only jack him up some, just like he always does," said a forth.

"Betcha!" said some one else.

"Yer on!" came a reply from across the room.

There was some wagering starting up, and Henry heard one buck, two bucks, two beers, can of snoose, and a jug of redeye tossed verbally out onto the table as he walked by. The man who had called him over was motioning to him with a wave of his hand. "Here you go, Whitey. It's clean," the man said, handing him a fork. "Here, have a seat." He was pointing at the bench across the table.

Henry thanked him and sat down. His two table companions were silent, while he hungrily devoured his pancakes. They knew full well that a person can't eat and talk at the same time. Eating's serious business in the woods; food is energy. Besides, Henry wasn't in a talking mood. Right now, Hack's immediate future was heavy on his mind.

The men were getting up, one by one, and stomping out on their calks. Cookie limped about, picking up the leavings. In about ten minutes Slim re-entered with Hack still in tow. Hack looked peaked, but relieved as he approached Cookie to get his breakfast.

Slim headed straight for Henry and sat down on the bench next to him. Studying Henry with curious eyes, he slid a snoose can from his back pocket, lifted the lid, and with long fingers like knotted steal cable, pinched out a wad and poked it between his gums and lower lip. "Hack tells me you got experience in the Rockies," he said. His speech was slow and deliberate, almost a drawl— not Okie, not Missourian, not Texan, or cowpoker—more like a stew of all of those with a touch of the Canuck chop and some old-time Swede vowel extension stirred in—northwestern-big-woods way of saying.

"Six years of it with the best horse logger that ever lived," said Henry, somewhat surprised at his feeling of pride.

"Good goin'. By gawd, that'll grow a man up fast enough. Woody prob'ly told ya, we don't yard with hay-burners in these parts, no more. That's mostly all done with a donkey and high-lead shows now.

"Yeah, like you said, Woody told me. I've done more than work with horses. I've put in more time than I care to think about on the end of a misery harp," said Henry, well aware of his exaggeration. That was another bit of advice from Woody: "Stretch the point an' blow yer horn louder than ol' Gabriel ever thought of. Then take ever'thing ever'body else says an' divide by two er three, an' you might come close to actual fact," he had said.

"Glad to know yer a friend of Woody's; damned good man, ol' Woody. I knew Woody when he was one of the best. To damn bad it don't none of it rub off on his kin. A friend of Woody's is a friend of mine, an' any relative of his gets more chances with me than most." He raised his voice when he said this and glared over at Hack. Hack heard but pretended he didn't as he gulped down his coffee and chewed his cakes.

The man who'd called Henry over spoke up and introduced himself as Arkie and said that the shy boy with him was named "Junior-the-whistle-punk". Arkie looked to be around forty and wore a long, heavy beard. Junior-the-whistle-punk, was only a barefaced boy, no older than fourteen, who was trying his damndest to show a mustache. He'd touched the soot on a stove pipe with the tip of his finger and wiped the smudge off on the peach fuzz under his nose. Arkie looked at the boy and said: "C'mon, Punkie, gotta go to work. See ya at dinner time, Slim. Good luck today, Whitey." Arkie pushed his plate aside and got up and departed, obediently tailed by silent little Junior-the-whistle-punk.

"Well, you came here fer work, an' I got plenty of the stuff. Pays a good faller five 'n a half bucks a day, along with the best grub in these parts. Hope you're as good with a saw as ya claim to be," said Slim with a slight sly smile.

"Like I said, I can hold my own."

"Yeah, I wouldn't doubt that you have—up until *today*."

Now, there it was again, no doubt about it. It was that same silly smirk lifting the corners of his lips that had lifted Hack's at the mention of the name of Abe. Henry watched Slim's Adam's apple wiggle ever so slightly, savoring the trickle of liquidized Copenhagen. He knew, good and well, that Slim was waiting for him to say "why?" or "what do you mean?" or something of the sort, but he held his words, determined not to give in to these furtive little insinuations. He'd wait things out and see how they developed—work a little bit more on his patience.

Now, thinking he failed in arousing Henry's curiosity, Slim said: "Okay, Whitey, finish up here then put on your corks, and I'll meet you outside in a quarter hour.

Henry sent a silent message of thanks in the direction of Woody, because he felt that this crew was about as good a bunch as there was. Ol' Woody'd never steer a man wrong. Woody might make a mistake and say that Crescent City was the place to go to when somewhere beyond Remote actually was, but this was only because his decrepit body relegated him to a life on the fringes of his broad world of the big woods.

But Slim didn't leave right away; it seemed Henry spurred his curiosity. "Been to school, ain'tcha?" he said.

"After a fashion."

"Mind if I ask where?"

Henry remembered some old words of the Professor's: "If they question your credentials simply tell them you served your time at Professor's University and are now a master of letters. This will give you a license to hunt on the king's preserve. If they ask you for papers tell them what to wipe with them."

"Don't mind at all. I spent six years at Professor's University."

"You don't say. Professor's, huh? I think I mighta heard o' that. Where abouts is it located?"

"England, originally. It was English and moved to this country. But it's all shut down now."

Slim's face formed a puzzled expression, and he blinked a few times. Slim was no dummy and this tale didn't ring right. But what the hell, he was used to tales that didn't ring right. Besides, who was he, who didn't have one day's schooling behind him, to question an educated man. But later, he mentioned these words to others, and the rumor spread and followed Henry until the end of his time in the big woods, that he'd been a high-born man who was educated in some fancy English university. This tall tale never bothered Henry in the least, because when he thought about it in a certain way, it was close enough to the truth.

"Why you loggin', if ya don't mind my askin'?" asked Slim.

"Because I love the woods."

Slim smiled. "Good reason. Hell of a good reason," he said with complete understanding. That was the last question he ever asked Henry about his past, because here was a place where a man could hide from the past if he wished—and many did—while others simply forgot it, and few ever fretted much on it. Here lived the timber folk of the big woods, boundless people in a place that had never known boundaries. A place where no old culture held predominant sway, unless it be the universal woodland one. Here lived a grouping of people whose roots tapped deep into the forested soil of the old world but grew their leaves in the light of the new—elemental people. Such people do not live at the mercy of the elements; they live in them and with them and are constituted by them. Here was a small gathering, remnants of a vanishing tribe that pledged itself to no nation that would reserve it and jumped across manmade borders as if they were muddy little creeks. Dryads taken the form of man, they came from Oklahoma, Arkansas, North Carolina, West Virginia and the Yankee states. Here were Latvians, Scandinavians, Germans, Hungarians, Irish, Italians, Dutchmen, Russians, Englishmen, Scots, and Frenchmen. Here, too, the Chinaman and the Indian, among others. In this place of the big woods, in the manner of mountain-bred rivers, something old and diverse merged along the way and became newer, broader, deeper, and spoke a common language.

Here was a world peopled mainly by males, men living deep in the fertile womb of a female demigod. Though it was beyond their vision to know this, instinctively they called the forest "she." She was innocent and vulnerable and far more delicate than she appeared. Her capacity for forgiveness exceeded any man's comprehension.

In this place, they called themselves by different names. They dropped such titles as Carpenter, Sawyer, Shepherd, and Mason and assumed new ones. For here worked the whistle punk, choker setter, hook tender, biscuit shooter, high climber, rigger, faller, bucker, loader, boom cat, bull whacker, bull cook, greaser, pine top, river hog, gypsy tender, pea souper, donkey puncher, riggin' slinger, topper, toggler, sled tender, sniper, snooper, and the monkey men: the monkey wrencher, the grease monkey, the powder monkey and the pond monkey, among all the others.

Also, to this place, came those desperate men, trying to lose the devil in these deep, dark woods, only to find him here, because the devil followed. The devil loves deep, dark places—new places. He delights to shine his light into them—see what's for the claiming and the taking.

And some men, not blinded by the devil's light, saw through the light into the darkness and knew that the usurper had come. These seers said: "We have seen the devil and he has changed his name again. Now he goes by 'Company.'"

Chapter 4 ABE

It was working-day time, long before sunlight. Just as Henry suspected, the time had finally come, and before him now loomed the man named Abe. His first sight of this man was like a tall black shadow emerging from the dark forest, where he kept his solitary camp.

Slim did the introduction: "Whitey, say hello to Abe. Abe, say howdy-do to Whitey here."

The face he looked at was expressionless. The eyes were still and deep and as dark as the new moon. Those eyes could be looked into. If a man's eyes are his windows to the world, they're also the world's windows to the man. For the moment, Henry avoided looking directly into those eyes.

"Hello, Abe."

Abe simply nodded his head. Henry was relieved when the full lips lifted ever so slightly at the tips, lending a delicate curve to the bushy black mustache that dropped down over the corners of his mouth and merged into a thick copse of mutton chops.

"Whitey's goin' to be yer new partner," said Slim to Abe. "Reckon ya can keep him busy?"

"Reckon I can try." He drew out his words in a long, slow cadence with a voice mellow and smooth that sounded as though it was pulled from out of a cool well. Hearing it the first time, Henry envisioned a pail of thick creamy butter his mother used to serve up.

Now commenced the measuring art by which one man takes the measure of another. Abe looked Henry over, first up then down, as though sizing him up like a redwood to fall. Henry knew the look and practiced the art, himself. He could always tell how he sized up by reading the expression of the measurer, studying his body language. But not here. This expression remained neutral and the body didn't talk; this man was a subtle master of the art.

"Okay, Whitey, you came lookin' for work, an' now you found it. He's all yers now, Abe." With these words, Slim turned and strode hurriedly away, in the fashion of a man with lots to do, and joined up with three others who were waiting for him at a trail head. Each man was decked out in corks and black cotton pants. Their pant legs were rolled up to mid calf to keep them free of the sharp calks. Wool plaid coats were worn over cotton shirts. Some wore canvas hats, others wore felt ones. These were pushed up into cone shapes with the brims turned down, to shed off mist and rain. They all held stout axes. Slim said something Henry could not hear, and the men chuckled and tossed their wide-faced grins in his direction. Then, with Slim leading the way, they shouldered their axes and disappeared up the trail into the tall timber.

Abe was outfitted much like them, except he wore no coat. He wore a gray flannel button-down shirt, and though it was cool in the early morning dim, his sleeves were rolled up. Instead of a brimmed hat, he wore a wool watch cap. He carried an axe exactly like the one Henry bought from Woody. "Got us a good one all staked out," he drawled. "C'mon, follow me. We gotta go get the harp outa the filin' shack."

Henry followed as Abe led the way toward the bunkhouse and then rounded it and proceeded to a small lean-to that was built against its backside. The man walked with a deliberate stride in his tall cork boots, animal like, picking them up and setting them down as easy and light as a big black bear. His pants were stagged off even with his boot tops and were frayed. His long wool socks were topped with a red band, which he turned down to form a tuft at the boot top.

My God, Henry said to himself, *I'd sure as hell want this guy on my side if I happened to be cornered by a grizzly bear. No chance of that though; hell, no bear would be that stupid.*

"Abe, are there any grizzlies around these parts?" Henry asked. It seemed like a sensible question; he was only curious and some conversation might break the ice. He'd heard that there were once grizzlies near the mill town in New Mexico, but now they were all gone from there.

Abe didn't answer. He only chuckled to himself and ignored the question. He pushed open a low rickety door that sliced the morning calm with a loud squeak. Then he removed his cap and stuffed it in his rear pocket. To Henry's amazement, he was as bald as an old madrone tree.

"Wait here; I'll get the saw an' stuff," he said. Soon he came out with a ten-foot crosscut saw—the infamous "misery harps" of the northwestern big woods. These were used for falling the great trees. Slender and springy, they sang a siren song, a song that didn't come cheap. Many a noble but frail-hearted man had succumbed to the singing and paid the price of his life for the song he heard during the heat of exhaustive labor.

Abe gently laid the saw down and re-entered the filing shack. He re-emerged with a heavy sledge hammer, sixty pounds of steel wedges, and two corked whiskey bottles that were filled full of oil and had leather straps tied tightly about their necks. The wedges were nested in leather pockets, made from the cut-off tops of old calk boots, which were laced and bound by leather thongs. Except for the oil bottles, he set the gear down with the saw. He handed one of the bottles to Henry. The other bottle he tied to a belt loop on his left side. Henry picked up the cue and did the same. Then Abe went back into the shack and came out carrying two slender boards. The boards were about seven feet long by six inches wide and sleeved on one end with steel. He held one board under each arm.

"Here, you tote the springboards," said Abe and handed them to Henry. Then he stooped, and with one hand, picked up the leather pockets that contained the wedges. With the other hand, he hefted the harp. Without looking at Henry, and as though more to himself, he muttered: "A man should always shoulder his own saw." He hoisted the harp so that it lay over his left shoulder and drooped down in a long arc over his back with its razor-sharp teeth pointing outward. He bent his elbow to forty-five degrees and held the saw's handle about two and a half feet in front of his chest. This left one hand free. He reached down and picked up the sledge and then slid its long handle through the handle of the harp, so that it nested against his side directly under his left armpit.

"I'll take the wedges," said Henry.

"It'd spoil the balance," muttered Abe without even so much as a glance at Henry.

The wedges, secured in their leather bags, rode against Abe's back near his waist, off the ends of the heavy leather thong. This thong was looped around the saw handle and slung over the same shoulder that held the saw. Now, his right hand free once more, he stooped and picked up his axe. Every move was made with precision.

Henry stood transfixed as he witnessed the spectacle. The process didn't take Abe more than a few seconds. Now he stood there as effortless and well balanced as a dancer and packing all the gear a timberfaller needed, except for springboards.

Abe glanced at Henry askance. Henry picked up the hint and quickly laid the springboards across his left shoulder and took up his axe with his right hand.

"C'mon," ordered Abe. Then at a brisk clip, with Henry on his heels, he headed up the trail into the dark woods after Slim and the crew. For some reason, Henry couldn't help feeling like a dinghy, slack-towed astern of a mighty timber cruiser.

When they came to the edge of the timber, Abe stepped right on in. He vanished like a phantom.

Henry hesitated. Standing at the edge of the clearing, he tried to look into the forest, but it was too dark. He watched Abe disappear into the trees, as though he had been swallowed up. He tilted back his head and followed the upward flow of the giant trees to where they merged and vanished into the dark sky. He had never felt so small. He wanted to follow Abe, step on into those trees, but his feet were rooted to the ground.

It was only one step. Why should one step be so hard? One step . . . The step off the farm had been hard. Stretching steps across the Great Plains and then lifting steps up and over the Rockies hadn't always been easy. Now, countless steps merged and faded and dissipated like particles riding waves. And the farm, the plains, the Rockies, all these fell and cascaded, washing away all the steps of his past. One more step to take—just one. By God, why was it so hard? He felt as though he was stepping off into some deep dark mystery with no bottom, no surface, no returning. A shiver ran up and down his back and his back hairs stood on end. Suddenly some words hit his ear:

"Hop . . . Turn your rabbit loose, Henry. Step out and in . . . Hold your tail high, so the hawk can see it—and hop! Oh, but it's a hard little hop, eh?"

The words peeled through his mind and vibrated his skull as if a swinging clapper were suspended in his head. He recognized the quick clip in the accent. He'd know the Professor's voice among a million men. The old boy was back. It seemed the Professor was right next to him, speaking directly into his ear, but when he turned his head—no Professor.

Off to the right, about fifty feet, lay a windfall where a huge Douglas fir had come uprooted in some long-ago storm. Now it lay there, composting into bygone forests and into forests to come, an old nurse tree, laying full length, sprouting a brood of saplings that were growing up out of it, sipping away its juice. Its root system formed a tangled dirt-clogged bulwark. Twenty feet in the air, perched on a thick root, legs hanging down, sat the Professor. It was a precarious place for an old man to sit, but the Professor didn't seem worried. The root didn't even bow under his weight.

"But you're not just a rabbit, are you, Henry? You're also a traveling man, and a traveling man is all you are right now, and traveling men step, not hop. Your rabbit's in the woods, you know. Follow that rabbit and the curtain will open. You've come a long way, my dandy man, too bloody far to hold up in the wings," said the Professor. "It's a nick in time in there, where eternity is falling away and the days are numbered. It's just a wee bit of a world, where a midget can be a giant, and a giant can be whatever the hell he wants to be. Be careful. Don't step too high or you might overstep the stage. It's a brand new act but getting older." He motioned with a quick thrust of his thumb. "The scene's right there, just the other side of that curtain, suspended, waiting—starts with a step. Oh, it's a tragedy, lad, a tragedy! Go play. Step in."

Curtain? Henry saw no curtain.

The Professor chuckled. "Go on, lad, step right on up there and elbow your way into your niche. Time is a line that you can belly up to—order what you will. But it's a line on the move and won't wait for a stumblebum. It meets itself coming and going in you, you know. So belly on up. And when you do, you'll likely be amazed at how wide that line is—and how deep. Hesitate and you'll likely miss the nick. Follow that rabbit. Lift your knee, lad, and stretch your step."

And Henry did. He swallowed hard; his chest heaved; his heart skipped a beat; he lifted his knee and took a big, long step. In mid-stride he heard the Professor say: *"Into,"* Henry's foot hit the ground with a thud, "the place where you'll meet your death." A chill suddenly ran up his spine. He turned back to face the windfall, and he wasn't certain but he thought he saw something shimmer, like the folds of an invisible curtain closing behind him, meeting in the middle, sealing the seam. The old nurse tree was still there, and the Professor's perch was there, but the Professor was gone. And Henry knew, beyond the flicker of a doubt, there was no stepping back through that curtain. It would never open again. He'd made the step just in the nick of time.

Henry couldn't know—how could one know such a thing? -- but this step was a moment, long anticipated. In this moment, in this step, the dark forest breathed in and he breathed out, and the forest breathed out and he breathed in. It breathed him and he breathed it. He filled his lungs with cool, fresh air, and then he swallowed and filled his belly. From somewhere up the trail, he heard Abe's mellow voice: "Are you with me, Whitey?" It was as if the forest spoke.

Many steep steps later, the sun was just about to break the horizon, but its dawning couldn't be watched from these deep woods. Giant trees stood upon a soft green carpet of fern. Nestled in the cover of the trees, small thickets of broad-leaved rhododendron bushes were beginning to show clusters of pink flowers, glowing white in the dim light. Vine maples clustered and tangled their spindly limbs; their flowers were drooping, and the tiny double-nutted samaras were emerging like rabbit's ears out of burrows. A thin ground fog rose and slowly melted, as if the soil was breathing vapors.

The Professor's rumor of death didn't burden Henry for long; on this side of the curtain, death was a constant factor. Strewed through the standing lay the fallen, their roots of life dead and drying in the wind and rotting in the rain; their tangled limbs, brittle and clutching at the air as though trying to hang onto something, anything, to avoid the inevitable; their bodies melting, sinking into teaming humus. Henry couldn't see it yet because he was too new to this place, but he was walking through the workings of an inside-out stomach. Mushrooms and fungi of all sizes, shapes, and descriptions floating in a sea of bacteria devoured every fallen leaf, twig, and tree and then through their own deaths, excreted it all back to where it came from: into the soil and the air. The infirm and crippled leaned against the deeply rooted in the manner of wounded soldiers supported by comrades. Here death and life were as two sides of the same coin, but merging, taking no sides, losing distinctions. There was no head, no tail; what stood over his head lay under his feet and settled in his lungs—only the forest, everywhere.

Life soared; death oozed. Thin trails iridescent with slime ran this way and that through the trees and under the brush and crisscrossed like road markings on a map, then disappeared into leaf mold and damp humus oozing the musty smell of old, old death in decay. At the trails' ends lay prides of blind slugs, big as overripe cucumbers, slowly stretching and contracting, sleeping on their rotten beds, digesting their night's forage, waiting for the new night when the darkness becomes so heavy and thick even silence seems to ooze. Slugs . . . the woodsman's worms. The woodsman . . . food for slugs.

The jabbering of unseen crows filtered through the thick canopy of fir boughs high overhead. A squirrel chirped. The country had a rich aroma to it that was so strong Henry could taste it on his tongue. He flared his nostrils and breathed in prehistoric air, air that superceded all this living and dying. Passivity filled space with profound substance. It was, however, a passivity felt by a man, or breathed by a man, but not for himself, not his to own, more like a feeling felt for something else—breathing for something else, too, breathing it in and becoming it and breathing it back out—then leaving it to go its own way. Leaving . . . He had never felt so close to home—nor so far away. He felt as naked as a weathered bone. A profound sense of place filled him like marrow in a ripe bone. A place he could never fill if he grew forever. In this place a restless, roving spirit in mankind descends and merges and mixes with the spirit in humus, jells, and alchemizes into woodsy folk.

Suddenly the sound of axes at work, on up the trail, reminded Henry that he remained in a world where men lived.

Abe threw his head slightly to his left and spoke over his shoulder. "Hey, Whitey, caughtcha peerin' at my noggin a while ago. Betcha wonder how a young buck like me come to be so skin-headed, don'tcha? Well you don't have to wonder no more, because I'm gonna tell ya. But you got to promise not to tell no one else. Okay?"

"Okay." It was a meek reply. Henry felt embarrassed that he got caught "peerin'."

"Plain truth is, I rubbed it all off on the bedpost. You know what they say 'bout us kind o' boys."

Henry thought he heard him chuckle, but wasn't sure.

They continued walking on past Slim and his crew, who were busily at work, chopping limbs from a windfall. Suddenly they stepped right out into blue sky. The forest left off and opened up to an area that had been cut clear of trees. It was as though a giant door had opened overhead and let in a flood of light. The heavy light hit Henry like a sledge. The trees, like fallen soldiers—limbs hacked away, stripped—lay pointing down the steep mountainside toward the shimmering river far below. He and Abe were walking the crest of a long hogback ridge that ran east-west and paralleled the river. It was plain to see that the ridge side was being logged off with the plan to use the river to transport the logs to market.

Henry was at a loss to understand how they planned to get these huge logs to the river without the use of animals. Even with animals, most of this ridge was way too steep to log off. *This is curious as hell,* he thought.

Abe stopped and stood next to a large Dougfir, standing on the high side of the logged-off unit. He lay down his saw and the rest of the gear he was carrying, but held onto his axe. "Here he is," he said. "He ain't the biggest but he's a good clean one an' he should fall true. He's been a waitin' here a long time for us, ain't he?"

"Hundreds of years."

Henry was looking at the tree, but Abe was concentrating on the redheaded axe, Henry held. "Where abouts did you get her?" he said.

"Get what?"

"The axe."

"Bought her off of Woody Leather."

"Ol' Woody hisself, ya say." Abe smiled and held up his own axe. "She's got a twin. Meet Ruby."

The two axes were identical, redheaded and all.

"Well, I'll be damned, can't tell one from the other." Henry hadn't noticed that the two axes were exactly the same, till Abe mentioned it. "Where did you get yours?"

"From the man who created her," said Abe. "C'mon let's put 'em to work."

Once again, it was thank heaven for Woody. That night in Medford, over beers, he had explained all about how they fell timber in these parts. He even drew illustrations on napkins. Henry had never worked off springboards before. No profit in trying to hide his inexperience with these kinds of trees from a man like Abe, because no doubt about who was in the lead here, so he said: "Where do you want the springboards to go?"

In a second, about half the time it takes to take a shallow breath, Abe swung Ruby. She buried her tooth in the bare wood higher than his head. Then, quicker than the eye can follow, a twist of the wrist, freeing the blade, another swing, another bite slightly above the first, another twist of the wrist, a wedge of wood slips out clean and falls to the ground, leaving a perfect pie-shaped gouge. "Notch in right there," said Abe.

Henry was watching Abe's hands. *God almighty, those hands could take an anvil apart!*

Henry had the uphill side. Abe took the downhill side. This meant that Abe had to work his way up. With the same flawless precision as before, he cut the first notch and then inserted the metal tip of a springboard and stood upon it. Then he cut in another notch, higher up, to where the two men could stand directly even with one another upon their boards on opposite sides of the tree.

They'd leave more wood in this stump alone than was in a whole tree, back in the Rockies. But they had to cut high; the saw work was too hard down next to the ground. Closer to the base of the tree, down where it flared, the wood was tougher and harder and full of heavy pitch deposits that gummed the sharpest saw. Though nothing here was easy, a good logger always picked the easiest way in order to save time, because in these parts the favorite saying was: "Time is money."

Together, Henry and Abe chopped out the face, so the tree would know exactly where to fall—the tree always falls upon its face.

After the axework, the sawing began in earnest. "Stay in tune," said Abe. Working high on their springboards, they took up the misery harp, each by his separate handle, and began their mournful tune and cut in from the backside toward the fresh-chopped face. But for Henry, the tune was too fast.

The saw was heavy, springy, the balance felt off, and the grip didn't fit his hands. The springboard was narrow, hard to grip and hard on the ankles. In his mind, Henry could see the sneaky smirk covering Hack's big mouth as he made his vague references about the man named Abe. In his ears, he could still hear the loggers giggling like schoolgirls and see their snaggletooth grins. The bastards had set him up! Good God, no mortal man could work up to this slave driver! Henry's shoulders started burning from heaving on the saw. His ankles ached from gripping the board. Then his stomach turned over. He couldn't believe it. *Sick . . . Blast it all, I'm getting sick!* The tree was beginning to blur. Nausea was rising in his gut, headed for his throat. He swallowed hard. *I'm going to fall off this blasted springboard! Dig with the corks! Dig with the damned corks! Grip it! Hold it! Hang on! Steady up with the saw. Don't wobble on the board. Don't you dare ask this guy for pity!*

Determined, Henry gripped the saw handle tighter with his hands and gripped the springboard tighter with his feet. This was a test of a man's mettle to see where he'd fit into this non-verbalized hierarchy of the big woods.

Puke's rising. Swallow the crap back. You son of a bitch! You calloused son of a bitch over there on the other side of this tree! Take this, you bastard! Take your own medicine! Henry worked the harp for all he was worth: push, pull, push, pull. He lay into it on the push and lay against it on the pull, leaning and raring. His eyes glazed over. Suddenly, faster than he could swallow, up came the vomit, and out went Cookie's pancakes and all that good bacon, followed by the coffee and whatever water was left in his body that he hadn't already sweat away. Out over the saw and down the hill it went and out of sight into the brush below, but he didn't skip a single stroke. Push, pull, push, pull.

A funny thing: the puking cleared his stomach and got rid of all that sloppy weight; now he felt better. *These pricks are not going to drum me out of the woods or debase me through disgrace; I'll show them! After I'm finished with him, it'll take the whole damned crew to pour this cur into bed tonight.*

More desperate than determined now, he lay harder on the saw, concentrating action into words: *pull, push, pull, push, pull, push, pull, push,* giving it all he had for what seemed like an interminable series of strokes. His blood ran like red lava and suddenly his muscles tightened up and lumped like burls. His face flashed hot. Then he belched and puked again. He actually found himself wondering what the hell it was he could possibly be throwing up this time. Couldn't be any more of the breakfast, so it must be what was left of Woody's pork chops and gravy. Again he lay into the saw, but this time more because he needed something to lean against. It seemed like hours, but only a few moments passed, when, through the miserable music of the harp, Henry heard Abe sing out: "Whitey, get ready to spring like a grasshopper." Good thing too, because Henry had puked up the last of his determination and was just plain ol' desperate.

Then the death rattle began. The giant started to softly moan, the moan became a groan, then the groan rose into a loud shriek that sounded as if someone had just opened a giant door with rusty old hinges. But by the time "he" shrieked, the two men were well clear, for they sprang from the springboards between the moan and the groan, and stood well aside as the tall fir crashed down upon the ground. In no more time than it takes to breath in and out, five hundred years fell away. The forest king's stately crown was now litter upon the floor. Like a shot bullet, a hamadryad fled its husk, and the dryads flew away with the birds. Down went the tall tree and up stood the stunted stump. And the sun came down like a liquid torrent, hitting soil that hadn't known heavy light through the revolving millenniums. This ground doesn't like bright light, so it'll push up blackberry vines and bearberry bushes, and viny maples thick with wide leaves will grow and spread like the ribs of an umbrella, and myriads others like them will come to shield the ground. It'll suck up the rain and succor moist grubs, and the grubs will rise from the ground and devour the rotting stumps. And the endless wind will blow, and the seeds of other trees will grow wings and fly in the wind, and some will land and sprout into seedlings, and the seedlings will grow tall, and the day will come when this space will say "tree" once again.

In future times, after the bodies of these fallers have gone back into the humus, here will rise and stand the forest—same forest as before—if freedom is allowed to run its course.

Abe yelled, "Tim-b-e-r-r-r!" at the top of his lungs, and it seemed like a victory cry, or a war whoop.

Henry swallowed his putrid saliva. His legs wobbled like rubber stilts. *Christamighty, how can the guy find it in himself to yell like that?* Henry was only glad the tree was down and dreaded the next one.

Then he heard Abe say: "Must be pushin' noon. I'm hungry."

For the first time of many to come, the two men sat together with their backs against the stump and looked out over the tree they had felled. Abe reached for his nosebag and said: "Let's eat."

Just the thought of food was disgusting. His throat burned. His mouth tasted like innards. His own putrid breath nearly made him gag. "I'm not hungry. Here, you can have mine." Henry pushed his nosebag toward Abe.

But Abe politely declined. "Better hang onto it," he said. "You'll prob'ly want it later an' be sorry." Then he paused for a moment and looked out over the canyon, as though studying the ridgeline on the other side. Still looking far off, he said: "This is a long high ridge we're aworkin' here, an' when we're done with it we'll go over to that one over there on the other side of the river, an' when we're done over there we'll move onto another one some other place—don't know where, don't care. So, Whitey, I got some words for ya if you wanna hear . . ." Abe paused and held his words.

What the hell is he getting at? -- Henry nodded.

Abe drawled out in that slow rolling way he had: "Whether you be a sawin' with me or another man, don't lean into the harp an' then haul on it the way you do. Ride it. Ride it, my man. An' Whitey . . ."

"Yes."

"Ain't no grizzly ever crapped in these woods that I know about, 'cept some grizzly sorts of men I do know about."

Hearing these words, Henry understood that Abe hadn't done one single thing to him, intentionally. Abe wasn't out to prove anything or show up anybody. He did his job, and that was that. Henry felt his hard feeling's toward the man soften and melt.

Abe stood up, leaving Henry to contemplate his words. He walked off a few paces, turned his back to Henry and took a piss. He pulled a red bandanna from his back pocket, walked over to the canteen, soaked it with water, and squeezed it over his head, letting the water run down his face and neck and over his suspenders and into his shirt. He removed his shirt then poured some water on it and wrung it out. Then he wiped his head with the bandanna, as though polishing it like a knob.

Henry watched in silence. He had come to these woods expecting these kinds of trees, but nothing had prepared him for men such as this. Now he sat in awe, watching this one and wondering if there were others like him. Abe was one of the extant *homoarboreal*. Bulging arms hung from shoulders that humped up in muscle like knotty burls and spread out from a thick neck. His midsection rippled over fibrous sinew and bone then tapered into a straight narrow trunk. He stood square off and steady and planted his corks into the ground like roots. As though powered by hydraulics of thick pitch, he moved in an easy deliberate fashion that left no waste. From within, he gazed out through deep, dark pools that contained no turbulence or conflicting undercurrents and flashed with sparkles when light hit their ripples. On the surface, he was tough as bark, but his core was clear-all-heart and ran his length. Except for eyebrows and a thick mustache and curly mutton chops, he was completely hairless. He stood there in the sun, black as a winter oak, looking off, grinning at nothing in particular. He referred to trees by gender, calling them: "he", "him", "she", and "her".

Abe pointed at another fir, even larger than the one they had just felled. "See that one over there?" he said. "She's our next one. An' Whitey. . ?"

"Yes."

Abe gazed seriously at Henry and said: "Could you keep it down over on yer side? You woke me up two times on that last one."

These words were unbelievable. *Keep it down? Keep what down? Woke him up?* Was Abe being coy, or what? What was the guy doing, taking a nap over there? "What? What the hell do you mean, I woke you up?"

"Yep. That's what I said. Woke me up two times. Pukin' sounds unsettle me. Make me feel jumpy when I hear 'em up close like that."

Henry heard him chuckle as he ambled off. "Hey, Abe," he called after.

Abe stopped and looked back. Henry started to say that Whitey was not his name, that he heard it that very morning for the first time, when someone he didn't even know called it out to him. But for some strange reason he held back his words. Funny as it sounded, he liked the ring of it. *If it's Whitey they want, then Whitey they can have.*

A new place, a new name, a new start. He smiled at the whole idea. Everything new, just like it should be—beginning, always beginning, beginning is leaving. A growing tree constantly begins right where it leaves off. A story he'd recently read flashed through his mind. It had to do with Indians and how some of the nations had a custom wherein a boy's name was changed after he completed

some great feat on his way to becoming a man. The name change was to mark
the passing from one kind of life to another, and though he'd have a new man-
name, the boy-name would be left behind but never forgotten so it remained as
something of what he was. The new name, if he lived up to it, would bring him
wisdom and the strength and the courage to express it truthfully. Henry had to
admit that those Indians were usually given high names to live up to, such as
Eagle Flys High, Bear Stand Up, Stong Buffalo, and that the color of one's hair
wasn't so honorable a designation. But what the hell . . . After all, he'd just fell
his first giant, even if it did make him puke and wake up his partner. Abe was
waiting. Henry looked him in the face and held his gaze.

"Yeah . . . whatcha want?" asked Abe.

"I'll keep it down, so you can get your sleep."

"I'd appreciate that, Whitey," said Abe, walking away.

Whitey was never so grateful to see a day end in his life. It was all he could do
just to follow Abe back down the hill to the camp. Every muscle ached and his
head hurt and his feet were numb. He wanted to sit down beside the trail, and
almost did several times, but Abe kept going with that same tireless stride. Light
was fading.

The windows glowed with lantern light when they arrived back at camp. Moths
were fluttering, and chirping crickets were harmonizing with the tree frogs.
Several vultures descended and silently settled into some alders overhanging the
river, bowing them under their weight. The flowing water murmured along its
banks, and Whitey could taste the fresh coolness of it in the air.

"Here's where we part company." Abe halted and stood in the same spot where
they had met that morning. "I go that way," he said, pointing off at a slight trail
that disappeared into the woods. He looked at Whitey askance as though waiting
for him to respond.

Whitey didn't know if he liked this man or not. He was pretty certain that Abe
didn't much like him; but then, he couldn't read the guy. That's probably why he
was so uncertain about all this liking and disliking stuff. But he was certain of
one thing: Abe demanded his respect and piqued his curiosity. Right here in front
of him stood one hell of a challenge and he liked a good challenge. And so it was
almost as if someone else was listening in when he heard himself say: "Where do
we meet in the morning?"

"Oh . . . you comin'?" Abe sounded surprised.

"Sure I'm coming. Is that okay with you?"

"Yeah, sure . . . okay by me."

"Did you think I wouldn't? Slim said that I was your new partner, you know."

"Hell man, I ain't even got no *old* partner. He meant partner fer the *day*. I ain't
had the same *partner* more'n one day at a time since before I can remember. The
others have taken to tradin' off. "

"You mean kinda like sharing?"

Abe grinned. "Yeah, sorta like that. But more like sharin' spinach 'cause you don't like the taste of it an' can't eat it all."

"Well," said Whitey, "I happen to like spinach, but I'm a little bit stingy when it comes to sharing my partner."

For a moment, Abe didn't respond; he just stood and appeared to be in thought. Then he stared Whitey in the eye and smiled ever so slightly, then said: "Half hour earlier, same place. Want to get to sawin' with the first light."

Abe turned and walked off into the woods, leaving Whitey standing alone. Whitey wasn't certain, but he thought he heard him chuckle as he disappeared from sight.

The sun set early, and a short-lived moon was hanging low in the sky, about to drop off the edge of the world, and the dark was coming down, coming down heavy, like it always does in the big woods. His little tent was waiting, and Abe was glad to see it. Tenderly, he lay the saw down, and then set aside the rest of his gear. He sighed loudly from the relief of casting off the load and stretched his weary muscles. He grunted when he sat down on the tarp. He looked toward the fire pit, but starting a fire seemed like too much effort. He reached through the darkness and pulled a leather pouch from the tent, untied the string that secured its opening, and removed his file. Then he laid the saw upon its back and started to hone it, lightly, smooth and even, back and forth, like a bow on fiddle strings. Black on black, fingers stroking through the night, invisibility was no problem—he knew exactly where the file was. He knew by the pitch just which tooth was coming sharp. His neck was stiff, his shoulders ached, his back ached, his sides hurt, and his legs felt as stiff as springboards. Why, he hadn't felt this good after a day's work in a long while, and Whitey was coming back because he was stingy and didn't want to share his partner. Those were his exact words: "my partner." He smiled at the thought and started humming an old melody that he didn't know the words to, as he always did when he tuned the harp. Right there, on the third tooth from the southward end, he made up his mind to stay on for another day—at least another day. This saw would be sharp as wolf fangs in no time. It needed to be—it had work to do.

Abe never talked while sawing; he was a perfect picture of moving muscle and easy concentration. He displayed no exertion whatever, and Whitey discovered that the sweeps of the saw had a flow and rhythm to them. After a few days, his sore muscles eased, and he began to slowly tune into Abe's rhythm and allow himself to be led by it, and so he began to ride the saw as Abe had told him to do. It was an easy rhythm being played back and forth through the harp. Past times, faces of people he'd known, and words he'd heard them speak played in his mind like little songs. Some words of the Professor's tuned in: "Henry, people push and pull too hard and exhaust excessive steam into the things they do simply because they *believe* that's what they have to do. Like an old choo-choo, they end up spewing most of their time away, without going very far. So much for belief, eh . . ." He'd said those words back then, and in a certain way he was saying them again now. Funny thing: they made more sense now than they had back then. Here was a man on the other side of this tree who seemed to personify the vague moral behind those straightforward words. He appeared to neither work nor spew, but with easy cadence made music with a misery harp.

Whitey discovered he could go on like this for hour on hour, lost in the present moment to thoughts and dreams of bygone times or to future aspirations, awash in the aroma of new-cut wood, pitch, and his own sweat. And the forest gave way tree by tree. All too soon, the passive giant began to groan and sigh, and with a shriek, go crashing to the forest floor. The birds flew away to sing their requiem from other boughs. Then Abe shouldered the saw and moved onto another tree of his choosing and Whitey followed. Soon the buckers and bushelers moved in with their saws and axes and scurried about the carcass like minimites, hewing its limbs into heaps. They bucked it into logs of various lengths, though not too long for the donkey to handle. Then the choker setters came and choked it with cable and chain, to be yarded up or down the hillside to the river or landing.

Like Abe said they would, they worked the ridge that year, cutting out a pocket of trees here and there, but leaving plenty standing in between. As he watched the goings on, Whitey learned the operations and marveled at the genius of these big woods loggers. He figured that with enough power and plenty of wire rope, along with block and tackle and a stout fulcrum, they could figure out ways to move a mountain if it should ever come to that, and they had a hundred different ways to do it.

The primary leverage they employed was called a "spar tree," or simply the "spar" or the "tree." Yarding power was a "donkey." Until recently, the donkey was fed wood and ran on steam, but now it guzzled gasoline. The donkey was the workhorse of the operation. It was constructed of nothing more than some motorized spools of heavy cable coiled within spinning drums, which were mounted between two parallel runners made from logs called "skids." Spinning one spool to haul the chokers out, spinning another to haul them back in, this donkey never balked unless the operator jammed his gears. When the chokers came back in they were choking logs.

It was the spar and its rigging that fascinated Whitey, and he pledged to himself that he was going to become a highclimber. In the big woods that was a far-fetched ambition, because only a very few of the very best ever climbed that high. Funny how fate works: an idea comes into a man's head in the form of a notion or an aspiration. Caught up by his ego, he thinks it's all his idea and it never occurs to him that he's being *told*—maybe it's a *good* telling and maybe *not*. Whitey had no idea how high his highclimbing ambitions were due to take him or how far the fall can be from way up there. For now he studied the climber and the climber's art.

First of all, the highclimber selected the tree of his choice to serve as the spar. This tree had to be a prime tree without fault: tall, clean of limbs for at least two hundred feet high, strong, and in a strategic location. He went through the soon-to-be unit and selected it before the fallers moved in. Using his axe, he marked this tree with a large X, so the fallers could know to leave it standing while they cut down all the others. This area to be cut was a "logging unit" or a "side." The logging work involved was the "show."

Then, the unit felled and the fallers having moved on into other parts of the woods, the climber returned with his rigging crew to rig the tree. He attached steel spurs to his heels, longer and sharper than those of a fighting cock's. To a wide belt about his waist was clinched the climbing rope, which girdled the tree. Leaning out against the belt strap, repeatedly swinging the rope upward, lifting his knees and stepping higher and digging in his spurs for footing, he scurried up the tree like a squirrel. He tailed his saw and axe from a rope attached to the belt, chopping off any limbs along the way, though usually these didn't begin before he reached the point where he topped the tree. There were some, less refined highclimbers, who topped it with a blast of dynamite. They drilled their holes and buried the sticks, but the sticks had long fuses, and the climber was on the ground and well clear of the action when she blew.

The refined climber was a maestro who took his chances with the action. Working two hundred feet up, with the precision of a diamond cutter, he topped the tree with axe and saw about a third of the distance from the top. He chopped out the face and sawed in from the backside and drove in his wedges if it pinched his saw. When the top started to lean ever so slightly, he withdrew his saw, and then he quickly dropped down a few feet in case the bole split and spread. Then the top fell away, but not without a severe kickback that set the spar to swaying in an eighty-foot radius or more. At this point the climber had unleashed forces beyond his control, and all he could do was dig in and hold on and pray to his god. He had just dethroned an old queen. A crown of boughs fell away and crashed far below him—more than a few times the climber fell with it. Or he was sometimes left hanging in death, wrapped up in the binds of his rope and squeezed against the tree that had split and spread.

With the tree topped, and if still alive, the climber descended the spar by leaping out to clear the spurs and flipping slack into his rope. In a few quick flips and downhill jumps he was on the ground. Then he called on help from the donkey puncher and the crew. He went back up the spar, packing a stout steel pulley, a steel strap to hang it by, and a long length of small wire rope. Using this pulley rigging and working from above, all the remainder of the rigging needed to create a spar tree was hoisted up to him. He tied the spar to the ground with cable, pulled taut by the donkey and cats. The cables were the "guy lines." They looped the spar and were secured to omni-directional stumps, holding it ridged and eliminating the dangerous sway, which could shatter the spar. It was guyed at the top and it was guyed in the middle to keep it from buckling when the donkey puncher applied his power against it. Last to go up was the high-lead block and rigging, and this weighed a ton or more.

It took several days to rig the spar. When finished, it all appeared like a huge, very tall antenna mounted upon a slanting roof. It was the marriage of wood and steel. It was a marriage that did not beget posterity.

Well above the guy lines, nearer to the top of the spar, the climber rigged the heavy cable that looped the span from the donkey. Along this span traveled the choker cables, hanging down from the high-lead and swinging and dancing in the air like a long-legged spider flying on its string. This kind of rigging was called "high-lead logging," and when it was complete the spar was "rigged"—time to start up the show.

The donkey operator, or puncher, or engineer (he was called all three) simply spun the donkey's drums and took up and doled out slack in the high-lead to move the chokers back or forth along the line and up or down the hill to the landing. The choker setters worked out in the unit. They choked the logs by looping them with cables, which were designed to tighten like a noose on a neck when stressed by a surge of power from the donkey's spinning drums.

The whistle punk—most often a young boy, keen of eye, ear, and concentration—stood within sight of the donkey puncher as well as the choker setters. Then he relayed signals to the donkey for the choker setters by tugs on a line that tooted a code through a whistle on its roof. It made the woods ring a lively but monotonous tune, to which the choker setters danced for their livelihood—and their lives. Far too many young loggers died on that crowded dance floor, poor dancers who got out of step and were stepped on by their eight-thousand-pound dancing partner.

The gyppo was the Gypsy entrepreneur of the big woods; he plied his trade for profit. If he didn't make it in one place he'd try to make it in another. He was always trying to make it, always moving on. Depending upon his skill, plus luck, a gyppo could go broke or make a decent wage plying this trade. But, whether he financially lived or died, the gyppo who did it was a logger, and at the end of the day, one could be certain he had earned his wealth or his poverty.

If the whistle punk was the lowest, then the highclimber was the most esteemed logger in the woods. Most often he was the gyppo himself. These were the pioneer years of spar tree logging. The highclimber's was the job with the most skill and greatest risk, and the highclimber was the one who received the greatest praise. Fame and fortune followed on the heels of the great ones—while death always lurked, ready to spring in from the blindside.

The desired job for some in the crew was that of donkey operator because it paid fair, considering the man got to work with the machine, but the machine did all the work. So in Slim's camp, Slim was the climber, and a fine one he was too, while Hack operated the donkey and thus avoided the heavy work. But no one begrudged Hack; after all, he had been with Slim for going on twelve years. He'd started out as a whistle punk and worked through good times and thin all the way up to the job of his dreams; and though still young, he was considered a senior man. In the nomenclature of the woods: "He'd earned his whiskers." Whitey and Abe were two of the several fallers and buckers.

Some of the camps had their own saw filers, but in this small camp, the men sharpened their own saws. Abe said he wouldn't have it any other way. Slim, being the gyppo, was the master of all trades, except cooking. Come day's end, after they killed the machinery, he turned into a mechanic and did his own monkey wrenching. He gave it guts, feathers, and all, working endless hours for his slight reward. The break of dawn, often as not, caught him washing grease and oil from his hands so he could put on his calks for the day's work without soiling their rawhide strings with greasy fingers. Like others of his breed, he esteemed himself independent and freewheeling, and preferred to imagine that he was a free man who answered only to himself. Truth was he worked for the banker. But he answered to the company lawyers, because there were conditions and quotas written into his contract, and the contract paid his banker's note.

Back in the early years, squads of itinerant whores worked the big woods circuit, traveling camp to camp for brief but welcome interludes to the interminable card game and tall tale contest. But this activity ceased as the towns progressed in number and size. The woodland nymphs left the woods, because they could lie in one soft spot and rest their heads on feather pillows in the towns and let the business come to them. Why bruise your wares along the bumpy and somewhat dangerous rides to the camps? So progress was good for them but hard on the loggers. As might be expected, this gave rise to hot but unquenched libido in the camps. To relieve the pressure, a promiscuous little whore was handed around. Pussy Palm was her name, though some nicknamed her Fanny Five Fingers. And a cheap lay she was. Of course, the muffled sounds and desperate sighs produced by such furtive activities were absorbed by, and added only a subtle strain to, the cacophony of snores, wheezes, coughs, and sneezes that filled the atmosphere and shook the rafters.

A bunkhouse at night, filled to the brim with the essence of wet wool socks, boot grease and spittoons, and the sounds of loggers, most with corrupted nose and throat tissue from overindulgence in snoose and snuff, was not a fit place for serene dreamers.

Some few of those with less gregarious natures, or persistent insomnia, chose to camp out rather than sleep in the bunkhouse. One day over lunch, while sitting under the shade of a cool cedar with Abe, Whitey voiced his displeasure with bunkhouse living. He said he was going to town the very next Sunday and buying himself a tent and the basic necessities for a more solitary life about the campfire rather than the potbellied stove. To his surprise, Abe invited him to pitch his tent next to his own and stoke a mutual fire. Whitey was inwardly thrilled at the prospect.

"There be one condition if we're gonna be full-fledged partners," Abe said. "The condition is that we don't buck no windfalls on a board-foot pay scale unless we, ourselves, do the markin' for the buckin'. We don't let no bull-buck do it. If he marks 'em, he bucks 'em. Should he object, we pack our soogans an' shoulder our sacks. If he wants to mark the ones we fall, then we got no qualms."

Whitey knew that a good faller could read his timber like an easy book and knows just where to fall it so it won't bind the saw in the bucking. A man could waste away a day trying to buck a fallen tree in a stressed spot where it bound up and pinched the saw. He couldn't carry enough wedges to work his way out, and it was useless labor and poor, too, if the man was working by the board feet. Though Whitey had never seen one, he had heard of bull-bucks who insisted on marking all the felled timber. They could mark the cut where it was hard to work the saw, rendering life miserable for a logger, until he gave up and quit. An unscrupulous bull-buck used this petty power to run off a man he didn't like but who was too good a hand to find a reason for canning.

Windfalls fell where the wind said and they were often full of stress. But a good faller laid his tree right where he wanted it; he could drive in a stake with it or lay it on a dime. He laid it down nice and cozy without stress or binds.

"Do you have that condition with Slim?" asked Whitey.

"Nope, don't need it," Abe said. "Besides, Slim pays us by the day, because there's too much fussin' an' fightin' when men get paid on production. That's why I work so hard for him. But I been t' places where a man needed his conditions all laid out." Abe slowly shook his head in disgust. "Yessir, I sure have, at them gawddamned company camps."

That Saturday night, Whitey spent the last night of his life in a crowded bunkhouse, all smelly with smoke, snoose, dirty socks, and unwashed men. Come Sunday morning he entered into a new relationship: a partnership liberal with thought, conservative with words. Early every Sunday, right after breakfast, Cookie took the old pickup to town and loaded it to the gunnels with all the necessary supplies to keep a crew of hungry loggers' energies up and going. This Sunday, he had a welcome hitchhiker.

Whitey returned at the end of the day with something more than a tent and the usual fare of necessities. Snuggled discreetly amongst the coffee, toilet paper, fresh fruit, underwear, and new socks and gloves, feigning the innocence of a fleecy wolf, lurked a small package of hot chocolate. He'd spotted it on the counter right next to the coffee and tossed it in the sack and then forgot about it. So innocuous to touch and smell, only one pinch apiece in a cup of hot water that very first evening left both Abe and Whitey henceforth addicted. To their mutual despair, they ran out midweek, but toughed it through to Sunday, when Whitey again returned from a hasty trip to town with a bulging sack packed full with their tasty bane. It was held in special reserve each day until that time, after supper in the bunkhouse, when stars danced in tune with the fire, or water drops tapped rhythmically overhead against the suspended tarp. Then out of its hiding place it came, and each man doled out his individual pinch to fix him up and ready weary muscles for sleep and sugar-sweetened dreams.

Solitude is sweet. But solitude had been difficult in the bunkhouse. There was always too much coming and going and men chipping their teeth on palaver and tall tale contests. Whitey learned soon enough where it was that Woody had honed his tall-tale-telling skills. The tall tale tellers were the clowns of the big woods. They made sad men laugh and lightened up heavy souls that were dragging in the dirt from hard work. After dinner, while digesting the heavy starchy stuff that fed their aching muscles, the men circled around the table and the warm stove or reclined on their bunks, and then the clowns stepped in and competed for center ring.

These clowns were far from mute. They reached way down deep and stirred up a light-hearted stew of witticisms with their wits and ladled it out with their tongues. The men opened up their hungry ears and gobbled up the sweetened bons mots and fed their aching spirits. In this sylvan world men labored like brutes so they could live in the tall trees they loved, while falling away their world with their labor. It was the senseless tall tale tellers who made the only sense here and kept a comic peace. They kept the too-serious brute at bay and the men away from one another's throats. Everybody knew this, but nobody spoke about it.

Abe and Whitey were ironclad partners now, and each stood his springboard and held up his end of the saw. Day followed day and blended gently into one another. The evening routine was one of congregating at the chow table and then listening to some of the tall tale tellings.

Hack had told Whitey on the ride to camp that a man could die real easy if he joined on with Slim, because he employed the best damned cook in the woods, and if the man wasn't careful he might eat himself to death. This wasn't as exaggerated as it sounded at the time. Now Whitey saw what Hack was talking about. An undeclared gorging contest was played out, where each man measured his virility against his ability to eat himself into a stupor. The man who devoured the most was, of course, the most man. It was not unheard of for such a man to shovel his grave with his spoon, and finally eat himself into oblivion during a hard-fought contest lasting for several days. In such cases, the "great logger" was buried with honors, but instead of a cross as a grave marker, a wooden spoon was fashioned and pounded in at the grave head. Many years later, weekend trekkers would stumble upon a huge spoon petrifying on the forest floor and surmise that giants had once lived there. And so began the beliefs and myths about giants in the old-time forests.

After the socializing, the two partners returned to their mutual fire between the two canvass tents and settled in over their hot chocolate fix. Then Whitey set about sharpening their axes while Abe honed the pampered harp, which he kept wrapped in a special holster he had fashioned from canvas and old soogans. He was widely recognized as "the best damned filer in the woods." He engrossed himself in it and always hummed along. He said he loved to hear the music of the file, and Whitey noticed that it did have a distinctive rhythm that varied according to Abe's mood.

One time, Abe didn't hum while he filed the saw. He seemed to be watching his hands and concentrating. Whitey tried to watch his hands too, but they moved faster than the eye. When he finished, Abe looked up, smiled, and said: "Took four hundred and sixty-two strokes." A few days later, on a long summer day, Whitey had some time on his hands. He walked out to a tree he and Abe felled that day and counted the rings in the stump. He counted three hundred and ninety-four. When he told Abe about this, Abe dropped his eyes and said: "I can't handle numbers over fifty." Whitey forgot about the stump. But later, right out of the blue, Abe said: "You know that story about Adam eatin' that apple?"

"Yes," said Whitey, feeling somewhat surprised by the words. "I know about it."

"I think he ate it because he loved the taste of apples," said Abe.

And Whitey understood. Not another word was spoken about this subject for as long as they remained partners. They toed the line where they stood, because this is the place where they met, and never spoke of their pasts or contemplated the future. Few words were said and most of the time none at all. It was a sublime routine that mere words could not improve upon, and each man knew it well. The mornings began where the evenings ended: they arose then met at the cold fire, ate breakfast together at the cookhouse, took up their nosebags, shouldered the harp and tied on their gear, and then off they headed into the tall timber.

Abe never went to town. He preferred the silence around the camp on the days when most of the others went home to their wives, if they were married, or to the towns to loiter in the bistros and whore around if they were bachelors. Whitey went in, on occasion, but only for supplies or to have some beers—never to whore. He did his best to rise above his persistent urges. Going to a whorehouse to "have a good game of ball busting" wasn't a thing he could take lightly like the others could. Perhaps this was because he didn't care for most of the games men like to play. Cards were monotonous and bored him after ten minutes, and the word games in the tall tale tellings became redundant. Or perhaps it was because the memory of Peppa, his gentle lover, lay dark and heavy, yet sweet as molasses, upon his soul.

From Abe, he learned the skills of a logger and a woodsman of the big woods. He even took to dressing exactly like him and stagged off his pants and wore socks with wide, colored bands rolled down into a tuft at the boot tops to expose a flash of color when he stretched his steps. When dressed for work, from a slight distance in poor light, it was hard to tell one from the other. Whitey was a full-fledged and respected member of the culture of the big woods, for it locked no one out. A man had only to rise up to it to open its door and enter. These seasons of solitude were exactly what he needed to forget and grow.

Somewhere along the way, Whitey felt an urge to take up the books again, and to Abe's surprise, he brought home an occasional book from his jaunts to town. Like many of the others, Abe couldn't read his name, and to see Whitey, his partner on the saw, silently reading within the glow of fire or lantern light gave him an uneasy feeling. He always knew that Whitey was there, present and tuned to him when at the saw. But this reading thing perplexed him, for it seemed to him that Whitey's presence was lost and gone off to some place else like something mystical. Because of this, he never mentioned the books and pretended to not even take notice of them. But his curiosity overcame his reservations on one warm evening in July, when the sun was still shining at bedtime and the moon glowed overhead. There was Whitey, sitting with his back resting against the tree, lost in one of his books. Finally, Abe said: "Whatcha readin' about in that book?" He wasn't even certain Whitey could hear and was relieved when he looked up and smiled.

"Some words I like that were written down by a man a few years back."

"Oh." Abe studied the book in Whitey's hands. "Never learned readin' m'self, ya know."

Thinking Abe was in a talking mood, Whitey started to close the book.

"No . . . no, you go right ahead an' read an' pay me no mind," said Abe, feeling like he had blurted in.

Suddenly it occurred to Whitey that he had a way of shutting Abe out when he read. *So why not take him with me?* he thought. So he said: "Ever heard poetry, Abe?"

"Yep. That be one of the things that finally ran me outa the bunk house. My ears got to ringin' with it all."

"I don't mean only word rhymes like Zimm and Hack and some of the others play with in their tall tales; I mean poetic thought."

Abe slowly shook his head. "Is that whatcha got there, poetic thought?" He leaned forward a bit, trying to get a better peek at the book.

"Yep, and I think there's some here that you'd like. It was written down by a man during his own time so men like us could read his thoughts in our time. That way, the man dies but his mind lives. Let's see . . . ummm, it's in here somewhere, just read it a moment ago." He had Abe interested now so he quickly turned back a couple pages. "Ahh, here it is. You ready?"

Abe shyly nodded, because no one had ever read to him before, except for those times when he was a gandy dancer on the railroad, and the gang boss read his name off a roster call every morning and evening. He didn't know what to expect and wondered if he would be able to understand reading.

Whitey started reading slow and easy so Abe could easily follow:

"Earth spoke in my dream. She said:
'They claimed that I was theirs to eat.
My flesh was to be their meat.
So they sat themselves down at their
table and sharpened their teeth
on avarice and lust and plunder.
But I was not at the feast.
Uninvited, I did not attend,
though I was there at the end,
when they lay down to sleep off their hunger.
Besides, who is he who can prepare me?
Who is this man of soil and clay who
would eat his own bed?
I look around. I do not see him or the likes of him,
because all as such are dead.
And so, I eat them instead.'
I never awoke from that dreary dream,
because I am one of those men, dead.
I look around, but I cannot see me."

Whitey lifted his eyes and met the soft gaze of Abe. Abe lowered his toward the book, resting against Whitey's leg. "It says *that* in there?" said Abe, in a subdued tone.

Whitey nodded.

Abe looked into Whitey's eyes, and Whitey read the child-like astonishment there.

"Read it again," Abe said.

And Whitey did, in the same slow easy cadence, while Abe sat stock still with his attention riveted to the words he heard. When Whitey finished there were a few moments of silence.

"What's avarice?" Abe asked.

"Avarice means to be greedy after things and to want to own them."

Abe nodded and then looked off silently into the trees for a long while. Then he said: "An' I always thought poetry was just rhymin' a bunch of words in them silly stories they tell in the bunkhouse."

"For the *most* part, those tall tales *are* just word rhyming, depends on the teller. Many of the greatest poets make use of it and play with it in much the same way. It sugar-coats their thoughts so that people will chew on them and maybe even taste their message."

"Is poetry like prayin'?"

"What?" asked Whitey, not getting the drift

Abe looked Whitey in the eye. "I mean, is poetry like prayin' with readin'?"

Abe didn't smile nor did his eyes twinkle. He was as open in this moment as Whitey had ever seen him. Whitey felt off balance with the question because he didn't know the answer, and yet he was the one who could read. "Well . . . I guess I'd have to say that I can't say. I've never thought of it exactly that way."

"Are *you* a poet?" Abe sincerely asked.

Whitey didn't expect this kind of profound response from Abe. He'd hoped to capture his attention and interest him in reading in much the same way the Professor had captured his own attention. But Abe's reaction surprised him. "No, I'm not a poet, but I wish I were," he said. "I can read them, though, and try to go up to them. A man whom I suspect may have been one gave me that ability for a gift."

"Who was that?"

"A man everyone called the Professor. He was an Englishman and had been a real professor at some of the universities back in England."

"How was it ya knew him?"

"Met him in the Rockies. When I came to those mountains I was only sixteen. I was bedraggled, half starved, and without two copper pennies to rub together. There was a mill town there. Everything but the whorehouse was owned by the company that owned the mill. I went to the hiring hall, looking for work. The woods boss said they'd hire me as a full-time trail swamper, for which they'd pay me, and part-time toilet cleaner, which would come free on my part. But I needed boots, clothes, and an axe and the company agreed to withhold the cost of those things from my wage. Said I could board in the company's bunkhouse for eighteen cents a day. I was going to jump on it. Like I said, I was damned desperate in those days. But a tall lanky man was standing nearby and heard the conversation. It was the Professor. He was a horse logger who contracted to the company. He needed to hire his own swamper and had come down to the hiring hall to see if he could scalp somebody away from the company. 'Save a soul,' he called it.

"Well, the Professor took me to the side and told me that what the company withheld from my wage plus the price of board would come to more than I earned. He said the things I bought would wear out and then I'd need more. Said the company would be more than willing to extend my note in exchange for my labor. The company would own my ass. 'And you won't even have to clean out my toilet. Perhaps I'll clean yours,' he said.

"So I went to work for him. But I still had the problem of a place to stay, so he loaned me a tattered old tent. A few months later he told me to throw out my bedroll in the corner, and he let me lodge in his cabin and even fed me for free on the condition I let him educate me. 'Toilet-cleaning time,' he called it. He said he intended to turn me into a scholar, if he had to turn me inside out to get the job done; said he liked big challenges and wanted to see if he could accomplish the impossible in his lifetime. Seems he had a hankering to teach, because that's what he had been schooled to do back in England." Whitey thought for a moment, remembering, then, drawing up a special moment like a gem on a string; he chuckled softly and said: "'First and foremost,' he told me, 'we are going to exorcise that whinny talk that your tongue twangs out of your mouth before my eardrums go numb.'"

"Did he finish the job?" asked Abe, grinning.

"I can't comment on the scholar part but one thing's for sure: he damned well turned me inside out. Godamighty, I had no idea of the deal we struck! 'Our agreement,' he called it. I near belonged to him for over six years." Whitey paused in thought, slowly shook his head and said: "Hell's fire, I did belong to him—hook, line, and sinker. It was just the same as if I were his property. The work in the woods was easy compared to the mind-stretching he put me through in that book-filled cabin of his. I forgot what sleep was like. The Professor did four things: he logged, read books, thought, and visited the whorehouse. You notice I didn't say he slept. Sleep seemed to be something he didn't need, so I guess he figured no one else needed it."

"Sounds like a strange sort."

"Yeah, he was as strange as they come. Most people considered him downright weird. He himself said he was a stone's throw away from insanity. Said it scared the hell out of him because just the thought of going insane drove him downright crazy. I once asked him why he left England. He got a far-away look, leaned back in his rocking chair, tapped the bowl of his pipe, and said he hadn't the faintest idea why he left, other than to say he had a longing that stirred his soul like a ladle in porridge. Said it made him hunger for the feeling of freedom, and he wanted to go to the edge of the world, where things were still soft and wild— where he could hang his head over its rim and breathe fresh air. Said his cronies in England told him he was out of his mind if he left. He said that sounded mighty good to him because out of his mind was right where he wanted to be."

Abe smiled, chuckled under his breath, and slowly nodded his head. Then he said: "Not so strange. That Professor fella wasn't weird; wern't so crazy, neither—only different. Sounds like he was a right good partner."

"No, a damned dictator is what he was," said Whitey, grinning.

The two men were quiet for a few moments, listening to a cricket chirp. Abe stoked the coals then said: "Whatcha got naggin' at ya, Whitey?"

"Nagging at me? What do you mean?"

"Prob'ly none of my business. I mean, I know the Professor is dead an' all, but people die all the time, leavin' others behind. An' I know firsthand how it hurts. But it ain't something that nags at a man. Know what I mean?"

Whitey knew exactly what Abe meant. He didn't know how Abe saw through him, but he knew that somehow Abe could see his pain, his nagging guilt. He lowered his eyes and they turned misty while he said: "I had a special friend. She was just a little whorehouse girl, but my godamighty she did work her way into me." The words came hard. "And now I can't get her out. Hell, I don't want to get her out. She's *dead*. Some drunked-up drifter knifed her just to have a good time, watching her die. I should've taken her away from that kind of life, but I didn't, and so she died."

Abe was silent, thinking. Then he said: "Don't you think if you *should've* been with her ya would've been?" There was a pause. Whitey raised his eyes and Abe was staring right at him. Their eyes locked and Abe said: "Should'ves will drive a good man to bad. No end to 'em. They'll pile up on ya, go to spoilin', get to stinkin', because should'ves ain't somethin' a man can use. They belong some place else."

Whitey pulled his gaze away and stared into the fire, thinking about the crux of Abe's words. As though from far away, he heard Abe say: "How do ya read an' not say the words?"

"I say them, only I say them inside myself."

"You say them inside?"

"Yes, that's right," Whitey said, smiling at Abe's apparent confusion.

But Abe surprised him again, for he wasn't the least bit confused—entranced maybe, but never confused. "You told me once thatcha was stingy an' that sounds like a mighty stingy self inside there to me. Kinda like not sharin' candy."

Abe said this in all sincerity and with such a straight face that for a moment Whitey was left speechless. It was as if he'd inserted a key into a secret slot of Abe's mind and unlocked a closet of longings that were suddenly reflected in the words of an old poem. Those longings contained questions and finally they'd found a place to seek answers. Then he said: "Tell you what, Abe. I don't want to get branded as stingy any more, so from now on, whenever I come across something that I think might appeal to you, I'll call you over and share it out loud. That way, we'll both get to eat the same piece of candy. How's that?"

Abe nodded his approval. And so, for several years to come, the big woods of the Coast Range resounded to the words of the poets, even if there were only two sets of human ears to listen to them.

So it went, this new but odd partnership in literature: Whitey read aloud, and Abe leaned back against his tree with a far-off look, often humming a low melody. Whitey even got the strange feeling, at times, that Abe's comprehension exceeded his own, and where he groped, Abe stroked, as though stirring the fire or honing a sharp edge. Perhaps here was the *true* scholar. Whitey figured he could learn a great deal from a man such as this.

Late that night, just about the time the North Star was setting, the Professor showed up. Whitey was sort of surprised to see him. He hadn't been around since just after Abe arrived on the scene. Seemed that the old drifter had finally drifted off to some other sphere. But here he was, riding Ol' Dan, his favorite Percheron.

Ol' Dan, that same old horse that grew too arthritic to go on any longer. The Professor had been forced to shoot him. The last time he'd seen Ol' Dan, the buzzards were carrying him off into the sky. Now, wouldn't you just look at him! That horse was prancing, acting like a frisky colt, heading off on a trail ride. Several raven-black feathers hung down from his bridle gear, attached by what looked to be threads of fine catgut—or spider strings, maybe. When he tossed his head the feathers fluttered about. And funny thing: the Professor didn't look nearly as old as he was. His hair was sandy colored, thick, and curled out below the rim of his hat and fell down his neck. His face was smooth, cheeks full. But his eyes were the same: clear and dark and as full of wonder as the night sky.

Whitey wanted to speak, to hug him, give him a big squeeze and tell him how much he loved him, how much he missed him, but he was as frozen and mute as a dead man.

But not the Professor. He was as spunky as ever. He didn't dismount. He slumped over, rested his forearm on the saddle horn, and stared down at Whitey. "How do you do, Henry? I came to finally say good-bye," he said. "I guess it is bloody well time for me to go. I can't hang around forever, you know." Then he chuckled to himself, and said: "Simply because there's no such thing as forever if you have no time. But thanks for letting me tag along this far." He motioned with a sideways nod of his head in the direction of Abe's tent. "That timber tramp over there, I leave you in his hands; or perhaps I should say, in his steps. And mighty fine hands and long steps they are. In his own way, he'll take over where I left off."

What does he mean? As usual, Whitey didn't have the foggiest idea of what the Professor was talking about. He wanted to speak but couldn't find his tongue.

"What's that you say? Take over what? you say. Why you, Henry, take over with you. Or more precisely, a part of you I never got to: the *heart*. We ran out of time you and me, remember. I taught you how to see. He'll teach you how to feel – to listen. We have a job to do, we three. My part in it is finished and so now I'll go my way, and so will he one day. You're the one with the destiny – one last job to do – a mission. I'll bet you thought you were finally free. Only free of me, my sad little prodigy. Always lessons, Henry . . . Only lessons . . . Lessons about everything . . . But, really, *nothing* to learn, and *that* is something that you don't know, so far . . . So, *nothing* to teach . . . *Nothing* – tis Lucifer's fire . . . Learn *that.*"

Then he reined Ol' Dan around and headed down the trail. But he didn't go very far before he whoaed to a stop, turned his head, looked back, and said: "However, should you need me, I won't be far away." Then he urged Ol' Dan along. But before they rode off into the canyon, Whitey heard the Professor yell back over his shoulder: "Simply because there's no such bloody thing as far away." Horse and man vanished into laughter.

Chapter 6 The Fish

In the deeps of winter, The Fish was killed. His name was Carlo Glass, but he was a full-blooded Red Salmon Indian, and so the loggers called him The Fish. He lived solitary in a hollowed-out tree, porched with a suspended tarp. He slept under a soogan thrown over a bed of spruce boughs and moss, and he rarely said a word. It wasn't because he was naturally taciturn or shy that he held his silence. He was the last of the Tree People, a once noble but now extinguished tiny tribe, which had dwelled in these forested mountains since the dawn of time. There'd never lived a man more alone upon Earth than Carlo since the death of Adam. History lived in him; but he did not speak of this and kept it to himself, thinking there was no man left alive who could comprehend it or even want to, because what white people called *"his* story" the Tree People called *"the* story.

Some who were near said that the moment when he died was the first time anybody had ever seen Carlo smile, but when Whitey went to pay his last respects there was only the grin of death upon the corpse's face. Somebody had weighted down his eyelids with coins, and it was as if Carlo stared up through the unblinking round-eyed gawk of a fish. Carlo told him once that there was really no Red Salmon tribe. There was only the nameless Tree People, and Carlo was his whiteman name and was simply a sound-word made by flipping the tongue while grunting. Perhaps the reason he had smiled in that last moment was because he was falling somewhere in the forest, like a good son of the Tree People should.

At the time, Whitey could only feel deep remorse at the loss of a good man. But in later years, after he learned the history Carlo held secret, he would think back on that moment from time to time, and the irony in it would cause him to smile as he wondered if the Tree was there to hear Carlo fall.

The Tree People were rememberers. It was only through the power of memory that they could pass on and save their story, keeping their mind deep and their memory keen and their story forever fresh in the re-singing. With Carlo, the story of the Tree People was *his* story. The story-singing had finally ended in this place and so his story was all he had left. So it was now up to him to remember for his people.

They were a reclusive people who weathered the harsh climate and challenged the pitched terrain until they became one with the Tree. The whites called them the Red Salmon Indians, because they loved the red roe and red flesh of this fish that swarmed in the shallows of the river and darkened the water with thousands of black backs, when they came up from the sea for their death and rebirth. The whites said that the Tree People had eaten so much of this fish that it turned them red. But they called themselves the Tree People and had for almost as long as the rememberers sang the story. Their skin was the reddish-brown hue of the cedar tree. The young ones were as smooth and soft to touch as saplings, and the old ones were wrinkled and grooved, like the tallest of trees.

The stories were once many and long that sang of how it was they became the Tree People. One of the stories sang of a time when the people lived in a far-off place, beside the white owl. Monsters rode in the wind and these had teeth and stingers that stung flesh and burned the eyes and skin. And they were food for bears with claws like knives. There was nothing to cast a shadow and so no place to hide from tormentors. There were no trails to follow, neither in nor out, because as soon as one was cleared it filled right back up again with ice and snow debris. They would have perished in that place had they not heard a calling, like notes upon a flute or as wind though trees and rushes, in the far distance, that was first low and then high. And they were pulled by it and followed it through many hardships, going first this way and then that. But the singing came no closer and it was as though it came from all directions. People grew weary in the wanderings and died, or they were killed by monsters and demons, or hopelessly sank away under the snow.

The tribe despaired. One day, during the time of freezing rocks, the elders called a prayer council. The people came together and sounded the drums, and they sang with the drums and the drums lifted their voices and merged them, and so they prayed as one person. That was the day when the midnight sky descended and gathered itself into a form. The people were astonished and afraid. What they saw was as black as nothing, and filled the sky, and its feathers shimmered and glittered with light. Its beak was long and thick and curved, like an old man's. Its eyes were as calm as a child's. Its raspy voice rattled and crackled like lightening. "Follow me," it said.

"Why should we follow you?" asked the people.

"I will lead you to the music you seek," answered the bird.

"Who are you?" asked the people.

"I am the one who clears the way. Follow my call."

"What is your name?" they asked.

"*You* are the namers. Name me," it answered.

And so the people named it as it sounded, calling it: "Throat Clearer" and followed the bird. It flew always before them—high, but appeared as darkness going down. Curved wings stretched from horizon tip to horizon tip. A sliver of light shone beneath its belly, as though under a door. The trail was long and full of trials. Of all those who started out none were at its end.

Finally they came to this place and found the Tree silently waiting. And when they arrived the great bird sounded a terrible rattle: "*Craaaaaaak, cruuk, craaak*," and sank into the deeps of the sea as if dead. It pained their ears and filled them with misery and woe and a sense of finality. The people trembled in fear and hid their faces.

The Tree spoke to them, as in a whispering wind, and said: "Do not fear my messenger. When you hear it call, clear your throat and call back, and it will answer you with your death. But for now, clear your throat and sing to me the music you have followed, and I will spin a web that you may live within, free from fear of monsters and the unseen demons that bite and burn your bodies."

So the people sat down that day in a circle so that none should be ahead that others would be behind, and in one clear voice they sang their music.

Tree held back the sharp-fanged winds with her own body and kept the people cool with her shade when the fire monster flew high in the sky. There were berries on the bushes, grass in the meadows, fish people in the waters, and the bird tribes lined the riverbanks with eggs. In the soft bodies of the old trees that were lying upon the ground, going back to Earth, there were voles, fat grubs, roots, and plump mushrooms. Between the fallen trees, buried in the softness of Earth, were truffles and different kinds of grubs and roots and sprouts. Rushes edged the lakes and bark slabs lay scattered about on the ground for making lodges, and much fodder for feeding the lodge fires fell freely for the gathering. Babies were born fat and dark and warm. The children's eyes were as deep and soft as a woodland fawn's, and they grew tall and strong-limbed and lived almost as long as the trees.

The people buried the fish bones and threw the mussel shells into the swift river, and wood smoke lingered in the air and mixed with the evergreens and kept the biting bugs at bay. There was laughter in the village and much lazing around between the huts. From time to time, they heard the one that clears the way off deep in the forest, and the people bent their necks and faced the ground and closed their eyes and covered their ears with their hands. But some brave ones cleared their throats of phlegm and called back with a song that they had been taught as children. They sang: "Throat Clearer, Throat Clearer, I hear you. Carry me home. Spread your wings and we will fly, *together*. Carry me high away."

These people all lived in the same lodge, and they were called: "Throat Clearers". They said that, if called from the heart, Throat Clearer would clear the way of all the flam and needless residue. But to call him in, a man had to kill himself and then listen—listen through the closed door of the heart for the answer; the answer would open the door into the forest. And so these people grew patient and silent and still, and they listened . . . In their silence, they waited only to hear the clearing call. In the *waiting*, they found wisdom and they knew beyond belief that in the end, if not before, the answer would surely come.

For the Tree People, in those days, as always with Carlo, all trees were one Tree. Therefore, one did not simply cut down a tree; he cut down Tree. And Tree gladly gave herself to a man to be cut down, for though one, she was many. There was, however, a condition: before the chopping started, the man had to tell the tree his purpose for taking it so that Tree would understand.

Carlo could even remember the old songs, when the entire tribe sang the night away to the sound of wooden drums fashioned from all the different trees. Each drum was unique and sang its individual song. Several men and squaws sat in a circle, each with a drum. In a slow and easy cadence, they began to beat the drums and chant. The rhythm of the chant danced out into the trees and went from tree to tree, touching each and every one within its reach. At first, only the men sang, and they sang low and slow. Then the beat quickened to double and triple its pace, and the chanting grew more shrill and warbled as the women and children joined in. No signal was given, yet no drummer missed a beat, and no chanter sang off key, and no two songs were ever the same. The people drummed and sang as one.

The faster rhythm flew away like a bird hawk, pushing the slower before it, until the entire forest was touched, and all trees were joined together by silver threads of euphony. Then, there was no fear. The people knew they were safe, because a web of enchantment bound the forest as though spun by a giant night spider, and in the early-morning dew it caught the light and gleaned it into rays that glowed silver and gold and cast innumerable tiny rainbows.

These were Carlo's memories, but they were vague and seemed far away, for he was a child when the evil ninety-proof spirits of the whiskey bottle broke through the web of enchantment. A break in the web of enchantment weakens the entire structure. The songs became solemn and confused. More often, when one drummer's arm was going up another's was coming down. His memories also held those days when various men of the tribe could be seen coming home from the settlement at the river's mouth, trailing their wives behind, whose love they had sold for sips. The eyes of these men were filled with the red glare of the whiskey demon, and when their wives gave birth, the babies of these mothers were born pale and poor, and they were marked with festering sores, and they were cold, and they died fast. In a short time, the singing ceased altogether.

One day, a group of men came to the village who called themselves "Company." Some of these men were hard-eyed and carried guns. They told the Tree People that they could stay upon the land of their ancestors, along the banks of the swift river, with the prerequisite that they help fall the trees. And the Tree People were perplexed, for to force one's will upon another was an evil they had never practiced and so had no natural defenses against it. Some quickly agreed, because they would be rewarded with sips. Those who refused were carried away by Company. Though many protested, it was as though their protests were carried off in muddy spring freshets. Though they beseeched Wind, River, Rain, Mountain, Sun, Moon, Great Water, Rock, Raven, and prayed to Tree with all their might, it was as if all these were dead to them and their cries went unheeded.

Company came in and took its liberties with their forest home and with the Tree People. It built large dams and splashed the river, once in the spring, once in the winter, and again the next spring. After the third time, the black-backed salmon with the red flesh they loved was never seen in the water again by the Tree People. And the great sleek sea-river fish that doesn't die unless it's killed, and carries rainbows on its silver sides and fills the streams with its seeds, shunned the river, went back, and lived only in the sea.

All those who stayed as slaves for Company were now dead from hard work and hard liquor. The medicinal herbs lost their magic, and the soothing leaves stung like bees, and the wise old medicine men were as quacks. The fire monster had his way. Saplings wilted. Berries dried and died on the vines. All those who were carried away were dead from pellagrous sores and sore hearts. Only Carlo remained to the end, and now he too was dead.

But Tree is one. Time is many. Tree is greater than time. No many-things are greater than Tree. Tree is old, old, old—and wise and true. Time can only sigh as it flows through her leaves. The time of the Tree People had been as a passing breeze, a wind-whisper in the limbs, and so would be Company. The old wise ones, the shamans of the tribe and the Throat Clearers, had said that a man should *be* as Tree, if he could. "If he cannot, he should at least strive to be so," they said. The young would ask: "What sort of *being* is that?" The Tree People had no word for *Truth*, so the wise ones would reply: "Never lie."

Though its design is hidden in mystery, Tree is not cruel, and she never deserts her people, and to that person who perseveres, the mysteries unravel themselves, and all knowledge is revealed in that final link that ends the links of the chain of moments, if not before.

In that place of the last link, Carlo learned that he had been appointed messenger to the Tree People. For he alone persevered and stood straight and unfallen and held his shoulders square and shunned the bottle spirit and was not carried away with the tribe. Each and every time he felled a tree or chokered up a log, he said to Tree: "I do this to you so that I can stay here in our home and leave with you at the end." And so, he stayed with Tree the only way he could and keened over her in hard days and sacrificed his reason and he knew there was a purpose to sorrow but did not claim to know the purpose, because the shamans had said: "Never lie." So he proved himself worthy of the Tree People.

In that open place of the final link, Carlo finally saw Everything, before it sunders into things; he saw Knowledge before it sunders into knowing; he saw Integrity before it sunders into integrals; he saw Unity before it sunders into units.

It was as though a voice spoke from that place and asked him what he had learned, when he was bound within the links of the chain. And he knew what it was, but he did not speak of it. His silence was his answer. For within his solitude, he had remained single while becoming many. Now the circle was complete; he was again one with the Tree People.

The last of a race always has one last job to do and Carlo's one last job to do was to carry the message for his people that if they had stood fast and tall and spread their limbs to interlock when Company came as a hard wind, and had they demanded a *good* reason of it they would have received no good answer. And so, they could never have been uprooted and scattered by the storm—though their moments may have ended right where they stood. Then, from the west, he heard the sound of ululation beyond a far-off dark ridge, and he felt a great surge and flow, and he spread his arms as though to swim, and to his amazement, his arms were as the diaphanous fins of a swift rainbow-sided fish. Up the mountain stream he went, trailing his colors through the currents. From somewhere, he heard Throat Clearer call out a loud and deep rattle and he felt his answering call deep in his throat, rumbling down through his chest and seizing his heart. And then, there was the deep green forest. In that moment, he smiled.

If those loggers, who glimpsed that final smile, had known how to listen, they would've heard these last few words: "*I* will clear the trail."

The story of the Tree People would have died with Carlo, except Abe knew it, and Abe never forgot a *good* story. Carlo perceived that the usurpers could not understand *the story* and would be uninterested if told of it. Not being rememberers, they would heap it upon the slash pile of forgetfulness. Late one evening, a few months before Carlo's death, Abe walked up to his hollow tree and found Carlo outside under his canvas awning. He was sitting cross-legged, his back as straight as a post, bare-footed, no hat, staring into the gathering gloom and listening to the sound of a lone hoot owl, singing a dirge off somewhere in the forest.

It was going to be a cold night and threatened rain. As usual, Carlo lit no fire, so Abe scrounged around for wood and started one up. Neither man uttered a word. Abe was going to leave Carlo alone in his reverie. However, when he took a step toward the trail that led down the hill, Carlo spoke up. In a clear voice, sonorous and deep, as though he answered the owl, he started telling the story of the Tree People. Abe sat down against a tree and listened while watching the fire shadows dance. The fire cast its glow upon Carlo's features as he stared through it blank-faced into another place, another world. When he finished, Carlo hung his head as though in deep sorrow and said not another word to Abe after that.

Several years later, somewhere along the banks of the Klaskanine, on another late evening when misty rain hung in the air, gathered in the trees, then rolled down the boughs and fell in large drumming drops upon the canvas awning, Abe entered the world of the Tree People for a time. Owls were warbling vespers from the treetops, and tree frogs chirped from the dark. He was staring blankly into the fire, when he spoke up out of that deep place and entrusted the story to Whitey. In later years, Whitey passed it on to some of those whom he considered worthy of it. Others with merit picked it up from there and wove it into their rhymes. So it happened that in the tall tellings of the timberjacks, the Tree People continued to walk upon Earth.

Though the styles are not the same, there is only a subtle difference between those tellings and the singings.

Slim was dejected by it, but Hack was devastated by the death of The Fish. He lost his usual imperturbability and lamented in morose silence. He blamed himself, entirely. He was opening the throttle at the time, urging on the donkey, spinning the drum, stressing the cables, trying to dislodge a big heavy log that had nosed into the frozen ground. This is what broke the spar, snapped the lines and sent them whipping, and dropped the high-lead rigging on top of The Fish. He said he should have known better, considering the weather was so cold with ice and snow. Spars were known to shatter in such weather. He announced his decision to quit, but Slim managed to convince him that it was no man's fault that another man dies, unless he was trying to kill him. Slim said: "If it's anyone's fault then it be God's, and can't any man find fault with God, though many fools have tried." They spent that evening consoling one another over a bottle of redeye that Hack had stowed away to wait for some special occasion. This occasion seemed special enough, even if it wasn't what he'd had in mind when he stashed it.

Slim wouldn't allow drinking in his crew at any time and saw no reason whatsoever for liquor to be anywhere within the confines of the camp and made a real point of it: "Want booze, go to town. One sip here an' yer canned, *period*!" It was a hard and fast rule and brooked no offenders. But in this particular case, every logger understood and didn't hold it against Slim for breaking his own law, and he didn't even think to ask Hack why it was he had it stashed in the first place. The pathetic irony of it all was that Slim and Hack washed away their guilt and sorrow with a bottle of the very stuff that The Fish's tribe used to wash away theirs, but washed away a tiny nation to boot. They went to work with sore heads the next day.

But for whatever else he may have been, The Fish was a logger to these loggers, and he knew full well there were no safe jobs in the woods. Later, when Abe went through Carlo's hollow tree looking for his belongings, he found one change of clothes. So they dug a deep hole and bedded it with spruce boughs and buried the last of the Tree People upon the riverbank, beneath the red cedars, wrapped in a soogan, wearing his corkies, and one change of clothes in his traveling sack.

The cold winter passed. The wet Chinook winds had come and gone, and the Chinook salmon was on its way inland. The torrents of spring left a part of their run-off in the backup behind the splash dam on the river. It was fat-river time, time for the big event called a "splash." The climactic day arrived, the day when a season's work worth of logs was sluiced down the river to the mill sites in Coquille, Marshfield, and points in between. The greatest number finally settled in the Coos estuary, where the tugs boomed them up into rafts that were almost as wide as the river and hundreds of feet long. The tug captain revved his engines and spun his propellers and towed the rafts to where the big black Asian ships wait to fill their empty, hungry gullets.

A splash was a show worth seeing, so Slim gave the entire crew time off to watch the grand event.

Splash dams were marvels of engineering, constructed from braced logs and timbers, cross-bolted and woven together by an ingenious web of steel cable and rigged with hinged gates that could be lowered and raised by water pressure and levers. In effect, they shut up the river with wooden gates. On the selected day, the gates are opened, and the splash releases the backup in one big whooshing wave of pent-up water, splashing several months' accumulation of logs away with it. Very few men could construct these dams; theirs was a direct descendant of the same genius that built the ancient arched aqueducts. These times, instead of for Rome, they worked for the boom companies that contracted with the timber company to turn the rivers into log flumes.

Abe and Whitey left the saw in the woods this morning and joined the rest of the crew on the hillside, just down river from the splash. When the boom company men opened the gates, a cheer resounded through the woods. A wave of logs surged through the dam helter-skelter, rolling and tumbling down the canyon on their way to the millponds, far below. The splash was on its way. It gouged out the river bottom and gnawed away its banks. It sliced away the overhangs where the little rainbows hid in shadows. It washed the silt from farmer's meadows and from the stump ranches, and spit it out the river's mouth like thick, brown snoose and over the salty bar, where it landed in the sea's spittoon. It turned the ocean brownish-gray for a hundred miles or more.

Hogs rode the logs. "River hogs," so called. Agile young hogs, much more like long-legged birds walking and jumping on the backs of hippos and alligators through currents, rapids, and slack water. Whoever it was that attached their handle to them must have never watched them work a splash. The hogs carried long pikes and peaveys for rolling and pushing logs this way and that, keeping them apart and free-flowing. They corralled them into booms. Their job was to keep the boom from jamming up into a water-tangled bird's nest of debris. But jam up they often did, and many log jams couldn't be untangled with any amount of dynamite and were never set free, even in the highest of succeeding "century" floods. These only jammed it tighter. It took time's relentless rot to undo the doings of force. The skilled hogs loved nothing more than to show off for the land-locked loggers, but through the years many a poor ol' river hog was butchered and ground to sausage between the logs and the river bottom.

Astonished and wide-eyed, Whitey had never seen such a spectacle. His heart leaped with the splash, and his blood surged with the river. He cheered with the rest and threw his hat into the air, too.

But Abe was strangely silent, downright glum. He watched until the splash was out of sight, then without a word, turned on his heels and walked off into the woods toward his saw.

Experienced loggers were hard to come by during the booming twenties, and sometimes Slim had to disregard his better judgment to keep his crew full. The replacement for The Fish was a bandy-legged boy, barely dry behind the ears. He'd served his time as a whistle punk and wanted to climb up the hierarchy. At his age that was all the way up to choker setting.

Setting chokers was as rigorous and dangerous as most any job in the woods.

Snapping limbs and flying logs and swinging cable required diligence and animal reflexes, so these were bright young men; but rarely were they as young as this one. His handle was Bugger. Tonight, Bugger and Junior-the-whistle-punk were sitting together on a bench, taking their usual ribbing from the older, more worldly boys.

Said someone loud enough so that all could hear: "Hey, Bugger, got yourself a girlie friend?"

Bugger only grinned, saying nothing. He knew there was no way to win a word contest against this bunch.

Said another: "Punkie, what 'er you sittin' there grinnin' about? How many you got?"

Someone else piped up: "Neither one o' these pollywogs would know what to do with a gal."

Now it was Hack's turn: "Well, let's show 'em. Hey Zimm," he said good and loud, "you still got them photographs you showed me, the ones that show ever'thing, an' I do mean it all."

"I got 'em stashed," said Zimm. "Why ya' askin', you wanna' stare at 'em again?"

"Well, yeah. But first let's hold 'em up in front of these two tadpoles' faces. Then we'll tie their hands behind their backs so's they can't jack off an' relieve the pressure, an' then point 'em towards Marshfield where all them good lookin' little bow-legged gals work. We'll watch these two go t' runnin' an' place bets to see which one gets to town first."

"Five bucks on the long-legged Punk," hollered out someone.

"I'll take that bet, 'cause ol' Bugger's older an' hornier," hollered another.

And so it went, placing bets for a while. The two awkward boys sat red-faced, grinning and squirming on their buns as if they'd just wiped their bungs with nettle leaves.

"Fellers, I'm hotter 'n a wild cat with a red-hot noodle stuffed up its ass. Why, I'm so danged horny I'd diddle the town of Florence if'n I could find her hole," added a fourth.

A fifth confessed: "I found it once, but it was too tiny for me. It's called the Siuslaw Bay. Cold and wet, it is."

Someone else bragged: "Besides cold, she's deep, too. I'm agonna get me on down to town come July Fourth an' cozy up to one of them warm ones."

From the back of the room: "Hey Zimm, where the hell ya' hidin' them photographs?"

As usual, it was ol' dirty-minded Hack who made the initial wisecrack that stirred up this series of salacious witticisms, and now they teased his own hot libido into action.

Hack was a big man in the big woods; no way could he fit into little ones. He was a carouser, a cockster, and one of the tallest of the tall tale tellers. He was tireless at a party, always the first to arrive and the last to leave. But he lost his poop real quick on the job, and Slim considered him downright irresponsible. Gregarious to a fault, loving to wedge himself into a crowd and cavort around in a tangle of people, he mixed his snores with the men in the bunkhouse. For simplicity's sake, Hack *believed* without question or doubt, and so fiction was fact for him. That's because belief requires little effort and he didn't want to do any more work than he had to. This way, he was able to believe in something or another and also it's opposite, so that they neutralized in him, leaving him clueless and completely carefree. On those rare occasions when he saw a need to put some labor into it, he could *make*-believe impeccably: "kiddin' around," he called it—"plain ol' bullshit," according to others. But in a certain sense, he lived far from the crowd, way down deep in the spontaneity of the present; therefore, his time-sense was different from the norm. Sired by a timberbeast, conceived and born under a cedar tree, and raised among the river canyons, he grew up to be naturally religious and worshiped life with fervor and trusted it completely, and though the ground shook when he walked, he tramped his world lightly. He'd told may a lie but never one for personal gain.

Hack was the type of peccant the proselytizers of the world work to save from their wicked urges and ways. Unlike the worldly saviors, he held no vision of how things *should be*. It wasn't *his* to *change* anything, or *anybody*—a fatal mistake, as it all turned out. The deep forest was his church, the tallest tree the steeple, and the turnings of the days were the pages of his bible. It never occurred to the saviors to look for him in there, so he avoided conversion.

Among his allotments was a rare gift, which was the ability to laugh at his own ridiculous self, so he'd never known a moment's disconcertion—but he knew sorrow. The way Hack figured it, as long as he could laugh, he'd have some fun in life being as ridiculous as he pleased in a funny world. He never took a thing that wasn't his and he worked, however reluctantly, for every dime he ever had. He treated his women friends with nothing but respect—didn't use it all if she couldn't take it, paid her up full, and tipped generously. Even though he loved them one and all he never confused this with Love itself. This he offered up to his forest queen with all of his heart, and she considered him her lover of lovers. But, finally, inevitably, the page turned up that didn't contain his lover and his heart was as delicate as a thimble berry and just as easy to crumble.

Even though Hack held all beliefs, he also held one big disbelief: he disbelieved in change and insisted that things always stay as they are, and so he was always unprepared. For him, the *days* turned but the world didn't. Perhaps it's better to love without a lover, because a true lover living with a lover who leaves him leaves him with no place to live and he soon languishes in helpless, homeless solitude. Solitude becomes confinement; memory-making ends and with it purpose ends and then life stagnates and starts to rot like a snag. Like a ruminant on loco weed, he re-dreams the poison of lost dreams for his spirits nourishment. For him there is no other than his lover, no other upon whom to lay blame for his sorrow. And so the heavy weight of his shame becomes his alone to shoulder. No man's *that* big.

Not long ago, Hack would've been headed to Medford on the Fourth, but Woody was gone now, and he'd lost contact with his gal friends down there. So in this moment, Hack was thinking of the brothels that the bunkhouse stories said lined the waterfront along the bay of the Coos, at Marshfield. Word was that a man could hop from one to another and catch a high-living saloon in between. To Hack it sounded like the carnival had come to town. But he'd never been to Marshfield and didn't want to go alone, so he thought of Whitey and Abe. Now there'd be good company to take along, because he heard that Marshfield was full of tough whores, tough longshoremen, and tough cops. It was the tough cop part that bothered him. Question was: how could he talk these two stay-at-homes into going? Well, he figured he could sure as hell try.

"How much ya gotta pay fer decent lays these days?" Zimm asked, addressing anyone who might know.

"Last time I gave it a go, a beginner cost you four dollars," came an answer.

"Cost ya more'n that on the holidays, I bet," said someone else.

"Hell, way I feel, at five bucks a shot, fifty bucks'd just get me warmed up an' agoin' good," someone said.

"I'm not forkin' over no five bucks less'n it's for top-notch stuff," said yet another.

"Hell, you wouldn't know top-notch stuff if it sat smack down on yer face an' swallowed yer head," said Hack.

Laughter filled the room.

Hack put on his hat and walked out the door, into the freshness of the June night, and left the rest to debate the supply and demand of the marketplace.

Hack's stride was remindful of a big up-right circus bear, who bends forward at the waist, droops his shoulders, and swings his arms in long arcs, while throwing each foot ahead and then dropping it like a plantigrade goose: *whump, whump, whump, whump*. It covered fast ground and forced most men to trot just to keep up, but it wasn't a pretty sight to look on.

Abe heard him coming a long way off. "I hear ol' logs-for-legs Hack alumberin' up the trail," he said.

"Shall we offer him some hot chocolate?" asked Whitey.

Abe shot Whitey an incredulous glance. "That mooch? You gotta be kiddin'! No way we'd ever get rid of him after that. He'd hang aroun' here each and ever' night. Hide it, *quick*!

Whitey quickly tucked the hot chocolate sack under the edge of the ground tarp, just as Hack entered the firelight. Hack cocked his head, twitched his nose and sniffed the air. "What's that I smell?" he asked, looking all around.

"What? You smell somethin'? I don't smell nothin'. You smell somethin', Whitey?"

"Just the summer air."

"I smell somethin' sweet," said Hack, still peering about suspiciously.

"That's the June air, Hack. If you dragged your carcass out of that smelly old bunkhouse more often you'd know what it was," said Whitey.

"Oh," said Hack and plopped his big rear down next to Whitey and sat right on the sack of hot chocolate. Abe and Whitey exchanged furtive glances, but Hack didn't notice anything. "How's about the three of us goin' into Marshfield during the Fourth of, uh . . . uh, got any coffee?"

"Yeah, got some coffee," said Abe as he removed the pot of boiling water from the coals. He then poured it into a cup and dumped some fresh coffee grindings on it and stirred it with a spoon. "This is called strain with yer teeth aroun' here."

"Anyway, as I was about to say, the Fourth of July's comin' up so how's about the three of us headin' into town?" Hack took a sip. "Ahhh, just the way I like it," he said. He looked around. "Got anything to dip in it, like cinnamon bread or somethin' like that?"

"No," said Abe.

Hack wrinkled his brow in disappointment, and then said: "Well, how about it, you guys wanna go?"

"What the hell's in Marshfield that ain't here?" answered Abe.

As if perplexed by the question, Hack wrinkled his brow, looked at Abe, and said: "Touch. Touch is what's there and ain't here, Abe. It's all about touch. Does a man good once in a while, to touch somethin' besides tree bark, ya know."

"Well, I know what yer talkin' about touchin', an' I know what you intend to touch it with," said Abe.

"Now here's a man who knows a good thing," said Hack to Whitey.

"I didn't say I was goin'," said Abe.

"Well ya are ain'tcha?"

"Hell, no. I got plenty to do right here."

"Here? What the hell ya gotta do here?"

"Sharpen my saw an' my axe, an' grease my corks, an' wash my clothes an' my soogans to name a few."

"Ohhh, Abe. You can do them kinda things anytime. Gosh dang it, I hear there be lots o' purdy gals in Marshfield. Just imagine this: yer promenadin' down the boardwalk with a good looker on each arm." Hack held out an elbow. "Just you boys think about it. A redhead here," then he held out the other elbow, "an' a blonde one here, an' each one wantin' a big piece of whatcha got. Give her all she can handle. Those are workin' gals, ya know—gotta earn their dough—a little bit of touchin' here an' there, an' a whole lot of rubbin' everywhere, is what they get paid to do. Find the kind who love their work, an' spread the wealth around. Why, it's good fer the economy. Take two or more on at the same time an' work 'em from both ends an' sideways; drop in a few drops of engine oil, so's to make the slidin' an' the slippin' real easy. Make 'em squeal." Hack's eyes were glassy, dreamy, and trance-like. He got lost in his own visions and went silent for a few moments, then found himself, shook off the trance, cleared his throat, and said: "There now, how's about that? Just imagine. C'mon, just imagine. Imagine how nice it'll be, an' tell me whatcha gotta say."

The fire flickered and danced about. Colored sparks: red, orange, yellow, with just a touch of green took wing – tiny fireflies, flying away.

In Whitey's head it was as though a voice said: *"Just imagine . . . imagine . . . imagine up the sweet dreams. Take a breath. Pucker your lips. Blow against the world, and set it to spinning. Now, puff a little harder, and spin it faster than time. Now, like a finger, take the tip of your mind and touch the world—be delicate—and slow it back down. Slow it way down. Go back. Re-dream the sweet dreams."*

Whitey stared into the fire, and same as Hack's had, his eyes turned glassy. An owl's hooting drifted through the forest and faded. The fire pulled him in and melted him away from here, into the time of the mind. *Yeah, just imagine . . . imagine: olive skin, hair as black as the new moon night, full lips smiling just for me, and eyes sparkling and dancing just for me. It's Saturday night, end of a long week's work, summertime, air's warm. I'm riding into the mill town high upon the back of Greymantle, the Professor's broad-shouldered Percheron. Oh, how I do love these Saturday nights!*

Greymantle's got a hot trot going. I think he has an eye for that big-rumped Belgian mare that lives at the stables. He'd give her a lively roll in the hay, too, if he weren't a gelding. But I'll bet he does his share of flirting—and imagining. I'm sure as hell glad I'm not a gelding—blood's running hot.

"I think that coffee's makin' you too hot," said Abe to Hack. "You better drink some of that spring water, there in the water jug."

"Ain't my throat that's hot—my gut, neither," said Hack.

"Pour it down the front of yer pants then."

Abe and Hack laugh.

"It just might help. I got me a hankerin' for somethin' wet, ya know," said Hack. "Just have somethin' a little bit warmer than spring water in mind."

More laughter.

But Whitey's not laughing—his imaginings are sweet, not funny. The fire's flickering, flashing in his eyes. Like a brand, the old scene burns its way into his mind: *Ahh, it's an easy evening. Wind's in my face, and I'm headed for the heaven of Peppa's company. And there's the Professor, right alongside, riding Ol' Dan. Look at the old goat, sitting in the saddle and grinning like a skunk in an outhouse. He's thinking about the saddles he's going to be lying in. The Professor likes to play the field. But not me. Peppa was my first -- (and she was my last—none in between).*

"Abe, you don't know what yer missin'."

Abe looks at Hack as though confused. "If I don't know it, then how can I miss it?"

But Whitey doesn't look; Whitey doesn't hear all the jabber. Time is here, and time is there; it's everywhere in the moment—makes a line coming and going. It covers a man like coarse skin; he sloughs it off like lizard's scales. Whoever said that a man can't toe two lines of time at once? -- maybe even more than two . . . sorta like he can touch more than two sunbeams at the same time.

Almost there. We're riding past the saloon. Honky-tonk music is flowing out of the open door, mixed with the laughter of men and the giggles of the flappers. Real jubilee going on in there. No time for the saloon right now, not for me, though the Professor will amble back here for a toot or two. Says he likes to wet his whistle before he wets his pistol.

Move it along Greymantle; Peppa's waiting. Almost there, me to the quilts, you to the straw.

"Gawl dang it, Abe, ya miss it in sorta the same way ya'd miss a sip of good whiskey, if'n ya never had yerself a sip of the best there is."

"Well, I've had enough sips to know that I'd never miss 'em, the best or the worst, even if I were to go from now to whenever without sippin' another."

"Not the same thing, not nearly the same thing. Whisky an' pussy ain't . . . Oh, what the hell . . . Gawl . . ." Hack shrugs his shoulders and slowly shakes his head. "Ya miss the whole point. Can't *touch* whiskey," he mumbles.

It's getting late. Abe yawns and stretches, hoping Hack will get the point.

But right over there, in that other place, that other time, it's a youthful night, still early, and full of promise: *Oh, boy, won'tcha just look at that! There she is, waiting on the porch of that big two-story house down at the end of the street, sitting on the bench, waiting like she always does on these Saturday nights. A slight breeze is blowing her hair. Jeesus amighty, won'tcha look at it shimmer! It's sprinkled with moon dust . . . no, gold dust . . . maybe stars . . . She's wearing the lacy senorita dress, the one that flows out from the hips and falls to the ground, the same one she was wearing that night the Professor introduced us. She dressed up extra nice that night, because the Professor was bringing me in for the first time, and she knew I was on my way, and she wanted me to walk down the line and choose her, out of all the others. She'd already chosen me. She needn't have worried: I'll always choose her. It's a special dress that she wears only for me, only on these Saturday nights.*

"You ain't got no imagination, Abe."

"I got a full day's work ahead of me tomorrow is what I got."

"No imag . . ."

But Hack doesn't get to say it again, because Abe doesn't need to hear it again. Stretching once more, Abe says: "Tomorrow comes early, Hack, real early," and yawns.

But Whitey's not yawning. *There's a white flower in her hair, bet she picked it from a meadow just for me—and look! It's glowing in the moonlight—a daisy I think . . . or perhaps a moon flower . . . God, how fine she is! I can't wait to touch her, taste her, smell her. She sees me coming; look at her smile; she thinks I'm a king. She couldn't care less that I'm a swamper working for this old down-and-out horse logger for next-to-nothing wages. Won't you just look at those eyes dance! Just look at . . .* "Whitey . . ."

Whitey heard the name like an echo through the canyon. Peppa heard it, too. Her smile faded. She tilted her head and her eyes looked puzzled and her lips moved, as though saying: "Whitey . . ? Who's Whitey?" And then she was gone like vapor, and the big white house was gone, and the mill town was suddenly a ghost town, and the Professor . . . even big ol' Greymantle. All were gone.

But Hack wasn't gone. He was saying: "How 'bout you, Whitey? You got any imagination? C'mon, talk ol' Abe into it. Tell him what he's missin'."

And Whitey understood that Peppa didn't know him. It was yellow-haired Henry who Peppa loved. One thing was for certain: Henry had gone right up onto that porch, swooped up Peppa, and they were all coupled up under the quilts, this very moment. After all, didn't the Professor say there's no such place as far away?

Whitey said: "Can't find the words to tell him what he's missing."

"Oh, hell, c'mon you two. Neither one o' you guys got even a sliver of imagination."

"Maybe I'll go," said Whitey. "Only maybe. I'm not making any promises, but just maybe."

Encouraged, Hack said: "They'll be crazy about ya, Whitey." Then Hack looked at Abe with one of those well-how-about-you looks. But he didn't catch Abe's eye. Abe was looking at Whitey with disbelief.

Abe lowered his eyes, slowly shook his head, frowned and said: "Well, they won't like *me*."

"Oh, hell, Abe, you don't know that. Why the hell won't they?" Hack glanced at Whitey; his eyes were pleading for assistance. "Right, Whitey?"

Whitey shrugged his shoulders and grinned. "Why would any gal like someone that ugly," he teased.

"Aww, come on, Whitey an' help me talk him into it."

"Naa, his mind is set like a mountain, and a mortal man can't move a mountain."

Disappointed, Hack slumped, sipping his coffee, searching for convincing words. A bat fluttered back and forth through the sparks in the firelight as though it were gulping the sparks. "Well, I'm sure glad *yer* comin'. We'll have the time of our lives," he said to Whitey.

Perhaps it's a gift, like a basket of fruit from a benevolent god, that the sweet memories hold their taste the longest. It's ambrosia for a traveling man's imagination, keeps him from starving during the lean years. Or perhaps the good god is a well-meaning trickster and causes a man to forget too easily the hard-earned lessons he should most remember and thus dooms him to repeat them.

Whitey most remembered the warmth and gentle touch of Peppa, giggles under the quilts, and whispers of love. Right now, he wanted to forget his sorrow and even perhaps his love, but remember the touch. So, like Hack, on this warm feminine night, he felt his lust stir. "I'll think on it, Hack," he said.

After Hack left, Whitey asked Abe why he was so reluctant to go, and Abe hesitantly admitted that he had told a big fib on that day he said he rubbed off his hair on a bedpost. "Fact is I ain't never been with no woman," he said. "My hair fell out on its own free will." When Whitey asked him why it was he'd never known a gal, at first Abe couldn't answer, but finally he said it was because all he'd ever done was drift and work, neither of which activities lent themselves to womanly contact. But Whitey had learned that a man can at least seek that contact out, and was convinced that Abe was afraid of rejection.

"Abe, why don't you put some thought into it? There's nothing gentler than the feel of a good woman. It's a feel a man shouldn't live his life through without experiencing at least once."

Abe raised his eyebrows. "You sound like you plan to go with ol' Hack."

Whitey sighed. "Thinking on it. It's been a long time."

Abe mulled his thoughts for a moment, and said: "Oh hell, I'm not so sure if I should go along. Know what I mean?"

Surprisingly, Abe was giving a little, so Whitey said: "Hell, they might not like me either. It's not like I'm riding high into town on a big gray horse. Let's both think on it, okay?"

Abe and Whitey threw out their soogans and slept under the trees and stars on this night. The dying fire cast its glow off the tall-shafted trunks all about, and before long the darkness was as heavy as the silence. And like the black silence, the forest both rose up and settled down all around them. The forest is far more than just trees. The old forest is one world that contains many worlds, and in the gathering dark, unseen by eyes born into bright light, a world nodded off to sleep with the two men, while another stirred: mice scurried hole to hole; countless moths emerged from bark and foliage and spread out like a dark cloud; bats swooped and swerved; owls opened their large round eyes and lifted off on quiet wings, looking for voles; slugs went foraging; and salamanders raised their noses up out of the humus and sniffed the air. It's the changing of shifts; the hunt and feast goes on; the old forest never sleeps.

The creek under-washed its banks where it meandered through the meadow. Spittle bugs infested the grass with their foamy beds. Tall daisies waved their white heads and peered through big yellow eyes. Rainbows and cutthroat, about seven inches long, darted between cut banks and hid in the shadows. This was Friday, and Abe had the day off because Slim had granted the crew an extra day to celebrate the Fourth of July. Tomorrow he was going to town and he'd finally know the feel of a woman, or so went the plan. But he was not just a little apprehensive, for there was something about this plan that didn't smell just right. It started out with one big stink against it, considering it was concocted by Hack. But Whitey was going, and for some reason he didn't want to be left alone this time. So he was going too, and Hack was thrilled and Whitey was pleased, but still he wondered about the whole affair.

Abe was on his way to his favorite place. It was where the creek cut the meadow's edge and then rippled down over some boulders and a slide of stony slab into a deep pool. The pool was shaded by bigleaf maples, a few white-barked alders, some chinquapins, and flowered-out dogwoods. It was a place, as yet, undiscovered by saw and axe, located a few miles off on the other side of the ridge that they had just logged. He called it the Maple Pond and came here every Sunday, on warm days, and washed the sweat of six days of toil from his body. But it was more than just a pool to wash up in; there was something special about it that drew him. He came here to wash his soul of impure thoughts, because here he forgot the saw and the axe and the labor and a woodsy world he loved that seemed to be falling away.

All week long, Abe anticipated his dip. The water was as cold as ice and as clear as crystal, and when it engulfed him it was as though he were suspended in starlight and all the world was pure again. Pure fact was: he was called here, through his early-morning dreams, by the amorous little undine of this pool, who loved his soul and bathed his body with her wet kisses. So it was that today he came to wash inside and out and frolic.

He walked along the stream's edge, cutting a swath through the daisies, while looking for the little fishes, which, like little wishes, disappeared in flashes down the current—dreams come from up stream. It seemed to him the daisies stared up at him through their big round eyeballs and shook their heads like mute witnesses who saw through him and knew of his plans and these thoughts that burdened his heart.

At a certain spot along the bank he knelt and then reached down to the stream's edge and pulled out a fist full of bright green leaves, which were strung along delicate threads of stem that tied into a common root stalk. He examined them closely for a moment, and then he ate them. It was watercress, and Abe revered it, because without this, he'd surely have died during that first time he crossed the Siskiyous all alone. Close to starvation, he'd sat down in despair along the bank of a stream much like this one. He was on his way to the Pacific, but didn't know at the time if he was three miles from the beaches or three hundred. There he'd sat for a long while, pondering how he might catch some of the small trout he saw dart by, when suddenly a lucent green glow within the water caught his eye. As he looked closer, he saw that it was emitting from a string of green leaves and white flowers just under the water's surface. They clung to wispy stalks, and flowed out from the bank's side and swayed from side to side, like a maiden's long hair. At that time, he thought the glow in the leaves was reflected light, even though it was a rainy day and the air was gloomy. But now he knew the leaves glowed from within. They literally lit up the pure water and the glow mesmerized him, and he did not feel so cold and his loneliness went away. Being a desperate man, he'd scooped out a handful and hesitantly eaten it. It was his first taste of watercress. Never before or since had he tasted anything sweeter, not even the hot chocolate. It filled his muscle and bone with new energy and spiced his spirit. It was as though something succored him on that gloomy day.

He slept along the creek, under a low-hanging cedar, through several days and nights, and renewed his sagging soul. Finally the clouds broke up and the sun was back. He stuffed his pockets with watercress and walked through the mountains and down to the ocean.

He had gorged himself on it back then, but he tasted it only sparingly these days. It was pure power. The glow was mesmerizing, seducing, light energy, indestructible and life-giving. But this was all from the inside. Outside, it was tender and susceptible. Quick to retreat from corruption, it thrived only in the purest of flowing water. In any water that was tainted, if it grew at all, it didn't glow. So he came to deify it, and he honored it by eating it, and he considered that a bite now and then would keep him healthy, strong, and steadfast—but only if he remained pure. He couldn't describe purity, but he thought he could feel it.

These days, something was amiss. More often now, the green leaves of water hemlock mixed theirs with those of watercress, aped its appearance and crowded it. In such places, one had to pick his handfuls with discretion. But that was not the case here in this stream—this one still ran pure. Its bottom was pebbly with periwinkles.

It was late morning and getting warm under the big yellow sun, when he came to the Maple Pond. The cascade tumbled and mumbled through the slate and hit the pool, tinkling like tiny bells. When it dropped into the pool, the water bubbled and shimmered and glistened and the maple leaves overhead caught its rhythm and swayed to and fro. When the sunlight fell on the maples, their broad thin leaves took it in and held it, allowing only the green rays to go their way, and finally merge into the waters of the pool transhueing them to liquid green. The chinquapins added a pinch of gold. Everything in the pool and the air all around was bathed in the iridescent green light of the forest's soul.

Abe stepped casually into this place, tread lightly across a soft green carpet of filtered filigree, and then sat on the mossy bank, where he removed his clothes, stepped out, and waded into the translucent water. The icy water sent a quick chill up his spine and made him shiver. The leaves all about suddenly shook like timbrels. Limbs in the chinquapins vibrated like harp strings. Hamas hummed. Zephyrs skipped through, tossing seeds and flower pedals to the ground. Unseen by him, a zillion dryads, like countless birds of every color and every shape, fluttered through the trees and danced upon leaves and filled the air with susurration. To Abe's ear, it sounded like a soft rustling in the leaves; but there was no breeze.

The evening before the big holiday, the crew lined up for turns at getting haircuts. Cookie was also the camp barber. Abe, Whitey, and Hack took their turns with the rest. First in line was Hack. Then Cookie cut Whitey's hair, and next he put a nice neat edge to Abe's mutton chops. He told the three of them to behave themselves.

The next morning, as the sun slowly opened his sleepy red eye and peeked over the highest ridge, there was a short debate about who got to sit in the rumble seat. A flip of the coin declared the debate winner. So with Hack and Abe up front and Whitey filling up the rear, off they went, dressed in their best and looking mighty rakish in the buffed and polished automobile. Then it was up and out of the river canyon, along the high ridge, winding through the trees, then down the western slope, following the routes of the river hogs. All the way to the bay they went, and then down the tacky skid road of the waterfront.

This skid road wasn't bordered by firs and hemlocks, like it was back in timberjack days when the firs and hemlocks grew all the way down to the water's edge. These days, it was bordered by rows of bistros, rows of honky-tonks, and rows of red lights. Once a skid road always a skid road, so "Skid Road" it was still called.

With spirits high in hopes of adventure and sweet strokes, Hack proudly docked his dusty automobile.

The waterfront was quite a place. It was a place for fools, where the wise could indulge themselves in foolery for a time, should it strike their fancy. It was a place where fresh water from the mountain slope met the brine, fresh in from the sea.

Henry had come here in search of old memories, renewal perhaps, expecting the past to repeat itself. So much for déjà vu . . . The foyer reeked of smoke, whiskey, cheap perfume, and passed gas. There were several whores slouching about, in various stages of tasteless dishabille, all of whom gave the three loggers incredulous stares when they walked through the door. No one came forward, touting her wares, teasing with a sly smile. There was no lineup of pretty girls. All eyes were locked on Abe. Two surly longshoremen whispered to one another, glancing askance at the three men, motioning towards them, then scurried over and hurriedly whispered back and forth to a concerned-looking woman. She headed in their direction, all in a huff, sneering like a hard-faced witch.

She was just another madam afraid of petty politic, but it was easy to see she fancied herself the Skid Road queen. She tried to hide her ugliness behind a coating of makeup. Bright pink lipstick matched her rouged cheeks. Her eyelids were painted black. A hawk-like nose that had been broken several times was centered between the dull red eyes of a heavy drinker. Perfume vapors mixed with her whisky breath.

Grinning ear to ear, Hack immediately stepped out to greet her, but she didn't return the smile. She motioned with a stiff swing of her head, and then led him off to the corner of the smoky room where she'd been whispering with the two men. Those two were now sneaking out the front door. Hack began to talk to the woman. The twinkle in his eye faded.

Abe watched. They were arguing. The madam was stiff, shaking her head. Hack was pretending to be jolly. Abe knew the argument centered on him, and now he was sorry he ever came, and he only wanted to go home. That voice in his head was saying: *"You're out of your place, Abe—told you so. Gotta learn to listen better."*

Hack returned alone and looking glum. Arms crossed, feet apart and planted, the madam watched.

"Says we gotta scoot out an' scoot fast," said Hack, dejectedly. He lowered his eyes and looked at his feet.

"We have to leave . . ? Why?" said Whitey.

Hack was nervous and shame-faced. He glanced at the madam, caught her stare, and then looked at his feet again, muttering: "Well . . . uh, not *we* exactly. I mean . . . not you an' me." He meant his words for Whitey's ears. But Abe heard anyway and without speaking, edged toward the door.

Whitey was astonished. "Are you telling me the goddamned truth?" he said, frowning.

"Yeah, afraid so. Says it's not her doin's, but she's scared the tar-an'-feather boys'll tear hell out of this place an' put her back on the street, if . . . well, you know . . . if she allows Abe to . . . you know . . . Anyway, she says we likely don't have long till they come."

Hacks words burned like hot pokers. Whitey felt the heat of exasperation surge, then fill his veins and quicken his pulse and singe his mind. His ears were ringing. He wanted to strike out and hit somebody or something, but didn't know who or what. For a moment, he thought he might bash the hell out of Hack for bringing them here in the first place, if only to relieve the pressure. He curled his fingers into a tight-knotted fist. Through his peripheral, he could see Abe edging near the door, and for the first time in his life, he felt ashamed to look at a man, and ironically the man was his friend and partner. It was as though he instantly inherited some accumulated profusion of racial guilt from some old relative to whom he had never considered himself heir-apparent. He felt stricken numb, thoughts grew torpid, and his words oozed out like cold molasses. He clinched his teeth, and muttered: "Till *who* comes? Who the hell's *coming*?" To his own ears it sounded as if another person spoke.

"The tar-an'-feather boys. Says they'll be here to tar our asses, too, if we don't get the hell and gone from . . ."

"Bullshit! Shut up, Hack! I hear you! Just shut your mouth!" The exasperation finally burst into rage, and Hack stood in its way. Whitey shoved Hack aside and started for the madam, who now looked not nearly so tough anymore as horrified, and who was about to poop in her lacy silk pants. His voice rose up: "You damned bi . . ." The madam tucked her tail and scurried away. But before Whitey could curse the bitch, he felt a vise-like grip, as long broad fingers, hard as steel, closed in on his shoulder. It was Abe.

"No Whitey, not on my account. It ain't worth it, my friend. It's a dumb ol' fight, an' ain't no need for you or me either one to go an' join in." His voice was soft and soothing.

Whitey looked into those eyes of Abe's; they were as calm and serene now as ever, but hauntingly sad. He'd seen that same sadness many times before, but had never known why it was there or fathomed its source. Now he understood. However, along with the sadness, he now saw another look expressed in there, one that he'd never seen there before: Abe was beseeching him. He started to say something, but Abe squeezed his shoulder all the tighter, causing him to forget his words.

"C'mon, Whitey. Hack ain't in no fight, neither. Let's get out o' here an' go back to the woods, where we belong." Holding his grip on Whitey's shoulder, Abe guided him out the door.

And so out into the night went the three skid road kings, and the Skid Road queen rushed up and slammed the door hard behind them.

Chapter 8   What's a Buford?

"BUFORD . . . BUFORD . . ? WHAT'S A BUFORD?" It was a rhetorical question that appeared as a headline on the front page of the local newspaper almost a year before. The only answer to it was that Buford was a brain-dead bigot who had just been elected mayor by default, and it was the electorate of the town who were the fault. Though now they wanted to get rid of him, they were stuck with him for a term or until he did something "outrageous" enough to warrant drumming him from office. Problem was: he still had three years to go in his term, and the city fathers couldn't agree on exactly what set of circumstances constituted the word "outrageous." Anything they could come up with in this regard had been committed at least once by more than one of their number, and of course, no self-respecting citizen wants to be included in the category "outrageous" right along with Buford. But, whether drunk or sober, he came to all the town meetings, and they were stuck with him for a term.

Reality was: Buford wasn't really the mayor at all. That position belonged to another man. The real mayor had been mayor for sixteen years. He was an upstanding citizen whose father had been mayor for many terms and handed over the sinecure to his son. President of the Rotary, exalted bull at the Elks Club, and manager of the family's prosperous stevedore supply and marine outfitters business, it was he who took the brunt of the blame when the company located its new million-dollar plywood plant over the hill in Roseburg. It had been a hard-fought bidding battle, lasting for four years.

"How outrageous!" screamed the local news headlines.

"Why, Roseburg did nothing at all to deserve it! Roseburg is downright backwoods!" said the worried mayor, who was coming up for reelection.

"Doesn't even have a bay," said the harbormaster.

"Unfair to labor!" griped the longshoreman's union.

Lose out to Roseburg? Outrageous! Outrageous!

The incensed community voiced its discontent: "Vote the bastards out! Get rid of all incumbents! Down with the mayor!"

In their grand announcement, the company stated that Marshfield was a "close runner-up." But this did nothing to soothe the ruffled feelings of the local voting gentry. "Vote the bum out!" was the civic cry. So the mayor lost his title, right along with a humongous land sale, considering a big part of his bay front land holdings were earmarked for the new mill's location. If the voters had known just how ungodly hard he had worked, wheedling, cajoling, bribing, and begging to get this plant, they would have gone much lighter on him. But it was: "Jobs! Jobs! He *cost* us jobs!" And unfortunately for the poor mayor, cost jobs cost votes.

The mayor wasn't a bad sort, just the typical political sort, and the town didn't deserve what it did to itself. As punishment, and during a fit of economic moroseness from counting income that wasn't but might have been and was never to be, they temporarily handed over the reins of local government to a bawdy longshoreman by the name of Buford Bunner. But Buford had no experience at anything except whoring and brawling and gambling at cards. This fiasco came about because Buford was the only challenger in the mayor's race, and this was because anyone with a lick of sense knew the job was a sinecure and was the inherited property of the longstanding owner. So Buford ran on a lark, as a little joke to impress his drinking buddies and because he had nothing to loose anyway, and he won by a lark. Flimflam ace that he was, Buford considered a little joke for a big lark to be one-hell-of-a-deal.

So, Buford . . . Buford. . ? What's a Buford? started out as an editor's witty whimsy, and became a whimper which turned into outright communal lamentation before Buford's reign ended.

News travels fast along the waterfront, and now here stood Buford with his gang of henchmen, doing his self-appointed mayoral duties and facing the three loggers head-on as they stood on the whorehouse steps. It was plain to see that the dull-witted gang had not anticipated what walked out of the whorehouse door. The whore slammed the door, and there on the steps stood one of the largest alongside two of the most formidable men they'd ever laid eyes on. To a man, they gasped, cringed, and instantly sobered up, and there was no little amount of jockeying for position as each one sidled toward the rear of the mob, leaving Buford on the point, alone. Buford was a long way from being a woodsman, but he'd heard rumors of the bulls of the woods. Now, here he stood face to face and eye to eye with three damned Brahmas! He silently cursed his luck. But he was top dog, by gawd! He had to stand his ground or lose his position. God, it's lonely at the top. Scary, too.

Right now, Buford sorta wished he wasn't the mayor; he sure-as-hell wished he hadn't made that eloquent declamation over beers at the Barge Inn Saloon & Eatery no more than ten minutes before. The two stooges had run over from the brothel and whispered in Buford's ear: "Boy, have we got news for you! There's a nig on the docks."

"No sambos on the waterfront!" he had proclaimed with gusto. "No sambos on the waterfront!" parroted the inebriated chant, as the local voting citizenry, gathered together there in the confines of the saloon, bombasted its mandate and determined to see it instituted.

Several henchmen formed a committee and elected to "clean-up the town." "Is this war, men?" yelled Buford. "War! War! War!" came back his answer. His blood ran hot with anticipation from excitement of impending battle. Together they marched in staggered step out the saloon's batwing doors. With heads held high and shoulders back, gallantly they charged. Gutter to the left of them, trashcans to the right of them, onward went the brigand brigade. Not a single soldier dropped out; volunteers joined up along the way. Down the street along the bay, boldly they marched, right up to the gates of the house where it was rumored the infraction was taking place. Fists shook toward heaven and a bone-chilling oath pierced the air and electrified the ether: "No sambos on the waterfront!"

They halted at the brothel's steps—a file of rank soldiers shoulder to shoulder—and waited, waited, waited for the madam to do her part and deliver the heathen.

Right now, to a soldier, they wished they could turn their tails and retreat right back up the street again without completely losing face. Each and every one thanked his lucky stars that others of his ilk were coming up behind. Still, despite their numbers, a fight would be no contest, and as it turned out, many in the bunch surely owed their lives to Abe that there would be none. Both Whitey and Hack were more than ready to rip, twist, tear, slam, gouge, grind, crunch, crush, break, maim, pulverize, cripple, and finally: kill for pleasure.

Buford summoned up all his pseudo courage, but alas, when he spoke his voice broke three times and gave the coward in him away. Raising his arm, he pointed at the three loggers with a shaky index finger and said: "My name's Buford Bunner an' I happen to be the mayor of this here town. You fellers may (*break*) not know it, but we (*break and clear throat*) don't allow no (*break and clear throat and gulp real hard*) sambos on this here front.

Hack clenched his fists and held himself against the adrenalin flow and mentally calculated that it would take him about five seconds to tear the talkative bastard's head off, and then he could use it, like it was the jawbone of an ass, to pound the hell out of some of the others. However, Whitey gave in to his adrenalin and started to surge ahead. But Abe had him by the wrist. When Whitey felt the grip tighten he held himself in check. Then Abe took Hack by the wrist and held them both, while he quietly said: "Go easy, boys. If we fight 'em we can lick 'em, but we can't lick the cops because they got guns. They'll likely shoot me in the ass an' kick the two of you out of town. So think about it, do ya want t' get kicked out of town?"

His meaning was not lost on the two of them, and it was quick-thinking, fast-talking Hack who came up with the solution to their dilemma and diffused the powder keg. Making a show of it, he jerked free of Abe's grip and addressed the mob: "Listen, fellers, only reason we're here is because this here feller," he pointed at Abe, "is down here lookin' fer his sister."

The mob was filled with petty hecklers. One randy fellow near the rear of the press yelled: "Ain't diddled his sister, but his ma's here."

Hack only laughed with the rest, and said: "Then his sister must be around here, too, because they're a close-knit family.

This one really tickled the crowd's funny bone, and another brave soul in the back shouted: "Then let him stay, so's I can have him, too. Already had me his sis an' his ma."

Now this nonsense was about the funniest thing this bunch had ever heard. They were all having a good old time, laughing at the top of their lungs and jostling one another around. To Buford's relief the tide was changing. He fancied himself the man of the hour and grinned ear to ear. Hack spoke to Abe and Whitey now, but kept his voice low, so the gang couldn't hear: "You guys hightail it out of this stink hole. Get back to the camp any ol' way ya can. I'm goin' with this bunch."

Before Abe could protest Hack's plan, Hack turned to the rest, and addressing Buford in particular, said: "How's about me comin' with you fellers? We'll have a few beers then you can point the way to this feller's sis, that is, if'n it don't rub off."

This one really made the mob howl, and Buford was overjoyed with relief, because not only was he the kingpin, but he occupied the foremost spot and stood closer to Whitey than any one of the others. He tried not to look at Whitey, but for some reason he couldn't help himself. It was as though those pale eyes were sucking him out of his skin and putting him in another place, another scene, a watching scene, watching, pulling him in closer, watching powerful hands break him apart piece after painful piece, bone by bone. The man behind the eyes wanted to realize that scene—to remove it from his mind and place it in the moment—to live it—to enjoy it. Buford could hear the crunching of limbs and the tearing of sinew in his inner ear. It hurt to look into those eyes. If that tall bull charged it would be right at him. All the stevedores on the docks wouldn't be able to stop him from doing what Buford knew full well he was aching to do. Buford wasn't so simple as to not know that right now the huge talkative logger over there was his best friend, to whom he probably owed his life. Buford heard someone say: "It don't rub off; I can vouch fer that," followed by some more uproarious laughter. He tried to laugh, but like a burr, his laugh stuck in his throat and wouldn't come up and wouldn't go down. It hurt. He gulped and swallowed cotton.

Hack then stepped down and walked toward them, grinning like a turncoat skunk with halitosis. "C'mon boys. Let's go have us a high time," he said.

Now, having become the Pied Piper of obnoxious drunks, Hack forgot his amorous imaginings—touch would wait for another time. He marched off down the street, playing the music of his verbal wit, with a bunch of drunk harbor rats titubating in his tracks. Abe and Whitey stood in front of the brothel and watched him go.

"I hope he *lives* through this night," said Abe.

Whitey said: "I hope he *kills* Buford."

Chapter 9 The Gandy Dancer

It was a long walk to Coquille; not a word was spoken. Whitey couldn't understand his newfound sense of shame. It's hard to find words for what you know but don't understand. Shame's all he could think about. It damned near brought tears to his eyes. So, like the tears, he held it in, where it grew hot and built up pressure. He'd beat the ground with his fists or rage at the nearest tree and tear at its bark if he were alone, but Abe was at his side, strolling along as though he were enjoying the walk through the warm evening. They kept off the road, wherever possible, and cut through the low-lying marshlands, laced with tidal sloughs and humming with mosquitoes nearly the size of dragonflies. But both men considered the mosquitoes to be better company than that swarm they'd just come from. They sat beneath a madrone tree on the outskirts of town and waited through the dawn for the new day.

Abe spoke the only words that were spoken all night long. Sitting under the tree, he said: "Don't paint yerself in with them boys. You ain't the color ya think ya are. It ain't so much in what you look at with your eyes, it's whatcha feel about it."

It was the day for Cookie to make his timeworn trip to town for supplies. Abe and Whitey killed time in a greasy spoon, and then they sat on the curb outside the grocery store. It was a long wait, because Cookie had made arrangements with Arkie to pick him up at his home, along with Zimm who wanted to spend the holiday in a domestic scene. Wishing to stretch their holiday, they'd talked him into coming in later than usual. On the way in, he had a flat tire and stopped by the rubber shop to get the spare repaired.

Abe and Whitey began to think Cookie wasn't coming. The beat-up old pickup, bouncing down Coquille's dusty main street, was a pretty picture. Even ol' Cookie was pretty. Whitey dropped all of his usual reserve. "Gawdamn ya, ya old mulligan mixer," he said, "you're a sight for sore eyes! Take us *home!*"

The two loggers welcomed him with such unexpected glee that it warmed the heart of the stodgy old cook and made his eyes twinkle. It even made the outermost corners of his mouth turn up, ever so slightly. He said: "Got in trouble didn'tcha?" Abe and Whitey nodded their heads. "Told ya so," he mumbled.

They helped him load the supplies in the back, and then piled in with them. Cookie headed out to Arkie's place.

Zimm was no dummy; he knew where to spend a holiday. Arkie's wife was a hefty Swede of hardy Northwestern upbringings and loved to cook the good old timberjack fare. The kind that puts meat on bones and fat on meat if not worked into muscle. Bred out by timberbeasts, she'd once been one herself, bending her steps between the far-flung camps. She held Cookie's job before Cookie did and had taught him all of her recipes when his turn turned up. That 's where Arkie met her, in the hash hall over a heap of pork gravy, golden brown and hot, poured over buttered sourdough biscuits and sprinkled with nutmeg. It was love at first taste. Then he wed her and bought the house in town for her as a wedding present, and so they would have some place to spend their honeymoon and build a nest and raise a brood on the downhill side of their lives. Both had toiled long and hard and considered that they had earned their respectability.

When the pickup pulled into the driveway, the three hedonists were sitting on the porch, side by side, burping and digesting and enjoying the waning hours of the warm day. It was plain to see that Arkie and Zimm were bursting from two days of gorging on good grub and guzzling thick, home-brewed malt beer.

Of course, they were all curious about why Abe and Whitey were parked in the pickup's bed. When they heard the story from Whitey they became incensed and talked of "goin' back there and kickin' ass." Arkie and Zimm could've made short work of it. Cookie figured he could get in a few quick kicks before his lame leg gave out. Then he'd still have one active leg and two good arms with fists on the end of each to use. Even Biscuit Betty, Arkie's wife, was going to do some kicking of her own, and she could do it, too; she'd done her share of ass-kickin'.

But Abe reminded them that the present whereabouts of Hack were unknown, and were they to go charging into town kickin' ass, someone just might tie an anchor to Hack's big ol' ass and drop him like a sinker log into the bay. He convinced them that they still worked for Slim, and if they all ended up in the Marshfield jailhouse, Slim wouldn't be able to run his business. So it was that, like a good choker setter, he chokered their emotions and yarded them in.

Zimm and Arkie squeezed into the cab with Cookie, while Abe and Whitey reclaimed their seats in the back among the supplies. The poor old pickup, loaded to the gunnels with oversized loggers and merchandise and sitting on its axles, labored its way back up the long hill, along the serpentine trail of ruts and bumps.

Sitting in the pickup bed, Whitey still couldn't get his mind off the events on the waterfront. It seemed to him as though he was tried to his limits that night in Marshfield and found lacking. He'd wanted to grab that madam, hold her up, and shake some sense into her. He'd wanted to grab Buford and shake the life out of him. Didn't get to do either one. Now he felt unfulfilled. Never had he known such rage as he'd felt back there and the sterile powerlessness to express it. Still, he knew that he did the right thing for the sake of Abe, as well as himself, and had Abe to thank for holding him in check. Yet he couldn't help chewing on the vision of Buford's smirk. It was bitter cud. He finally spit it off his tongue: "I'm going back to that town, soon as I get the chance! I'm going to find that bastard and break his son-of-a-bitchin' neck!"

"*Naa,*" replied Abe.

"Don't *naa* me, Abe. Just you wait and see."

"Whatcha want to go do somthin' like that for? Ya miss them fellas that much?"

Now, even Abe's nonchalance was starting to perturb Whitey. He spoke more for effect than substance when he said: "Because I *hate* a bastard like that! That's why, Abe."

Abe was silent for a long while. He knew Whitey needed to purge some bad humors. Then he tilted his head back and looked up at the sky. "Look at them stars astartin' to glow up above ya, Whitey, an' tell me ya can hate anythin' to the point of hurtin' it."

"Okay. You want to hear it? Okay. Here it is: I hate the son of . . ." But, before Whitey could finish, Abe cut him off.

"I said to look at the stars, first. *Look*," Abe ordered.

They were still in the coastal valley with a broad view of the sky. Wide fields lay on each side where dairy cattle stood like dark shadows. The air was clear and cool and carried the musty smell of tidal mud flats. Whitey obeyed Abe's order. He tilted his head and raised his eyes. There weren't many stars out yet, but it was a new moon time, a good time for stars, and there was going to be a billion of them pretty soon. The ones that shone now were big ones and looked like fawn eyes caught in a headlight beam. The truck jolted along and the wind blew through his hair. It occurred to him that those were the same stars that lit his way when he left the farm. They'd soothed him out on the prairie, during that long trek when he began to fear there was no end to flat land—no mountains. They were the same ones that shone over the Professor's cabin and the same ones he and Peppa had known together. After all this time and all this way, these same stars were still back there, in that time, in his mind, shining over those places right now, and they were here, too. And they had been right where they are for uncountable numbers of men and women and years. The whole incident with Buford suddenly seemed damned petty. He recognized his folly and knew his words were beneath him and even felt a little ashamed of himself in the face of Abe—and the stars.

Still, a sense of stubbornness strangely lingered, and in spite of himself, he weakly said: "I hate them." Whitey heard the words as though someone else, a trite someone, afraid of starlight, who didn't want to leave the comfort of his warm dark gut, had spoken them. He also heard the sound of laughter.

Abe was a quiet man and withdrawn from most men. He didn't laugh much. Hack could make him laugh, but that was about it. After all this time of being partners, he still held back from Whitey, and Whitey knew not to probe. So this was one of the few times Whitey ever heard him laugh, right out loud; and to his chagrin, he was the one being laughed at.

"Whitey," said Abe, after clearing his laughter, "I suspected you might have a lot of the stubborn streak in ya. Felt it through the harp on that first day. Now I know it t' be a fact."

"What the hell are you talking about?" said Whitey.

Abe wasn't going to allow Whitey to hold onto his rancor, no matter how hard he tried.

"Okay, I'll tell you what I'm talkin' about. It's the least I can do, seein's you were so willin' to go against yerself an' fight a war for me. Way I see it, Whitey, we be too much akin inside our skin, an' I don't hate no one, so how can you, considerin' we be kin folk?" It was me they ran out o' town, ya know—not you.'"

"Considering your words, they ran us both out, so *who* they ran out of town doesn't make any difference to me, Abe."

"Tell ya a story. Wanna hear?" said Abe.

Whitey perked up and snapped out of his brooding. This was a different Abe sitting across from him from the one who stood opposite the tree upon his springboard. This Abe was going to talk. And Whitey was going to listen.

So began Abe's story: "Whitey, I was born in a big ol' city called Baltimore. Lived in a tarpaper shack among a bunch more shacks just like it. My pa stomped around barefoot all day in clay, makin' bricks down at the brick factory while my mama made babies. The reason she made babies was because she loved so much it flowed over. She needed them babies so's to have somewhere to put it all. I was the oldest of a whole bunch of brothers an' sisters. Some lived; some didn't. Livin' was just as hard as it can get. Funny thing, though, I can't remember my pa much. S'pose cause he weren't home much. But my mama, Whitey, oh, that be a differrn't thing. There's been times when thinkin' on my mama was all that kept me agoin' an' from just layin' down an' dyin' like an old stray dog on a cold winter night. But I didn't lay down. I knew she wouldn't have none of that."

Abe paused for a few moments and looked up at the stars. Whitey kept his silence. The story continued: "Well, she only had so much milk an' that went to the youngest, so the rest had to fend for themself's, soon as they were able. So I'd run the street an' do what I could t'get a penny, an' I wasn't too proud to steal me one when I could. Thought o' starvin' sorta makes a boy do things, ya know . . ."

"Well, one day she called me to her side an' she said, 'Time to go, son. Time to find yer home. You got a long way to go an' you can't get there from here.' At first, I didn't pick up what it was she meant, 'cause hell, I was home. So I just thought she was sayin' to go out an' try to find somethin' to eat." Abe slowly shook his head. "That weren't what she meant this time, because she'd say that outright. She was tryin' to tell me somethin'. 'Time for you to go, son,' she said again. 'Your daddy an' me, we can't take care of you no more. We be too poor— don't wantcha to end up like us.' Well, I s'pose you can guess, Whitey, this made my bones hurt. I was gonna cry, but my mama stopped me. She said, 'Don't you do that, Abraham, don't never you cry no more. Might be reason for a baby to cry if it be hungry and needs milk or burpin' because cryin's all it knows, but sure ain't no reason for no grow'd man to cry.'

"Tell ya what, Whitey, with these words she ran me up a tree, and there I sat, like a little black bear in the top of a tree, feelin' sorely sorry. But now, I understand that ol' mama bear. She puts that little guy in a place where he can't get down real quick an' leaves him there. Then she moves off into the woods where he can never find her again. He sits up there for a spell, confused an' lonely, but then he begins to look around. As far as he can see in all directions are mountains an' trees an' meadows full of grass and streams a runnin' through. He's astartin' to understand what his ol' mama knew all along: it's better to spend ten minutes amovin' on out than ten years asittin' on yer rear. So he climbs down through the limbs to the ground, picks a direction, an' heads off. He might fall over the first cliff he comes to, or maybe he'll grow into a mighty big ol' bear. One thing though's fer absolutely sure: he can't suck on his mama's tit no more.

"That little ol' bear don't hate nothin', because his mama didn't teach him to hate. But my mama, she weren't no bear, she was a fine woman, an' she'd say to me, she said it a hun'red times if she said it once, she'd say: 'Abraham, when you wake up in the mornin' always say to yerself that you love ever'body an' ever'body loves you right back. Then you say the same thing again before you go to bed at night. Now, you do this each day; promise me ya will. No matter how hard an' mean things be, you say this.' I promised. So I have, an' I do.

"Now, I think I know what she was tryin' to teach me. I know that I know somethin' that most men jus' make believe like they *don't* know: there ain't nothin' but love. Love's all there is. That's where things come from. Ain't nobody goin' to make me hate by makin' me hate them, no matter how hard they try.

"You think it be different with them fellers down there on that waterfront, Whitey? They live too high in their heads an' they're gonna take their falls. *They* be the ones got the problem. Poor men protectin' their little bit of turf, because they think they need turf. Ain't none of it true. Take yerself, you got turf needs protectin'?" Slowly shaking his head: "Naa, not an inch.

"When I left Baltimore, I caught some trains an' went to wherever they took me. Ever' place was the same place, with poor men protectin' their turf, actin' like fools. 'Scram on out of here,' they'd say. 'This place is mine.' Didn't matter what color they was. Them men in town on the waterfront, they say: 'Get on out of here. You leave off with these here whores, because they be part of our turf.' They do me a big favor, because that weren't for me, an' I knew it. This is for me: these camps an' my saw an' Ruby an' the woods."

Abe tilted his head some and raised his eyes to the sky. "Them stars up there, too, my friend, let's see them take those away from me. Whose turf are *those* shinin' on?" He looked Whitey in the eye as though to emphasize his next words: "Them men they run me off because they love me an' can't help themselves. They really say: 'Abe go back to where you belong, this place here ain't for you. You hang aroun' here an' it might change yer color. You give in to temptation too easy, boy. So scoot!' See what I mean, Whitey? By them doin' wrong, they make me see what is right."

Abe paused for a moment, collecting his thoughts. Then he said: "Somethin' else my mama told me more'n once. She said: 'Abraham, clinch your tongue with your teeth an' keep your words in your craw. You just do your best an' forgive the rest, an' then see what happens next.' But she never told me what to do. So most of the time, I don't know if what I do is right or wrong at the time I do it, an' I don't know if I really do my best. I'll tell you what I know: I know these woods ain't never told me to scoot, an' these boys in these camps, they only tell me I gotta hold up my end of the saw, an' that is somethin' I can do. Ain't no slave-owner types in the big woods, Whitey, slave *drivers* maybe. Out here, I don't have to drink out of no black man's dipper, because out here that right up there be the only dipper." Abe smiled and pointed overhead into the eastern sky at the Big Dipper, which was just beginning to glow. "Out here, we all get down on our knees an' stick our butts up in the air an' lower our heads an' drink outa the same stream, don't we?"

"I guess we do."

"So don't you go fightin' no battles on my count, because like I said, I ain't in no fight. Tell ya this too: I ain't goin' t' jump into one that don't make a bit of sense. If'n they wanta come at me through my front door, I'll leave by my back one. They ain't gonna get to *me*."

Whitey sat there, dumbed by amazement. Across from him, seated in the bed of an old jalopy of a pickup truck, bouncing down some second-rate logging road, was a man whom he had never heard utter more than four or five sentences in succession, showing himself to be, if not a poet, then a man as sage as any. Abe was one of those who spoke only from his heart, and like a redwood, his heart ran his length. It was all-clear-first-grade stuff. His pureness was as uplifting yet unassuming as a water ouzel. Now, it was clear to him why Abe didn't talk much. It wasn't because he had nothing much to say, like everybody thought. It was because he couldn't find anyone with heart enough to grasp and hold what he had to say. So, Abe obeyed his mama and kept his tongue between his teeth and his words in his craw.

Abe paused in thought, as though carefully choosing his next words. "Do you ever dream, Whitey? I mean, while yer awake." Abe didn't wait for an answer. "Well I do," he said. "I dream while I'm asleep, an' I dream while I'm awake. I dream most all the time. When I climb up on my springboard and grab the saw grip, well, then I go to dreamin'. I feel my mama arockin' that ol' chair of hers just like when I was a kid. I rock forward against the feel of the saw an' back again, then against the saw an' back again. Before I know it, an' before I'm ready an' done, that ol' tree is startin' to squeak an' groan, as it gives up its soul. I don't want the tree to fall. I'd rather have a tree standin' there than just some empty air. I just want to go on arockin' an' ahearin' the ol' hum in my ear. But sometimes, that don't seem right, Whitey, because all that sort of thing don't seem like it's goin' nowhere no more. An' I just keep on fallin' trees. Makin' more air."

Abe paused and slowly shook his head, while he stared at his legs. He pulled up his knees and tilted back his head and looked at the stars for a minute. Then he said: "I'm tellin' ya all this, so's ya can answer a question. You're the only one I ever knew, besides Sydney Garbo, who might be able to tell me what she meant by that, when she told me I had a long ways to go. I never got the chance to ask Sydney, so I'm askin' you."

Abe quit talking and looked at Whitey, eye to eye. His eyes were wide, and Whitey felt a deep sadness in them that plumbed their depths. Neither man looked away. Abe's expression beseeched an answer, but Whitey didn't know the answer. His experience, though similar in some ways, had been different from Abe's. He couldn't remember his own mother ever even hugging him, much less rocking him to sleep with a song. He wondered if she had, and if he had just forgotten. He knew that she loved him. They simply weren't the hugging and singing kind of people. It occurred to him that he and Abe had much to teach one another because they were so different in unspeakable ways. Yet there was a sameness that could only be felt like magnetism between two poles. As he thought on this, the words Abe had just now asked for came as though on their own volition, and Whitey heard the answer right along with Abe. The words were like tiny things, hanging there in the air for a moment, then they drifted off on the breeze: "Abe, if your mama were sitting here in this pickup bed with us right now, she'd most likely say: 'Abraham, my boy, you done come so far I think you might have arrived right to where you always been, right where you belong.'"

Both men remained silent for a moment, eye locked on eye, each reflecting starlight into the other. Finally, Abe lowered his and said: "I don't know about all this dreamin' I do. I mean, I'm not so sure it be right. Do you dream, same as me, both day and night?"

"Well, Abe, I can't really say I do. When I'm up there on the board, saw grip in my hand and rocking, I'm mostly just trying like hell to keep up with you."

Abe chuckled softly and said: "You know how Hack an' Zimm an' some of the others are always tryin' to tell the biggest fib, an' they call it tall tale tellin'?"

Whitey nodded.

It was getting darker, but Abe could see Whitey's eyes flash and his white hair move to the rhythm of his nod.

"Well, I got a tall tale to tell, too, but it's not a big ol' fib like theirs are. Want to hear about ol' Lester an' my gandy dancin' days a workin' on the rail gangs?"

"Yes, I'd like that," Whitey said. He pulled his knees up, laid his forearms over them, and clasped his hands, as a person will do when settling in for a good story around the campfire.

Abe cleared his throat and started his tale about the gandy dancer: "To be one of them gandy dancers, a man had to make music with his gandy tools, which was all steel on steel. A man had to get the rhythm an' stay with it an' dance the whole day long, just to keep his job. Before long, I could do that real easy, but the boys that couldn't hear the music couldn't dance. They'd get out of step, fall behind, an' get run off by the boss. Then they'd be in the first boxcar they could find, goin' to somewhere else. A boy had to dance real good fer his dinner.

"Them ol' railroad bosses was mean as polecats, an' I didn't like 'em much. The days were hot with no shade to get under, an' the music didn't suit me, neither. I guess I just don't appreciate the sounds of tinny bells an' chimes—too much gawldang steel hittin' steel. I like hummin', like the wind ablowin' nice an' low. I was younger then, an' I think what I wanted to hear was the music my mama made when she hummed to me, so while I worked I hummed along, best I could.

"One day, one of them gang bosses says to me, he points an' says: 'You there, you look like a good strong buck-nig, so come on over here. I'm a gonna put you to sawin.' Then he leads me over to the place where they pile up the timbers fer sawin' into sleepers. He says: 'I'm gonna make life real easy fer you, buck-nig. All you gotta do is hold onto one end of this here saw and then saw faster than that buck on the other end.' Well, on the other end was another one of us buck-nigs about my age, though smaller. He had long legs an' arms. Boy, was he tough, an' could he saw! Weren't no way I could out-saw him, but after a while, I learned to keep up."

"I know the feeling," interjected Whitey."

Abe smiled. "Together, we made that saw hum a good loud tune—just like you an' me."

Whitey felt a surge of pride; he knew he had just been supremely complimented. But he said nothing, and Abe continued: "Well, man, there was the music I could dance to or sleep to. But I knew that any day the boss could pull me off and put me back to gandy dancin'. I sure didn't want that, so I got to wonderin' where I could saw all I wanted all the time. Well, my partner's name was Lester, so one day I told Lester what I was a thinkin' about. Lester was real smart, an' he'd been thinkin' the same thing, so he right out an' says: 'Let's go be timberjacks, Abe.' Hell, I didn't even know what that was, so I says: 'Okay.' I didn't want to sound dumb or nothin', you know. Lester says: 'Them timberjacks, they get to work in the shade all day long. Ever thought on that?' I says: 'Where can we be these timberjacks?' Lester looks at me real odd an' says: 'Where they cut down trees, Abe. Where ya think?' I says: 'Where's this place at?' Then he looks at me real odd again, an' I'm startin' to feel sorta dumb. He looks at the pile of timbers to be cut up, an' he looks back at me an' grins, then he says: 'Same place these here things come from.' I asked him if he had any money comin', an' he says: 'A little bit.' He's astandin' there grinnin' real big at the thought of it all. 'How about you?' he says. I says: 'Same as you, got me a little bit.' He says: 'Don't cost nothin' to ride them boxes an' walk when you got to.' I liked what I was hearin', an' so I says: 'Man, we're atalkin' down the same railroad track.'

"Funny how things happen, Whitey, because the very next mornin', almost like we asked him to, the ol' boss-man walks up an' he looks at Lester an' me, then says: 'Buck-nigs, looks like you just ain't havin' no fun asawin', an' I need me a couple o' dancers today.'" Abe chuckled at his memory, and Whitey could see his eyes twinkle. "Ol' Lester, well he looks at that man an' says like he's real dumb, he says: 'Boss-man, where these here big ol' timbers come from, anyhow?' The boss-man scratches his head an' says: 'Prob'ly from Northern California, Eureka, up around where they say them big trees are, I guess. Why you want to know?' Lester looks at me, then he looks at him and says: 'Cause that's where we're agoin'. Right, Abe?' I say: 'Yeah, man. We're goin' to be timberjacks.' So we quit right then an' there, though they made us gandy dance for the rest of the day before they'd pay us.

"After work, we go to the paymaster tent an' draw our pay. I'm all ready to head down the tracks. I got change in my pocket an' thoughts of bein' a timberjack in my head. But Lester, he ain't so inclined. He's feelin' smart-alicky, so he goes walkin' back toward where some gandy dancers are still workin', an' when he sees that boss fella he points an' yells: 'Hey, hogo.'"

Whitey interrupted. "Hey *hogo*?"

"Yeah." Abe touched the long fingers of one hand against the other and megaphoned his mouth as though he were yelling into the distance. "'Heey, hoogoo,' he hollers an' the ol' . . .'"

"Wait a minute," said Whitey, interrupting again. "What the hell's a hogo?"

Abe shrugged his shoulders. "Damned if I know," he said. "Lester never said. It was a word Lester used for people he didn't much like. Where he got it from, I don't know. Mighta made it up for all I know. Why?"

"Just wondered," said Whitey, shrugging his shoulders.

"Anyways, the ol' boss-man, he hears Lester, an' he looks all around to see who Lester's acallin' a hogo. So Lester hollers again." Once more, Abe encircled his mouth with his hands and pretended to holler. "'Hey you, hogo.' The boss-man can't believe what he hears, so he points at himself, an' it looked to me like he was sayin': 'Who me?' Then Lester points right at him and yells: 'Yeah, you there, hogo.' Now, you can see this ol' boy get real mad, because his face gets all twisted up an' turns bright red."

"He must've known what a hogo was," said Whitey.

Abe laughed softly. "You must be right, because it sure as to hell got him all riled up. Ol' Lester clenches his fist, pulls up his shirt sleeve, an' bends his elbow, an' then goes to jerkin' his arm up and down from the waist, kinda like a stud shoven' his big ol' pecker in a mare. Then he yells: 'Up yer rosy pink hogo.'"

"Wait a minute," interjected Whitey. "I think I just figured out what a hogo is."

Again, Abe laughed softly. Whitey could tell that Abe was enjoying his little stroll through this piece of his past as much as he was enjoying hearing the telling of it. "Maybe . . . don't know fer sure. Like I said, I never asked what a hogo was."

Both men laughed softly. Their laughter drifted off and mixed with the unseen dust trailing behind.

"Anyways, ol' hogo comes achargin' down the tracks after us like a runaway locomotive, an' Lester turns his tail an' goes runnin' up the tracks as fast as his long ol' legs'd carry him. He's gigglin', an' I'm runnin' like hell, tryin' to keep up." Abe shook his head and uttered that long slow low chuckle of his again. "What a sight that musta been: one mad man chasin' two crazy ones down the tracks, legs a pumpin', tryin' not to trip on the sleepers, way out in the middle of nowhere and smack-dab in the middle of nothin', except sand an' rocks an' sagebrush.

"All this runnin' goes on for a while till it occurs to me that two men were runnin' from one, an' the one weren't near as big as either one of the two. All a sudden, the whole thing seemed more stupid than crazy, so I stop an' turn around. That ol' boy was back there puffin' like a choo-choo, an' when he sees me turn around, his eyes grow real big, an' he begins to slow up real fast. So I go to walkin' toward him, an' he stops an' tries to say somethin', but he's puffin' so hard the words won't come out. I think it sinks into his scull that he's run off from his gang an' stands alone out on them tracks with only me an' Lester. He turns aroun' an' scoots off back down the tracks as hard as he can go, which ain't very hard at all, because he's all winded out by now an' can't even holler for help. I catch up to him real quick an' kick up with my foot, tryin' to get him in the caboose, but I miss, an' he gains some steps on me. So I catch up an' try it again, only this time I kick harder. But he's amovin', an' I only kick air. But I kicked too darn hard, an' so I lose my balance an' fall over backward. So there I sit, with my ass on a sleeper, watchin' that hogo stumblin' off down the tracks, wheezin' an' gaspin' for air.

"Behind me, I hear that damned Lester. He's a laughin' like he ain't got good sense. I look down there, an' I see him sittin' on one of the tracks with his legs off to the side, hollerin' hisself hoarse. He's a laughin' so loud that I'm a thinkin' he might wake all them sleepers up."

Abe paused for a moment, and Whitey held his silence. He knew that Abe was lost, for the moment, among his own ruminations and was sitting in the middle of nowhere between two tracks, held together by dreamless sleepers, laughing right along with Lester.

"Then we go to walkin' an' talkin', walkin' an' talkin', me an' Lester, down them tracks, for mile on mile, till we finally get to where the trains are runnin' so we can jump the boxes. Ol' Lester, he had done lots of that, almost as much as me, so knew how to work the tracks. Between the two of us, we knew all the tricks to that game. Our plan was not to go an' spend our money on nothin' except food an' we didn't need much of that.

"We got to L.A., finally, but should a kept right on agoin'." Abe's voice dropped. "Remember when I said Lester was real smart?"

"Yes. I remember."

The story's tone abruptly changed. The light-heartedness of a moment before sank into heaviness and grew ominous. Whitey tried to see Abe's eyes, but they were invisible, so he figured they were shut tight.

Abe sighed and continued: "Well, he was real dumb, to boot. He got to whorin' with them ol' street gals in L.A., an' they took all his money faster'n he could kick off his pants. Then he got upset with hisself. I told him it was awright, that we'd make do with mine. Didn't need much money. It was summertime. There were berries to eat an' we could prob'ly trap some rabbits.

"But Lester wouldn't listen. He tried to steal some money from a store. He took it in broad daylight. Tricked the shopkeep into leavin' his till, then emptied it into his pockets an' ran like a jackrabbit with that shopkeep ascreamin' bloody murder. Then he come back to our camp by the tracks an' pretended like nothin' had happened.

"I don't know how they knew, but them cops, they knew where to find him. Lester, he thought he plumb got away with it. Well, he was wrong 'cause them cops showed up that night at the camp an' shined flashlights in ever'body's face, an' they had that storekeep along. They kept askin' each time they shine a light on a man: 'Is this him?' The storekeep, he'd say: 'I ain't sure. Might be.' Then they get to where me an' Lester was, an' they shine the light on me. They say: 'This here him?' But that man, he don't know. Lester be next, an' he's shakin' all over an' his sweat's pourin' out; then he loses his nerve, so makes a run for it. They jumped him like a scared little long-legged rabbit, an' they shot him full o' buckshot. Lester died right there. Didn't even quiver.

"One of them cops comes over to me. I'm just standin' there like a dumb stump; I don't know what to do. I feel numb all over. I'm gawkin' at what was once Lester, lyin' there in the glow of the fire. They roll him over on his back, an' his toes are pointin' up in the air. I'm feelin' sick an' real scared. This cop says: 'Hey nigger, you with this here ex-nigger?' I say: 'No, sir, I ain't.' He says: 'You sayin' ya didn't know him?' I said: 'No, sir. I only seen him aroun' about.' This here cop, he looks at me real hard, an' then he says: 'I want you outa here right now, so get up your shit an' get yer black ass long gone.' I asks him if I can wait till mornin'. I want to look after Lester, bury him, maybe. 'Move,' says the cop, 'or I'll fill your lousy hide with buckshot.' Then he points his shotgun at me, an' I thought they was goin' to shoot me, too. I figger'd if I moved out in a hurry, they'd claim I was runnin' for it an' shoot me dead. So I says out loud to the bums standin' about, I says: 'Well fellers, this here man says I gotta leave your company. Been real nice knowin' ya.'

"Now, that cop, he looks at me real mean, an' he's aholdin' his gun real tight like an' his hands start to shake. I could see the killin' look in his face. He'd just killed an' he liked the feel of it. I was hopin' it would be as quick for me as it was for Lester, because I knew for certain I was about to get shot. I moved real slow, an' the first thing I did was put on my shoes, because I didn't want to look all hokey, like ol' dead Lester alayin' there, with my toes a stickin' way up in the air.

"The cop, he says: 'Move your ass north.' He said that because we were along the tracks in the north part of town under a bridge, an' he didn't want me to go towards town. I kept movin' real slow, slow as a slug, an' he kept on sayin': 'Hurry up, run.' Well, as you can imagine, I weren't about to run. If he was figgerin' to shoot me, I determined he'd shoot me walkin', an' he'd have to shoot me head on, so I didn't turn my back on him. I stuffed my sack an' backed on outa there real slow like. That cop, he kept on glarin' at me, all hard-eyed, holdin' his shotgun against his hip, just a wishin' I'd turn an' run. As I backed on out into the dark, I looked past him, an the last thing I saw in that camp, before I turned an' hightailed, were Lester's toes, apointin' toward the moon, turnin' frosty white in the moonlight."

Abe went quiet for a moment. He chuckled, and said. "Ain't it funny, somethin' like that? Sometimes I have trouble rememberin' what Lester's face looked like, an' I try real hard to remember it. But as hard as I try to forget, I can't forget them toes."

Whitey heard Abe softly click his tongue, and he knew he was probably shrugging his shoulders and slowly shaking his head the way he'd do when he felt exasperated about something. Then he heard him say: "Well, I've been pointed north ever since, Whitey. I rode the boxes, an' I walked some, an' sometimes, when I was afeelin' especially good, I'd get on one of them long, flat valley side roads, an' I'd start runnin', holdin' my gunnysack by my side." Abe paused for another moment and savored his thoughts. Then he continued: "On those days, I'd just run 'n run 'n run. That's the way I liked to travel, back then."

Whitey said: "I crossed the prairies a whole lot like that."

"Figgers. Then you know what I'm a sayin', don'tcha?"

Whitey didn't give an answer; Abe didn't expect one. He remembered the feeling that Abe was referring to. It was a free feeling of stretching your stride and feeling your legs under you as you ran off toward the horizon, holding an image always in front of you. It's a perfect image, contrived in your own imagination. It's a different image for different men, though some men seem to share the same image. While the miles slide by, and the dust settles in your tracks, it crosses your mind that it may all be false or that the reality could be far less than the image, or that the image is the only real thing and that you may never arrive anywhere at all, and you start to question your own sanity. But, boy, the running sure feels good!

Abe continued: "I asked aroun', an' most people said the same thing as the boss-man: the biggest trees were somewhere called Eureka. Well, hell, I didn't know where Eureka was; I didn't even know where *I* was. I'd never heard of no place called that, but I headed there anyhow, an' I finally got there. I ended up a little bit too far northeast at first, over around Weed, where there were sure lots of big trees, awright. I didn't know trees got like that. But ever'body I asked kept sayin' that the biggest trees were on out west where Eureka was an' that was out by the ocean. So I headed me west without a penny in my pocket—or a bread crust in there neither.

"There weren't no railroads goin' across them mountains, so I set out awalkin' an' walked all the way an' damned near starved to death before I made it. I didn't know the first thing about mountains. I got lost. But I learned about them mountains, an' I come to know them trees too, when I crossed them Siskiyous. So you see: it was a good thing I had to do it, though I almost didn't make it. I still can't say if I really know where I'm at. But I'm in the mountains now an' in the trees, an' that's enough.

"I hit the downside slopes, an' I crossed the Klamath, an' walked through the Redwood, an' I seen the ocean, an' I could o' died right there, an' it woulda been okay with me. I finally found Eureka, an' I found the surf, an' I found the biggest trees in the whole world. I'd found my home in the trees, an' I weren't never goin' to leave 'em.

"I was starvin' by this time. Winter was comin' on fast, so livin' off pickin's was not a solution. But I sure wasn't plannin' to steal an' end up like poor ol' Lester. It was either starve, beg, or get a job. I weren't goin' to beg. I needed shoes an' a good soogan an' clothes that'd keep me warm. Lucky for me some big ol' war was startin' up then an' so they were runnin' short of manpower in the woods. They also needed lots of lumber; anybody who claimed to be fit an' able could find work in the woods.

"Funny, when I look back on it, ever'body kept lookin' at me real odd-like, kinda like an' empty stare. I thought it was because they thought I was a bum, but soon I realized that there weren't no other black folk around that town. Far as I knew, I was the only one of 'em in the whole place. It took me a spell to get used to the way they'd look at me. It was like I was wearin' a mask an' they were tryin' to figger out who it was that was wearin' it. Know what I mean?"

Whitey couldn't say yes, so he said nothing.

Abe continued his story: "Well, I walked aroun' that town for a while, till I sees this cop acomin' an' then I says: 'Oh, oh,' to m'self because I thought I was in trouble. It even occurred to me that the L.A. cops had told the local cops to look for me. He was walkin' down the boardwalk straight towards me, so weren't nothin' I could do except stop. I didn't dare run; weren't nowhere to run to anyhow, because I was where I'd been headin' to all along. Anyway, this cop's lookin' right at me. He walks up an' says: 'Who are you?' But my tongue feels like it fills up my whole mouth. I can't make words. He says: 'Who you work for?' I'm really scared to tell him I ain't got no work. I don't know what to say, even if I could move my tongue, so I don't answer. I feel m'self startin' to shake. They throw bums out of lots of towns, you know. I sure looked like a bum, I guess."

Abe went silent for a long moment. "Anyway, he looks me all over. He even walks around me, lookin' at me like I'm a horse for sale. I'm ashakin' to where my knees are knockin'. He says to me, he says: 'Don't see many like you in these parts. Whatcha doin' here? Are you workin', lookin' for work, or passin' through? Answer me now, if you're not deaf an' dumb.' Well, I'm purdy sure by now he ain't out to catch me for the L.A. cops. So I finally get my tongue limbered up. I say: 'Well, sir, I'm not aworkin' right now, because I just got here, an' I come here because I heard that there was plenty o' work to do for a good worker like me.' He looks me in the eye an' says: 'You did, did ya?' I say: 'Know where.I can find me some work? I gotta make me some money, real fast.'

"The man starts to smile at me, an' I'm feelin' a whole lot better. You know, the way ya feel when a big dog you thought was mean wags his tail atcha. Boy, I can't even tell you how much relief I'm feelin'. It even seems like he's startin' to like me a little: ain't no killin' look in them blue eyes. 'Tired of bummin'?' he says. 'Tired of travelin', I say. He keeps on smilin'. I think I was even smilin' back at this point. Then he says: 'Ever done any loggin' work?' So I say: 'Well, no, sir, but I've done some gandy dancin' an' lots of timberjackin'. Yessir, I done lots of that there timberjackin' work.'"

Whitey started to laugh softly; he suspected what was coming. "What did he say to that?" he asked.

"Well, he gets this big ol' grin, an' he's lookin' at me, an' his eyes are just atwinklin' an' dancin' like they're full o' stars." Abe paused for a few moments. Whitey couldn't see him well but sensed he'd drifted a long way off. Then Abe abruptly recollected himself from his musings and continued: "He says to me, he says: 'How about timberjackin'off? Ever done any o' that?' Then he chuckles— kinda like 'yer doin' right now. 'Oh yes!' I say, 'I done me lots an' lots o' timberjackin'off!' Boy-o-boy, I'm a flyin' high, an' I say: 'In fact, my last boss told me I was better at that than anybody workin' for him'.'"

Whitey was laughing right out loud, and Abe joined in. The two men set among the milk, eggs, ham, bacon slabs, pork and beans, corn starch, flour, shortening, salt, pepper, sugar, confections, peanut butter, beefsteaks, fresh caught snapper (well-wrapped), toilet paper, tobacco products, canned goods, and sundry others, and mixed laughter into the stars for a long while. Their eyes were lucent with mirth tears. It occurred to Whitey that the men up front were wondering what they could possibly find so funny back there, especially considering the glum atmosphere they started out in.

Abe, laughing and talking, continued his tale: "Well, this ol' boy, he's laughin' till he hurts. I know I'm bein' kidded with; but I was concerned with *what* was bein' said, not with *how* we were sayin' it. He takes off his hat, an' I see he's got hair color of creek sand, an' he's about thirty-five or so. He's just havin' a great ol' time with me an' slaps his knees with his hat a few times. He asks me my name, so I tell him, an' he says: 'Well, Abe, reason I'm so curious is my brother's a logger. He runs a crew of loggers, uh, I mean, timberjacks, an' he's short on help these days. He told me to keep an eye open for young strong men that can swing an axe or push a saw an' send 'em in his direction if they need work. He pays better than most, but he'll work your tail off.' Then he looks at me an' grins real big an' says: 'He's especially in need of a good timberjackoff. How 'bout it?'

"I say, somethin' like: 'Oh good gawdamighty yes!' But he can't hear me what with him alaughin' so hard an' slappin' his knees an' all. But he read my lips. Then he told me to follow him, and said his name was Sidney Garbo.

"I was right when I thought the man was beginnin' to like me. He got me on with his brother's crew an' even grubstaked me for some clothes an' calks an' an axe. We became friends an' stayed so all through my years in the Redwoods, an' a friend of Sidney Garbo's was a friend of ever'body."

"Where's he at, still in Eureka?"

"No. If he was still there, then I'd still be there. When he wasn't policin' he logged. He got killed in the woods. Widowmaker got 'em. Can ya believe it: a logger with his savvy gettin' had by a damned widowmaker? There'd been some hard winds blowin' through, makin' widowmakers all over the place. Guess he didn't see that broke-off tree leanin' against the other. He was workin' downhill from it, choppin' out a face when she slipped loose and fell down. I was off buckin' on that day so I didn't see it happen. Those who did said he never knew what hit him. I say he knew; nothin' got by Sidney. Left a widow and two almost growed-up boys behind."

Whitey considered it was just as well that he couldn't see Abe's face very well right now, because he could feel the pain of Abe's loss and suspected there may be tears streaking his cheeks. Then he heard Abe say:

"Funny how it works, ain't it? I mean, how, when a man is most down an' in need of somethin', the somebody that can give it to him or show him the way always shows up."

"Yes. Funny how that works."

"You know, Whitey, I don't know why Sidney did it all. You know, helped me like he did—me, a man he'd never seen before in his life. I've wondered a thousand times why."

"I wouldn't let the why of it bother me much if I were you. More often than not, the hows and whys just can't reach the answer to their own questions. That's how the world keeps its mysteries secret, I think. One thing's not a mystery: he lived a good man."

"Yeah . . . but in this case I think there be an answer to all that mystery, an' Sidney, he knew what it was. Seems to me if I knew the answer, too, then I'd be a better man for knowin' it."

"Don't sell yourself short, Abe. Sounds to me like your friend didn't," said Whitey. But as he spoke he was peering into his mind at a wordless vision that was forming in there. Here, in the bed of a rough-riding old pickup, a vision of something contraput embodied itself in a scene, somewhere, someplace, which could only be right here for either himself or Abe. Right here sat Abe, a man in outward aspects who was stoic in nature and hard as rock, by his own words defining himself all together different from his appearances. Abe wasn't at all the solitary giant, standing his ground like a tree in a storm. He was nostalgic, and spent much of his time caught up in dreams of a home he'd lost. By his own admission, he feared himself to be a man given to too much mooning within his mind. *How different from me,* Whitey thought, *who ran away from a home I myself rejected. But I do moon. Yessiree, I can sure moon.*

So, here again, it happens that two men heading off in different directions meet upon a road and decide to travel along together; but somewhere down the line there's a fork around a sharp bend. Here they are, at some point along a curvy line called time, or life, or experience, or events, and like phantoms they merge and then move on in separate ways. It's a scheme that counters nature, as two great rivers that meet and cross. But now he felt he could merge with this person and be swept along with him, for a while. Present in this sad man was a singular strength and force of flow; and now, for the first time, Whitey felt an understanding like a firmness under his feet of the kind that a man feels for when he's crossing a swift river, and a long-lost mystery within the scheme came back home to his awareness.

He and Abe were merging, and they were crossing. As it had always been with him, divergence was certain, because a vagabond is contained within his own banks. Whitey already dreaded the inevitable parting. If he tried, he might postpone it. But this time, he'd recognize it when it came and not cling to what might've been. He wondered if all is really fixed, and if a man is only one soul instead of many, or even if there is a difference between the two distinctions. If he understood him right, Abe had just said that he didn't think there was.

Perhaps he was all that moved, suspended for a distance between his head and his mouth, flowing to and from some distant inland sea, and his entire life was contrived with this subtle scheme which adds or subtracts, according to his own inherent elements—his nature—rushing on here, meandering there, and changing its course against resistance, always flowing away.

In himself, he felt the powerful surge of the Professor, and gentle flow of Peppa, along with others he'd known, and he wondered if he'd left something of himself flowing along in them. *If that's the case, then one is many in the same way that a river is a watershed of many streams.* As he mused on the scheme, it occurred to him that he surely had and *they* carried *him* along with them, even now, for this is a scheme that flows down from the highlands and cannot fail; nothing can dam it.

"You know," said Abe, "I've never had many friends; I mean friends like you'd want for a brother. Lester was one, an' Sidney was one. Even though they be dead, you know, to me they're still my friends, because I dream about 'em a lot, when I'm awake and when I sleep. Know what I mean?"

"Yeah, Abe. I think I follow you on that."

"Thought ya might. Ya know it's real important, here where we're at, because it be where we make our memories, ain't it?"

Whitey didn't respond and fell silent. Abe disappeared into the soft starlit shadows and into his own shadowy world of self-contemplation. But his tall tale was far from over.

The old truck bumped, battered, and shook through the ruts; it twisted and gyrated on the hairpin turns; it squeaked and rattled and clanked. Cookie throttled full on the upward pull and feathered the brake against compression on the downhill coast. The forest slipped steadily by, absorbed and unseen, into the clear blackness of the night. The stars were not enough to light it, but they filled the cut in the trees overhead and twinkled down and danced around like they always had and always would.

The stars are restless spirits. Like everything else, they come bearing a message to a wondering wanderer—they speak. They say: "There are forces that lie beyond the senses of a man, but not beyond the sum of his perceptions. If you would know the spirit of a man, look for us in his eyes. There can be no pretension here, for we cannot be bought with money or fame. He who can see the stars knows where to find us. Compared to us, men are small in number. But the eyes of a great man contain us one and all."

Whitey sat and pondered his musings, his head tipped back, eyes toward the cleavage, suspecting that Abe was sound asleep. But Abe suddenly surprised him.

"Whitey?"

"Thought you were sleeping."

"I was. Just had me a little dream about you an' me an' ol' Hack all sitting around an' sippin' hot chocolate, listenin' to Hack tell fibs. Let's invite Hack up for some hot chocolate tomorrow night. Whatcha say?"

"Let's do that, Abe."

The two partners went silent. The pickup bounced along, until it finally pulled into the little logging camp, somewhere the other side of Remote.

Meanwhile, back at the Barge Inn Saloon & Eatery a gay old night of hoorayin' and hoopla and gut bustin', guzzlin' down Benson Bangers and Blarney Busters and Stumble Bummers, was in process. With his newfound pals, Hack was looking for respect and honor, and he knew just how to find it. "Keep adancin' your arm garters barkeep, an' keep 'em comin'. Pour 'em heavy on the blarney and heavy on the buster an' fill 'em to the brim an' see if ya' can make a stumblebum outta me!" Hack hollered out. And the dapper Dan behind the long mahogany bar, polished smooth and shiny with elbow grease from a million elbows or more, lifted the curled-up tips of his handlebars with a satisfied grin, weaved this way and that and danced his arm garters up and down like a cancan man and tipped his black and brown and green bottles and mingled the essences of his enslaved spirits and emancipated them into sparkling glasses. Over his head, a naked whore, caged within her picture frame, reclined upon a red Victorian couch. She was pleasingly plump and comely. Her dark eyes seemed to be watching the scene unfolding below while her lips wore a knowing smile.

Hack tipped his Blarney Buster bottoms-up toward the tavern ceiling, and without so much as moving his Adam's apple, swigged it down in one big gulp—he didn't even blink, nor did a single drop dribble from the corners of his mouth. A respectful gasp resounded throughout the room. He didn't know how many this one counted to, but he knew he had established himself the all-time king of the guzzlers in this saloon.

"No man on Earth can guzzle booze like a logger,, was an old longshore saying, a myth that they all believed in like sin but hated like hell to own up to. "An' we can cuss 'n swear ever' bit as gawdamn good as them bastards can, too," they'd claim. This wasn't true in the least. They could cuss more, no argument in that, but they couldn't make it flow and rhyme—no way; they tried too hard and so their King's English didn't come out anywhere near as polished. Each and every one feared he didn't measure up in the he-man department. Hack was determined to realize their fears for these wayward citizens of the docks, though it meant he bust his ample gut.

"Yessirree, Bufie." He slapped Buford on the back for the hundredth time. "I'm glad you did whatcha did. Only reason I'z with them two stumblebums is because they be too dumb t' drive an' made me bring 'em in here in my brand new automobile, so's they could load up their wangers an' blow their damn balls off. First, they said they'd beat shit outa me if'n I didn't oblige 'em. When I raised my dukes an' told 'em to come right at it, they chickened out an' said they'd flatten my tires with nails when I weren't alookin'. So what's a man to do? Tell you this: sure is great to have buddies to help a feller out. Yes-sir-ree, sure is, ol' buddy."

At first, Buford tried to keep up with Hack—silly Buford. Now, his eyes rolled about in a stupor. He tried to talk but couldn't, so he wiped his nose with his sleeve and grinned a skunk-eating-shit grin. Hack talked on: "Ain't because I got somethin' against them sambos, ya know. Hell's fire, man, I think ever'body should own at least one, if only to keep his corkies greased up and shiny."

The Citizen's Committee, seated at the table, roared with mirthful glee. Like a master snake charmer to a basket of snakes with bloated necks and heads, waving to and fro under his entrancing spell, Hack played them the music of his wit. But he carefully watched their eyes, for they were a venomous bunch, and he knew better than to trust them so much as an inch.

"Tell you boys the truth, ya spoiled my breakfast, because I was goin' to butter my pancakes with him," said Hack. And then he raised an elbow and guzzled down another Buster, then raised the other elbow and chased it with a beer, then leaned over, and let go his wad into the copper spittoon. Then without even taking a deep breath, he slammed his empty glasses on the table and yelled out: "Fill 'em up, barkeep."

The mouths all opened simultaneously and hissed out their appreciation of the merry tune.

The night wore down until Buford couldn't take any more of all this fun. Hack, however, didn't want to see him pass out completely and lose his senses, so he said: "Looks like ol' Bufie here's all hooted and hollered out. You fellers stay where yer at. I'll take care of my good buddy an' pour him in my automobile an' haul him home." The gay gang all nodded their approval. "That be okay with you

Bufe?" Buford grinned and dumbly nodded his head. So Hack helped his buddy out the saloon door, and disappeared from the sight of the Marshfield waterfront, forever.

In the early hours of dawn, a lone motorist was on his way to Coquille and saw something lying next to a solitary hemlock that lived alongside the road, and he got out to investigate. It was Buford, chained by his neck and padlocked to the tree like a mean dog. He lay naked and skunk-bit drunk under a greasy old soogan. The Samaritan flagged down some help, but when they tried to move him, Buford hollered to high heaven, and no one could figure out why. Turned out, someone had lubed his bung with axle grease and then corked it with a big, scaly pinecone. This couldn't simply be pulled out without spreading the scales, and these were tipped with prickles. It had to be removed, tiny piece by tiny piece, which took a long time of intricate work with scalpel and tweezers, all of which interfered with his civic responsibilities.

Buford had a problem getting up off his belly. Though he sorely tried, he was unable to sit in on the town meetings, much less officiate. His attendance began to suffer, and the upstanding citizenry were finally able to declare him a truant and drum him from office and get their Babbitt back. From that time on, Buford, when he thought on it, considered the whole incident with the three big loggers nothing but a big pain in the ass.

Chapter 10 The Longing Worm

Summer melted; fall fell away; winter froze then thawed. Now things were springing up again. Little blue-eyed Mary peeked out through the leaves of grass sprouting in the meadows, and the vanilla leaf's bright flower lit up the dark shade beneath the tall timber. This was a bright day, and the busy nest-builders were happy overhead.

The two men sat beneath an old cottonwood tree that was breaking out in fresh buds and perfuming the air with the spicy scent of flowing resin. Whitey was finishing his lunch, while Abe honed the misery harp, as he always did at lunchtime. "Keeping it sharp keeps the work lighter," he liked to say. "Besides, don't it sound sweet?"

Whitey had every good reason to feel springy on a day like this, but he was heavy instead, and he couldn't say why. He figured some talk would give him a lift, so he said: "How much longer is Slim going to stay parked here?"

"Can't say for certain. Prob'ly two, maybe three years." Abe replied without looking up or breaking the cadence of his strokes.

"Any idea where to after that?"

"Nope. None at all."

Whitey sat forward, picked up his axe, eyed its edge, and said: "You know, Abe, to tell the truth, I'm growing a little weary of this wandering life."

"Oh, I don't think so," said Abe, still not looking up.

Abe's bluntness set Whitey back a little bit. "Oh, *you* don't, huh? Well, *I* think so, and *I'm* the one that knows what it is *I* think. Seems to me, more and more, that I should settle down in town."

"And do what? Get married an' raise kids I s'pose—be a genuine domestic man. Maybe run for mayor; beat out ol' Buford. If you win the election you could go to hullabalooin' with the merchandisers." Abe chuckled at the thought. "Now that's a good one to ponder on," he said. "When I come for a social call, maybe you'll let me purchase discount." Abe smiled a self-satisfied smile at his choice of words. Then he shook his head, and said: "Sounds to me like you don't know whatcher thinkin' at all. Only a short minute ago you were complainin' because we're still parked here." He slowly ran his finger along the saw's teeth. Then he looked up into Whitey's face and seemed to study him for a moment.

"Hell if I know what I'd do in town," said Whitey, trying to avoid Abe's eyes by dropping his own. Perhaps I could open up a filing shop and sharpen saws or something like that, and then just see what happens from there."

Abe threw back his head and showed off his big white teeth in a deep unsettling belly laugh. Abe was laughing a lot these days and Whitey was glad to hear it, but not this time. Right now, Whitey wasn't humored; this time he was the brunt of the joke. But he understood. He knew his words had a ridiculous ring to them. Judging from Abe's mirth, and that laughter, it was entertaining, too.

Abe read Whitey's mounting frustration in his face, so he ceased his laughter.

After all, Whitey had a problem and had really come to him for help, so why tease him? He figured he might as well get to the crux of the problem. Its solution was simple enough. "Don't mean to laugh at yer whims, Whitey," he said, apologetically. "Can't help it if I'm in a good mood. Tell me, just where is this ideal town you plan to settle down in? Marshfield, maybe? Then I s'pose you'll invite me to town. Then, me, you an' the missus, we'll have a nice time promenadin' down the boardwalk; go t' church an' sing along. Why, maybe I can even help you sharpen a few saws an' help cover the overhead, ya might say."

Unable to restrain himself, Abe released a pent-up chuckle at the vision of his thoughts. Then in a more serious tone he said: "Tell you what, though: Before you go, why don'tcha climb up this mountain, far as you can get, an' dig up one of them young mountain hemlocks agrowin' up there. Then take it to town an' plant it in your yard, an' sometime later I'll sneak in an' see who lasted the longest, you or the tree."

Whitey's face turned pink. "Not Marshfield, for Christ's sake! I had Roseburg or Springfield more in mind." His own words embarrassed him. He felt truly foolish and expected another belly laugh at any moment. He realized in this moment what Abe already knew: he didn't have any town in mind, and didn't mean a word he was saying. What he was doing was whining about nothing, but he didn't know what it was that prompted him to talk crazy like this. He hoped Abe did. As he pondered his own foolishness he even chuckled at himself and then said: "That hemlock wouldn't last a single season."

Said Abe: "It would outlast you." Whitey was starting to sound sensible, good humor works wonders. "Hell, man, don't matter what town you're talkin' about, they all be the same. They be full of yellow people, blue people, purple people, red people, orange people, black people, grey people, brown people, white people, an' people all the colors of the rainbow, for all I know, except for one. They ain't got no green people. Know that for fact. A green person might die in one tryin' to get out if he gets caught up in there. But one way or 'nother he'll never stay. Can't. He can't grow there."

"Why not?" said Whitey, puzzled by the words. He wasn't even going to try to make sense out of this. He'd let Abe explain his way out.

As if ignoring the question, Abe didn't answer. He picked up his file and started to hone the harp again. The birds went silent and sat in the treetops, listening to the sharp, lively tune—perhaps taking a lesson. The fluid motion of the long nimble fingers pulled at Whitey's attention, and like the birds, he became entranced by the music. He clean forgot his melancholy and the subject of discussion—that saw would be sharp as a razor in no time.

But Abe hadn't forgotten: "Don't know why not. Just know . . . Maybe it's the dogs."

Now it was Whitey who released a throaty chuckle. "Dogs? What the hell do dogs have to do with living in town?" Was Abe still teasing, or what?

Fact was: Abe was far from jesting. Straight-faced, he said: "They all the time bark at themselves in the night. Just listen some time, when yer passin' through an' tryin' to sleep. You can most always hear at least one barkin', barkin' away at nothin' at all. Man that listens can't hear nothin' but dogs abarkin'. It's a sad sound, sorta like the sound of somethin' in a cage, barkin' at ever'thin' outside it."

"Don't listen then," said Whitey, grinning.

Abe looked at him with a puzzled expression, and said: "Why would I not want to listen?"

"So you won't hear the dogs."

Abe slightly shook his head and shrugged his shoulders. He gave Whitey an incredulous sideways glance, and then looked away. Whitey wasn't certain, but it appeared like Abe rolled his eyes. He looked back again, and said: "Whitey, if a man closes off his listenin', how the hell does he know what's goin' on in the dark—or anywhere else?"

"What are you listening so hard to hear, Abe?

Again Abe didn't answer and let the subject drop. He didn't say that in his listening, during the dreamless hours of night, he strained to hear the timber wolves sing. He'd heard them before: on two occasions in the Trinitys and once in the Klamaths. The wildness of their song had made his backbone tingle back then, and it tingled now as he thought about it. When he spoke of it to others, they only laughed and said there were no timber wolves in these mountains any more, and that they had all been eliminated, because they were a threat to man and his belongings. "Hell's fire, Abe," an all-knowing old jack once said, "they strychnined them damned wolfs out of this here country, a long time ago, so's they wouldn't get the stump ranchers cows 'n chickens. If'n ya go off lookin' fer wolfs, better look out lessen they find you first an' eatcha, boy."

But these were the words of an old geezer, and Abe knew better, because he'd heard the wolves—howling. They were always far off, along a distant ridge and there was nothing malicious in their song. Were they calling to somebody, to one another—to something? To whom were they singing? Why sing? To throw your voice out to be carried away by the wind, to go wherever it may, seemed so careless, fearless, and free. They probably sang just for the feeling of it.

When he persisted in his claim, some had told him to describe what he heard. How ridiculous! It would be easier to describe the colors of the sunset to a blind man. So his attempts to talk about them began to sound silly to him, and he decided to keep his wolf fetish a secret. More than anything else, he wanted to see the source of the song he heard. But he knew this was going to take no little effort. They were probably wise and wary, these that were left, and the sound they made was the sound of the primeval forest—not until it was gone would the last of them be dead.

Sometimes, after lying very still for a long time, listening, he'd hear the howling, just as he drifted off into sleep. But he didn't want to go to sleep in it; he wanted to wake up in it. To howl with wolves . . . The vision filled him with a terrible anticipation that he could not fathom. Someone had mentioned that there were timber wolves up north and there was some consensus on this, but no one knew how far. So after the death of Sidney Garbo, he headed north in hopes of coming to the place where he could hear them every night, but there were no more wolves up here than down there. Now, the question perplexed him as to how far north he should go, because the farther north he went the farther south he left the tall redwoods.

Whitey was perking up. Seemed he'd decided that living in town wasn't so good an idea after all, and Abe didn't want to say what it was he listened for in the night, so he quit the subject and leaned back against the tree. Nearby, a chipmunk's big dark eyes were peeking out between some bunchberry flowers; its nose twitched its whiskers this way and that as it scented the tasty aroma of sandwich in the air. Whitey took some breadcrumbs and laid them next to his feet. Excited, but nervously holding its banded tail up at quick attention, it trotted up in starts and stops and quickly snitched a jawful. Then it trotted off several feet with its prize, where it squatted on its haunches and nibbled it away. Soon it scampered back for more, a little bit braver. Whitey fed it with his fingers.

Peeking out from the corner of his eye, Abe watched Whitey and his new friend. *They tame fast when you give them food*, he thought. He went on filing, thinking about what to say next and how to say it. He knew that it was going to take more than talk and words for Whitey to come to terms with his *longing worm*.

Oh, that tenacious ol' longing worm! It's a parasite of the first order. It was going to take the timberbeast to kill it.

Abe knew the feel of the longing worm, and he knew the mistake. It's a curious worm, but greedy, that burrows into the heart of a vagabond like it were a juicy red apple. Like a fruit grub, it feels a hunger to seek out then settle into and devour the heart of the very thing that gives the man his substance as a vagabond. It eats the core and chews away the longing and defecates wanting, which slowly piles up to fill in the empty place. This, of course, means the end of the vagabond. Any true vagabond who succumbs to the longing worm and settles down in some town, thinking to satisfy his emptiness there, becomes less than true, if any true vagabond is capable of such a desperate act. That's why he laughed at Whitey. Of all the vagabonds he'd ever known, he'd met only a few true ones, and Whitey was probably the most impeccable of these true few. So he laughed, not so much *at* Whitey, as at the absurdity of his words.

Whitey didn't understand this feeling gnawing like a leaf grub at his heart. He sat there like a truthful liar, claiming he had wants that were diametrically opposite from what he felt, only because he hadn't yet come to terms with the longing worm. But then Whitey had never known bondage to the worm. Even the way off the farm had been prepared for him, and what had seemed to him like breaking away was only taking an advantage of a given opportunity to purge his longing and fill the new space with more of the same. But his own life had been different. There'd been those times when the hungry worm had eaten away his guts looking for food. It's a tenacious worm, and home-brewed remedies can't expel it. Salt and vinegar won't purge it, and molasses mixed with sugar and sweet milk and poured out on the ground won't lure it out. It seemed to Abe that had it devoured him completely, and had he digested away in its gullet, he'd have found no peace in that busy grave. So, fighting against it, he came to know the worm, and how not to feed it, and that the same worm that he knew how to not feed was, right now, nibbling at Whitey.

He well understood that Whitey didn't know he had a longing worm hatching in his heart and mistook it for longing itself: the worm eats the longing simply because it *wants* it. It's a mistake that confuses longing with wanting, which can trap a good vagabond and root him to the world with his ass bare to the axe, like one of these vulnerable trees. Truth of the matter was that Whitey didn't want anything and probably couldn't if he tried. It was time to call forth the timberbeast, because the timberbeast is wild and free and cannot want and can save the longing from the worm. This was the only way he knew to starve out that damned worm. So he said: "Thing is, Whitey, the way I see it, you ain't white, an' I ain't black."

Just as Abe thought he would, Whitey chuckled and said: "Oh! Then what colors are we, Abe?"

"Green."

"Green? (*chuckle, chuckle*) Why green?"

"I don't know *why* green. I'm not the one does the color'n. Just *are* is all. Green people all have somethin' in common. They can't park their ass in one place, but what they start to grow moss on their backs, an' that moss gets old an' turns to brown or grey or black or white, an' they're all times longin' to go someplace where it's greener. Sometimes they think they can settle down with a yellow person or a blue one, an' so they try to mix colors, but they can't an' still be green. They can't be no other color from what they are, so before they know what's happened they're off lookin' for more green people."

"That's called looking for greener pastures, Abe."

"That's what the folks in town call it, an' they're talkin' about fields of dollars. I ain't.

"You know what? You're starting to sound a lot like somebody else I once knew: sorta weird."

"If you mean that Professor fella, then I thank you, I think," said Abe, grinning.

"Well, how about blue people?" asked Whitey, thinking he'd play along with Abe's little game.

"Can't say. I don't know much about blue people. Like I said, I'm green, an' so are you. Lots o' people like to think they're green an' make believe like they are, but they're not. They ain't got the grit."

"Tell me then, how am I going to find these green people, because to me, you sure don't look green and neither do I?"

"Don't look. Feel. You may love 'em or you may hate 'em, but you'll feel right bein' where yer at if you be with green people. Tell ya this: look away an' you can't be guaranteed they'll still be there when you look back again, 'cause green people got themselves a problem."

"What's their problem?"

Abe puckered his lips and lowered his eyes to the saw. He thought for a moment, and said: "Well, it's sorta like they got a worm up their bung an' it makes 'em squirm. They can't sit still for long." He ran his index finger along the serrated edge of the saw. He lay the saw aside and picked up his axe. "Okay, Ruby, it's yer turn," he said. He stroked her with the file and Ruby softly sighed. Then he touched her lips with his fingers, smiled, and looked up into Whitey's eyes with an expression of satisfaction. "There, she couldn't be prettier. Let's get back to work."

That night, over hot chocolate, Abe said: "Whatcha say, Whitey, wanta blow up our balloons an' head off up north? I've been athinkin' that I ain't never seen the Columbia."

Whitey raised his eyebrows. "Quit Slim? I thought you couldn't be yarded away from here with a team of cats."

"Why not? Hell, we can always come back. Slim'll make a place for us. C'mon, let's go."

"Feeling a little itchy are you, Abe?"

"I'm a gettin' moss on the north side of my ass. Gotta move my butt aroun' a bit an' change exposure."

The tone in his voice convinced Whitey that his partner was serious. He wasn't so certain he wanted to pull stakes, but if Abe left, he'd go with him; of *this* he was certain. "I'll think on it."

"Then think tonight, 'cause I'm givin' Slim notice tomorrow."

"Okay, I'll go. But Slim isn't going to like it."

Abe slowly nodded.

The next day, they gave two weeks notice to a distraught Slim Hoskings.

Chapter 11 The Timberbeasts

Unknown to Whitey, but intuited by Abe, a broad world was waning like a bright dimming moon, a vigorous innocent world, a world graced with majesty, crowned with beauty that stood royally tall, too high for the halls of the sky to hold on a shrinking planet. It was the world where roamed the timberbeast, the camp jumper, the timber tramp, and the bull of the woods. Abe knew this world. It was his home. But his home was falling down, and now, before it was too late, he determined to introduce it to Whitey.

The years that followed the jump from Slim's camp were ones of howling with the timberbeasts. The timberbeast was the timberjack archetype. Not since that primordial day when the divine leagued with the beast and made mankind had such beings as these roamed and ruled the big woods. They were probably the freest human beings ever to tramp Earth. Over the ridges they went and across the steep little river valleys. From camp to camp they tramped, these two timberbeasts, *howling* all the way. Abe and Whitey fell a wide swath in those years.

Logging of the era was a constant shuffle of ramshackle camps that squatted knee-deep in mud during winter and spring, and smothered with dust and swarming bugs the rest of the year. Overnight, one of these camps would lay in, deep within the heart of some dense woodland at the end of a makeshift road, near the head of a river. Like a big-bellied leaf worm with a thousand steel teeth, it began to eat its way outward, fulfilling its contractual obligations only when the leaf was digested. Then, as though gorged and looking for more, away it crawled, leaving its shed-away skin behind in the form of a dilapidated shack here, a garbage dump there, heaped tangles of played-out steel cable, dead rotting machines, donkey skids, holes of composting defecates where the outhouses once stood, and maybe even a grave or two. All left behind for the tenacious blackberry vines to lay claim to.

Loggers moved with the camps and jumped them in between. The rumor mill was the telegraph of the big woods and its grist was exaggeration. It was a coarsely-ground grain. The wise peregrine was wary and selected his meal with discretion. It fed him good information about what gyppo was where, what kind of shape they were in, and how good or how bad the food was.

Each camp took on its individual personality, which reflected its gyppo. But not all were gyppos; some were large corporate camps, more permanent in nature than the gyppo camps. These company camps came close to being towns, and more than a few did become towns. The company camps often occupied a river valley for twenty years or more, until they faded away with the trees. Whether gyppo camp or corporate camp, some were God-fearing, some pagan, some sober, some soused, some sordid, some spick 'n' span; all were hard work.

There was some security in laying in with a good camp that suit your nature and when it moved moving with it. Alas, such was not the nature of the timberbeast. For him, the trees were always taller on the other side of the hill where the camp of his dreams was sure to be. Each job he took was a grubstake just to get him enough money to get him down the road and up and over that hill. When the moon came full, peeking down through the trees, lighting up the trail, he got a hankering, blew up his shoulder sack with all his worldly accumulation, then, with a pocket full of change and with a balloon on his back, back out he went again, exactly the same way he'd come in, trying to follow the wandering moon. But his moon was a will-o'-the-wisp. The nearest honky-tonk town probably drained his grubstake pocket, while he drained the whiskey barrel.

Most of his kind laid buried at the end of it all in unmarked graves with none except the tearful angel of mercy to mourn over them. Whether they finally saved their grubstakes or not, perhaps only she knows

Oh, the old, long-gone incorrigible timberbeast . . . He strove only to do as he pleased without probing thrusts of the beak from noisy, nosy woodpecker types. He asked of the gyppo only that he be fair: that he pay a fair wage, and that he finally pay. He asked of the barkeep only that he be generous and not water down his redeye. The personal inclination of others was none of his concern. But he cleared the hard, steep trails and made them wide and easy going and the relentless crowds surged in from the east. In the manner of all wild things, he retreated. He fell back until he was trapped between two surges. His world finally fell away along the cliff sides that butt up against the shores of the Pacific, where the driftwood gathers in piles, leaving him nowhere else to go.

Those were high years, indeed, well suited to two wayward souls, walking the roads and trails, working the camp of their choosing. Abe and Whitey downed many a cup of hot chocolate on cold windswept nights with the sideways rain beating on the tarps, shaking the evergreen boughs, and they exhausted many a poet's words, to boot. In summer, they pitched their camps under the big-leaf maples, when they could, because these were cool but let the light shine through. In winter, they looked for a droopy-branched cedar, because these shed the rain. Days were long and nights were short, but hard labor goes unmindful when spent in good company.

Hack's remark that everybody knew Abe was an uncharacteristic understatement. Whitey discovered that the name Abe was one of no little significance in the small but wide world of the timberbeast. Woodsmen sang its praises far and wide. But in the physical presence of Abe, awe rose up like a fog, and a hush fell over those same singers. During these times, Abe taught Whitey all he knew of the woods and the woodsy culture.

On a cool misty day, with the sun peeking through the overcast, they took some seats upon a high mossy bank and rested their eyes on the queen of rivers herself. Whitey would have jumped even this, because those grand Olympics were over there, somewhere. Mountains so high, he heard, they pierced the sky with glacier fields of snow. On hot days, a man could hear their thunders rumbling from a long ways off, if he put his ear to a tall tree and held his breath.

But Abe knew better. He'd heard more tall tale contests than Whitey had, and knew that country across the river to be like all the rest: a smorgasbord of gyppo camps and huge company town camps and ever-increasing acreages of stumps and blackberry filling up low-lying hills right up to the slopes of those Olympics and creeping up them as well. In short, the Olympics had two timberlines—one near the top and one near the bottom—and he didn't want to see it. Instead of rolling thunder, mellow and deep, there would be only the constant, high-pitched tooty-toot-toot of the whistle punk and the monotonous roar of the donkeys. There wouldn't be any timber wolves there, howling in the night. So he turned his back to all that, and faced the south from where he had come, because he was a true timberbeast and intended to go out the same way he came in. Whitey followed—for now.

So it was with Abe, that he longed to stretch his steps and point his toes northward, until he finally bumped face-first into the tall North Pole and then to dig in his spurs and highclimb even that, rig it if he had to. Then he'd look about and see what could be seen from there. But the gravity of his soul pulled him ever downward, whirling like a maple-key and looking in all directions for a place to plant his root and grow, and where he could say: "This is it for me, homeland of the green people—the place where a man can keep on the move an' never leave home."

Those such as Abe lift their knees and kick their calks and follow their moon toward the abode of the evergreen man. Theirs is the green in an apple tree. So how are they to know that the evergreen man is as the man in a moon of green cheese, gone away into yesterday, seen today and not tomorrow, changing his face in the passing moment? Their quest appears as a land which fades, then recurs, appears to *be* and then recedes to *be* gone again—and on and on. To the man who searches for that abode, it seems that just as he's found it it's dropped off beyond his horizon. Like a bullwhacker, his vision goads his soul. As a hungry crawdad grabs a worm on a hook with his claw and hangs on for all he's worth—the current be damned—the tenacious timberbeast grips his vision. He's pulled north, then south, then north, then south, trying to stay in the greenish light, edging westward all along the way, and he appears to be a hopeless vagabond, always chasing back parts. Fact is, he's a true son of the sun whose bright soul is forever at home and needn't move at all, because all things turn their faces to him. He moves the moon. It revolves around him. It is reflected light.

Chapter 12 The Bull Of The Woods

In the big woods country a man doesn't get the blues. Here, he looks forward to the blues, anticipates them, dreams about them, talks about them. He bends back his neck and strains his eyes, looking up through the trees for the slightest smidgen of the blues. Here, the grays come down on a man and spread out over him like a heavy, wet blanket. More than a few men have been known to suffocate to death under that blanket—but never a logger. With the grays comes the endless Pacific rain, raining down on the Coast Range: drops of nectar to the evergreens; cloud-tears to a miserable man; just the way his world is, to a logger.

The woodsman of the big woods had to be like the giant trees—passive in the face of the rain. The alternative was to go insane.

So if it wasn't the rain that had Abe so broody, then what?

Whitey had the grays. These were dreary days. It was as though Earth had lost her star and was struggling hard to hold her own against an encroaching fatal gloom. In the dying days of winter, the weather was a tumult of alternating spasms of sleet, snow, rain, wind, and snow-rain mix that turned everything, including a man's spirit, into thick muck. His corkies had soaked through a month ago and hadn't dried out since. He'd forgotten what warm dry socks felt like, and knew it was futile to curse the weather—weather was a logger's lot. Why, a logger worth his salt doesn't even know *weather*. But this cold, wet stuff was trying his patience, and he couldn't help but feel that, somehow, it was due to the place and circumstance. If they were to shoulder their sacks and go over the hill, the sun would probably be shining there.

But Abe was reticent and being downright mulish, ever since they turned back at the Columbia. God Almighty only knew why. Abe's solemn eyes were always inward these days and Whitey felt shut out. There wasn't a single reason to remain in this rotten place that he could think of. In fact, there wasn't a reason to hire on with this haywire bunch in the first place. That was Abe's idea, too.

Any logger who knows his business can take a quick look around and see the skill of the gyppo, simply by eying his camp. This place was way down low on the bad side of extremes. To Whitey, it seemed as though they had waded into a thick miasmatic soup that could cook a man's soul, that rainy day they entered the camp. The devil fell with the rain, turning heaven to hell in this portentous place. Hillsides were scraped and dozed to the bone, trees broken off, seed trees gouged, logs heaped like tossed cordwood. Raw soil was festering in the draws and bottoms, pouring its life away. The downpour formed deep freshets on the uphill side and washed blood-thick muck into the road, and then it ran down the road a ways and branched off into a gully wash, then hurried down the gully on its way to the Alsea. Ramshackle shacks. Filthy, stinking shithouse. *Slim would sit right down and cry at the sight of this*, Whitey had thought.

Whitey remembered the day with regrets. The bunkhouse reeked of redeye whisky when they walked in. Most of the men were in the camp and they were all drunk or close to it, including the gyppo. He and Abe only intended to warm up with a cup of hot coffee then move on down the trail, find a cozy spot under a cedar, and sit out the Chinooks, for a week, or two, or three, or maybe more, with a good book, plenty of food, and lots of hot chocolate. This sounded mighty good at the time, and it sounded a hell of a lot better now, and Whitey was anxious to get down the trail and find that tree—but Abe wasn't.

The gyppo here was a man called Dewey, silent, tall, long-armed with large powerful hands and long fingers. He had a hard chiseled look to him, like that of a bird of prey, and an eye to match. He seemed disposed to have Abe and Whitey do what Whitey wanted and get on out to where that tree was. Sitting slump-shouldered alone on a bench, he lowered his brow and glared at them through surly eyes. When Whitey walked by, he thought he heard Dewey growl down deep in his throat. Abe removed his slicker, and then sauntered off a short distance and struck up a friendly conversation with a young boy, fourteen, maybe fifteen, years old, while Whitey socialized with some of the crew.

Whitey finished his coffee and was anxious to make a hasty exit, when Abe walked over and asked Dewey if he was hiring. Whitey couldn't believe what he was hearing. Obviously, neither could Dewey.

Dewey squinted his eyes and curled his fingers into fists. His upper lip formed into a sneer. He squared his shoulders. A hush filled the room. Rising, he said: "You gotta be kiddin' you big ni . . ." But what Dewey was going to say went unsaid, because right then, a runt of a man with a scruffy head of hair and dark quick eyes, got up from where he was sitting in the far corner of the room. He hurriedly walked over to Dewey, reached up and tapped him on the shoulder, and beckoned for him to follow. Dewey hesitated, glared at Abe, grunted something incoherent and followed the runt. They walked off to where stood a man so huge that to call him a giant would not be an exaggeration.

Whitey watched as the giant stooped forward so the runt could whisper in his ear. It took a long time. The runt was straining and his face turned red. But the big man was patient and slowly nodded his head, as though signaling his comprehension. And then he relayed what he was hearing to Dewey. After a few moments of this strange activity, Dewey returned, but spoke to Whitey and not Abe, and reluctantly hired them on.

Whitey was curious about what was said over there that made Dewey change his mind, but not curious enough to investigate. Besides, he didn't like to talk to any of these screwballs and preferred to keep his distance. Just having meals with them was noxious enough, and the food wasn't any better than the company. But a month of lousy food, bad company, poor work conditions, and inclement weather had come and gone and they were still parked here, and all because Abe was being bullheaded. This place was the bottom of the pit where the black bile settles. The obvious rancor of the gyppo plus the infernal weather was enshrouding them both in a heavy, wet air of melancholy. So why Abe stayed only the damned devil knew. And those damned clouds just kept dropping those miserable damned tears right down onto his head.

Nothing made sense, and Abe wouldn't talk about it, and Whitey was tired of complaining, and a logger never bitched about the weather. *Well, to hell with damned codes!* "Bet *this* is the only place it's raining. We're sitting in the piss-hole of the world, and I'll wager it never stops," he mumbled, just loud enough for Abe to hear.

However, Abe went unaffected by the griping and just sat there with his back against his tree and said nothing. His watch cap was soaked, but he didn't seem to care or even to notice it. Water dripped off the tip of his nose like a leaky faucet and into his coffee when he tilted his cup, but he seemed to not notice that either.

The two men sat facing each other with their backs against a couple of scrawny beat-up cedars that were left uncut for lack of market value and somehow had survived the ravishing. They might possibly make it to become big trees if the cable gouges on their trunks escaped the fungus rot.

Dewey's logging techniques were all raw power and no finesse. They were saw, fall, gouge, doze, dig, scrape, pull, pile, and heap. The area looked as though a major campaign of The Great War had happened right here. Not much was left standing and even this was damaged. Dewey's thought process was: *Why go around when you can go through?* It was the code he lived his life by.

Dewey had been born too deep in for his own good—where everything is a threat—where the world is perceived as the devil, out to take what you have and what you have is all there is to you. It's a fearful place—makes a man want to hide. These perceptions manifested a man stricken by diverse maladies, not the least of which was his propensity to hide himself in redeye whiskey. He put forth a bull-of-the-woods swagger and virility, but in reality he held a morbid fear of being exposed for what he was and losing his control over others, and he hated his soul for harboring his fears. The man who hates his own soul hates everything, right up to and including God Himself. So, absorbed by hate, Dewey could not change, because hate is a tyrannical dictator that allows no movement and simmers in the thick slop of its own hot rage.

Dewey seethed with rage. He swam through rage, and he wallowed in rage like a hog in muck. But he needed his rage. It was his security. For who could take his rage from him? Like a walking stick, rage gave him something to hold onto, to lean on and prop him up in the world.

Hate, to be pure, must hate *itself* as much as any. In this respect, Dewey was as pure as dark crystal. He was in the final stages of rotting alive, and his logging techniques mirrored the extent of his putrefaction.

In a certain sense, Abe and Dewey were closer than either could imagine. They were as siblings, children of bark and fiber and dwellers in the forest. But in another sense, they were as far apart as Cain and Able. If Abe was like a black oak—heavy-hearted and firmly-planted, Dewey was like a cedar with a bad case of heart-rot—decaying from the inside out, sweet aroma gone to stench, eaten at by bugs, and vulnerable to the storms that blow.

That place where sympathy homes itself in the psyche of a man was a cold void in Dewey without a single star to spark it. He couldn't even pretend to intellectualize it like so many men do, so for him, it was absent even as a concept. It was plain to see that he was not going to experience the birth pains of so deep-set an emotion as sympathy within the time frame of this life, and probably, if there were a way to tell, not in many to come.

He killed a striker during the wobbly wars. It happened up around Aberdeen, one terrible night, during a mob fight. He was among a gang of company men who charged some strikers and chased them off, but he got too fired up during the heat of the chase and didn't know when to quit. He ran a man down and beat him senseless; then he pounded the poor fella's head against a cement wall and cracked his skull like an egg. Dewey got off scot-free, without so much as a trial, because this was a company town and everyone said it was self-defense. The man he killed was half his size.

The wobblies were a worker movement that was hard bent on unionizing the woods industries. No doubt, it was a radical movement, but these were radical times. It was refuted to harbor communists in its ranks and even to be controlled by such, which may or may not have been the truth. Hysteria prevailed on both sides, and hysteria tends to exaggerate the truth, and the truth exaggerated becomes truth out-of-round, and truth out-of-round is not true Truth any more.

In the eyes of the labor movement, the dead wobbly had died at his post, like a good warrior should, and many in the union tribe swore vengeance on his killer.

Dewey was an imposing sight to look on, being tall and long-limbed. He had muscles as hard as knots from a life of hard labor: swinging axes, pushing and pulling saws, packing steel cable around, choking logs and then yarding them in. His eyes were as red as a dragon's. He always wore his corks. But it only takes a little squirt of a wobbly, crouched behind a stump—just one little wobbly, drunk or sober, with one good eye, one limber index finger, and one gun with one bullet, and one split second of time—to fall the biggest, meanest, strongest, machismo bull of the woods in the forest. Dewey caught a case of wobbly horrors and began to see a vindicator behind every tree. So he left the Grays Harbor country, and now hid himself in the woods, south and east of Newport, along the banks of the Alsea, where he logged his quota and kept the company happy.

He drank redeye straight from a jug. He craved that tight, wet hole and loved to tease it, tickle it with his tongue, tip it up, and suck it dry. People said that when he drank, he got mean as Satan and this is why he drank. "Look out for Dewey when he's tippin' the jug," they said, "'cause he'd as soon stomp ya into mincemeat with his calks as not."

Fact was, his bullyness was only a front, a high wide facade to hide his insecurities behind, and he had to be sober to hold it up. He was dangerous when sober, meek when drunk. That's why he always drank alone. Whisky was his one and only true love: she was tart and sweet, and she was hot and fast. She licked his throat with her long wet tongue, and she made his cold heart feel hot. Then she made him feel good and satisfied. She soothed him. She sucked the stimulant from his hard rage and turned him soft and mellow. She boiled his urine and heated his groin. She put no demands upon him. She was always ready. The more he had her, the more he wanted her. She made him want to curl up and sleep when he was finished with her. As long as he had her, he could live with himself.

With a disgusted expression, Abe flicked his wrist and sent the rest of the coffee flying from his cup, where it mixed with the falling rain. "Shit's gone cold," he said, breaking his long silence. "Need a warmer-upper. Yer mud still warm?"

"Yeah, almost." Whitey reached under his rubber raincoat, pulled out his thermos, and poured some into Abe's cup.

Abe took a sip and settled back against his tree. Then, looking Whitey in the eye, something he hadn't done for a long while, he said: "Whitey, I don't cotton to this here shithole any mor'n you do, so I don't blame ya for complainin'. When a man's standin' in muck up to his ass, he'd best be thinkin' about stuffin' his balloon an' gettin' on down the road, that's fer sure. But we ain't in no muck here, because we're standin' in shit, an' I gotta kick it offa my boots before I go."

The words were as hard as the stone-faced stare, and they set Whitey back hard against his tree. Was this the same Abe who sat placidly inside himself like an imperturbable Buddha? The same man who said Buford and the rest of those waterfront thugs were his friends and teachers? Who the hell was this? Did the dreaming giant stir? If so, what stirred him?

This transformation Whitey witnessed was downright awesome. He was speechless.

Abe lowered his eyes to the cup in his hand, slacking the tension. "We ain't even been here a month yet," he said softly.

Abe appeared to be drifting off again. So Whitey spoke up. "It's been *damned near* a month," he said. He raised his voice and said the words clear and sharp, hoping to snap Abe back. Abe didn't respond.

Abe's words seemed contradictory. So Whitey gave up on trying to make sense of the situation and left him alone, to drift off once more into his melancholy.

The time stretched out, and the coffee in the thermos got cold, but the two kept their seats against the poor cedars. The sawing could wait. *Thoughts* were important now. The rain began to slack off, and a gray mist rose, like pestilential vapors, from the soft, torn dirt. It permeated Whitey's bones. He looked at Abe with an expression of two parts perplexity, one part jest, and said: "Let's see if I get this straight. You're standing in shit up to your ass, and you don't think you've stood in it long enough." Adding some body language to his words, he lifted the corner of his mouth into a sideways mock smile, cocked his head, and shrugged his shoulders. Abe appeared unaffected.

Abe looked down at the ground and softly said: "The boy. I ain't leavin' without that boy, 'cause I'm afraid if we don't take him with us he'll never leave this place. Dewey will most likely see to that when he's done with him."

Oh my God, yes! Blind! Blind! Blind . . ! How the hell could I be so damned blind? In a sudden flash of recognition, Whitey understood this onus that weighed on Abe, and now it was not Abe he wondered about nearly so much as himself. He silently cursed his own insensitivity. Just as Abe had, he'd watched the disgusting goings on, yet he had been blind, all this time, to what Abe had seen in a moment. But now he saw: there was Dewey, pruriently eyeing the little punk, stroking the boy with those red eyes, penetrating him, and always paying him way too much attention—man to boy attention of the wrong kind—grabbing at the boy's ass every chance he got, sneaking up behind him, then reaching through his legs and crotching him, making him jump and squeal and making his balls sore. Dewey'd laugh as though it was all in innocent fun, even urged the others to *tease* him in the same way, so as to camouflage his pederastic inclinations. Dewey didn't care what he screwed. The easier it came, the better. If it was warm and had a hole somewhere it was for the dicking. Had the forlorn boy sulking around, wide-eyed as an owl, his tail tucked between his skinny legs.

Abe looked up and gave Whitey that hard-eyed stare again, but this time Whitey knew it wasn't meant for him. Abe said: "You can go if that's whatcha want. I'll catch up later. I ain't leavin' here without the boy, an' I ain't been here long enough to get his confidence. Things won't get out o' hand long as one of us is aroun' here to keep his eye on things, Whitey. Should it come to it, I'll drag him away from here acomin' easy or akickin' hard, tell you that."

As he looked into Abe's face, Whitey felt a surge of embarrassment. Abe couldn't possibly be serious about him leaving alone—leaving Abe and the boy behind. "Yeah, this is no place to strand a stranded boy, is it?" he said.

As serious as he had been up until now, Abe's countenance grew even sterner. His lips drew taut, and his dark eyes waned dull, without even a hint of sparkle. He spoke through his teeth. "Tell me about it, man. Tell me about it," he said.

Abe's eyes turned in on themselves. Many men hold an evil secret. They lock it up in dark corners of their beings, where they keep it in chains and never allow it to live in the light. They think they might starve it until it dies away. But these diabolical things never die—like sin, they feed on darkness. Now, one of these was clutching at Abe's gut, trying to pull its way out of the pit. Abe fingered his cup and fixed his gaze at the pool of black coffee, grown cold, but saw instead something in the dark past that would never grow cold. Like a furtive shadow, an old scene crossed his mind and made him shudder. Dark memories, vague and dreamy, of a nightmare that wasn't dreamed, nor washed away by purging tears, were stirring again. Up they welled toward the surface of his mind's eye: dark ditch of a place, railroad tracks between boxcars in a run-down switching yard, hard steel, gravel-rock, mean-eyed bums, hard-knuckled fingers, hands holding, groping, probing, men grunting, laughter, smell of garlic and dog shit—

unspeakable! Unspeakable! Pain and shame . . .

Oh, the demons, the demons in the mind! Jesus, save us from the demons.

Remembering, Abe's gut contracted into a knot. Guilt, fear, and shame are the soul's black holes and bend its light back toward their heavy cores. There, they contain the man as captive within their dark horizons, while what escapes their gravities goes lost and floundering within the reciprocating light of events. But the courageous man who holds them up to the light sees, perhaps, better than others. In this moment, another young boy came to view, just a little bit younger than this little whistle punk, dreaming the world was a better place than it was, but afraid it wasn't and unable to imagine how bad it could be. He had been unable to help that young boy, because the boy had been too young. But he could help this one, because the man wasn't.

All of a sudden, a flash of color, deep and pale, gray and blue, still and serene, cut the darkness like a fire bolt and it was as if cold water poured out and extinguished the horrid vision. Abe awoke in Whitey's eyes. He knew they had probed his soul, intuited his thoughts. He withdrew himself with effort, shuddered, shook off the trance, and looked his partner in the face. Whitey's expression was telling him he understood. There would be no more questions. This time, he was not alone.

"Knew some bums once," Abe drawled soft and low, "and these here are them again. Different names, different faces, same damned bums."

At last, Whitey understood something in Abe that had long perplexed him. Abe was not only the man of peace, setting sang-froid within a content and serene soul. He was also a man at war, fighting like a Turk against the demons invading his memory. When he said he slept or dreamed, what he meant was a truce, or perhaps a victory, like liberating the Holy Land and purifying his recollections for a time. So, to maintain his truce and stay in his sweet dreams, he had developed a selective memory, which meant he consciously blocked out sizeable portions of his life in favor of a select few. This could easily be the case with a man who had known degradation. So he practiced love. Love was his redeemer— the Messiah he longed for, waited for, and knew would come. And a devotee of Love is the first to fight for honor. Love is his sword. Now, it seemed to Whitey, he could almost hear war drums beating.

"You know, I'm beginning to like that punk a whole lot. Think I'd like to get to know him better, maybe even make a new friend," Whitey said, with a reassuring smile. He sloshed out what was left of his coffee, stood up, and stretched. "Perhaps he'd like to drop by tonight and have a cup or two of that hot chocolate with us. Why don't you ask him?"

They headed for the misery harp. The rain tapered off, and the sun started playing peek-a-boo through the cloud layer, which was thinning and beginning to glow. Vapor rose from the warming black ground so fast it almost seemed to hiss.

Two weeks went by. The sun rose higher in the sky, heading north. The air warmed up and dried out and the knee-deep mud turned into ankle-deep dust. Corks dried out. Slickers were rolled up and stowed away. And the moods of the two men weren't nearly so muggy as they had been.

It was dusk. Moths were flying. The campfire flickered. They had pitched their tents under the boughs of a solitary cedar that stood in a grassy meadow. Whitey lay on his back in the grass, pillowing his head with a rolled-up soogan, looking up at the sky, watching and sniffing the air and listening. In the wet moss, in the grass, in the convoluted bark of the old Dougfirs, in the draping boughs of the big cedar, under the ferns, in the boggy places, peeking and peeping out between last year's leaves, the tiny frogs of early spring were singing. And for each frog that started to sing, a star came out to dance. Soon, Earth sang with frogs, and the dance floor of heaven was crowded with glittery-dressed dancers. The heavy fog bank along the Pacific lifted, grew heavy, rolled over, and tumbled in and put an early end to the party overhead, but the frogs sang on, beneath their damp blanket.

As with the frogs, the fog didn't dampen Whitey's spirits. His heart felt like partying and stayed to dance the night away. Because tomorrow they were finally leaving this pathetic place, and their newfound young friend was coming along, too. *And that settles that,* he figured.

The fog washed in the piscatorial scents of the sea, and these mixed with the musty ones of the forest, and a chilly stew of odors steeped the ambience. Whitey sat up and threw the soogan over his shoulders and tossed another log on the fire. He glanced over at Abe. Obviously, Abe wasn't in a musical mood. Though his mood had improved considerably from what it was, tonight Abe was solemn and sat under the tree, deep in thought. Whitey started to say something to perk him up, and then decided that the mood of this night would do a better job on Abe's morale than words could.

If Whitey understood the Deweys of the world as well as Abe did he probably wouldn't be so light-hearted. Or instead of dancing a merry jig, perhaps his heart would be stepping to a quick marshal tune. He was mistaken, however, about Abe not being in a musical frame of mind.

Abe reached over and picked up Ruby and laid her heads in his lap, gripping her handle with his knees. He gently fingered her lips, feeling her keenness. He removed his fine-ridged file from its holster, laid it against her, and started to stroke her. Up and down he stroked, too and fro, slow and easy, and the strokes were even, well-timed and rhythmic. Ruby grew warm and clinched her lips tighter and tighter, and the more Abe stroked the warmer her metal became, until she was downright hot and getting sharper, and finally just as sharp as she could stand to be. As though from pure pleasure, with each stroke of the file against her lips, she squealed high and moaned low. Abe's cadence did the rest, and Ruby went out and sang with the frogs.

If Whitey had been ignorant of the Deweys of the world yesterday, today he was going to learn one-hell-of-a lesson. In the pre-morning dark, he and Abe skipped the usual breakfast routine, rolled up the tent, and packed their gear. Then, just as the air began to glow, they shouldered their balloons, picked up their axes, and walked down the trail to the road. Kicking up puffs of dust, they walked to the spot near the log landing where they'd prearranged to meet Punkie. The boy was there as planned. He crept out from behind a tree trunk. All the worldly belongings he owned barely bulged the gunnysack that was dragging through the dirt at his side.

His real name was Kevin. In the big woods, there are lots of kids called Punk, and yet there's no one named Punk. It's easy to forget your name and become just another Punk. Whether Kevin or Punk, he knew this: he wanted out of here. When he peeked around the trunk and saw Abe and Whitey coming, a welcome sense of relief began to purge his overwhelming fear of Dewey. For the first time in a long while, he started to feel free again, and not like he was cowering in some dark corner, afraid to show himself. Dewey had never struck him, but then he was always careful to give him no reason. Dewey's persistent teasing and cursing at him were unbearable enough, so he didn't dare to encourage the lash, because he knew Dewey would use it. And if he used it he might not know when to stop. He sensed a violence in the man that he didn't want to trigger, and a craving he couldn't comprehend. So his entire existence, since coming to the camp those three months before, had been like being confronted by a cougar: he was very much afraid to stay put, but just as much, he was afraid to turn tail and run.

It was like he belonged to Dewey, as though Dewey had staked some kind of property claim on him that the others respected. But now, he had some friends who didn't seem to recognize property claims. He knew Dewey hated the attention that Abe and Whitey had given him these past two weeks. Dewey especially hated the obvious fact that he responded to it by spending all the time he could in their company. But still, he went to their camp every evening and drank hot chocolate and talked and laughed. Dewey was simmering and picking up steam. Last night, he finally came to a hard boil and blew his top.

Last night—good gawd, he'd never forget! Maybe he'd never be able to think about anything else. At supper he'd sat on the bench between Abe and Whitey. He didn't know exactly why it was he squeezed in there, but he knew at the time it wasn't smart. Dewey always insisted that he sit next to him and made a big show of it with the others, so's everyone would know not to sit in that spot. "This here's m' pup," Dewey would brag, as though he were a puppy on a leash. But last night, Dewey had sat across the table and glared at him sitting there between his new friends. Dewey was all red-faced and tight-lipped, and he sensed that Dewey's inner rage was beginning to steam up. When Abe and Whitey rose to leave, he wanted more than anything to go with them, and almost did, but Whitey had placed his hand upon his shoulder and said: "Sleep good tonight, Punkie, because tomorrow's a long day." Then they had said goodnight to everyone and left the bunkhouse. He wanted to run after them, to clutch them by their pant legs, and not let go even if they tried to shake him off. *Wait for me! Wait for me!* The words rushed in and jammed like a log jam in his throat. Then, Dewey got outright ugly and just sat there, sullen and squinty-eyed, watching the two men leave. The others, with the exception of The Little Willy, were talking and joking around, unaware of the mounting crisis. Dewey glared and quivered, like a dog that's about to snarl and just might bite—then he snarled: "You ungrateful little ass." He rose from the bench and walked around the table real slow and deliberate. The men knew by now that he was mad as rabid hell; they stopped talking and watched.

Good gawdamighty, what a gawd-awful memory!

He had felt so awful and alone on that long bench with those two big empty spaces on each side of him! He felt his anus suck up into his gut until he thought he might turn inside out. His body went rigid as a snag.

Right then, Dewey bit: out snaked his long arm and hard fingers. He was frozen to the spot and could only watch as Dewey's hand came toward his eyes. Then everything went dark as the calloused hand closed and covered his face like a black cloud. He felt his face contort as fingers with hard nails squeezed his cheeks and dug into the sides of his head. The nails pierced his flesh like steel tongs biting into a soft little cedar log, lying severed and alone in a pile of debris. Then the helpless feel of raw power, the surge, the sudden jerk, the pull of taut cable, and being yarded up a ravaged hillside. Poor little lightweight cedar stick, headed for the slash heap.

The power lifted him by his face, up from the bench, forcing him to stand on tip toes. But he couldn't stand straight, being wedged between the table and the bench, so he just managed the best he could and sort of dangled there, contorted, which made him feel all the more pathetic and helpless. He managed to peek through the fingers and then quickly closed his eyelids, but not before whiskey-red eyes with smudges of faded blue, centered with tiny black points, pierced his brain like heaved pikes.

He began to feel sick. Then Dewey twisted his head to the side and put his lips against his ear and snarled: "You listen to me, you bastard brat of a two-bit whore! Don't know what in damned hell's good for ya, do ya? What is itcha think a big nig like that one wants with a juicy white boy like you? An' after he's done with ya, that albino whore of his will use up what little bit's left!"

What a pitiless vision to have branded into your brain! Dewey's words hit his ear like a bell clapper, set his entire head to ringing. The table edge cut his hip, and the bench pinched his legs. He wanted to sit down, and tried, but the powerful hand only gripped the tighter, and he thought his head was going to rip right off of his shoulders. Then Dewey pushed him sideward, and he fell against The Little Willy who was still sitting on the bench. The Little Willy held out his hands and braced his fall, so he wouldn't go sprawling. His feet left the floor, and he ended up straddled on the bench where Abe had been sitting. Then he heard Dewey mumble something like: "Stupid little asshole, you better listen to me." Dewey walked off toward his bunk. A hush filled the room.

Then he cried. He didn't want to, tried not to, but he couldn't help himself. The tears came, and his stomach heaved up sobs and shook his sides until they hurt. Feeling ashamed of his helplessness, and knowing the men were watching, he laid his face against the table and covered his head with his arms. He didn't know how long he sat there like that, but he finally heard Tall Tex cleaning off the table. Then he faintly heard the men, talking among themselves, getting up a card game and pretending as though they were unaffected by what had just happened, but knowing full well that Dewey's show had been as much for them as anybody.

When the tears quit flowing and the sobs subsided, without looking at anyone, he slinked off to his bunk next to Dewey's and crawled under the blankets fully-clothed, boots and all. He felt Dewey's presence over there and knew that Dewey lay stretched out on his own bunk, savoring his wrath. Somewhere in the night, the sobbing left him but sleep never came. So, among the coughs and snores of the loggers, he prayed the night away.

His mother was a good, hard-working Christian woman who feared God but was terrified of Jesus. "You must pray, Kevin. You must pray each day and every night, or Jesus will not favor you and give you the things you ask for." Now, the old words he'd heard so many times in his past pierced his head, as though she sat on his bunk. "What do I say?" he had asked. To him, it felt awkward, talking to Someone who didn't talk back, and it seemed more like talking to himself. Asking for things and special favors seemed sorta like begging. "Ask for forgiveness and tell Him you love Him," came his mother's answer, "and He will be there with you when you need Him. He will protect you from your fears."

So he had lied to his mother and told her he prayed to Jesus, when he really never did. But the lie seemed to satisfy her and put her at ease, thinking that her child was a "little friend of Jesus." Truth was: he thought his mother could have picked her friends with more discretion, considering how hard she labored for all her poverty and loneliness, and had only her own name to give him.

Now, the most fearsome force in the whole wide world lurked not five feet away, and he knew, without a doubt, it was because he had lied to his mother and called Jesus his friend when He wasn't. Then he remembered his mother saying it was never too late to call on Jesus and He would forgive sins. He'd never known what sins were, until just now. His had been a real whopper! So he decided, here and now, to pray, while he lay curled on his side, shaking. *Jesus, this is Punk . . . I mean, Kevin. Oh gawd, Jesus, I'm sorry! I'll never lie again. I'll never ignore ya no more, an' I'll pray to ya every day. Please let Abe an' Whitey get me out. Oh, please! Gawddamn, I'm sorry, Jesus! I love ya, Jesus. Are you here, Jesus?*

In the night, he heard Dewey moving, and then he heard his feet hit the floor. He heard him grunt. He heard his heavy steps going toward the door, and he heard the door open and shut as Dewey headed out to his whiskey cache.

Though only a boy, Punkie was like any other man whose subjective qualities sleep fitfully in the dark night, waiting for a dawn. And so, this was the world he lived in. The coming of light is long and dreaded, but anticipated. The next morning was unadulterated terror. He took his seat next to Dewey, but neither Abe nor Whitey showed up. This was all according to plan. They had told him they would skip breakfast that day and get their gear all packed in the first light and then meet him at the log landing, where the crew assembled each morning for orders from Dewey. There, Whitey was going to state their intentions to leave. He fully intended to crowd in behind Abe and Whitey's legs and hide there when Dewey got the news.

Dewey was swollen-faced and sour. He'd drank heavily during the night and stunk of unwashed sweat and whiskey and didn't say a single word to anybody during breakfast. He sat, face to his plate, stuffing down food and making grunting sounds. It wasn't the first time Whitey or Abe hadn't showed up for a meal, so Dewey appeared to suspect nothing.

Kevin's legs were shaking so hard he was afraid Dewey might feel him through the bench. Jumpy as a long-tailed cat in a room full of rocking chairs, he was about to come plum clean out of his skin. Any moment, somebody was going to look into his eyes and see his thoughts in there and yell out: "Hey, ever'body, the Punk here's plannin' to skip out!" *Oh, good gawd!* And he could hear Dewey saying: "Is that a gawdamned fact?" Then he'd lose all his composure and be so afraid of what might happen to him, should Dewey catch him in a direct lie, that he'd just let it all burst out and tell him the whole plan. But none of that happened. Dewey finished his breakfast, pushed his plate away, then belched out essence of sausage and egg spiced with redeye, and got up and left the room. One by one, the others rose and followed.

As soon as he was alone, he'd quickly stuffed his clothes into his gunnysack, ran to the door, and peeked out. The crew was walking away, except for Buster Tooker, who sat on a bunk lacing up his calks. He went back to his bunk, grabbed his sack, and squeezed out a side window that was out of sight from Buster. He then kept the building between him and the others as he scurried across the logged-off area into some dark woods about a hundred yards away.

There was only a slight glow through the timber. The first dim light rays would soon be threading between the branches high above. Close to the ground, a tiny patch of Indian pipe, ahead of its season, gathered dew and glistened. Overhead, an owl soared through the tall trunks, dark and quiet as a fleeting shadow, headed for its roost. The trunks stood ominously silent in the gloom, like giant colonnades from some mysterious bygone time.

Like a nervous chipmunk, Kevin scurried, tree trunk to tree trunk. Then he held his arms at his side, and stood behind a tree, as straight and stiff as a picket pin, for a few moments. And this is the way he went, scurry, stop, freeze, fret, and scurry again, all the way to the landing. Once there, he hid behind a stump, shaking like a puppy, until he saw Abe and Whitey approaching. Then he gripped his sack and walked out onto the landing site.

Now he was secure. Now he felt relief and happiness. No more fearful shakes. His friends were coming for him, carrying their axes and shouldering their gear: "Oh, thank You, sweet Jesus! Thank You! I'll pray to You forever!"

Chapter 13   The Little Willy

Dewey ramrodded the most haywire, scoundrel-infested outfit of hooligans and stumblebums in the Northwest woods. The crew numbered nine men, not counting Punk. Abe and Whitey didn't consider themselves part of this crew. It was a small crew, compared to most, because Dewey was afraid of losing control over a larger one.

First on the roster was Slick, Dewey's sly brother.

Noble James was on it. He wasn't the least little bit noble.

And Tall Tex was on the list. Tall Tex had an unwashed tongue. He preferred telling a lie to the truth, even when there was no point or gain to the lie, and even when the lie was obvious. He was five feet seven and hailed from Oklahoma.

Buster Tooker was a flim-flam man from Walla Walla, who took too many gullible gamblers to the cleaners cheating at cards. There'd be a lot of guns pointing in his direction, but he was sneaky and a good hider, and so their owners didn't know where to point them.

Harry Butts carried his hair-braininess in his genes, considering it was his parents, Mr. and Mrs. Butts, who named him Harry. Harry was something of a namby-pamby who wallowed around in his sentiments, and so at any given time, didn't know if he was coming or going. He spent most of his time doing neither.

Purdy John Jones was a baby-faced roughneck. He spent much of his time primping in front of a hand mirror that he carried in his pocket. He was a Mormon from Utah and was wanted by the law in Washington, Oregon, Nevada, Idaho, California, and Wyoming for wedding various gals in each of those states without divorcing any of the others. He wasn't wanted in Utah and was trying to grubstake himself here to hightail it there, but kept losing all his money to Buster.

Also listed on the roster was a churlish character, named Hawk Babcock. Hawk was a small man with a ruffled head of thick hair that was remindful of feathers. His nose was long and narrow and curved down to a point, and he had two beady eyes, deep-set on each side that darted first this way and that. As a result of a throat injury, he tilted his head back when he talked and spoke with a high-pitched voice. He claimed that he hurt his throat working in the woods when a cable snapped and whipped and throttled him. But the word about was that he got into a barroom brawl over in Idaho, and someone's big fist changed his tone. Then, one dark night, he snuck up on the man who hit him and stabbed him in the back. He'd been on the run ever since. Of course, Hawk denied this; but still, his eyes always darted to and fro.

Last on the list was The Little Willy. This was as odd a character as ever worked in the big woods. He was actually a couple of titmen. One's retardation was inside, the other's was outside, but he was always referred to in the singular, because the two behaved as though one. Rarely was one seen without the other. One was a man, as big as a man can be, whose name was William Little, called Willy. The other was a nubbin of a man, named Willy Monday. These two had a symbiotic relationship, because Willy Monday talked with a stumblebum for a tongue and tripped over each and every word, so chose not to talk at all, except to Willy Little. Willy Little was the only man Willy Monday had ever known who didn't poke fun at his tongue, and who possessed the patience to bear with him as he stuttered out his thoughts. But Willy Little contained a severe stutter in his thought processes.

One night, many years before, Willy Monday came much too close to losing his useless tongue. A lively storm was blowing through the San Juans, tossing up waves and swirling the foam. In a seedy saloon on Seattle's skid row, three mean drunked-up Finns, fishermen blown in off the sound, were killing time till the storm died. Willy was working the crowd, performing for drinks—walking on his hands, dancing jigs, pantomiming—whatever it took to earn a swig. The Finns got it into their heads they'd cut out Willy's tongue and feed it to the saloon's resident tomcat. The whole thing started out as a bad joke: "I know why this tongue-twisted twerp can't talk. An Irishman's got a bigger tongue than pecker. His mouth's stuffed too damned full an' he can't wiggle his talker," said the first Finn.

"Let's do this little frigger a favor an' jerk his worm outa its hole an' use it fer fish bait," said the second Finn.

Whiskey spoke up. And then it all turned heavy, deadly serious: "No self-respectin' fish'd nibble on the damned thing. But I betcha that ol' Tom over there'd gobble it right down. Befitting end to an Irish tongue, I'd say." And the third and meanest of the three Finns reached into his pocket for his jackknife.

Carried away by their tide of whiskey-purged braggadocio, the Finns threw Willy flat down on his back and then piled on top. Two of them sat on his arms, pinning him to the floor. Willy clinched his teeth. The third Finn sat astraddle of his belly and forced his mouth open with a long-necked beer bottle, reached in and grabbed his tongue, and pulled it out so far he almost tore it out by the roots. Willy could only groan and moan and flail with his legs and pound the floor planks with the heels of his brogans. The crowd stood and watched. Ring-tailed Tom sat on the bar, waiting, licking his chops. The tongue-grabber brandished his blade and grinned like the devil. "Here, kitty, kitty, kitty," he said.

But it was Willy Little who came, quicker than any cat. Not being a thinking man, Willy Little couldn't think of a single reason why he shouldn't help the pathetic runt—he acted out of pure instinct. He grabbed the two arm-holders by their collars and rammed their heads into the knifer's and co-conked them all three. Then he picked up Willy Monday, threw him over his shoulder, and got him the hell and gone out of that whiskey hole. Through the pouring-down rain and straight for the woods they headed. The Willys had been together ever since.

Willy Little was only doing what had to be done when he connected those heads; he didn't intend to hurt anybody. But it was a long time before any of those Finns woke up. It's rumored that the would-be knifer never did wake up.

Willy Monday started doing the thinking for the two, which he was mighty good at, while Willy Little did the talking, which he could do after a fashion. Thus, with a little Willy doing the thinking and a Willy Little doing the talking, "The Little Willy" came into being. The two Willys were almost always considered one in the same, but when one was referred to apart from the other, he was called the big Little Willy, if it was William Little being referred to, and the little Little Willy, if Willy Monday was the subject. But rarely was one considered separate from the other. The Little Willy was an innocuous but shiftless fellow whose biggest problem was the whiskey bottle.

Dewey wasn't just crazy like a bull whacker can get when he's over imbibed and out to strut his stuff, and striding high on liquid courage he oversteps his gait and steps into big-bull trouble he can't whack himself out of. He was also insane, and besides this, his booze-pickled brain was too slow on the uptake. He actually thought this crew would back him up and follow him into any fray, when in fact they were really the last bunch a sane man would turn his backside on for any reason.

Dewey's learning was somewhere around zero, but his math was good enough to tell him that ten against two were good numbers. He had run these numbers through his head several times, because he was a naturally suspicious man who suspected that those two no-counts, Abe and Whitey, hated his guts and would do him in if they could - of course he suspected this of almost everybody. But he trusted his crew, because he figured they were entirely dependent upon him, considering no one else would hire any of them. The fact was, they feared him entirely, and not a one of them had the fortitude to tell Dewey that he was leaving for greener pastures, and so they stayed on. They thought Dewey would beat the crap out of any one of them that upset him, and they had good reason to think so, because he'd told them many times that this is exactly what he would do. His brother was no exception and feared him as much as the others did.

What Dewey couldn't comprehend was the difference between not fighting *against* him and fighting *for* him. This fine line of consideration could not enter his gross thought.

Dewey had actually been looking for a showdown with Abe and Whitey. The way he saw it, Abe wouldn't even be in the fray, because he intended to subtract him real quick with one mighty Herculean charge. He figured he'd have to ambush Abe real quick to get him, because as soon as he saw him coming that blackie was certain to run like a cottontail from an eagle. The crew could take hold of Whitey, until he finished up with the black. Then he'd spike the bastard with the sharp point of his peavey and give it a quick turn and hook him in the ass and then roll that albino, like a worthless log, into the fires of red hell! Such are the workings of the mind of a crazy man.

The crew was gearing up for the day at the outfit shack, from where Dewey could see the landing and the rendezvous going on down there. He saw those two sonso'bitches approaching down the hill with their sacks ballooned and that little turncoat Punk asneaking out of the trees to join up with them. The day of reckoning was at hand. Simmering hate boiled over, scalded his perceptions, and he despised all men with a burning passion. He hated his crew, his brother, Punkie, Whitey, but most of all, he hated Abe. He grabbed up his peavey, grinned truculently, and snorted. Then he clenched his teeth and hissed: "You bastards, get yer axes an' follow me. I'm agonna skewer me some dark meat an' see if that sucker's got black blood."

The others could well see what Dewey was looking at, and they all did as he said—for the moment. Dewey strode off. The crew followed well behind, like a tug-towed log boom, harnessed by a long cable of fear. The Little Willy was bringing up the far rear and was just about to jump the boomsticks.

The woods smelled musky, as wet mossy wood will as it dries. The dew in the dirt was dried already, leaving dust. The decked logs near the landing effused the air with the scent of pitch. The sky was deep purple overhead, black in the west, and the east was all aglow. As though under the spell of a magic lantern, there was no shadow to fill in space and link things up, so each man, and everything else besides, stood solitary and magnified larger than the image. The cool night air still hugged the ground, and the men moved through their breath vapors. Dewey, breathing hard with fury through a throat still hot with redeye, snorted between breaths, and like Lucifer's steed, set the air before his face ablaze.

Absorbed by thoughtless rancor, Dewey couldn't realize that these men behind him didn't have the slightest intention of confronting Abe or Whitey. Even Harry Butts wasn't that dumb.

They met near the cold deck. In this moment, the sun began to peek over the ridge behind Abe and Whitey.

Whitey spoke: "Dewey, we're drawing our pay this morning and taking Punkie with us."

In this moment Dewey ambushed Abe. He was the only one that moved. The crew froze in place and gawked. Slick put a brief thought into it, but realized that if Dewey was charging on Abe that left Whitey for him, and that's as far as his thought dared to progress. He locked his knees and stood with the others and helplessly looked on.

The Little Willy stopped and stood well behind the rest. The Little Willy was far from big, but he was deep enough to harbor a genius, and this genius had seen this moment's arrival for several days and had no intention of getting involved. Being a lover of tall tales, he was well familiar with Abe's reputation. He was the one who had convinced Dewey to hire Abe and Whitey. So in a warped sort of way he felt somewhat responsible for all this hullabaloo. "You wanta double yer production? Right there stand the two best fallers in the woods. The company will kiss yer ass from here t' hell an' back," had been his message to Dewey on that day when Abe and Whitey arrived. But that was then. Now he was thinking he should have kept his mouth shut.

The Little Willy took several backward steps, placing some distance between himself and the developing drama, dropped his axes to the ground, and stared with amazement at the unfolding scene.

Poor, silly Dewey: to imagine he could ambush the likes of Abe. He walked toward Abe saying: "Then take the worthless little skin bag and the lot of you get the hell and gone out of here. I'm canning yer asses without pay." Then he stopped about fifteen feet away and glared like a hawk at Abe.

Abe wasn't listening to Dewey's lying words and he wasn't intimidated by his eyes. He was watching his body, reading its language. When Dewey stopped, he squirmed his feet to plant his calks, slightly bent his knees, gathered the muscles in his shoulders, ever so slightly raised his chin, and the fingers on his hands griped the peavey so tightly the knuckles turned pale. In the very second he saw him lower his gaze from his eyes to his heart, Abe knew Dewey was on his way.

In the manner of a charging, dimwitted bull following its horns instead of its brain, Dewey sneered. A low rumble filled his chest and rose up and made his throat vibrate. It mustered his strength and keyed his pugnacious instincts. Just the sound of it was known to make proud men tremble, surrender their honor, fall to their knees and beg for mercy. But not this time . . . This time, there was no begging, and there would be no mercy. He snorted and lunged, thrusting the peavey at Abe with all of his might.

But a man-created bull can't charge on a grizzly bear; bull's spirit's been bred away. The bear is wild and free, and he'll move faster than that bull will ever see. He'll simply step aside and watch the bull run blindly by, and he'll swing out a paw, and with one sharp claw, he'll eviscerate that bull on the spot before it can even stop. A dim-witted bull can never better a wary ol' grizzly bear. Not today; not on any day.

With the nimbleness and silence of a cat, Abe leaped to the side and dropped to one knee. The peavey's point pierced the air a hair's-breadth away from his right eye and grazed his ear; the free-swinging hook hit his arm just below the shoulder and snagged his shirt, tearing it.

Dewey had missed and his inertia met no resistance, and he went charging by, stumbling forward, clumsily off balance. Then, when Dewey was about two or three steps behind him, Abe struck. In a scintillating second, the razor-sharp axe named Ruby, gleaming like a double-headed gem in the early light, swished in an even arc parallel to the ground precisely the height of Abe's shoulder. And like a hot blade through warm butter buns, she sliced a neat swath through the nates of Dewey's butt. It was all so clean and quick, Dewey didn't even know he'd been struck. He regained his balance, eyes bulging wide in astonishment and blood-red with rage. He quickly turned to face Abe again.

Abe stood and turned to face Dewey, holding Ruby at his side; he knew Dewey was done with. "Best ya drop the peavey an' lie down, Dewey," he said.

In blind stupid fury, Dewey planted his calks, lowered his head, and gathered himself to charge once more, but when he braced to lunge he couldn't move. He felt the gush of something thick and warm down his backside and in his boots.

He reached behind and felt his rump then held out his bloody hand and stared at it in disbelief. Astonishment bleached his face. Blood was oozing from the gap in the back of his trousers and dripping into the dust, where it rolled up into dirty globules. He looked at the ground and saw the bloody muck gathering around his feet, and then he suddenly felt the pain. A newfound sense of horror and defeat rose up in his heart and displaced his rage. His body convulsed with shock; his knees buckled, and with a mournful groan he fell flat on his face with his limbs spread out. Moaning, he lay on his belly and squirmed under the rising sun like an unearthed worm.

The crew stood for a moment, frozen dumb as stumps, eyes wide, mouths gaping, faces drained of blood. Then, as a flock of birds that through some unknown signal turns and darts off in unison, they dropped their axes and saws and turned and flew away. Leaving their deserted leader to his fate, they ran for all they were worth toward the bunkhouse and points beyond. All, that is, except for The Little Willy who stood fast.

The little Little Willy was raptured and was frozen to the spot. He saw what had just transpired better than any other man. For him, it was as though the scene had expanded like a lung and breathed him in, and he was the scene, and he not only saw it in its most minute detail, he also felt it. Daydreams, aspirations, cravings, the thickets in his brain, were cut away by the arc of that axe. Everything he'd ever imagined himself to be was felled. It was the end of the time of the mind, and for the fist time in his life he stood tall. And the big Little Willy always stood with the little Little Willy.

Whitey stood and gawked, as astonished as any of the rest. He was too close to the action. It went by him like a flurry. He needed to catch up. His trance was shattered by Abe's calm words: "Whitey, go get Slick an' see that he pays for us an' Punkie. I'll tend to Dewey." Abe then stooped to examine Dewey's dorsal side.

Punk had disappeared. During the melee, he'd jumped behind a log and was cowering there, curled up on the ground, quaking in fear from the sounds of screams and moans. He heard murmurs and the quick shuffle of running feet. At the soothing sound of Abe's voice, his entire system relaxed so fast he lost his bladder and bowel control, and embarrassment replaced fear.

Whitey responded to Abe's order and took out after Slick. Slick, though, had a good lead on him and was dashing headlong for the bunkhouse. The rest of the crew skirted the bunkhouse and headed for the safety of the woods beyond. Slick flung open the door and vanished through it, like a rodent into its dark burrow. Whitey figured he had him trapped for sure. He charged in, slamming the door behind, but the latch didn't catch, and it flew open again. He couldn't see Slick, who was hiding himself, so he stood in the aisle between the rows of bunks, held his breath, and listened.

Slick's panic had drained his lungs. Whitey heard him gasping for air under one of the bunks where he had squirmed. So he got down on his hands and knees and crawled along the aisle way, looking first under the bunk to his left then the one on his right. The open door let in light, and the rising sun beamed the aisle way. But it was gloomy under the bunks, hard to see, so Whitey took to probing with his axe. Holding the handle end against his palm, he slid the blade along the floor, so that should it encounter Slick's body, it would hit him without cutting, and yet it would flush him like a grouse. Then he'd grab him.

Slick was wheezing so hard, it seemed to fill the whole room. He didn't know who it was that was after him, but imagined in his horror that it was Abe, and that it was Abe's axe he heard scraping against the wooden floor—ever so slowly seeking him out and coming closer—ever closer. Blind panic filled his shallow soul, overflowed, and he flushed in a flurry. His body flew in every direction, and he might have come completely apart and shattered into tiny pieces had not the bunk been over him to hold him together. Forgetting where he was, and imagining the bunk's weight as Abe's, he screamed and lunged again, sending the bunk flying.

This explosion of activity was more than Whitey expected and it caught him off guard. A mattress flew through the air and landed square on his back, throwing him off balance. Through the corner of his eye, he glimpsed Slick fly by, springing like a blacktail across the bunks. He fully expected the desperate man to run smack against the far wall, but this didn't happen. Using some primordial instinct, that led him straight to the light at the exit of the burrow, Slick darted out the open door and disappeared from sight again.

Whitey threw off the mattress and went after him. But he didn't know which direction Slick had turned. *Left or right . . .?* He knew he sure as hell didn't go back up the road toward Abe. He paused just outside the door and looked up the road at Abe who was hunched over Dewey, examining his ass. The boy was standing along side. Then he saw The Little Willy looking in his direction and pointing to his left. Whitey spun and rounded the bunkhouse corner just in time to see Slick's foot disappear around a big old Dougfir seed tree, standing solitary, about forty yards beyond the back of the building. Whitey headed for the tree, but when he passed it, Slick was not in sight. But he should have been, because this was the only tree in a hundred-yard radius. All else was logged off, and he'd see him if he had continued on, so he knew that Slick had rounded the tree like a squirrel who intends to keep the tree between it and its pursuer.

Whitey quickly reversed direction and headed back the way he had come and darted around the tree on a hard run. Then he skidded to a stop, reversed directions again, and headed in the opposite direction, hoping to catch Slick unawares. He surprised Slick, as Slick came sneaking around the other side. Slick reversed his direction with astonishing speed, and ran back around the tree with Whitey hard after. They circled the tree several times, with Slick barely managing to keep out of reach. Slick was tall and lanky and had the long legs of a jack rabbet; he could run and jump like one, too. This wasn't going to be easy.

Whitey was beginning to tire, but Slick knew the raw endurance and adrenalin flow that fire-hot fear brews and managed to keep his distance. Whitey stopped and turned in his tracks again, hoping to surprise Slick coming around head-on, and then nape him before he could stop and turn. And he almost got him. Slick rounded the tree, saw Whitey, skidded to a stop, turned, and jumped. Whitey reached for his neck but missed and his hand made a downward sweep and grabbed him by the seat of his pants. But Slick pulled free of his grasp, leaving Whitey holding the torn-off flap of his back pocket.

About this time, the absurdity of it all began to impress Whitey. *This is pretty damned ridiculous,* he thought. The humor of a grown man, with an axe, chasing another around and around a lonely old fir tree, trying to catch him by the seat of his pants in order to collect some wages, caused a chuckle to well in his parched throat. He could've laughed right out loud in the midst of the silly scene, had he not been gulping for air. He stopped.

Sensing that his pursuer had halted, Slick stopped on the opposite side, facing the tree, poised, suspended between his right and his left, and ready to turn in either direction. He was as tense as a drawn bowstring, in grave danger of splitting himself right up the middle. So there they stood, the pursuer and the pursued, breathing hard, each man facing the other through the living wood.

Whitey caught his breath and said: "Slick, if you keep on running around this tree, I'm going to start chopping it down, and then where the hell do you plan to go?" Slick didn't answer, but Whitey could hear him gasping. "Damn it all, Slick, all we want is our pay, so come out from behind this tree and pay us!"

From the other side of the tree, he heard a meek voice say: "Yer agonna axe me."

"I am not going to axe you, Slick. Here, I'll show you." Saying this, Whitey gently tossed his axe out to where Slick could see it. "There, that should prove my words."

"Yer agonna beat shit out o' me then."

"Slick, only reason I might beat the shit out of you is if you don't pay us. And if you keep running around this tree, I'm going to knock the pee-wadlins out of you, to boot. Just come on around here and unlock the damn box, and pay the three of us, so's we can get on our way out of here. That's all we wanted from the start. If you don't do that, I'm going to pick up that axe and go to chopping." Slick was silent, and Whitey knew he was considering his predicament, so he added some frosting to his persuasion. "Slick," he said real slow so the words would sink in, "look at it this way. Abe's going to be coming down here any minute to see what the hell the holdup is all about. Who'd you rather get caught by, me, or him?"

Slick immediately walked around the tree. He looked pathetic: his face was drawn, and it was as white as a ghost. His shoulders were slumped, and he cringed like a whipped slave. Whitey actually felt sorry for the man, and said: "What the hell's wrong with you, Slick? You didn't do anything against us."

When he heard these words, Slick stood straighter and squared his shoulders, and got a look to his face like he suddenly realized that he had been cringing for a long time. He walked to the place where Dewey hid the key, and he opened the moneybox and paid them in full. Then he reached in and took out ten more dollars. "Here," he said, "this is a bonus for the punk."

Like Slick, The Little Willy wasn't an evil sort, just a coward trapped under the intimidating spell of Dewey. But, with one swing of his axe, Abe severed the spell and set The Little Willy free, which meant the end of The Little Willy, though the two Willys remained fast friends until the end of their days. They had plenty of time in the bunkhouses to reflect on the little coward they had once been. They made a pact, and shook hands on it, to kick their mutual dissipations, and never to fall from the grace of man again; for they saw those of Dewey's ilk as abominations, low-born beasts living in the form of a man. Abe and Whitey's ken were seen as men, worthy of that designation: man—even, perhaps, transcending it in subtle ways. The Willys swore off striving for effect and swore instead to strive for the sake of their spirits and to serve their fellow men by simply being the best men they could be. And they made a mighty good go of it, so that when their ends finally came they had established some communication in that respect.

Their friendship changed from one based on mere symbiosis to one deeply rooted in conscious love. It was only then that they were able to part, if they so chose, and go their separate ways. Though they chose to stay together, this newfound freedom did not supercede the awareness of either.

Willy Little quit drinking, cussing, smoking, fighting, chewing, philandering, lying, gambling, stealing, whoring, carousing, farting in public for the fun of it, and sloughed off all his peccadilloes in general and devoted himself to his work. He became a downright respected and sought-after logger.

Willy Monday did the same, but this Willy knew how to read and write a little bit, having had a bit of schooling. He didn't know exactly why, but words became his passion. He even made a trip to town just to purchase a dictionary. So, with a sharpened raven feather for a quill and berry juice for ink, and for reasons he didn't understand, he started scribbling on the bark skin of fresh bark slabs and playing around at making up word rhymes. Surprisingly, the rhyming came easy to him, and the more he fiddled around with it the simpler it was. Then he discovered a strange thing: if he talked in rhymes he didn't stutter, because he could simply read out the words from out of his vision, sort of like reading script written in light against a blackboard.

Willy Monday's problem, all along, had simply been one of having been born with two overriding souls, which behaved in the manner of estranged marriage partners, living under the same roof, neither of which denies the existence of the other but refuses to recognize its counterpart's independent authority. Like a double-headed axe, they turned their backs on one another and faced in opposite directions with Willy square in the middle between the two. But he couldn't get a handle on things. What a *dilemma*! He was consciously diametrical, and he was aware of each, but each one fought for its turn and tried to squeeze in front of the other. They would surface at the same time. He thought he was confused. He didn't suspect that he was split, though he'd battled like a riled-up Irishman all of his life for reconciliation, for consistency.

One soul saw things as being *in here* and claimed that all was *of* it; the other saw the same things as being *out there* and claimed that all was *for* it. The one soul said: *"I have arrived;"* the other: *"I am on my way."* These two spent all the time arguing with one another as to who was right and represented the truth and was, therefore, the greatest and eligible to receive the light of Willy's cognizance. Of course, to each the other was irrational. Back and forth they went and polarized Willy's tongue. When he tried to speak, his concepts jumbled and two words came at once and tangled with one another like wrestling contortionists.

Poor Willy Monday never had a moment's peace. Language was a trial. Thought-to-word required all his concentration. However, while other men merely talked and parroted one another's words because talk was easy, wordless Willy was forced to watch and listen, and to consider the clashing echoes in his mind. A woodsman among woodsmen, Willy lived in his own recondite niche of the forest. Though, to him, it was as if he'd been exiled into hell, and he cursed his situation, in his solitude he became a master of watching and listening—and considering. And the considering was like a file, moving back and forth and back and forth, and the more of it he did, rather than wearing away (being made from immortal stuff), the finer the ridges of the file became. How was lonely little Willy to know that all those years in solitude were ones of edging his perceptions to a fine, razor sharpness—that the Maker of him was not cruel, after all?

And so, his double-headed conflict was finally unified, and it saw eye to eye, and it rhymed, and needing no associations to prop it, it was constantly present.

At long last, in that endless silent moment, when Abe swung Ruby and felled a tyrant, it was as if those conjugal aspects of The Little Willy bent back their necks and looked over their heads and saw exactly the same thing for the first time. Finally there was no doubt or excuse for argument, estrangement felt unnatural, and they turned and faced one another eye to eye and simultaneously exclaimed: *"Oh, we see!"* In that moment, each soul took the measure of the other, and to their mutual astonishment they were equal parts of one and they were reciprocal wholes. It was love at first sight and they came together and copulated and reproduced countless-fold. In a split second, the echoes stopped clashing and the mountains became silent and serene—empty. Caged-up words flew away like freed birds. Then Willy heard a knocking tapping lightly on his noggin, and he said: "Come in my friend." And for the first time in his life he heard his voice without a stutter. A door opened. Forgotten old memories entered in and were new again. His perceptions sprouted wings and Willy Monday was heaven bound.

All the hubbub ceased, and Willy's world abruptly changed. Things, all things, each and every thing, were all at once, and were first here then there then gone, taking turns like notes in a song, or as rhyming words in a tall tale told by a master teller who knows all words. Chaos gave birth to harmonious symmetry, and within himself, he discovered the predilections of a poet.

As Willy harmonized, harmony became the one constant that he knew. Even the doings in the world began to harmonize. He was a member of the band, playing the symbols. He found his lost voice, and it was a clear resonant voice and deep and sounded as though it belonged to a much larger man. His words flowed out like honey. He began to speak out, always in rhyme, and sounded more like a man singing than a man talking. He came to be called Rhymin' Little Willy or simply Rhymin' Willy by most people.

So it finally came down to this: Willy Little wasn't called Little Willy any more, because he was far bigger than most men. And Rhymin' Willy became the foremost teller of the tall tale contests in the bunkhouses, because even the best of the old tall tale tellers, try as they may, couldn't make their tales flow in substance or rhyme the way he could. They were all astonished and would exclaim: "Gawdamighty, Rhymin' Willy! How the hell do ya do that?" Of course they couldn't understand that he did it the way he did because he had to, it being the only way he could speak. And because he spoke only in rhymes, he spoke only when spoken to.

Rhymin' Willy told thousands of tales, sometimes several a night. In the early days, all of his tales had to do with timberjacks, loggers, and life in the big woods. Timberjack lore, like the lore of old England, was passed along mouth to mouth and its heroes grew with the telling, until they became too large to record on mere paper. And so most escaped posterity. The lonely logger could only hold them in his heart and in his mind and in the striving vision of his soul, and in his passing, hand them off to the chief time keeper to store in Time's deep treasury where the timeless golden leaves are kept, and where they are due to grow eyeball to eyeball high to Beowulf himself, and vie with him for the imaginations of future men. If these future men are keen, they will see the moral contained in the theme: the timberjack, like the old English dragon slayers, killed off his giants, then was no more.

As huge as he was, his heart was too large for its frame, so it could not be contained and strained itself beyond its limits one hot day at the end of a long hard pull on the misery harp. Thus, it was not Willy Little's fate to become an old man, and he died while still young, as gentle giants so often do.

Rhymin' Willy took up the solitary life of a troubadour and traveled to and fro and from camp to camp, singing his rhymes to any who would listen. He knew the time of the clock by the lengths of shadows and the positions of stars, the week by the waning and waxing of the moon, the month by the texture of the air, and the season by the colors of leaves and types of flowers and the comings and goings of birds. Today's sun is yesterday's sun, but today's sun is new, so for

Willy, each day was a brand new day to wake up to. And the way he figured it, that sun up there shined its light on each and every thing according to the thing's own nature. The evergreen tree bathed in light till it turned the light green, the mushroom received the exact amount it wanted, and if the worm rejected it that was the worm's business. His brogans were worn; his pants were baggy; his pockets were empty; his coat was soiled and threadbare; and he wore an old felt hat pushed up into a cone. He walked wherever he went and refused the many rides which were offered, because walking along the narrow roads and the trails through the trees was when he did his best musing—"trampin' along," he called it. There's no word for his profession, so when someone who didn't know him asked him what his occupation was, he'd just smile and say: "Trampin'." Once, when asked what it was he did as a tramp, he grinned real big, removed his hat, scratched his scruffy head, and said: "Never said I was a tramp. 'Cept fer the word there be no such thing as that. Trampin' is where I said I'm *at*. But we recon' the answer to yer question be: nothin' at all do I do we'd say, 'cause I don't do the day. We take our ass in tow, draggin' nothing more than that. From here to there we go, with an empty sack slung o'er our back, hopin' maybe to fill it full with just a pinch o' Truth, for future proof that I passed through this way."

Willy was a humble little fellow, so at first he was only dimly aware that he had been appointed and groomed and allotted the duties of a teller. And he was faithful to his calling. When the muse dropped in to visit, he sat himself down on the spot and listened with all of his will. He slowly nodded his head and muttered: *"Uummm-huh, ummmmmm-huuu, mmmmmm,"* over and over, in complete agreement, until the muse departed. There he sat, upon a mossy stump, deep in some unnamed woods or in the ditch alongside of 101 or 99, and roads in between, up to his neck amongst the wild carrot, and patches of chicory, oblivious to the societies of the world, recording songs in his mind. If he was sitting in a ditch, tourists speeding by on the busy road to the beaches most often mistook him for a derelict.

The raunchy old timberjack camps were giving way to new settlements, but the settlers hungered for the wild and wooly flavor of the disappearing camps. Willy held a standing invitation to all the gritty mill towns, where he filled up the newly-built gymnasiums with lovers of wild and wooly songs. Willy's name spread like a forest fire, and others emulated him and their numbers grew, and so the tall tale teller's circuit was born.

Word of Willy's movements preceded him like a fast-flowing ocean wave. A town knew when he was headed its way, and children were posted as sentries to watch for him. While waiting, they played in the trees, dipped their toes in the streams, and skipped along the trails like woodland elves; and when they saw him coming, they scattered and went running through the village streets and alerted the populace with excited cries of: "Here he comes! Here comes Rhymin' Willy! Here comes the Rhymin' Little Willy!" Then the belfry bell rang, cars beeped their horns, trucks blasted their air horns, and the mill tooted its whistles.

And in he sauntered, flashing that ear-to-ear grin of his, with a balloon slung over his shoulder and a dancing throng of children and mothers at his heels. He never wanted. To take in Rhymin' Little Willy, for a night or two, was considered to be no little honor.

Willy only told a tale once, as was the way of the old-time tall tale tellers. Then, like blowing on a dandelion, he let the words fly softly away with the wandering muse, for her to do with as she pleased. It never even occurred to him to lay claim to his tales. The way Willy saw it, he was given the right to copy not to *copyright*.

A lady once approached Willy—it was plain to see that she loved him—and asked him why he didn't record his words. He said: "We would, if only we could, but I don't remember 'em."

"Then write them down with a pen," suggested the lady.

Willy said: "Then I'd have to think, and if I think, we lose the rhythm."

"Tell me what town you're headed to next. I'll take my car and be there when you arrive," said the lady.

Willy said: "Ma'am, we'd gladly tell ya if only we could, but time's not a block o' wood; we can't chop out a nick and put it in our pocket. This's not our show that's aplaying, but we're the one who's in it; so I don't know a single thing, beyond this single minute."

All of Willy's tales would have been lost to later generations if it had not become fashionable to recite the tall tale tellers at social get-togethers. Anybody who could recite the Rhyming Little Willy held center stage. Few had such good memories. So people began taking pads and pencils to his tellings. In later years, his followers retraced his steps and collected his tales from as many of his scribes as they could find. The followers collaborated and compiled his leavings into a collection that was so voluminous that even the most ardent of his disciples was flabbergasted. After his death, he was recognized as far and above the greatest of the old timberbeast myth-makers.

As time went on, Willy's tales began to change and were most often about glacial mountains, or cool ocean winds blowing in off the lips of storms, and of migrant geese singing their clarion chorus down to Earth. Or his verses were of wide rivers full of salmon and running clear and free through the same ancient canyons and forests the dinosaurs had known. It was as if he were tallying these aspects of Earth.

There were diverse tales of this kind and they sparkled like little gems in men's minds. The woodsy people passed them along like heirlooms. And the future dwellers of these lands were mighty glad of his leavings, too. In their time, they came to treasure them more than diamonds, because Earth was changing and this is not the way she was to be when they lived. But Willy's early tales were of the early times, and were most often about men larger than man, and this is one of his first:

THE BULL OF THE WOODS
He stood shoulder high to a redwood tree;
Didn't saw no logs, bucked 'em again' his knee;
Wore gloves o' iron an' a shirt o' steel;
Britches o' tin an' spikes 'neath his heal;
When he talked he bellowed like a chargin' bull;
Caused a man's bung t' shrink an' his guts t' pull;
Laid claim t' the grizzly an' the devil as kin;
But he was meaner than them an' loved t' sin;
Beat his jacks with a wire-rope whip;
Broke thar backs oe'r the slightest slip;
Bullied all men, each an' ever' one;
Uprooted trees an' spit snoose on the sun;
Drank up the Rogue like it was his fountain;
Got hungry an' ate up the Big Rock Candy Mountain;
Hated all men an' they hated him, too;
Wobblies tried t' sink him in the Coos Bay slough;
The wobblies couldn't get him 'cause he was way too big;
So what the wobblies couldn't do ol' Abraham did:
Grabbed him by the head, an' grabbed him by the foot;
Chopped off his tail, an' that's all she took.

And this is one of his last:

THE HONKY-TONK OF UNITY
Oh, the ragtime's great though fer some a bit randy,
So come ye m' lady an' m' lively li'l laddie;
Pick up yer feet an' make yerselves handy;
The music plays on an' it sounds mighty dandy;
So step lively t' the tune an' beat o' the gandies.
Go dancin' through the trees, prancin' through the leaves.
Oh, tis a gay, high steppin' li'l jubilee!
Jus' come t' the dance an' you'll see,
How tis ya dance in perfect harmony
With: cricket, bug, slug an' bumblebee;
Oak, cedar, apple an' bramble tree;
Nightshade, larkspur, hemlock and tansy;
Buttercup, primrose, sunflower and pansy,
Huckle, salal, bane an' thimbleberry;
Nettle, yarrow, watercress an' rosemary;
Peas in a pod, goldenrod and chokecherry,
Puppy, pussy, hamster an' caged canary;
Warbler, phoebe, hooty owl an' towhee;
Killdeer, veery, sparrow an' chickadee;
Now, then, when? An' eternity;

Up, down, aroun', an' polarity;
This, that, what? And ubiquity;
Us, them, you, all, an' me.
Oh, the gandy dancer dances with all that be;
Out in the honky-tonk of Unity.

The great tall tale tellers are powers in the world, because through the magic wand of their tongues, mortal men obtain to immortality. The Abes and the Whiteys of the world, and even the Deweys, live on in song.

It's rumored that towards the end of his days, on one clear day, Rhymin' Willy tread the highest and most solitary of forest trails and saw the glade where the High Teller Is and this is proven in his rhymes. But who could lay claim to such vision on the part of another? This will prove to be true only if Willy himself bent his step to the steepest trails and his will to all the trials along the way and completed the tall tales circuit of Time and tread above even the timberline, being simply a Teller's teller, and is his *self* told in rhyme. For now, this much is known at least: Rhymin' Little Willy was far from little.

No one knows what finally happened to Dewey. Rumors and tall tales persist. Of them all, the one that sounds most likely tells that having lost face and reputation, he lost everything. So he changed his infamous name and went up to the Ketchikan country, after his buns mended, where he hired on to various outfits as a choker setter or bucker or bushler, or whatever. But he'd lost his black heart, and with it went his rage, leaving him all alone with his self-pity. For such was the infirmity of his soul that if he couldn't be the bulliest bull in the woods he simply couldn't care to *be*.

He became a man tired of the heavy drag of his own spirit. He couldn't hold a job long. Liquor was his only intake. He lost his muscle, and his loose ragged clothes draped his marasmic body. Near his end, he took to sitting on the docks with his hands folded in his lap, while he watched the fishing boats come and go, and he endlessly twiddled his thumbs, as though in a stupor.

Then, one cold day, he drank some antifreeze while parked on the end of one of those long piers, but it was a cheap brand and below zero it lost its chemistry. That night, a chill wind off the gulf, mixed with sleet and snow, froze him to the dock like an icicle. When the early morning sun thawed their butts, and the icicles dropped, one by one, into the salty water, Dewey took his turn with the rest, and the swift tides hauled away the great old bull of the woods to feed the king crab.

Or so they tell . . . But who knows?

Chapter 14 Going Separate Ways

The great timberbeast was losing his howl. These days Abe was just trying to keep up with Whitey. He had accomplished his goal and starved out Whitey's worm. It had been a great adventure, tramping with this vagabond, but the irony of it all was that he couldn't starve out his own hungry grub. He wanted to settle in, or at least leave off his old ways: ways that he saw coming to an end in this changing world. He had gone as far north as he was ever going to go in his life, and now he just wanted to go home.

Like every timberbeast, he too dreamed about that dream camp which sits at the base of the Big Rock Candy Mountain right along side the Buttermilk River. If not his dream camp, for Abe, Slim's camp was his stable camp at least: a place in the timber where he could go and rest his weary beast. Now, he was feeling as tired as he had ever felt in his entire life. It wasn't a physical fatigue; it was his spirit that was dragging. He knew full well that his partnership with Whitey had become like an out-of-balance double-headed axe; the two of them pointed off in different directions at different kinds of lives and Whitey was hell-bent-for-leather.

Punkie was good company, entertaining too. He added some spice to the evening jawboning over the dinner plates, considering he was something of a tall tale teller, himself. Problem was: the tales were most often about himself, didn't rhyme, and he told them in such a way that it seemed as if he actually believed them, or, at the very least, wanted others to. So, they were considerably shorter than they were tall, but Abe and Whitey took them in stride and tossed grins along with little winks back and forth across the campfire. What the heck, he was only a punk and had lots of time to grow out of it.

Several months after the run-in with Dewey, another camp jumper, at still another camp, said over a cup of coffee one day that Slim had finished his contract and taken on a new one. He moved his camp to somewhere along the banks of the Rogue, around Agness, but not before he almost went broke.

He lost another man, "A feller name o' Zimmermann," the timberbeast said. Apparently, Zimm finally succeeded in talking Slim into letting him be the catskinner, but Zimm was a jack with no knack for cats and so the cat skinned him instead. He was making a turn on fairly steep grade, ran a track upon a high stump, hit the throttle instead of the brake, and the cat, so un-cat-like, lost its balance and fell onto its back with Zimm under it. Seems he tried to jump clear but didn't jump far enough.

If losing The Fish was hard on Slim, losing Zimm was devastating. Zimm had been with him almost as long as Hack -- started out as a whistle punk. Slim knew that Zimm didn't have any machine sense, but against his better judgment, he let Zimm nag him into the catskinner job when a press of duties forced him to give it up and fill it with someone other than himself. There were experienced catskinners out there, waiting in a long line for a job with the ever-popular Slim.

Zimm, however, was persuasive, and in the end Slim felt he hadn't taken the time to train him right and turned him loose too soon.

Slim got sick, grew disconsolate, quit working, and left camp for days at a stretch to go into town on binges. "Why, ya'd think ol' Slim wanted t' go broke, what with the way he was behavin'," said the timberbeast. This was probably true, because to Slim his gyppo camp was his life, so losing it would constitute a form of vicarious suicide. Going bust was better than facing another dead man and it would make bitter meat for his hungry guilt.

Slim was probably the best damned all-around logger in the world, who loved what he did—but he wasn't hard-boiled enough for the trade. Despite his stoic boss-like mannerisms, his vulnerability, as well as his ultimate salvation lay in his tender sensitivities. He himself had taken all the risks and been close shaved by death more times than a few; he'd lost count on that score. He could face the prospect of old grinning death by grinning right back at it, but he couldn't face the reality of it in another. Loosing a man on the job was his one great fear. In this respect, he lived in the penumbra of its cold shadow, and when death visited a man he loved, who worked for him, he moved into the miserable umbra of his guilt.

Slim would have lost everything he had, but Hack Leatherwood let off his drollery for a while, stepped into Slim's place and filled his calks, and rescued it all for him, in spite of him. The logger telling the story was hired by Hack and worked for him as a hook tender for a season. He said Hack surprised the hell out of everybody. But Abe and Whitey only smiled knowingly to one another.

After a year or so Slim must've drowned his sorrows because he climbed back onto the wagon, sobered up, came back to work, and actually worked under Hack's direction for a while, until he felt better, and probably, if the full truth were known, to learn what he could of Hack's management techniques. These days, they were down around Agness somewhere along the swift Rogue and doing well again.

When he heard the story, Abe became incurably homesick. Two weeks later, with Punkie in tow, Abe and Whitey stuffed their sacks and headed out for the lumber boom town of Powers, which was a place that, to Whitey, had the old familiar feel of the mill town in the Rockies, before it got *respectable*.

From Powers, they jumped a log truck headed off in the pre-morning dark for a load over the hill and down by the river around Agness. Punkie sat inside on the passenger seat, while Abe and Whitey hung onto the mirror hangers for balance and rode the step-ups.

The driver was a good one. His feet danced on the pedals, and he walked through the gears as though on tippy toes: first the main, then the auxiliary, then the brownie when needed. The roar of the rig changed its pitch with each well-timed flick of the wrist and barked on the double clutch. It was a shifting formula of his own choosing, and it urged the little Cummings diesel to sing out its notes, first higher then lower through the turn, higher on the hill, then lower on the down grade, and stretch them out along the straightaway. It was a merry tune, and like a busy bee, sang of commerce. The sound of it echoed through the woods and lost itself in a lulling hum among the ridges. Fine dust hung in the still air and glittered in the bright new light and hid the road behind.

By lucky chance, the rig was headed straight for Slim's operations. They stepped off the running boards into a hearty welcome home that couldn't have been deeper felt had they been the first robins of a cold late spring. It was as if time hadn't passed. They took up exactly where they'd left off. This was Saturday, so the camp threw a gay jubilee that night to celebrate their homecoming. Slim actually allowed the crew to break out some liquor. He reasoned they could sleep it all off in their bunks the next day.

But time *had* passed. Its passing could be seen in Slim: he was changed. His face showed more lines and deeper, and his eyes looked away from the logger and inward more often, to a place where the logger couldn't go. It was as though a subtle air of fatigue had clouded in around him, and he was given to long sighs during quiet moments. But not ol' Hack. Ever the harlequin without a mask, he hadn't changed a bit, with the exception that his ass was a bit bigger. If he didn't know better, any insightful person could still swear Hack didn't have a serious bone in his overgrown body.

To Slim, his camp was his home, and like a master house builder, he had a knack for finding just the right spot to place it. This one sat along a small stream that trickled down a slight incline to where it emptied out into the wide Rogue. Whitey felt as though he had come home, and Abe *claimed* he had—but had he?

After all these years of being partners and sharing experiences, Whitey thought they had purged their mutual restraints. But Abe grew pensive and didn't at all behave like a man who was settled in before his hearth fire. More often than not, Whitey found him sitting on the riverbank, caught up in his daylight dreams, gazing across the river into the distant mountains. Whitey gave Abe his peace. He knew that Abe would come out with what it was he was holding in at the time of his own choosing.

On a warm day in early fall, when flocks of geese could be heard calling above the treetops, Abe said that he was done.

Though he'd anticipated these words, Whitey couldn't hide his disappointment. "What for, Abe? I thought you were happy here," he said.

Abe shrugged and said: "I am, an' I ain't.

"Then what is it?"

"I never told you this, but I almost quit once before, then changed my mind an' stayed on."

"Oh. . . When was that?"

Abe looked Whitey in the eye and smiled real big. "That same day when you showed up," he said.

"You almost quit when I showed up?"said Whitey, exaggerating surprise.

Abe uttered his characteristic chuckle. It rumbled out of his chest and up through his throat and seemed to hang in the air and then float softly away. "Nope. That's the day I changed my mind an' decided to stay on for a while longer. An' that was a while back from now."

"Going on seven years."

"Like I said," Abe paused and swallowed, "that was one of the best days I ever spent in these woods. Guess I just figgerd you brung it with ya, an' so I decided to stick around an' see if you had any more of them kind of days. An' you did. Yessirree, sure did, an' I thank ya for 'em, too."

Whitey couldn't remember crying in his life. He didn't cry when he ran away from the farm even though he knew he'd probably never see his folks again; he was headed for an adventure. He didn't even cry when the professor died; the professor was ready for death and his dying seemed natural. He had cried when Peppa died, but that was different: that was for Peppa; Peppa wasn't ready. Right now, he was afraid he couldn't keep from crying. He felt his insides go soft and warm, his throat contracted, and his eyes grew moist. He knew he had to say something fast or the tears would well up. Then he wondered what was so wrong in crying. Why not cry? What would be wrong with that? Was he ashamed for Abe to see him cry? If he cried perhaps Abe would stay. He'd bawl his guts out for that. But he choked back his tears and said: "Am I all out of those kinds of days?" Then, to his amazement, looking into the dark eyes of Abe, he saw a moisture drop form in the inside corner of each and glisten like pearls as they rolled down his cheeks.

Abe reached up his index finger and wiped the tears away, but more followed. "Damn it all! Didn't want to do that," he said. He reached into his hip pocket and pulled out the big red bandanna that he used to sponge down his neck and head, then turned his head and wiped his face. He turned back to look Whitey in the eye once more, holding his rag on the ready at his side, and said: "Fact is: I'm all out of 'em. I'm older than you, ya know. You got lots left"". Besides, I jus' don't fit it the way you do an' prob'ly never did. Don't know quite how to put it . . ." He paused, searching for the right words, then said: "Yer the timberjack. An' it's come down to this: yer the *only* timberjack I know, an' ya just might be the best I *ever* knew."

Whitey started to speak, but Abe raised his hand slightly, requesting silence, so he held his words. Abe spoke: "When I first come to this country, all them years ago, it was so damn big there was no end to it an' plumb full o' trees. Biggest, purdiest trees I ever seen. Why, I couldn't believe it was real. A man could lose hisself in all them trees an' work his heart out an' feel good about it, because he knew it went on forever. Seemed a man could never cut down too many because took too long to fall one. Longer it took, the better. Can't say why it seems so, Whitey, but the country don't look so big no more an' neither do the trees, an' I think I done gone an' cut too many of 'em down. I don't want to leave these trees, but I'm afraid they're goin' to leave me. A man can't go from here to there no more an' be in trees all the way. Don't laugh at me when I say this, but sometimes, on a quiet day when there ain't no wind whistlin' or bugs abuzzin' an' I hold my breath an' listen real hard, I swear to Christ I can hear their hearts beat—swear I can. I'm just not so sure about this that I do no more."

"I've never laughed at you, Abe, not ever. Laughed with you plenty of times.

Abe nodded, and said: "Best times I ever had."

"Maybe that's your own heartbeat you hear," said Whitey, trying against hope to dissuade Abe.

"Yeah . . ." said Abe with a far-away look to his eyes. "Yeah, that thought's occurred to me, too. Kinda scary ain't it?" There was a long moment of silence before Abe said: "Real soon, Slim's goin' to want me to start knockin' 'em down with them power saws they're agettin', an' I ain't goin' to do it. Them machines, Whitey, . . . Them machines are startin' to eat up ever'thing, an' I don't want 'em to eat me, too. Way I see it, I best quit so ol' Slim won't have to go again' his grain an' tie the can to m' butt."

The talk seemed to soothe Abe. He sauntered over to the canteen, soaked his rag, wiped his head and neck, and then washed his face clean of dried tears. He glanced toward Whitey and smiled. Then he went over to the harp, balanced it over his shoulder, and said: "But for now, I can still hold up my end of the saw for a little bit longer. C'mon let's get back to work."

True to his word, Abe gave Slim notice and worked out the week. Slim tried mightily to talk him into staying on. "Damn it, Abe," he said, "I'll never make you stoop to usin' a blasted power saw. Just name your job and do it any old way that suits ya." He even recruited Hack to help. But Whitey knew they were wasting their time.

Abe drew his pay and left on Sunday morning. The day started out hot; thunderclouds were building. On that morning, standing on the bank of the river, with Slim waiting in his boat to ferry Abe across, Whitey asked Abe what he had gained from their years together as partners. Abe smiled, and with that familiar glisten in his eyes, said: "Well, I feel a whole lot greener."

Whitey stood on the bank alongside Punkie and watched Abe go. This was to be his last view of him, for they were never to see one another again.

The winds of the times were shifting through the big woods, flowing from another direction, blowing hotter, whispering through the limbs, whispering "war." Soon, the boulders in the rivers would hush their chuckle and the happy rifles start singing a dirge. The old days of peace, when a man could hide in the canyons and grow his soul amongst the tall trees, were at their end. These were the days of fire and wind, when the green leaves burned away and never returned again.

Abe and Whitey were fated to come together once more as soldiers in the first battle of a long war, during the terrible siege of the Great Red Wolf.

The thunder heads broke open and started booming like drums. Whitey watched until Abe disappeared into the evergreens on the river's south side.

Fate has its way, and so here the trail finally forked, and Abe went overland, back the way he had come. Up the crystal Illinois he went, then through the hot hills and canyons of the Kalmiopsis, then along the cool banks of the Chetco, and on down into the green redwoods of the Siskiyous, where he felt most at home.

A week later, Whitey hitched a ride out of camp with Slim, who was taking Punkie to visit his mother in Bandon. There, he said his farewells. He caught another ride and traveled the route of Highway 101 through the wind-blown hemlock and cedars along the coast, winding high along the cliffsides, then dropping down to skirt the dark sandy beaches that separated the weatherbeaten little coastal towns. On he went, twisting and turning through the curves, mile on mile, to the monotonous hum of an automobile engine, ever holding the Pacific off his left shoulder and Polaris off his right. He crossed the yawning mouths of a hundred rivers or more, and early one morning, he crossed the wide Columbia and was not to return this way again until the Great Red Wolf invaded the country and the alarum called him back and into war.

The Grays Harbor country was crawling with highlead logging shows. There were almost more spars than trees. If there was money in stumps, this would have been the wealthiest place on Earth. The toot, toot, toot, of the whistle punk echoed through every canyon that still held a stand of trees. Whitey settled in here for a time. Through the years, he'd helped Slim rig many a spar. Using Slim's techniques, he quickly established himself as the highclimber of choice. These days, the gyppo was most often a businessman who couldn't rig a spar, so they began to seek him out in droves. He was shuttled from camp to camp and treated like a king and paid like one, too. He became the foremost practitioner in the highclimber's fine art of rigging a highlead operation. When he finished a job, it was said to be "Whitey-rigged."

He did his work with his axe and a one-man harp and loggers vied for the privilege of helping to carry his gear to the tree—but *never*, never were they allowed to tote the saw; he always shouldered his own saw.

He even began to make a show of his art, and men crowded around the work area to watch him climb and top the tree. He dressed in clean fresh clothes on the day of a climb, and others began to emulate his appearance in the same way he had once copied Abe. He climbed the tree quickly and deliberately, not missing a step or wasting a moment. When he reached the point for the undercut, he hauled up his axe on the end of its line, dug in his spurs, and leaned back against the rope and cut out the face. Then, without breaking rhythm from first stroke to the last, he played the harp and cut away the crown.

And now the show began. As the crown hit the ground, he quickly climbed to the apex of the spar and pulled himself up and sat on it with his arms spread out, while the spar still swayed. It was during these days that he found out that he was, in fact, squeamish of heights, when one time he got the notion to stand up after the swaying stopped, but while the spar still quivered. He made it as far as his knees, then he looked down and became nauseated. Far below, the ground spun around. He almost lost his breakfast right there; then he swooned and nearly lost his grip. He wasn't to try this again for a long time.

The Grays Harbor country was over-logged. The loggers here were desperate after the meager pickings, and Whitey didn't like the way the wind blew through the country. He constantly edged northward, and finally settled in around the general area of Forks where the country and the people suited him better. He took the job he wanted in the camp he chose. The taking was his, because a huge ghost preceded his every step and cleared his way. It was the ghost of fame. It was as though his life had become a ball of yarn that was constantly being woven into the fabric of colorful legend by others, and then unraveled and spun again into a suit of epic proportion, fit to adorn Bunyan himself.

He lived, for the time being, as he always had, in the rhythm of the harp and the changing of the days in their seasons. But in a few years, the days changed. The hone and hum of the misery harp gave way to the new sound of the powersaw's shrill whine. On any busy day, the woods sounded like a nest of roused hornets and smelled of oily rags and gas fumes. A tree that used to take two good timberjacks a day's hard work to fall could now be felled by one greenhorn in a half-hour, and so the woods resounded far and wide to the constant call of "tim-b-e-r-r-r-r!"

The age of the machine was in full swing. This new-logger would never know the days when the saw sang, and the axe beat out the rhythm of a man's heart, and the timberbeast howled.

Chapter 15 The Great Red Wolf

It's the dog days of August, and the hot summer is a trailing hum and at the peak of things in their activity. The viney maples are blushing pink. Clusters of pearly everlasting are drying out, looking older and mortal.

Dragonflies are flying wingtip-to-wingtip maneuvers through stalks of cattails and tall fescue. Tiger swallowtails cavort in dalliance amongst the plump blackberries. Flocks of flighty gold finches, traveling through, flaunt their wealth up and down the brushy draws. On the polished surface of pools, groups of water skippers skip about and do-si-do. Garish painted ladies, adorned in cosmopolitan attire, flutter about and primp the purple pompadours on the thistles, as though preparing them for a hot night out on the town—or in this case, the wind.

Humble bees, honey and bumble, are working the teasel heads, salal, Indian paintbrush and berry briars in the high meadows. To one who stops to listen with open ear and closed thought, a steady ceaseless *huuuummmm* fills the ether—it's more than the bees. In endless service, the old Hindu sits unseen in the silent shadows of his mind and hums unheard amidst the busy marketplace—it's the commerce of creation. In this place, on this day, the oldest of old Hindus, long lost within his own lulling ancient hum, realizes the zenith of creation. He sits in bliss, knowing perfection.

He calls upon his friend who lives as the sun: "Vivasvan, my dear devotee, come here and embrace me..."

"What 'n the hell . . ?" Lighter than a cottonwood fluff, fringed like feather down, a slight wisp of smoke, rising, curling . . . "Sonofabitch . . ! Shit, oh shit! Fire! Fire! Gawdamn it, it's a fire!" The donkey puncher sits up high on the skids; he's watching for the log he's yarding in; he's the first to see. He rears back in his seat and yells at the top of his lungs, into the din of his engine. He screams out "Fire!" again and again then realizes that no one hears him. He pulls the shut-off chord and kills the engine's roar. Stupefied, he sits stuck to his seat and listens to himself scream: "Fire! Fire! Fire! Fire! Fire! Fire!" giving full voice to the dreaded word. A chorus goes up, ringing through the firs, as fifteen men hear and sing out the name: *fire*. The red wolf hears their call, gathers his strength, and leaps out from the dark wood.

In this moment, loggers are turned into fire warriors. Only the battle is on their minds. They grab for their axes and shoulder their spades and run down the hill to form the first battle line of a long war.

They were after that one last log before they saw the smoke, the last log before the end of day, a day that should have ended an hour before, but instead, a day that will not end before this generation of men.

The gyppo on this show was a desperate man, and desperate men always need more time to fill their needs with their wants. The weather hadn't cooperated; equipment kept breaking down; short-handed, he was running behind on his quota and so the company was pushing him hard. The company wasn't at all happy with his performance and his contract was coming up for bid. Maybe they wouldn't let him bid on his own job. He had equipment to pay for. One more log a day can make a big difference. One more log is a profit; one less log is a loss. *Loss* means no money.

Only *money* is money. *Time* is a facet on the compound eye of life. But the gyppo didn't consider this. And so this gyppo prayed every gyppo's daily prayer: *Lord, please gimme some time. Don't git me wrong, I ain't no timber hog but I just gotta yard in one more log. Time is money. Give me time, more time, more time in the short day. Only for that do I pray an' never for my wayward soul. So Lord, I'm goin' easy on ya; that ain't so much for You to do; just a wee bit more will see me through, an' pull me outa this deep ol' money hole. Oh, take my everlasting soul for just a tad more time!*

Now, cursing heaven and hell, fire warriors run for the fray, shouting out their oaths before them, as though to intimidate this tall red-crested Hector—this vile hero from within the walls of Hades.

For sixty days or more, a hard dry wind, fresh off the eastern deserts, rich with the scents of sage and juniper, has flowed through the gorge and down the steep western slopes of the Cascade Range. Off the mountains and across the wide valley it flows, where the wheat stalks wither and apples bake on trees. It grows heavy and hotter in the valley, and slows, and flows like hot goo up the slopes of the Coast Range, then down. The ocean's cool surge stops its onward flow and backs it up, rolling it back in over itself. It builds, grows heavy—settles—gets deep. A sea of heat, undulating, waves flowing through, sticking to everything. The red wolf lives here everywhere in this sea. He's gnawing on the forest, as a dog on a bone, sucking all moisture from its marrow, gathering strength. Look for him; you will not see him. He's invisible—till he springs. Then it's too late.

It stood as it always had: black under the overcast, green under the sun, ocean waves of trees, damp and cool and tenebrous within its own shade, flowing up mountains, reaching for the sky, riding out storms and sucking them dry, surging, lifting up and flowing over, falling and mixing and rising again and again and again, Dougfir, hemlock, spruce, cedar, the various true firs, and all of the named and nameless others—centuries layered upon centuries—time standing tall, unified. A forest-being, conscious and aware, stately, but defenseless as a seedling against a mere spark.

The choker setters saw what happened. They threw the choker cable around its neck and choked up that last log, a big heavy one the bullbuck ordered out. The whistle punk hooted orders to the donkey engineer to take up the cable slack in the highlead. Skidding slow and easy, the giant began to yard up the hill, headed toward the landing. It moved over and through everything in its path, until it came to a decaying old windfall, carcass of a long-dead cedar, lying perpendicular. It nosed in against that old cedar and stuck there. The donkey operator, feeling the engine strain, pushed forward the throttle and increased his power against the log. The log's nose bucked up, tearing at the bark on the old windfall, exposing her soft skin. The increased speed of the yarder caused the log to skid too fast across the windfall, and this created friction heat. Hot heat raped the tender pliant flesh and gave birth to an unwanted spark.

The three nimble choker setters jumped off to the side and ran down the hill about twenty yards away when the big log began to crawl up the steep face. They thought they were done for the day. They were glad. One told a joke. The others laughed. They shared a canteen of water. Then they saw the rising smoke. Agile young logger men, born in these mountains, as strong limbed as the trees, they dug in their corkies and raced toward the smoke with rescue on their minds, for they loved this forest as much as any man could. It was the only home they'd ever known. The vision of seeing it burn was a nightmare in their dreams. The red wolf was horror in their minds. Pumping knees and heaving wind, up the steep slope they went on hands, knees, and feet, closing the gap. To their amazement, the entire windfall was full of flame.

"The son-of-a-bitch must have been full of pitch!" one yelled to another. They shouted and cursed the fire, and having nothing else to fight with, they removed their shirts and began to beat it. This served no other purpose than to fan its vigor and spread its heat. They retreated slowly backwards as the flames advanced. From up the hill, the crew arrived to front the spreading blaze. Hoping to turn its flank, they formed a line before it. With shovels, they dug for dirt, but dirt lay a foot or more beneath thick dry humus, and they could find nothing to throw upon it as they dug, except more fodder.

"He's headed for the crown! The son-of-a-bastard is goin' for the crown," yelled the bullbuck. And in the twinkling of an eye, the red wolf fulfilled the bullbuck's prophecy and leaped three hundred feet high, into the dry treetops, where the wind blew. The crown would be his.

His flank turned, routed, the frantic gyppo dispatched a runner for reinforcements.

And so, the first battle line was drawn and then quickly breached by The Great Red Wolf—time to reconnoiter. The war had begun. Besieged, the sylvan queen sounded her muster call, and her subjects heard, and it was as music in their souls, because the natural forest is harmonious and can't sound out without singing.

Fire warriors came in legions. Abe came and Whitey came.

The fire was a grand event. It turned a page on time, closed a chapter, and opened the beginning of the end of the age of blind innocence. After this, Northwesterners would never view the great standing forest in quite the same way: as something limitless and permanent and at peace. People would come to see it more like the pearly everlasting: firmly footed in the soil, lasting throughout the ages by forever coming and going, fighting its way for a piece of the sun—if it is not picked and dried - - or burned.

The conflagration was a harbinger and marked the exact transition point between two eras: the age of ice was receded, and the age of fire was at hand. The forests of the Tillamook and the Oxbow once sheltered the saber tooth. Back then, ice tongues over one hundred feet thick were the forest's greatest foe. Ice crawls and creeps, but fire runs and leaps. Now, the forked tongue of heat licked the forest's flanks, but unlike the ice, there's no way to brace against fire: giving in a little here, gaining a bit over there. With ice, time was on her side—not with fire.

It came in fury. It was red and black and grey, but mostly it was sheeny red. It made heaven glow, and it cast its putrid breath over hundreds of miles and blackened the ass side of heaven. Its teeth were as lightning flashes. Its tongue was long and forked. It salivated hot ash. It growled and roared in a feeding frenzy. It filled its belly with the east wind. It defecated waste. It ran and it flew and it bounded. It traveled hell-bent-for-leather. Its voice was a roaring that began with a hiss and ended with a sizzle. Its laugh was like a cackle.

To the old-timers, and to the locals who knew it well, it was not an "it" at all. To such as these *it* was a "he," and long ago, their fathers named him "Red Wolf." They feared him. He'd come many times. But never before had he come like this. This time he would be called "The Great Red Wolf." There are those who claim he set a spark, touched it to nothing, lit the electron, congealed the atom that sent the globes to spinning and blazing into stars, dawned time, and fired the primeval gloom. Scripture says that on the coming day of doom he will slay the world. Some believe he will devour even himself.

Whether it was a *he* or an *it*, this was warfare. The whole thing started with a whiff of friction heat, and The Great Red Wolf leaped in through the spark. He was fed by living ages, and the forest queen was betrayed by her old ally: rain. Her new ally, men and women, rallied to the alarum, marching to her aid; and many thousands of them formed into long lines and returned the enemy's fire with volleys of their own. It was a valiant alliance for a time, but in the end, the war was lost.

Afterwards, some men on Earth bent their heads to their ledgers and calculated their arithmetic and saw a great loss of revenues. They stated that a million acres and many billions of dollars and board-feet had literally gone up in smoke and down in ash. But the fire warriors who'd fought The Great Red Wolf held their heads high, higher than numbers can count, so high they stood taller than the man in the moon. The man in the moon saw a scorched battlefield, like a terrible scar in the heavens, but the warriors, being mostly from sound logger stock and Christian upbringing, said the scar was on the ass side of God.

Two men don't meet on opposite ends of a misery harp out of pure chance. The fates aren't ruled by happenstance. Abe and Whitey were born together, before the world was dreamed up, conceived by the same spark that kindled the Earth Star. They were sons of fire, and it's the fate of such men to be consumed by fire. They were destined to finally part in the same way they had met—at opposite ends of a misery harp.

The harp plays on and on, while the world burns. It never stops. It plays the low note and the high note. Its music, like the fruit of the deadly-beautiful nightshade, can be bittersweet.

In the early days of the big burn, the primary staging camp was on the eastern front. The tiny town of Forest Grove was surging with confusion, commotion, and the press of bodies, vehicles, and make-shift shelters, as would be expected in a major theater of war. Men hollered, vehicles roared, horses whinnied, and mules brayed. It was motion in frenzy.

On a day in the hectic thick of it all, two buses departed a few hours apart. One bus headed northwest with crews to front the foe over in the mountains of the Tillamook country. The other bus headed southwest, to the opposite side of those mountains, down around the Oxbow. As tricky fate often has it, unknown to one another, Whitey rode in one and Abe in the other, headed for opposite sides of the same tall mountain, coming together again on the endings of a misery harp—Whitey to work the west side, Abe to work the east side. They came within a hundred yards, on that day, of embracing one another, one last time

Chapter 16 The River Beyond The Moon

Like he said he would, Abe quit logging. He spent some time walking the trails and called on some aging loggers he'd known in bygone years in the Redwood country. One morning, he paid his respects to Sydney Garbo's widow who was living in the mill town of Arcata. Then he headed east over the Siskiyous to the mountain hamlet of Happy Camp and the Civilian Conservation Corps camp located near there which was named Jolly Camp. Called the CCC, the Civilian Conservation Corps was a government organization that helped down-and-out young men to help themselves rise up, during these low economic times, when the greedy few had pulled the cornerstone from the economic temple, leaving the needy many stranded in the cold.

The forest service was attempting to strengthen its hand in order to exert more influence on how the forests were utilized. The CCC boys were trained in a variety of such jobs as carpentry, trail blazing, bridge building, and campground maintenance. They also learned to be foresters and they learned to be loggers and how to set chokers, to fall and buck trees, to be hooktenders, to be donkey punchers, and many other such jobs—but foremost, they learned how to fight fire. In this way, they were acclimated to the mountains and the woods culture. They also learned skills needed to enter into the demanding industries that exploited the forests.

These boys were not well received and were considered aliens and interlopers by the established gentry, most of whom, if the truth were admitted, had come from the same places these young men did and for the same reasons. Only the times were different. The flow from many rivers washes through every person's blood veins. We jetty out into the same ocean. We've each and all been refugees more than once, and most likely, will be again.

No one was more astonished than the Jolly Camp administrator on that day when a legend walked out of the trees into the camp and inquired about employment. Abe was welcomed with awe and open arms and settled into his new life as a mentor. They learned fast, these desperate young men, and like puppies, they wanted only to frolic and please their master.

When he heard the muster call, Whitey came on talaria. He worked the backfires due east of the town of Tillamook for a week then cleared firebreaks along the Trask. He'd seen the backfires lure their kin into the traps and devour them like cannibals, and he'd seen the red wolf leap upon the backfires and eat them alive like a beast devours its young. He'd seen enough of hell to last him forever—he *thought*.

In the thick of the melee, the fire marshals decided that protecting the rail line was a priority, so they assigned Whitey to head up a crew whose responsibility was to secure a long stretch of rail and a trestle bridge.

The railroad was the lifeline for moving machinery and materials between the eastern and the western fronts. The settlements to the west had their backs against the sea. The fighters to the east were fighting to keep the red wolf out of the towns and cities that strung along the line where the hills toe out into the valley. Hamlets in between were surrounded. It was a desperate situation all around.

Whitey's duty was to protect the rail line that bridged a river on a long high trestle. The trestle was the main thing; tracks and sleepers can be quickly replaced, but the trestle's construction occupied a large crew of hard-working men for over a year. It was made from logs and timbers and spanned the river canyon for several hundred feet. Going east from the trestle, the rails skirted the riverbank for a short distance, then veered away and ran through a shallow valley for about two miles before turning back to the river. Westbound, they left the river and entered into a long steep-faced canyon and didn't leave that canyon until they came to the Pacific. Should the fire burn over the roads, and run hard to the south, all the fire fighters and the coastal population from Newport through Tillamook to Seaside might be stranded. It was thought that, worse come to worse, entire towns could be evacuated by train. Protecting this trestle and all the others was of utmost importance.

Whitey's crew had been thrown together in haste, of men from diverse places and occupations. Some were willing warriors; some weren't. They numbered seventeen, and six of that number was a gang of tight-knit railroad men who were pulled from their jobs and assigned to the war. Some of the other men were pulled from their cars. Several of the railroad men considered themselves to be unwilling conscripts and their bitching and balking was relentless. It seemed to Whitey that all they wanted to do was sit on their asses, suck on snoose, spit, and bitch. They made it difficult for the others to put their hearts into the battle, and so it was a downhearted crew.

Whitey had bossed good crews and bad in the woods, but this was by far the sorriest of the bunch. To make matters worse, some of the railroad men resented having a logger in charge of them when their duty was protecting a rail line.

They'd been in there five days, clearing firebreaks along the hillsides above the trestle. The inferno had backed off all over, and the red wolf appeared to be beaten. But Whitey wasn't taking any chances; there was a strain to the air as though something was pulling it taut, stretching it to its limits. There had been no fire here, but ash was everywhere and constantly filtered in through the air. It subdued all color.

If the red wolf came, Whitey expected him to come from the south, because that's where the main battles were raging. But he could jump this canyon and come from the north—or he could race in from either up or down the tracks.

It never occurred to Whitey that the wolf could come from all directions at once, including above and below.

Not wanting to gamble with time, Whitey ordered some of the men to dig out several holes along the riverbank so they could quickly bury their food and supplies, should things turn desperate. As usual, the railroad men were indulging in more than their share of complaining, one in particular. But this was nothing new. This guy was born griping. Right now he was saying to the others: "Diggin' holes in sand . . . This is the most stupid damn thing I ever done in my life. That damned fire's finished, fer sure."

Whitey was digging along with the rest. He knew from experience that you don't confront a bitcher with words; that's exactly what he wants you to do. You either get rid of him before he sours the others, or you find some way to shut him up—and you shut him up good. He couldn't get rid of this one, quite yet, so he'd bide his time, see what it came to, and then do what needed doing.

The air was cool. The moon lit the trail. Far off to the east, the red and orange banner of the sun was unfurling, rising like an oriflamme. Their eyes were straight ahead, and they marched in file, and their heavy leather boots hit the ground with a timely step. Their arms swung in unison, some shouldered spear-sharp peaveys; others shouldered axes or pulaskies. When they passed, silence gave way to their heavy breathing, and the ground shook and rumbled like a drum roll under the beat of their feet. For these were fire warriors, going into battle.

Abe was in charge and led his troop down the steep face, descending in a long hard march that sliced it at an angle to a point three miles distance and over a thousand feet lower than the fire camp on the ridge top.

He didn't like the feel of the place: the canyon was ominous, deep and steep, drained by a small creek named Little River. On down the way, the Little River merged with the Big River and the Big River ran to the sea. The pitched walls were too steep and covered with loose shale to sustain much life and only scrawny firs and hemlocks competed for sun and dirt. The canyon floor, however, was a different story. Fed by soil that was long ago washed down from the slopes above, lived a thin stretch of forest.

This old strip of woods knew fire. Through the long eras, the creek that drained it had washed away black soot more than a few times. What it didn't know was man, but now men came. They came to its aid, for it had never before fronted fire such as this, and this time, the odds were weighted against it. This time, it needed allies. And it had allies. It had great allies, for its defense had been assigned to the CCC boys from Jolly Camp.

They were sixteen battle-weary men and a little brown mare. She was only about thirteen hands tall, but she carried her share, and she was woods-wise and never stumbled. She'd helped to pack down their gear, and she would pack it back out when the job was done. This time, they took her along in case somebody broke a leg or twisted a knee and needed a ride back out.

Her eyes were big and mellow, her eyelashes were long, her legs were slender and straight, and she had a big round rump. She loved to have her ears scratched and her withers rubbed and her rump patted, and horses don't usually smile but this one did, ever so slightly. They named her Mona Lisa. There wasn't a man in the crew who didn't love her, and they were determined to take her back to Jolly Camp. Abe didn't object, but he was hard-pressed to figure how they were going to get her in the bus. But right now, turning around and climbing back up and out of this canyon was on Abe's mind. But what would he say? How would he justify this decision to the fire marshal? After all, this was only a rear-guard action; the fire had never even reached this quiet place.

For almost two months, his Jolly Camp crew had battled the blaze in the shallow valleys up north, among the heavy forests near the place where that first spark was fired. Now, all seemed to be under control up that way. The lines were cleared; the backfires held; the enemy's flanks were turned; the red wolf appeared to retreat. Still, he didn't like the feel of the descent into something that can close in over a man and then devour him into its gullet.

This was their fourth day of clearing firebreaks in this canyon. Their assignment was to build a dam, a dam of emptiness, save for soil and rock, so that should the wolf get hungry again, he couldn't' run wild through this canyon and leap out into the expanse of forest down there beyond the Big River, and on into the Oxbow.

The fire wardens thought that Abe and his men should pack in supplies and spend the nights at the work site. "It's a steep hike in and out and you'll save a lot of time and energy if you stay put," they said. But Abe resisted this idea from its inception, and his were the final decisions. Time and energy be damned; a safe return to Jolly Camp was his priority. Though they packed in their gear and supplies the first morning, they'd left it all in the creek bottom, and walked back out each evening. He didn't want these men to be caught unawares at night in their sleep, down in a black hole, three miles away from the nearest road head.

As Abe thought on these matters, they reached the firebreaks and the spot along the Little River where they had left the gear the previous evening, and he opted to do his duty and stay. After all, this day, or at least tomorrow, should complete the job. He determined to push it hard today and finish it down here, even if this meant working into the night and feeling their way back out in the dark. He called a halt.

"Okay, boys, lighten yer loads for five," said Abe.

Some stood, some laid down, some sat with backs against trees, while others squatted on their hams.

On the seaward side of the mountain, overcast hung in the sky, obscuring the moon and stars and men in darkness. Whitey leaned against a stump and ate his canned beans and dreaded the coming day almost as much as he dreaded the restless nights. He'd seen better times than these. It was hard miserable work along the railroad. Days were hot as hell itself, and the nights were cold, and they didn't dare start up a fire. Sleep came hard, and he was glad another night was almost over—better to fight a red wolf than fight your sleep, he figured. He was soon to wish this night had never ended; today's light would be short-lived

No owls could be heard hooting. No crickets sang. Frogs weren't chirping. Metal spoons scraped against tin. Restless men, sore and tired from work and lack of sleep, sat about in the blackness, eating breakfast from cans. Bud the bitcher was bitching:

"Don't see why we can't light up a damn fire." Then he spat a wad. Then he continued: "I'm sick to death of raw food that tastes like tin rust."

"Aww, Bud, we're here to put out fires, not start them up," came a voice from the dark.

"The red wolf is as dead as my ass feels," said Bud.

"Don't count on it. I heard of them red wolfs ablowin' sky-high when they get like this. One over in Idaho a few years back damned near gobbled the whole state down. This sucker might just be layin' low, simmerin' an' gettin' stronger, waitin' for a hard puff of fresh air—then, WHOOOF! he'll singe the nose hairs in the nose of the man in the moon," came the voice from the dark.

"Blow, my ass," said Bud.

"Not here, please," came a reply.

Some chucking was heard.

Bud was pissed off. Bud hated good humor. He felt outnumbered, so he recruited reinforcements from some of his cronies. "How about it, Joe, if'n she blows you gonna stick yer head, like a dumb ostrich, into one of them holes we dug?" he said.

"Good way to get yer ass hairs singed," answered Joe.

"If'n she blows, I'm headed down the goddamned tracks, fast as my legs'll carry me," said Bud.

Bud's sour ambience contained a lucky vein. If it didn't, someone would have killed him, long before. But, with these words, his lode of luck ran out. Whitey was through with this nonsense. He'd told the men what to do if they were threatened and that was to get organized and listen for his instructions. They were to spare no energies in coming to this spot on the river and stay together. By no means was anyone to desert the rest.

"Take a blanket and a bucket with you when you go in the water. Soak the blanket and hang it over your shoulders. Use the buckets to throw water in the air and on each other." He had said it perfectly clear more than once. He didn't think it would amount to anything as desperate as all that, but a man can't take chances when he's caught up in the middle of a fire. Right now, Bud was saying he was going to do what he pretty damn well wanted to do, and what he wanted to do was dead wrong.

Whitey knew he needed a united front if this place fired up. He couldn't have these men going off willy-nilly. He was in charge and he was responsible—Bud wasn't responsible, and he didn't want to be. Like some high-headed moralist, Bud was doing all this *talking*, because talk is cheap, and easier than *doing*.

"I'll be right behind ya, Bud," someone said.

"No, ya'll be right behind me 'cause *I'll* be behind Bud," said someone else.

Bud felt better.

Whitey felt his nerve endings heat up, felt his juices boil.

"Gotta go do my mornin' constitution. Don't no one go to eatin' my delicious can of pork 'n beans." It was Bud talking again. Whitey heard him get up and watched his black silhouette head off down the tracks.

This was an alert crew. Abe had never been more proud of anything in his life than he was of this crew. Thrown together in haste by adversity, they had nonetheless formed a proud band—for were they not the CCC boys from Jolly Camp? For most of them, this was the only label in their life they could grasp and identify with. Like a royal title, it gave them something of themselves to be proud of.

The long descent was behind them and they felt good, and as they rested along the Little River, they settled into idle chatter. They were fanciful young dreamers.

Said one: "Look way over there, heaven's colorin' up. Hope we get blue sky today, as blue as pure ice. I'll crack me off a piece an' suck on it."

Said a second: "Not me, man. I'm a gonna soak my dogs in it."

Said a third: "You guys can have all the blue sky ya want. Blue sky means hot sun where I come from. Give me rain clouds, man. I'll take good ol' soakin'-wet rain clouds, full of sparklin' water drops that all drop right on top of me."

And so, the whimsical palaver continued through the period of five. Then Abe's firm mellow voice ordered them to their tasks. Like good soldiers, they put away dreams of comfort; in unison they rose and retrieved their gear.

So, in this early morning, with bold hearts full of false visions instead of caution, they put themselves to their duties. High above, an ashen gibbous moon shimmered and floated swiftly away, as though riding on strong convection.

Whitey watched Bud's form disappear into the night, then he quietly rose to his feet. Bud walked down the tracks about fifty yards to a place where a small log that had fallen off a railcar lay alongside. The log was about two feet in diameter, which was a good poop-stool height. Several of the men had been using it for a latrine bench. Bud slipped his suspenders off his shoulders and let his pants fall to his knees. He spit out his old snoose wad and replaced it with a brand-new pinch—a real big one. He planned to take his time. Then he sat down in his favorite spot, where he knew there weren't any slivers, put his hands on his knees, and strained.

"Uummmuhhhhhhh." . . . He was just getting into the feel of the relief of emptying his overfull gut of all its pork and beans, when something that felt like a huge raptor grabbed him. He felt the hooked claws of powerful talons close around his neck and over the top of his head, gripping, squeezing. To his horror, it lifted him straight up. The jolt and the shock caused him to lose complete control, and he emptied what was left in his gut down his legs and into his pants.

He swallowed his wad, all in one big gulp.

He struggled and tried to resist, but the grip on him was like a vise. He thought his head would shatter—a sense of total helplessness mixed with shock and fear. Suddenly, he felt himself spun around in the air, and then he was lying on his belly where he had just been sitting, and from the stench that filled his brain, he knew his face was either in or very near the pile of defecate; then, to his terrible discomfort in went his nose and into his nose *it* went. He wanted to scream but didn't dare open his mouth. How to breathe? To complicate matters, considering he'd just swallowed a palm full of snoose, he needed to spit in the worst possible way.

Then he heard Whitey's voice. It was a loud whisper in his ear. It said: "Listen to me, shit face. I want you to go back to the camp and sit your ass down like nothing happened and cheerfully say you're going to do exactly what Whitey says to do. Use those exact words. Do you understand? Nod your head if you do."

Bud nodded his head and each time he did so his nose dipped in and out.

"Go wash off in the river first."

Whitey could hear the men gasp when Bud came traipsing into camp and sat down and said: "Know what, fellas? I was just now sittin' out there on the crapper log, thinkin' that from here on I'm gonna do exactly what Whitey says to do. Yessir, you betcha; he says to do it, I do it."

The sky was white. Abe wiped his brow with his bandanna. A heaviness lingered in the air unlike anything he'd experienced before. He looked about, seeking the cause, but all appeared normal. Mona Lisa stood tied to a tree; her nose was buried in her nosebag. The men were busy, hard at work along the line, trying to maintain the feverish pace of the preceding days, wanting to get done and up and out of this place. With exhausted bodies, sore and hot, they faced the hill and bent to their spades, pulaskies, and axes. Up they went and down they bent, over and over again, chopping, scraping, digging, and gouging their way through the tangle of branches, brush, and humus, stripping the topsoil to clear the firebreak, as they had learned to do back in Jolly Camp, and as he instructed them to do now.

From where he stood Abe could survey the scene almost unimpeded. Everything looked orderly enough. The situation had improved considerably from just the day before. Though bodies were down, spirits were up; because it appeared that the task down here was nearing an end. All seemed quiet on the front, too quiet, and something in him didn't like the feel of it. Though it was hot as blazes, a cold shiver ran down his spine.

He leaned upon his axe, removed his hat, pulled his bandanna from its pocket and soaked it with his canteen, then squeezed it out over his head. The heat was stifling. He looked up. Overhead, a red bloated sun, as fat and oozy as a gorged tick, bobbled and danced around like a horizon star. For a brief moment, as though to escape fate, he returned to the cool old redwood forests he knew so well. There he stood among tall trees on a carpet of velvety green ferns and listened to the squirrels chirp. Then, a sudden increase in the sultry weight snapped him back to the fire line. There was something bad-wrong down here in this hellhole.

Suddenly, the world changed. The steady pick, pick, picking, sounds of pulaskies striking stone faded into heavy silence as clock time closed its orb and ceased its relentless flow. Silence was as thick as gumbo.

Abe was a man of the deep woods. He was no stranger to silence; he knew silence. But this was a different silence: a silence like nothing he knew. It was a silence that lay down on a man like a run-away log—he felt crushed by silence. The scene turned fluid-like and spectral. Strangely, men moved as though through thin water. He felt the surge and rhythm of his own heartbeat radiate from its center to his extremities, suddenly pulsing them into quickened life. He felt it in his toes, his legs, fingers and arms. His head seemed to swell and pulse. His vision cadenced with the pulsing beat. Oddly, the vision began to expand, contract, expand, contract; never before had he felt so alive. He heard his breathing going in and out, as if he were inside a bellows. His skin crawled and tickled with beads of sweat. His fingers clutched his axe and closed in upon his palm. Wide suspenders lay against his shoulders and held his pants up against his crotch. Sweat trickled down his legs. His feet were clammy-wet within their wool socks. Tall black corks laced up snug against his throbbing calves. His flesh felt thick and heavy. A noble line of men, faces to the ground, heaved against their labor like a rhythmical machine: up and down, up and down, up and down. Their breathing was like a soft whisper, undulating. Muscles bulged and veins swelled and turned blue against the strain of the heat. Mona Lisa, eyes wide and bulging, reared against her tie.

As a good woodsman will do when he suspects that something is amiss, Abe cocked an ear toward the silence and listened. And he heard and felt the sound of the old red drum, a sound older than the fist tick of time, the same sound that set the clock to ticking. *Doom, doom, doom, doom, doom, doom, doom!* His heart beat a slow sad dirge. His chest heaved with the beat.

Whitey had the crew all together. The camp was secure, and they were busily at work on the firebreak up along the north face. He was chopping at the underbrush and sweating profusely, but the cleansing scent of evergreens and freshly-chopped wood washed him. Suddenly, he heard a low whistling in the trees overhead, as if someone was softly blowing on a panpipe. The light dimmed and turned to amber. There was a rumbling sound, like low rolling thunder, or artillery, far away to the south. Then he heard somebody say: "Good gawdamighty!" The words were almost whispered, but the way they were said was enough to freeze those men within hearing range dead in their tracks.

Whitey raised his eyes toward the man who spoke, then followed his gaze across the river canyon to the ridgeline. There was a wall of flame coming over the ridge as far as he could see in either direction and reaching for heaven. He was astonished beyond words. The enemy had rallied his forces and they were rising up out of the ground like an army out of hell, madly charging across the ridge. Red panache flowed in the wind and over those flew a sea of red banners, flapping and swirling. There was no smoke. Air as clear as polished glass magnified the scene. Massive, blood-red chunks, like fireburgs, broke off and floated away on the currents. It was as if it all had sprung up from the bowels of Earth and was being sucked up into the sky by an unearthly force. The sky overhead was disappearing down the ugly black throat of some huge invisible sky-eating monster. He locked his knees and gripped his axe and faced the charge.

Silence was grave. All the men stood as still as posts along their line, with their eyes bulging, hair standing on end, and mouths agape, not breathing. Whitey was concerned that someone would try to outrun the wolf and break and run off, headed north, away from what they were seeing; this could stampede the others. *Gotta move fast!* His words cut the silence like a sharp sword: "Get down to the river!" he yelled. "Get down to the river!" They were all waiting for those words. Now, they knew what to do. Not a single man broke ranks. They stuck together and headed hell-bent for the river, crashing through the brush and trees along the way.

Abe was a mighty warrior within the play of man, and upon the warrior's stage of things every man's fate is death. There are no survivors in his world. But the warrior resists death for the sake of battle, and through his very resistance he generates his electricity and fires the spark of creativity. All his life, he sparred with death and parried its blows. Now it was the wolf; not the wolf he'd sought in the timber, but the wolf of fire, leaping high, flaring its nostrils, sucking deeply, filling its lungs for the exhale. He sensed it stretch and flex, felt the exhale upon his nape. It's the code of a warrior to anticipate the final stroke, but never to cower and hide from it.

He grasped his axe and dug in his corkies and bolted along the long line to startle his troop into action. As loud as he could, he screamed orders to retreat: "Out, out, out, get out of here! Out, out, out, get out of here! Out, out, out, get out of here!" But beyond doubtful reason, he knew one and all here were forsaken by fickle time.

Abe ran over to Mona Lisa and swung his axe, cutting the rope that held her. She bolted like a startled rabbit. The crew, dumbfounded, looked up in surprise, for they suspected nothing. He ran to a point at the head of the line and there paused until they gathered about. He gave no explanation and they asked for none. With all his strength and speed, propelled by a sense of overwhelming urgency, he headed at a diagonal, running northeast, ascending the eastern slope of the canyon for the top of the ridge and the staging camp. And then it blew.

Whitey was flabbergasted. In his wildest dreams, he never imagined it could fire up with such force, so fast. He'd fought many fires, but never had he seen anything to equal what he was witnessing. Trees were booming and fire brands fell like the devil's rain. In a red flash, the wolf leaped high above, over the river. The north side, where they'd just been, exploded in fire like it was doused with gasoline. The sky turned dark as midnight. The river ran blacker than blackberry ink. Thunder rumbled and boomed, in unison with the trees. Hot wind gusted and swirled.

At the river's edge, Whitey grabbed two men by the arms and pulled them close. "You two get two more to help you and go throw the supplies in those pits and cover them over with dirt—tents too. Go! Go!" Then he collared two more men and told them the same thing.

Everybody was grabbing up their blankets and buckets. Whitey started helping to bury the supplies. One of the railroad men was standing near him, fear-frozen in his tracks, frantic and shaking with terror.

"I'm goin' down the tracks!" yelled the man.

"Get in the river!" yelled Whitey.

"We're all agonna fry here! We'll boil in there! I'm a gettin' out!"

The man made to run, but Whitey grabbed him by his arm and spun him about. Then he picked him up and carried the man, kicking and flailing, down to the riverbank and threw him in the water. The man started to scramble out.

Whitey held up his axe and yelled: "Either you stay right there, or I'll run you down and chop off one of your goddamned legs!" And he wasn't bluffing. He figured he'd cut off the man's leg at the knee if he headed for the tracks, rather than see him get away and spook the crew into following him into certain death. The others were watching. They understood that the threat applied to everyone.

Abe cursed his own lack of instinct: "Too damned late, dammit it, too late!" He felt completely powerless. In a sudden flash, everything seemed vacuous, as though he stood suspended at the bottom of a vast hole that was exploding away from him. It was as though his body wanted to fly in all directions, and he had no weight and stood nowhere. Silence became ear-splitting. Then an unseen force, like a crashing dry wave, surged through and suddenly knocked him sprawling, along with all the rest.

Slowly, he recovered his feet and stood bewildered in shock and confusion— again the eerie silence. Fatigued, he gasped for air, but this breath singed his lungs. Then hell commenced to ascend to Earth. Axes and shovels grew too hot to hold, and the ground ignited under his feet. Rocks began to burn. Trees screamed.

Through the dark, Abe's mind saw the Big River, down at the canyon's mouth, and against all hope, he turned on his heels and bolted in that direction with his men in tow. Scree gave way under their feet, causing them to slide and fall, yelling and cursing and crying in desperation. The thick air suddenly filled with gray-black ash and poison smoke, as an entire forest exploded and boomed like a battery of cannons, propelling fire spears. Fire swept through the needles in the trees, hissing like a demon. No way to reach the cool river; it ran beyond the moon.

The fire welled up all about, and they were in its throes. Abe looked around through the heat and smoke. He could see a few of the men, close by, prone, fallen upon their axes. Some lay fetus fashion, hands over their heads and faces, returning to the womb. Others lay more upon their bellies, knees drawn under, heads tucked under their chests, held there by folding their hands up over their necks. Going to sleep's haven as the devil spread his ashen blanket.

Abe realized that he was down on his knees, in morbid supplication to this heat from Hades. Nearby, someone beseeched his god with a calm Christian prayer.

Whitey and his men were up to their waists in the river, wrapped in blankets, throwing buckets full of water over their heads, trying to cool the very air they breathed. Even so, their clothing was steaming and smoking and Whitey could smell his hair singeing. Some were cursing the devil; others were calling for God. All were fighting like warriors for their survival. They were good soldiers and followed Whitey's orders to the letter and listened through the ruckus for his commands.

In a split second, the wind shifted and the fire dropped like a rock, and when it hit the ground it shattered into pieces. The wind broke off in all directions. Wind devils spun like dancing dervish. Crosswinds met and crashed into one another and threw off heat and sparks and bolts of light, as though stars were colliding. Fire brands were coming in by the thousands, hissing through the sky and hissing when they hit the water. It was as if that great and final war predicted by the old prophets was being waged and hell's legions were defeating heaven's. Entire trees, blazing and ripped out by the roots and hurled by some God-awful force, flew through the sky, whirling and spinning. Whitey's mind almost boggled. It was the end of the world; it had to be! His feelings oscillated between wonderment and terror.

A tree crashed in, only a short distance away, with a tremendous sound, and showered the men with sparks. Booming and rumbling, it seemed as if Earth was breaking into pieces flying away, and that soon he, too, would be fire in the wind. A large tree flew by crashing into the river not far upstream, spewing steam like the caldrons of Hades. Right on its tail, another tree sailed in, directly over their heads, streaming a fire tail across the sky. It smashed into the north face, only a few yards away, shattering limbs and throwing off fire brands and sparks. A large chunk, full of flames, split off and landed in their midst, hitting two of the men and pinning them under the water. Whitey rushed to their aid. Only one of the men reemerged, dazed and incoherent; someone grabbed him in his arms and held him. Whitey floundered and flailed about in the water, desperately trying to find the missing man. He found him pinned under by the snag. He braced his feet and pushed the snag off the man and pulled him up. The man was puking up water, and appeared to be in great pain. He held the broken man by the hair of his head, keeping him where he could breathe, and continued to throw water with his free hand. He looked over to see who was helping the other man—it was Bud.

Abe heard the melodious hum of his mother above the fray and felt the softness of her stomach and the press of her ample breasts. The old rocker creaked with each rock, and her chubby toes left the floor on the upswing. She whispered words in his ear that he didn't understand, but knew they whispered her love.

Then he saw Lester's big ol' long toes, sticking up in the air, high as a line of mountain peaks, black, cold, tipped with ice and snow, and spanning the horizon. He crept up and peeked between the tallest ones and peered straight into the toothy grin of Lester. His teeth were as white as mother-of-pearl, and his flashing eyes reflected the campfire light while he laughed. "Didn't have no choice, Abe—no choice at all. Hell's fire, man, I weren't cut out t' be no timberjack," he said. "I'da just slowed ya down." Then he faded away, trailing his mirthful laughter. Lester had a way of always laughing at himself, as though he were his own private jester, humored by a fool.

Then Abe smelled the damp sweetness of wool shirts and socks, drying next to the fireplace and tasted the thick gravy in the chicken and dumplings that Edith Garbo always made when he came to dinner, because dumplings was his favorite. Now, there she was, pretty as ever, scurrying about with her apron on, carrying her ladle. Sidney's blue eyes twinkled across the table at him, and Abe knew he was conjuring up something to say that would probably tease him beyond his wit. Sidney was quite a teaser. He'd tease, and then he'd say: "Don't let it get yer goat, Abe; I only tease the people I like." The children sat in their proper places, speaking when spoken to. Sidney insisted on good manners at the supper table. "Food deserves respect," he'd tell them, "because we only get to borrow it for a while."

Then he felt his hands gripping hard to maintain their hold on this unseen surge of power from the opposite side of the big Dougfir: pull it through, ride it firm but easy, gather up the muscle and counter it with equal measure again and again and again, until the cadence of the rock and the lulling hum of the misery harp sing in the sweet dreams—*ride it, ride it, ride it, man! -- Don't let it work ya*. It was Whitey over there, upon his springboard, working the harp; only Whitey could play a song like this.

Suddenly, it was as though he received a soft caress and a light kiss from some gentle lover. Then she swirled about him and wrapped her long legs around him and hugged him close and soothed him and cooled him all over with her wet kisses. A green glow was all about, and he was swimming in the cool clear water of the maple tree pond that he used to love to go to, somewhere out beyond Remote. Water skippers skipped about by starts and stops, hugging the shoreline. Blossom petals dropped off the dogwoods and speckled the surface like stars.

Shy little rainbows and cutthroat, seeking cover, flashed like silver darts up the flowing stream and vanished under the overhanging banks. It was a pool in the river beyond the moon. He'd reached it after all. He watched, as its tiny whirlpools, eddies, and swirls flowed away, and he waxed nostalgic, as he was inclined to do at times, because he felt the agonizing fear that life was lost, and he would know it no more. Never in his time on Earth had he feared pain or death or even the loss of his honor—but oh the loss of life! Life . . . Sweet, fickle life. His love. To lose her . . . The thought of it had plagued him like a virus. As a jealous husband holds a beautiful wife, he'd held her, made tender love to her and did his best to keep her content so she would stay and hold him close, too, and requite his love. He'd never laid claim to anything—except for her. Now, he felt her slipping from his embrace and wondered where she was going and prayed she would return. "My love, my love," he softly said. For a fleeting moment, it seemed he heard something, like singing, faint and far away. Then, nothing.

He sighed and lowered his hands and grasped his knees in resignation. The heat from a fireball dried his final tear. He opened his eyes to look about for the last time, but saw only the fire that consumed them. Though the heat burnt his bones and boiled his blood, there was no feel of fire, no hell in it.

Treading the roadless places between the evergreens along the ridges and standing in the middle of the meadows under the sky, he'd seen the sun rise and set and the moon rise and set over and over again, and now it seemed as though Earth herself was setting, sinking through fire within her own horizons, into nothing. Soon he would sleep. As always, when waiting for sleep, he listened. He tilted back his head and listened for all he was worth, until there was only silence.

Scripture says that in the final moment if one calls out the name of God, God will appear and talk to him and die with him. But Abe never read scripture. Abe was an archaic man who never considered himself a man of God, therefore never knew His name. This requires a definition. He only followed the wonderings of his inclinations and let *them* define him. His own name was enough. Therefore he remained God's man and simply let it go at that. In order to follow one's inclinations one must listen into the beat of the heart. So now he listened. In listening he listened for that, which he had always listened for, in his dreams, both asleep and awake – the singing voices. Archaic men lord over archaic gods. These exist to serve their lords. When summoned they come running.

Through *this* night's silence, he heard the sounds of his aspirations like voices down deep and low then rising in pitch and trailing off as though carried by the wind, as a siren song along a far-off ridge. Then again, beginning low and going high, but closer this time. A pause, and then the singing again – coming closer.

With difficulty Abe opened his eyes. Silvern light, mellow and all a-glow, like moon water, flowed in and anointed him. Through the light he saw it in the air: sheeney black, nose straight ahead for speed, ears perked for direction, mouth slightly open for easy breathing, tounge lolling for cooling, tail held straight back for balance, long-legged for distance, eyes as deep as midnight. It was headed straight for him, hell-bent-for-leather. Stretching, contracting, pushing, pulling, muscles working—going with the flow. A chill griped him and he felt his hackles rise. It passed him by by a whisker's length and glanced at him askance. Abe knew an invitation when he saw one and a true timberbeast always goes out the way he came in. He crouched, gatherd up muscle, stretched his legs, leapt out, and fell in with it, running alongside, shoulder to shoulder. Up the canyon, through trees, and higher than the mountains they ran, over the sun, along the Milky Way, and fell a wide swath through Brahmaloka -- hardly slowed down. Far north of here, to where the river beyond the moon flows into the sea, they ran. They ran an' ran an' ran, *howling* all the way.

Some years later, the tall tale teller, Rhymin' Willy, told a tall tale. In it, he said that somewhere deep in the Coast Range lies a beautiful red-headed axe with silver lips, and her name is Ruby. She belonged to a timberjack king. Though she's cold and all alone, she's as sharp as ever, and as long as she's sharp she lives. She's waiting for the day that brings her the warm feel of the hands of another man and the gentle touch of his fingers on her lips, and she'll serve that man and do his bidding. "A man can fall tyrants with that axe," he said. But that man won't come, and she won't know the light again until the forest comes once more to what it once was.

And then Rhymin' Willy lowered his head and ended his tale with some words that sounded to those present more like a prayer than the words of an old tall tale teller. He said:
"Oh, soldier, soldier, fire warrior,
lyin' an' cryin' an' dyin' in a fiery grave,
shussh an' listen.
Hear the sighin'? -- The keenin'?
Tis the tongue o' the wind, lamentin',
lickin' sorrow from the soul of the brave,
so that it may rise an' laugh again.
The mournin' dove's perched out on his limb. Hear him?
Hear the hoot owl, in the thicket, singin' her sad refrain?
They sit an' sigh 'cause tis their's to remain.
Soldier, let *them* cry for you then."

Chapter 17 Tme To Strike The Tents

Whitey spent three sick and painful days in the Astoria hospital, eyes reddened and swollen, skin blistered and peeling off as from severe sunburn, eyebrows burnt away—mighty thankful to be alive. His hair was cut off as close to the skin as the nurse could come with her scissors, and it was turned a deep pink from the burn ointment they rubbed into his head. Fortunately his hardhat had saved his scalp. He was sore all over.

All the crew came through in about the same condition as himself, except for the man who was hit by the flying snag; his back was broken.

Natural instincts and the powerful will to live saw them through. That they were still alive was hard to believe, even now. The wolf raged and howled as the men cowered in the crevice of the river, just barely out of his reach. Dark forms entered the water and silently moved about and mingled with the men. It was hard to make out exactly what they were and it didn't matter, because no one was important here. The fire was a great equalizer. Some had antlers, others were shaggy-headed, some large, some small. As the wolf disappeared, they slowly departed and vanished forlornly into the waste.

Dog-tired dog soldiers crawled out of the river; they lay on the black sand along the riverbank, prayed for help, and waited for a search party. Prayers were answered three and a half days later. Their rescuers were astonished to find the crew still alive. In the meantime, Whitey and his men almost froze to death at night, because they were able to cover only two of the tents in the pits before the fire ran them into the river. The neediest took these. The soggy food was full of dirt and sand, but it kept their energies up enough to keep them from dying— barely. They drank the rank river water.

The trestle bridge never stood a chance. When Whitey saw it, his heart sank. Like some huge prehistoric animal killed by a predator, gnawed away down to its bones, ravaged by scavengers, its rib cage sticking up, bones shattered and scattered, cable hanging like tendons, the trestle was a pathetic sight. It was buckled in the middle and fallen in on itself. Parts of it still stood, burning, spewing smoke, blackened and charred and splitting. Timbers and logs and beams were sprawled ever which way down along the river.

Greatly relieved, Whitey thought the worst was over, but the worst had just begun, for him. On the second day of his stay in the hospital, he heard the rumor that an entire crew was missing, over on the other side, in the Little River district. On the third day, he heard that it was a CCC gang, the one from Jolly Camp. The last he'd heard, Abe was with that bunch, and it wasn't long ago when he'd heard it. This was grounds for concern.

It wasn't easy saying goodbye to the men he'd almost died with. It turned downright emotional. There were no words for their mutual feelings. He shook their hands and thanked them for being good soldiers. Some cried right out loud, including Bud. Bud . . . ol' bitchidy Bud. Bud wasn't a grouch—not really—not in his heart. In his heart dwelled a frustrated tall tale teller. But Bud had spent too much of his life living in the shallows and hadn't been able to stretch himself to the tales he wanted to tell. So he bitched because it was his way of settling for backstage—but now . . . the red wolf had devoured that old bitcher. As Whitey walked out the door, behind him he heard Bud say: "So long, captain."

In a drenching downpour, Whitey went straight to the Forest Service headquarters and inquired about transportation into the Little River area. When he told them why it was he wanted to go, one of the men present volunteered to take him. They were off within the hour.

The man who offered Whitey the ride was a fire marshal. He was almost as weary as Whitey, but his was more of a mental fatigue. In spite of this, he was anxious to be on his way.

The tires threw spray as they sped away from Astoria and headed up the south bank of the Columbia. They drove for a long while in silence. The rain increased with every mile and soon fell in torrents, as though it were in a hurry because it was late.

About halfway to Portland, the marshal broke his silence. Gazing out over the steering wheel, he mumbled: "Time to strike the tents." Whitey looked at him and he looked at Whitey. He figured Whitey didn't get his drift so he said: "We lost the battle. Time's come to move on out and get ready for the next one, I guess . . . hell, I don't know . . . hate to think about it." Then he sighed and said: "I saw that sucker blow. I witnessed something that will go down in the history books and hang forever right there in the middle of my damned head. I have something to tell my grandchildren, but they won't believe me, and I won't blame them."

He told Whitey of what he'd seen. He was way off in another area, working a high ridge at the time, planning its defense. What he saw put him into complete shock and sat him down while he gawked in disbelief. The thing was laying low then seemed to suddenly startle awake, jumped up, roared, and flew straight up into a cloud that was as black as tar and went higher than he could imagine. It was thirty or forty miles wide, and it mushroomed out in all directions. It rumbled and boomed with thunder. Lightening bolts zapped all about, shooting out of it like some kind of fancy light show. The warden said he was told that it split the atmosphere to forty thousand feet or more and giant hailstones as big and heavy as thunder eggs fell from it. From what he'd seen, he figured it took it about five seconds to leap that high. It made the jet stream boil. Air currents swept its fiery anvil out for many hundreds of miles, across jagged Cascade peaks and deserts of sage, juniper, and pine, turning light to dark in many places, and in some places, it literally rained down fire and ice. He said the blow set thousands more fires in scattered locations in several states, including on ships far out at sea. "But these rains are nipping at the devil's heals and all these fires should be under control real soon," he said. "Way too late," he added. The marshal went silent for a moment and stared off through the rain splattering on the windshield, and then he slowly shook his head and said: "He was one hell of a red wolf. He ate up the Tillamook, and he devoured the Oxbow, and he chewed a chunk out of my gut. I was born here, grew up in the Tillamook . . . and now she's gone . . . gawwdamn . . ." sighing greatly: "Goddamn it."

Whitey saw the furtive tears in the man's eyes; dolor etched his brow with long thin lines.

Telling the story fatigued the marshal, and there was little else to speak of, and he could tell by looking at Whitey that his rider knew fire better than he did. And Whitey knew that the fire marshal had lost something like a lover and with her went a big part of himself and that he was in deep mourning. They were not so different in that regard and he felt an ineffable sympathy with the man. So the long slow journey contained many thoughts but few spoken words.

Several crews had battled the wolf over in the Little River country and the marshal didn't know for certain which one was missing. Far as he knew, nothing was confirmed at this point, so it could be possible that the missing men had to wait it out in a river. He said that this had been the case with more than one crew when she blew. But he added this was the only crew still unaccounted for and a great deal of time had gone by. Still, Whitey tried to reassure himself by the fact that there were several crews, and perhaps the rumor had it wrong and it wasn't the Jolly Camp boys. Even if it were, Abe may have moved on some time before the fire and was off somewhere this very moment, sitting under a cedar, dipping his toes in a cool stream. Abe had that longing worm always eating at his innards, so more than likely this would be the case.

The winding road was long and slow. They had to go out around the burn and cross the Coast Range to Highway 47 and then south through Forest Grove and McMinnville then on down to Dallas. In the towns along the way, streams of thankful evacuees were returning to lands and homes. At McMinnville, the marshal stopped and at Whitey's urging called up the Little River fire camp. A woman manned the phone, and Whitey asked her if the missing crew had been located. She said that they had not. He asked her which crew it was.

"It was the Jolly Camp CCC boys. They went in, and they haven't come back out," she said. "If they're still in there, then . . ." Whitey could hear her clear her throat. "A search crew's out there. That's all I can say at this time," she said. "But we haven't given up on them, and we're still praying here . . ." Her voice caught and paused, and she swallowed back a sob. "We're praying an awful lot."

Whitey's heart was in his throat. He handed the phone back to the marshal. He could have asked her to read the roster containing the names of the missing men. But he didn't want to do that quite yet. The marshal inquired about road conditions. When they got back into the truck, he told Whitey that the road was passable with a four-wheeler and a winch. He could feel Whitey's concern and told him they had both of these; he would get him in there in good order and to not give up hope.

Near Dallas, a serpentine road snaked back into the mountains and the staging camp.

The way into the mountains was choked with struggling vehicles that were manned by men and women wearing the expression of a tired and beleaguered army that had shared the exhilaration of war, no quarter given—fight or die. They returned, in despair, going home, defeated. The queen is lost, and the enemy scourges the fields—but how they had fought! In another time, one old graybeard will turn upon his barstool; he'll peer into the tired old eyes of his companion and ask: "Where were you, old friend, when the Great Red Wolf came?" The other will lower his gaze toward his mug for a moment, and then he'll reply with sorrow and pride: "I saw that bastard blow." They'll wash down their lumps with gulps of beer, then one will call out over the bar: "Hey, barmarm, pour us up another round," and together they'll remember old visions burning through their minds.

Against this outward-bound tide of vehicles, the marshal shoved his pickup. Nosed down into the muddy ditches, trucks and autos of every description lined the route, mired to the axles, unable to move, given out like their weary operators who were sleeping inside them or alongside in soaked tents.

Even with the winch and four-wheel drive, the going was next to impossible. Being a fire marshal, the driver commanded the respect of a field commander, or they would never have completed the trip. When they bogged down, Whitey jumped out to push and others rallied to their aid. When necessary, they hooked the winch line to another vehicle and pulled free of the mire. When a vehicle blocked their way, they winched it free and left it to progress, if it could, while they continued to heave against the surge.

Many secondary roads ran down out of the side canyons, and like streams into a river, washed into the main route. Each of these roads was emptying vehicles into the flow, so the farther up they went the more the flow decreased. At long last, they moved unencumbered, with only rut and mud to impede them. There was only the occasional straggler, each with a sad tale to tell: men had died up there. "Fare you well, and push on my friends, for we are yet the living," said one in parting.

All Whitey could think about was Abe. How deeply in he had tied his feelings with his partner at the saw. He thought about the things they had shared together and talked about, and it occurred to him that, other than the Professor, Abe was the only man with whom he had ever communicated anything of value. How fortunate—to have communicated with a man. How rare. He knew, now, that Abe had shown him that one can live life close to the bone where the living is sweet. Like a tree, a man can grow heart if he tries.

If Abe was gone, Earth had lost one of her finest sons. She should be used to this, for their kind is not hers to keep. But, the rain was beating down in wind-driven torrents of tears and Whitey did not like this omen.

The fire marshal was a man fit for any command, and eventually, worn to the bone, he drove into the staging camp. The same lady that talked to them on the phone many hours prior was still at it when they arrived. She sat under a suspended tarp that draped down on three sides. Whitey thanked the marshal and approached her. Heavy movement of equipment on tracks and tires had chewed the area up into knee-deep muck. She was young. A tuft of hair, the color of fresh-cut cedar wood, protruded from the red woolen watch cap she wore. Her eyes were as round and blue and delicate looking as robin's eggs—but they were filled with sorrow. She was obviously fatigued, but the fatigue couldn't hide her strength, or her beauty.

"Hello," he said. "I'm down from the Columbia country to help in the search for the lost men. Have they been found?"

"Yes, they have," she said slowly. The strain in her voice told the tale. "The search party is caring for the remains. We'll have to wait till tomorrow to get them out."

"Remains . . ." The word stabbed his heart. "Can you show me on the map where they are? I'd like to go down there and help."

"Why don't you wait?" she said. "The search party will be back soon, and you can go in with them in the morning. I don't know what you could do down there, now."

"I'd like to go on down. How far is it?"

"About three miles, I think." She pulled out a map and spread it upon the table in front of her, pushing various assortments of papers and maps aside to make room. "Right about here," she said, pointing at a spot on the map.

Whitey studied the map. The station sat on a high ridge that dropped off fast to the west into a canyon that ran southwesterly. It grew steadily deeper as it went. A short distance beyond the point where her finger pointed, it merged with a larger canyon that ran due west. He could easily see the situation the men found themselves in: when it blew, the red wolf charged down that steep narrow canyon like a locomotive, sweeping everything before it. Even if they could have climbed the east face and reached high ground, time wasn't with them. It all happened too fast—just too damned fast.

"It was the Jolly Camp CCC boys," she said. Her voice was mellow and soothing. It took the sharp edge off the words.

"I know," said Whitey. "I talked to you on the phone several hours ago. I presume you have a roster."

She nodded her head.

Hesitation . . . then the dreaded question: "Is there an Abe listed on it?"

Again she nodded her head, paused, then said: "Abraham Biddle."

The rain let up. Whitey walked over to the edge of the canyon. He tried to look down into it but couldn't see far through the smoke-saturated mist. He pulled his coat tighter about him, turned up his collar, and headed down, sliding in the muck and black ooze. A wind came up and blew some of the dark mist away. Soon it stopped raining. He paused and looked around. Nothing stood except a few smoldering snags. All life was dead. He wondered if even an insect survived. All about, as.if in some nightmare, lay heaps of felled carcass, covered by their own black ash, sprawled head first down the canyon, as though a mighty hand had severed them clean and laid them down to sleep away their life. The entire canyon had exploded upward from the force of sheer heat, then it lay back down and incinerated to cinder.

He continued downward, veering across the canyon wall and descending slowly. After about a mile or two, he heard the sing-song sound of distant voices. The sound carried up from below, as though unseen devils were singing in hell.

He saw them. They were cursing and stumbling, sliding back one step for every two they took. The going was easy for Whitey, slanting down hill like he was, because he could slide with it. It was less effort for him to crawl over all the smoldering tree carcasses approaching from the slope side, so he yelled to let them know he was coming.

The crew stopped and stood, thankful for the brief rest and surprised to be meeting up with someone coming down. Here stood eleven forlorn men and two women. With the exception of his fire fighting crew when they crawled out of the river, Whitey had never seen a more sorry-looking bunch. Black ash, soaked in by rain, covered their faces and clothing. But their new-issue doughboy-type metal hats were washed clean and shiny by the rain.

A man, whom Whitey took to be the foreman, stepped away from the rest as he approached. "You lookin' for us?" the man asked.

"No, I'm looking for the place where the bodies are," said Whitey.

The man threw Whitey a look like he was seeing a crazy man. "Why in the name of blazes do you want to go down into that shit hole?"

Whitey sympathized with the man's astonishment. "I don't want to, but I need to. I lost a good friend down there," he explained.

"Oh, for God's sake!" The foreman dropped his eyes to his boots then peered back down the canyon, then at Whitey again. "If that's the case, I can guarantee you that you don't want to go down there. I'd advise against it. It's morbid as unholy hell." When he said this, a murmur ran through the crew and some hung their heads.

Whitey watched tears streaking the blackened faces. "Where are they?" he said.

"Oh, come on, man! Come back down with us in the morning, when we bring some sacks and sleds down to get 'em out. It's nothin' for a man to see alone, an' ain't no one, short of God Himself, who can do a single thing for them now. There ain't a thing to gain and plenty to lose, if you value your peace of mind."

Most of these people were young, probably about the same age as those of the crew that had died in this place. This was their first encounter with death. It was considerably difficult for them; death is hard on the living.

"I appreciate your concern, but I've come too far to turn back now. If you folks need some help in the morning, I'll be available. Right now, just point the way to the bodies. I have to say goodby - alone."

The foreman shook his head in resignation and pointed down the canyon. "In the very bottom, where she starts to flatten out. It's about a mile, mile 'n a half, from here. If you lose our tracks just look for a bunch of tarps spread out around."

Whitey expressed his thanks and started off down the canyon. "There isn't much to see under them tarps; you wouldn't know him," the foreman yelled after. Whitey knew the man was being kind and trying to spare him the same view he and the others had witnessed. But he held no intention of peeking under the tarps; Abe wasn't to be found, there. Without looking back, he raised his hand in acknowledgment and followed the tracks of the search party through the ooze. The rain started up again.

He hung his head and his tears fell freely with the rain. His knees trembled. Spasms raked his gut. Whitey rubbed his forehead with the ham of his hand. Then he wiped at his tears, and covered his face and eyes with his arm. He stood like this for a long time. But he couldn't hide in that darkness forever. He opened his eyes again to the stark vision of army-green tarps spread out upon a black landscape, sodden and smoldering under a low gray sky. About fifty feet away lay the grotesque remains of what was once a horse. The rain eased up. Drizzle filled the air.

It was as though he stood in a demon's dream. He had to stretch his soul, concentrate on life, in order to bear this vision without irreparable damage.

He closed his eyes and stood straight and still, listening to the soundlessness of the deep silence that engulfed him. He tried to recreate an image of his old friend, to see him, to feel him. Forsaken by gentle visions, he felt only forlorn and alone. The place was too heavy with the weight of death. He stood in the wrong place; it was in life where he had known Abe. *Concentrate on life,* he said to himself—or to his soul—or to God—or to whomever the listener is. The drizzle dissipated.

He asked himself the question he had avoided before: why did he *need* to see this? What was it that had pulled him here? Surely, not Abe. Abe would pull him into the living trees, and then lead him deep into the evergreens. This was no place to say goodby. Someday he'd go back to the place where they'd met and *there* he'd say goodby.

A presence pulled on his attention; a chill tingled up and down his backbone. He looked up and caught sight of a solitary bird, flying down the canyon. He strained his ears to hear it, but it didn't break the silence. He could see its head turning from side to side, surveying the scene from its elevated perspective. It was a big old mountain raven, a dark shadow in the mist, and appeared lonely up there. These kind most often travel in pairs. Perhaps it, too, lost a loved one. He felt an eerie empathy with the bird and watched it, as it disappeared against the dark clouds.

Rain fell again, though not quite as heavily as before. How good it sounded upon his metal hat. It echoed against the walls of his skull, filling his head with the rhythm of life. The music in the sound of falling rain had never been so soothing to him as it was this moment, standing in the middle of hell. He felt the urge to voice some words over this vast grave, but he was no good with such words unless they were someone else's, read from a book, and quoting old words that weren't his own didn't seem appropriate. So he spoke *to* Abe instead of *over* him and said: "Well Abe, I suppose that you had to go out some day some way but it took one hell of a red wolf to do the job. I'd wager that you chopped his tail off before he got to you."

He looked out over the tarps into the mist in the direction the raven had flown.

Heavy rain was sweeping in again. Whitey put his hat back on and listened for a moment to the tattoo of the drops upon it. The water in the rain seemed to wash away some of his despair. Where to go from here . . ? The battle was spent. The marshal was right: it was time to strike the tents, to count the standing and bury the felled, and move on.

Then, to the sound of the rain drumming taps upon his hat, he bent his knees, and like a good soldier, marched east by northeast up and out of the sorry spoils.

And so, The Great Red Wolf licked his chops and returned to his den. He lay down and curled up with his nose tucked under his tail to sleep and dream his dreams of fire and wait for another day and another spark.

The forest was dead. Snags stood everywhere, cooling in the rain and turning from black to silvery-gray in time. But before long, in the very next season, instead of heat blowing through the wind, seeds will ride it in. They will cover the ground and take root in soil, sprout, and the dirt will blaze up again with the bright flames of fireweed. But, instead of red, the blaze will be deep pink; and instead of like smoke, its aroma will be sweet; and instead of running in the wind, it will wave in the breeze and spread its seed.

So it is that what ends begins: the old Hindoo is young again.

```
              /\

             /  \
```

by Me
Jesus

I happen to myself.
Carl Jung

You think that you're important.
Castaneda

…you are both the observer and the observed.
Krishnamurti

For thou art like all Things and Nothing is unlike thee.
Jacob Boehme

Who knows what evil lurks in the hearts of men? The Shadow knows.
The Shadow

```
        1                  1

        1                  1

        1                  1

        1                  1
```
And the fair Paradisiacal Tree is gone, and it will be very hard to recover it again.
Jacob Boehme

BOOK TWO
Whitey's Tale

A prophecy and indirection, a thought impalpable to breathe as air,
A chorus of dryads, fading, departing, or hamadryads departing,
A murmuring, fateful, giant voice, out of the earth and sky,
Voice of a mighty dying tree in the redwood forest dense.
Thus on the northern coast,
In the echo of teamsters' calls and the clinking of chains,
   and the music of choppers' axes,
The falling trunk and limbs, the crash, the muffled shriek, the groan,
Such words combined from the redwood-tree, as of voices ecstatic,
   ancient and rustling,
The century-lasting, unseen dryads, singing, withdrawing,
All their recesses of forests and mountains leaving,
From the Cascade range to the Wahsatch, or Idaho far, or Utah,
To the deities of the modern henceforth yielding,
The chorus and indications, the vistas of coming humanity,
   the settlements, features all,
In the Mendocino woods I caught.

                  - Walt Whitman

The owner of the axe, as he released his hold on it, said that it was the apple of his eye; but I returned it sharper than I received it.

                  - Henry David Thoreau

I remember a short trip long ago, when I was fourteen. I was sitting in a pickup, squeezed between my father and a logger friend of his. In the gloom of the pre-dawn, we bumped along the winding road through the forest, ascending to the dreaded place where old-growth played out into a horizon of discord. The sun was soon to rise when we arrived. There, in the dim light of dawn, slash lay heaped and scattered like bones discarded by cave men. Soil festered as flesh torn by mighty cats. As far as I could see, not a single thing, neither seed tree nor bush, was left standing in place to mark the passing of a fine forest. A terror had emerged from the East like some conquering foreign king, armed with a new tactic for plunder and profit taking: clear-cutting.

Forgetting the youth between them, my father and his friend cursed this new thing, this corporation that was doing this, throwing vile at it with words, for words were the only weapons they had to use. But at the time, these were useless.

Sad to say, these men and others like them were fated to bear the blame for laying down this waste, even though they were blameless. This was their land, their home, what they knew, where they lived and worked and died. To leave would have been like cowards running away with no place else to go. And so, finally only the slash was theirs to keep.

Whitey's Tale honors this vanquished tribe of mountain people.

The author

Chapter 18 The Dead Gyppo

I had my children; I am content. Oh, they were such fine men and ladies: clear-hearted, fiber-fleshed, thin-skinned, long-limbed, thick-blooded, tough-hided, anchored with grit, stalwart in a storm.

But my grandchildren's eyes were on the stars – eyes that looked over my head and did not see me, into a future that did not include me. How could I blame them? I was old – patient – slow; they were so new – so hurried.

And so I lay down in my bed with my children, under my green quilt, where I went to re-dreaming the old dreams, and left the grandchildren to dream up the new...

First to arrive was the timberbeast who came seeking only to be with the great trees. He vanished without a trace unless it be only a slight hump in the green moss where a tuft of grass grows next to a cluster of starflower, as though the soil is richer in that mingling spot. The old timberbeast finally found what he sought, and the forest embraces him, wraps him in a lignin shroud and sanctifies him. A present-day tramp, out for a sauntering in the woods, may pass the little hump by or even pause and sit upon it for a while and feel a slight trace of longing. If he's true to tramping he'll muse on things old and fresh.

Then the timberjack came, carrying his long-handled double-headed axe and limber crosscut saw. He built his skidroad and threw up a few shacks along it, amongst the trees and stumps. Then he too vanished along the road of life and death but left a trace in the form of a skidroad and the tall tales he loved to tell.

Next to come was the old-time logger who resettled the shacks, and with a few nails and a few boards of lumber and a foundation, steadied them up and called them houses. He pulled up the skidroad's greasy cross skids, because he was not a bull whacker, and used them to heat his house through the rains and heavy snows. With his wagon wheels and machinery, he cut deep ruts where the cross skids used to lie. Along the riverbanks and the canyon sides, he lay down countless sleepers, hip to hip, for his rail cars to run over. His missus stretched a cotton line between the trees behind the house and hung out diapers to dry. His bachelor brother worked for the nomadic gyppo, who would have been as freewheeling as the extinct timberbeast had he not been wheeled onto the bumpy axle of profit and loss, which most often broke and stranded its rider in a deep rut. The old-logger left his trace in the form of the little houses and in the form of his heroes, heroes that he pulled up from the tall tales then sat them high in the cloudy sky.

Then the new-time logger came and occupied the houses and painted them. He built a small mill, and the first boards sawed were for the new church and one-room schoolhouse. He quarried the hillsides and graveled the road. The second sawing of boards built porches on the houses and these fronted the road. The people strolled the boardwalks and visited and gossiped. The trees were not so big, and the light was shining in, and the woods were not so dark as they had once been. He didn't need fearless heroes to light his way. And so the new-logger tried to forget about those heroes in the sky, tried to ignore them—but *my God* how he feared their judgment! In his attempt to hide from their wrath he placed his faith in the state.

The new-time logger called the place where he lived "community," but this was not enough distinction, so he *named* the place, and the place became a village, and the village became a town, and the town became a city, and the one-room schoolhouse became a school district, and the place lives on to this day at Coquille, Marcola, Oakridge, Gold Beach, Powers, Philomath, Coos Bay, Sweet Home, and many others.

The new-time logger grows old, too—he's leaving. Newer times will give a new name to his predecessor. But he leaves his trace in the form of towns and cities with little houses built against the weather and lined up along the back streets, which were once main streets to him, front streets to the old-time logger, skidroads to the timberjack, and deer trails to the timberbeast.

There are no survivors in the woods—only passers-through. And now, fifteen years after the great fire, the gyppo, who once seemed so immortal, was dead and gone, too. But he left his trace in a rare spirit to which a firm handshake will seal a deal and to which a bond is not simply something that is bought with currency and held in escrow by some detached party of the third part. He died away, leaving his trace imprinted within the nomenclature, like a dry seed that has flown its pod. Thus the name lives on, and many men still refer themselves to it, as if they could reseed that shriveled pod: "*Me*? What is it *I* do? Why *I'm* a gyppo logger," they proudly say. But in the same way a horse and a cow don't make a dude a cowboy, call himself what he will, an axe and a saw don't make a town dweller a gyppo.

He finally died along the narrow banks of the Nehalem, when old Swede Holstrom told Whitey that he was giving up his gyppo ways because of "too many years, too many headaches, and too few dollars. Payroll's gettin' bigger; trees are gettin' smaller an' fewer between. The boys all want to stay in town an' catch the crummies out. Guess I can't blame 'em, town's where the ladies are. A man can't run a gawddamn camp an' compete no more. She's all gone to hell. The company has gotcha by yer ass." Whitey never forgot the far-away look in the old man's eyes when he said what he said next: "Finally gotta scatter m' crew. *Gawdamn . . . Gawdamn . . .*"

And so, the dead gyppo didn't die of natural causes; he was killed. *Progress* killed him: too many paved roads, going in all directions. The men could live in town with the bars and their women, settle down and jump from town to town when the jumping urge hit them. But when they jumped, they jumped too fast. Their sights were set dead ahead, and they weren't really where they were at, and so they didn't see the trees in between the towns. Eventually they lost sight of the forest, completely.

The companies were doing most of their own logging, now that logging was getting easier, less remote. The few contractors they retained didn't need to put up camps. But Swede's was the final gyppo camp, and the day he shut it down, he dotted the last sentence at the end of a brief but hardy chapter in the tall tale of the big woods of the Northwest.

After the Tillabow War, Whitey returned to the life of a roving logger, but without the same vigor as before. A part of his heart left the world with Abe, the light part, and left him heavy-hearted. Though he and Abe finally went their different paths in life, Whitey had always expected he might see Abe again. The rumor mill brought him hints of Abe's whereabouts. Back then, he was able to look into the night sky whenever he wished, and know that somewhere Abe saw the same stars twinkling up there and that perhaps they were both sipping from that Big Dipper at the same time, and this thought was always consoling.

But after the fire, he felt broody, didn't work for months at a stretch, and pitched a lonely camp in deep woods where he lived with owls. Time grew sluggish and oozed along during these years. Besides the owls, books were his companions. He knew his brooding was a mistake of which Abe wouldn't approve. Still, he brooded. One thing he didn't do any more was practice *should'ves*. He'd kicked that habit for good.

He was inclined to think that the Professor's last words to him were just one of his little jokes or that the old boy was mistaken when he'd said that there was no such place as "far away". There *is so* such a place because he felt about as far away these days as a man can feel. He needed somebody but no one showed up: no ghostly Professor to haunt him, no Woody to teach him the ropes, and Abe remained unreachable no matter how deep his probing dreams. He felt as alone as God Himself, for Whom there is no "other".

As always, the seasons orchestrated their colorful rhythms and went dancing through hand in hand. Time heals hearts, protects their wounds with tender scars, and so gradually he regained some of his old pizzazz, left off his heavy brooding, but not his memories, and reapplied himself to his work. He stuck to the gyppo camps and avoided the busy places, which was becoming ever more difficult to do.

The demise of the gyppo left only one camp in operation, a corporate camp. It was located across the Willamette and up beyond the head waters of the Middle and South Santiams and over the Tombstone Pass, where it nestled in the narrow groove that separates east from west, fir from pine, blacktail from mule deer and salal from sage.

So there was one last place to jump, and like a good camp jumper will do, Whitey jumped. He blew up his balloon and shouldered his old axe—both heads still sharp—and he left the Nehalem in the heavy atmosphere of warm showers sweeping through. He crossed the Wilson and he crossed the Trask and Yamhill. Then he headed southeast along the unnamed creeks, logging roads, and mazes of deer trails. Tough-leaved iris lined the trails and shook their shaggy heads at him when he brushed them with his pant legs. Shooting stars streaked the mires. Starry-eyed dogwoods peeked down through the dripping branches, watching him leave the Coast Range. He never returned.

Whitey stepped down into the broad valley of the Willamette on a sunny day in May. The storms had passed. Mist hung in the draws like smoke. Overhead, the clouds were breaking up into innocuous big powder puffs.

Whitey was a man of masculine places: hard, steep rising places that peaked and probed the depths of the sky then dropped off into canyons where they tangled with heavy undergrowth. Places where rivers roared and charged, trees grew ridged and tall, and rain came in spasms. But the valley was soft to his touch and warm—pliant and willing. She oozed moisture. Brush bordered her edges and the Willamette cleft her down her middle. She gathered her flowers into well-defined patches as though sewing a quilt—blue camas patch here, yellow mustard over there, golden buttercups in bunches, purple bouquets of iris with fields of green in between, threaded together with grass. Then she speckled it all with white lambs.

The air was warming and zephyrs swirled. Old fence rows, propped up by tangles of Nootka rose and blackberry vine, met and crossed at right angles in blooming crab apple thickets, from where he heard the trumpets of solitary pheasant cocks. Breezes swept the apple tree boughs and filled the air with blossom flurries—smelled like perfume. Red-tail hawks stretched their wings and called for their mates over the scrub oak bushes on the hillsides. Buzzards soared way up high, searching out afterbirth and stillborn lambs. Large parties of red-breasted robins hopped about in the fields dipping for worms in the wet earth. Noisy killdeer ran along a little bit ahead, singing out soprano: "com'erre, com'erre, com'errre", leading him on, off and away. Give the feathered fakers a month and they'll be limping and dragging a wing in the dirt, acting mighty hurt – parenting; fools the foxes – usually. In every camas patch, a meadowlark tilted its head to the sky, stretched its golden throat, puffed up its breast and flashed its big black V, and tremoloed upon its flute. It's the vibrato virtuoso of spring fields and meadows. Doves dirged in the field oaks. Hover hawks hovered in place, searching out field mice.

Valleys are lulls between turbulent peaks. This one would be a good place for a mountain man, weary from climbing endless ridges, to kick his calks and soak his feet in one of the meandering rivers for a day, or a year, or a lifetime, or more. Maybe even go domestic. Unfortunately the breeze shifted and Whitey was goaded into hurrying his step, because to him, it started to smell like the entire valley was a big crack, dividing some big ass, hiding an anus somewhere that had just farted.

There was good money in stench, these days. Loggers fell it, truckers hauled it, mill workers chipped it, paper workers mulched it and spread it and glued it, brokers bought and sold it, shipping clerks shipped it, railroaders transported it, tugs towed it, shopkeepers marketed it, printers printed on it, newspapers columned their gossips on it and consumers wiped their bungs with it.

Several of the more enterprising valley communities won their bidding battles by dismembering land and slashing the throat of the property tax, thereby wooing and winning their corporate lady loves, who then handed them their perfumed pulp mills, amidst a great deal of pomp and ceremony. Not much of an ado perhaps, in the cosmic scheme of things: a battle won here, a skirmish lost there, myrmidons jumping ranks to follow the plunder, underpaid troops in revolt. But it was enough to turn the corporate victors into cosmic assholes. While owing a property tax that's next to none they levy a heavy one. Just ask the poor air.

Wanting to escape the stench, Whitey headed for a long line of cottonwood trees. He wasn't sorry; their buds were oozing out resin. He picked a bud and rubbed it under his nose, flared his nostrils, and breathed deeply. Cottonwoods lined up along the Calapooia where they mixed with willows, mottled alders and flowering maples. The day was bright and clear, and the woods were dappled by sunlight. Mallards and wood ducks jumped from the river, throwing out wakes of water and vanished in bolts of color. Water ouzels hopped from rock to rock and darted up the river's edge, then went dipping into the swirls and eddies. A kingfisher flew by, headed up the river, shaking the air with his rattle, packing the May sky upon his back and a fluffy cloud against his belly. Chickadees chackideed; black-hooded juncos flashed their white tail feathers. Willow's branches bent out over the murmuring stream and hid singing songbirds.

Hugging the river, he went away from the valley. On up beyond Brownsville he went, and through the Calapooia hills that tumble and roll away from the high-pitched Cascades. Then past Crawfordsville to where he left the Calapooia and turned north headed for the arborous village of Sweet Home.

The vagabond was no longer acceptable: his day had come and gone. He was increasingly classed with the bum and not the hobo or the tramp. And the tramp, like the hobo, was losing his distinction—a tramp saunters the trails; a hobo rides the rails. These days, the men who did such things were "bums." These days, a person had to live in one spot, where he could be easily found, and chain himself to his social security number, so he could be easily pulled up in line with the rest of the oysters and identified—as though there were security in society. This lifestyle does not dovetail with that of a tramp, so the fine art of vagabonding had become more subtle than ever. Only the most sublime of adherents could practice it, but these were few and getting fewer. The peregrine logger was vanishing with that falcon.

In the days of the tall timber, the vagabonds who loved the woods most of all were often called timber tramps. Vagabonds have always been and vagabonds will always be, because the vagabond is free, and there will always be some free men. But the timber tramp was a specialist whose speciality was under siege and whose retreats were becoming fewer and farther between.

A tramp is not a bum, and those who confuse the two are advised to study the difference: a bum stays where he can bum; a tramp never bums, and a tramp never stays. A bum offers his hand to clutch a handout; a tramp offers his hand. A bum can't hold down a job; a job can't hold down a tramp. A bum does not consider his appearance; a tramp is what appears. A bum treads heavily; a tramp steps lightly. A bum is an intoxicant; a tramp is an intranscendent. A bum is going to die; a tramp is as dead as he will ever be

Sweet Home was a town for timber tramps; it still welcomed the vagabonds. Nestled, like it was, off the big valley, in its little cove between the long toes of the high Cascades and along the banks of the Santiam, Sweet Home did not appear to count for much to the hurried tourists. Its gritty appearance contrasted with its savory-sounding name. If the tourists had come to savor the real Northwest of the times they could have sampled a good taste in this little mill town. The air was spiced with the smells of musty cold decks and of lumber fresh off the green chains and of wood turning to cinder in the wigwam burners. But they passed through, like salmon smote on their speedy way to the Pacific beaches, following the flow of the Santiam, hardly glancing side to side. The local Dairy Queen managed to hook a few by their appetites and reel them in for a sweetened feast.

In the fifties, Sweet Home was a bastion to those who loved the woods, but it was as a sweet sugar drop dissolving in a hard rain. It was here in this furtive little place, far from the beating drums down in the big valley, where the timber tramps halted for a brief time and mingled, just short of the Promised Land.

Whitey had to move. Like the spinning globe under his feet, there was no real choice in this regard. It was a law of his nature. If chained to a redwood, he'd uproot it or go insane. He came to Sweet Home because the camp at Lava Lake belonged to Carr Forest Products, Inc., and Sweet Home was where the company headquartered.

Early in the morning, Whitey heated river water over his campfire and washed himself clean with warm soapy water. Then he rinsed in the snow-fed river, put on his best clothes, which consisted of a red wool shirt, stagged-off black cotton pants, heavy wool socks, moccasin slippers, red suspenders, and a red and black, plaid wool jacket. He shaved close, combed his thick hair, and put on his metal doughboy hat. Then he went to the giant plywood mill and for the first and last time in his life, applied to a corporation for a job.

He filled out all the appropriate paperwork: name, date of birth, race, work history, workers compensation history (if any), marital status, place of birth, home address (if any), education, military service (the battle against the invasion of The Great Red Wolf didn't count), and all the rest that somehow seems to be so important to a person being allowed to do their chosen work. It was one of those bureaucratic-type places, where they screen dozens of applicants a day for the various jobs in the mills and logging operations and think they're screening the man.

A clerk took his application; she glanced up at him often as she perused it. "Excuse me please," she said, and got up and left the room. Shortly, a stocky middle-aged man appeared, introduced himself, and said he was the personnel director. He said, with a certain amount of disbelief, that he was looking at "quite some work history" and asked if it were accurate.

Whitey told him that it wasn't accurate in the least, because it was too general, owing to lack of space on the paper. He said that if the man cared to give him a writing pad he could detail it out for him. The director told him that would be unnecessary and hired him on the spot. Unable to contain his curiosity any longer, the director blurted: "Are you the great highclimber?" *How the hell do you answer a question like that?* So Whitey ignored the man's question and stated his desire to work out of the camp, as though casually negotiating a demand, and the director readily accepted. He told Whitey that the snowfall had been light that winter, and the work season was just getting underway up at the camp. He said that there was a crummy headed that way the very next morning and that Whitey could ride it up and go on the payroll immediately. It was hauling up a crew of men who were assigned to get the camp ready for the work season.

But this was too soon for Whitey. He'd traveled a good distance to come to these mountains, and he wanted to get acquainted with them. This was Tuesday, and he said he would be ready to go to work come Monday morning. Then he left, leaving a very curious personnel director watching after him.

Once again, these mountains were brand new. The last time he was in them was way back in twenty-three, on the train, coming out from New Mexico. Knowing them by reputation, Whitey purchased some snowshoes. Then he bent his knees to the road out of Sweet Home that headed east to the confluence of the Middle and South Santiams. Then up the Middle fork he went, following its steep winding banks through the Willamette National Forest. It was a forest rich in trees and scant with roads. The canopy of trees opened up occasionally and the ground drank up the light and fern sprouted everywhere. He pulled his hat down and his collar up, started climbing, and took the high way.

He bent his steps ever upward. He climbed through the silver fir and beyond the timberline, into the alpine tundra, realm of krummholz and the fast-flowering glacier lily and the grizzled old man of the mountains: the solitary mountain hemlock. That old tree's back is bent from heavy snows and all the storms of six hundred years or more. His limbs are stiff and hard to bend and icy winds have gnarled his features. His bark's tougher'n leather. High in the sky, this place of long winters and fleeting summers is where he makes his stand. But he stands above all the rest.

Taking his time, keeping the mossybacks to his left and walking upon the snow, Whitey descended the slopes somewhere north of Tombstone Pass. He found the camp on Sunday afternoon. It was squatting in a logged-off unit, cut out of some of the finest stands of Dougfir trees he had seen in a long while. He pitched his tent deep in a stand of the ancient firs, a quarter mile away from the camp, to avoid the noise of the camp's generator.

The company operated three sides out of that camp. When he showed up, shortly before daylight the next morning to report in and get his assignment, he saw a large gathering of loggers. All were dressed for the day's work in their heavy plaid coats, hickory shirts, stagged pants, corkies, and hardhats, like loggers everywhere. They were carrying their nosebags and standing around in small groups near three green crummies. On the doors of the crummies, stenciled in bright red, the name of the company caught the dim light and glowed. A solitary light bulb, mounted upon a tall pole, hued the scene in burnt-out yellow and cast long shadows.

It was as if the scene he witnessed was poised, ready to spring into action, but waiting in suspension, waiting for something other than for the crummies to rev up and haul it away into another day's work. Windows were glowing in the cabins and trailer houses, and the generator's roar tore into the crispy air. Snow still covered the ground and piled up into dirty heaps along the sides of the road to where the prep crew had dozed it.

Holding his nosebag and shouldering his axe, Whitey stepped out of the woods and walked down the road to where the men gathered. As he approached, he noticed that the gathering began to stir and murmur. Then two of the group pulled away from the rest and walked out to meet him. The others stood and watched through their breath vapors. The two were approaching Whitey, so he stopped, and they walked up to within five feet, but spoke no words as they looked him over. They looked him up; they looked him down; they looked at one another; then they looked him up and down again. They were both medium-sized men of about the same height, weight, and age, being in their late forties. He heard the one on his right say to the other: "Gawd, man, this's gotta be him."

Then the other said: "My name's Jacob Holt, an' this here's Ben Bishop. We're two of the side bosses here, an' we're curious as to who you might be."

This was all seeming mighty strange to Whitey. He'd only intended to show up in plenty of time to get his job assignment and catch a crummy. These were some of the oddest goings-on he'd ever seen. The loggers in this neck of the woods were a strange lot.

"Name's Whitey," he said. "You're just the fellas I need to see, because they told me down at the headquarters to show up here on Monday morning. Here I am."

He held out his hand and the three shook.

"You *the* Whitey?" said Ben, bluntly.

Whitey was beginning to understand. He was used to awed receptions and gawking stares, but not until now did he suspect that his fame had spread beyond the Coast Range.

"I've met other Whiteys," he said, smiling. "But I'm the one I know the best. If that's the one, then I'm *the* Whitey."

"Holy shit! It's gotta be," said Jacob to Ben.

Then Ben looked back over his shoulder at the crews and said in a loud tone: "Hey, Jeff, come on up here."

A short man, of about fifty years of age, broke off from the rest and briskly approached.

"Whatcha think, Jeff? Is it *him?*" said Ben.

Jeff looked Whitey over. A suspenseful moment passed. Whitey was starting to become humored by the goings-on and wondered if he was really going to turn out to be the "him" they were looking for. If Jeff said he wasn't what would that mean? He was half-tempted to remove his hat and twirl in a little circle, like a model, so Jeff could get a good three-dimensional view. But he held his humor and maintained a stoically indifferent manner.

Then Jeff smiled from ear to ear and removed his hat and deferentially nodded at Whitey. "Hell, yes. It's him. I'd know him anywhere. Seen him rig a tree once, up near Forks, an' again down by Astoria. It's him, okay."

"Then, I guess I don't need to introduce myself," said Whitey, holding out his hand to Jeff.

"Jeezus, man! Never thought I'd ever know you," said Jeff.

Whitey heard a commotion of talk go up from the crews, and then to his astonishment, they all hurried to form a long line and file by him, each one in turn, introducing himself and shaking his hand. He knew about the famous tall tale teller named Rhyming Willy and some of the others. He also knew that many of their tellings included his name. But he never mixed with the tall tale gatherings, and so he had no idea of the degree to which they embellished him, along with the likes of Abe, Slim, Hack, and Woody Leather.

Tall tales were told to men who couldn't read by men who couldn't write. The tellings were told over and over again in the old camps and grew through the years with each telling, because it was the intent of tall tale tellers to exaggerate and to be emulated and repeated by others, and they made no bones about this. Exaggeration, in the form of finely polished metaphor, was the art of the game. The idea was to mortar words into a foundation of symbols, and then to build upon that and pile them high—build a telling into the sky with handholds in it that a man could climb. But as the old camps died away with dying time, the tall tale tellers ended their days, too. Many were recorded in publications for an increasingly literate society, and the tellings began to be taken as quasi-fact. Then they quit growing taller and became tales.

An old order, a way of life, had passed quickly away in a quickening world, leaving its monuments in the form of totems sculpted into images by colorful songs that were only intended to brighten the dull dreary hours and lift the spirits of lonely tired men, crowded around the old potbellied stoves of the extinct bunkhouse. What was once verbal, fluid, and changeable now was written, rigid, and final. So it happens: what was once known by the growing heart becomes known only by the mind.

The woods and time had taken their toll. Whitey was one of the few of all the heroes and villains in the myths who'd come through the big woods still alive and active so he took on an aura of immortality for these new-breeds. To these men he was a tall tale read from books, a rumor and a mystery. They were hard pressed to separate fact from fiction and didn't even care to try. Plain fact was that Whitey considered himself a good highclimber and a good side boss. A savvy logger was all the reputation he ever laid claim to. But if one considers the doings of his life to be the telling of himself to himself, perhaps he was one of the biggest tall tale tellers of them all. Fact and fiction lose their distinctions in a life well-told because there is no mystery in either one alone. He understood full well how it is that people need their heroes. It was a role he'd never asked for nor sought after, and he felt completely humbled, as the long line of men and boys filed by so that each could touch him by shaking his hand. It was almost more than he could bear, and suddenly he longed to be obscure, standing upon his springboard once again, lightly riding the misery harp, harmonizing with a giant. An overwhelming sense of nostalgia engulfed him, and he choked back tears and peered out over the heads of the men who were filing by.

The eastern sky was starting to glow. In the far distance, out over the sloping unit and the camp, cast in shadow, stood the dark forms of the Three Sisters. They were adorned in white dresses of winter snows, dresses that flowed out and dropped all the way to the ground. The kind of dress a pretty Mexican girl might wear. As he watched, the sun began to rise behind the hip of the North Sister, tinting her in rosy pink.

These Sisters were the kind of ladies he'd like to get to know. And these Cascade loggers seemed like good woodsmen. He knew he'd found a home.

Chapter 19 The Camp at Lava Lake

The camp at Lava Lake was a big change from the old gyppo camps. Like the gyppo camps, many of the men here were true bachelors while others were camp bachelors who kept families in town. But many brought their families with them, so the camp was complete with women, children, dogs, and all the rest of the amenities of civilized life. Unlike the old camps that died on weekends and holidays, this one swelled with people, because wives and kids of the camp bachelors and sweethearts of the true bachelors loaded up their cars and left the valley towns and headed for the camp on Friday evening. Then the camp turned into one big playground, as the children from town mingled with the children of the camp for romps in the forest and late-evening games of kick-the-can out in the brushy unit.

Two rows of cabins, numbering sixteen, and seven rows of trailer houses, numbering eighty-four, comprised the camp. People socialized at the wash house, and at the cafe that was built off the back of the grocery supply and operated by one Mrs. Roberts. The mechanics labored out in the small truck shop along with the tire man, grease monkey, and the general flunky, whose job kept him busy sweeping up, washing trucks, and relining brakes for the fleet of cherry-red Diamond Ts.

The mechanics worked by night, because the trucks worked by day, and they pounded on steel with their hammers, and cursed when they hit a finger or toe or when a wrench slipped and skinned a hand. They revved the trucks to test the engines. The loggers and truckers needed their sleep and the mechanics were no help, so they located the shop about one hundred yards to the south side of the camp, along the logging road that fed in from the highway. At the edge of the forest, nearby the shop, the Forest Service dropped off horses and mules and held them in a wired-off corral before they moved them into the tall grass of the lake meadow.

About seventy yards east of the camp, and downhill from it, loomed the garbage dump, which simmered and stewed along the trail that cut through the brush and ended at the lake bottom. A tiny stream of seepage trickled out, like sweat, from the camp's over-worked sewage retainment and followed along side the trail. Its rising aroma mixed with the spicy fragrance of manzanita brush and wild lilac and perfumed the air along the way. The stream meandered in shades of copper, russet, and pink and finally disappeared into the dark secret abysses of the garbage dump.

A cat skinner had dozed out a deep pit at an angle and neatly pushed the dirt into steep-pitched earthen retainers along three sides, leaving the side facing the trail open for ease of disposal. The camp's humanity methodically filled it with all their unwanted leavings. At the end of its service, another cat skinner dozed the dykes back to re-cover the same area they came from. This left a large rounded mound that was due to slowly sink and reclaim its primeval level, leaving nothing to indicate that a community of people once settled here, back in the final days of the giant old trees.

To a woodland child, a chipmunk is the ultimate toy. He captures it and tames it with gentle strokes of a finger and tidbits of breadcrumbs. And the chipmunk succumbs to the enticements with surprising ease, because there is an affinity between the two. They are both of the woods, and their natures are closer than either could ever imagine. The children gathered at the dump to play, because it was rife in ground squirrels and chipmunks. These little rodents are real suckers for box-top traps, baited with bread and cheese. The traps are constructed by propping up a box with a stick that has a pull string attached.

A kid carried his new pet home, and the rodent had the run of the place, scampering across the sofa or raiding the cracker box. Then, during some quiet night it heard the call of the forest and craved for the feel of wood, pine needles, and molding leaves. In the early morning, a forlorn child discovered that his friend had hightailed it back to the garbage dump. Some of the less wary chipmunks had probably been domesticated by every kid in camp.

Carr owned the cabins, the shop, and the wash house. All else was held individually.

During the brief summer season, when the kids were out of school, the place took on all the aspects of a full-fledged community. But come September, back-to-school time, children and mothers emptied out in a sudden exodus for the towns. Then, some time in November, the snows blew in, and in early December, the camp bachelors and their single cohorts locked it up for the winter. Those who owned their houses hitched them up to their cars and pickups and headed down the hill, following the women to the various towns. Then, all depending on snow levels, some time in May or June, the cycle began to repeat itself.

The unit where the camp was located was logged off about ten years before. Manzanita, clusters of jack pine, and deer brush were filling it in. Bear grass grew in the spring. Viny maple tangled and threaded in and out through the shade at the perimeters, where the unit met the tall timber, edging it like lace around a doily. Beyond the perimeters stood undisturbed stands of Dougfirs. The cinder logging road to the highway skirted the camp's west side. Lava Lake lay in its bed, about two hundred yards to the east.

Springtime was cold with snow and rain, but the summers and autumns were dry.

The loggers came from the western valley towns, along the Willamette and the Umpqua. The truck drivers came from the east, beyond the Deschutes, out along the John Day, Deschutes, and Owyhee, where the sagebrush grows and the cowboys ride. The mechanics were split between the two, some coming from the east, others coming from the west. All together, they welded a woodland community, and there was talk and gossip and laughter and play and hard work. Men died here, and babies were conceived here, and one or two, who came in a big hurry, were born here. It was the only place ever like it.

Whitey made his own lonely camp across the road, deep in the same woods where he pitched the tent on that Sunday he arrived. There were burls on the boles and salamanders in the damp moss. This was one of those perfect cathedral-like old-growths. It stood exactly as it had on the day Eve was made. It survived her to strike wonder into the hearts of her children. Here, only the torpid heart stays grounded with the slugs and doesn't soar with the trees. The ground was a low carpet of moss and lace-fronded ferns and layed out as flat as a house floor.

The trees stood like giant marble columns. They soared to a height of over one hundred feet above his head before they sprouted limbs. Up there, they branched out their transept limbs, touched and intermingled, like gods locking arms, and swayed in a dance much too slow for a hurried-up man to perceive. So, what Whitey had to do was stay still for a spell and rest his back against one's bosom and hope to feel the heartbeat—their heart runs from tip to taproot. If a man can slow himself down and tune his beat to theirs, he can dance with them, swaying to the rhythm of a timeless classical tune. He can at least try and many men have tried. No one gets turned away at the dance hall door. They demand no I.D.

They capture the light of the rising sun in the rubies of their crowns and filter it through in rays of silver and gold. Then Earth turns and repositions the sun, and the day counts away its moments, and the colors dance and merge and change their hues as though moving through stained glass. Silver beams strike the ground like mellow lightening and set the lacy edges of the fern ablaze. Insects hum.

Gray witch's hair, hanging in long wispy strands high in the boughs, glows like golden ribbons. It's rumored that back in the age of Pan, witches held their conventicle and came out to dance the midnight hours away in places such as this, before dancing in the woods was outlawed. Some people claim they still do, secretly, in dark nights. Perhaps these strands tangled and were left behind by lawbreakers in some hasty dawn dissipation.

Here in these old trees, selected woods surround empty space and the birds and the squirrels serve the same purpose as the fine-tuned strings on a classical guitar. Songbirds stretch their throats and pluck their vocal cords. The notes go resonating through emptiness, fill it, overflow, wood absorbs them, holds them, mellows them, and lets them go again—and all the forest sings. The squirrels sing soprano. The needles are like tongues of the chorus, lapping it all up, singing it back, so that a man is hard pressed to know if one bird sings, or thousands. Little wonder those witches flew all the way from Wicca to come here to dance.

The Dark Age architecture of the great cathedrals and long arcades knew of this place; this was their archetype. Same with the old Greeks and even the older Egyptians. It's hard to say how those ancient people came to know. Perhaps they had their shamans who left their elemental bodies behind and flew through rock, fire, space, and Earth herself, to get here, and they were astonished at what they saw. They had a tale of wonders to tell and they flew back home and shared their vision with the builders who then emulated it in their works, because they sought favor with heaven. For this was the place, so said the shaman, where God holds up the sky.

"If we can not go to God, then we will bring God to us," said the engineers. So they constructed their silent cathedrals with soaring spires, stained glass, tall columns, and with menacing gargoyles, staring off into outer hell, warriors manning the ramparts so that evil could not enter the sanctum.

They built their impressive colonnades of marble, hacked out of living rock, which they claimed contained a heart. But how could that be true? Stone colonnades don't grow out of Earth. They don't sip juices from her teats. They don't stick out tiny green tongues and lick the sun's teats, too. They're seedless. They stand sundered and propped up and held together by beams and arches that crumble and fall with the first good quake. In these modern times, people travel from this new world to the old one so that they can pay their respects to those time-ravaged imitations and they disrespectfully fall these timeless trees to build temporary houses.

But you have to give those old devotees credit, because they did the best they could with their vicarious sanctums, and when they bowed their heads and touched the marble, they could at least imagine the heartbeat of God in there and hum to it—but it couldn't hum back.

Right here, on this very spot where Whitey stood, stood the culmination of time since long before Eve received her rib. It was created for her, and Adam judged it beautiful and named it, calling it "Forest." The name means: outside of closed doors. A man must open his door to enter it. That's Eve's hair up there, casting the light and hanging in the boughs, and Eve was no witch.

These old trees spread equally in all direction, and Whitey knew full well that those branches that grew over his head spread with equal abandon under his feet. His head's eyes looked up and saw branches; his mind's eye looked down and saw roots, branching. Where one set had their birds and bugs the other had their worms and grubs. One feeds the other. As above so below, and so soil was simply baser air. Clever scheme. It gives a man something of substance to stand on, in, under, and over, and try like hell to peer through. This ethereal surface is the merging place, the boiling caldron, where nothing-becomes-everything-becomes-nothing . . . And he was witness. No wonder everything expresses in diverse pairs: it's all reciprocal.

Now, Whitey, a modern man, had it over those ancient old shamans. He could stand here, in this hallowed place, body and soul, where they could only come as ethereal wisps. It was a good place for a modern-day anchorite to cast his anchor and ride out the wind for a short stretch of time, knowing that all too soon he, too, would be ancient and buried somewhere deep in the deeps of the ages. For now, however, here he'd sit and let *it* hum to him.

For the first few months, Whitey went into camp only when he needed such things as groceries or to shower in the bath house. Then he got to staying a little longer, as he came to know some of its citizens. Soon he began to look forward to his jaunts to camp and even started to hang around for a short while and perhaps have a meal at the cafe at the rear of the grocery store, or even share a beer or two with some of the bachelors. As he became used to the atmosphere of the place, he began to like the little transient mountain community. Before it finally died, he loved it.

He discovered that his job was ready and waiting when he arrived that Monday morning. They had, in fact, held it for him. It seems that the personnel director was especially impressed with his application form. His experience, and the literate fashion in which he completed the form was unusual, indeed. So the man showed it around and there were some who suspected this may be the Whitey of tall tales, even though he had never been known to be in these parts. It was known that he still lived, but no one could say where he was. It had to be him or a prankster, and the director said that the man he had met was "sure as to hell no prankster."

On a hunch that he was who they thought he was, and knowing if it was, he would be where he said when he said, they held one of the side boss jobs open for him. Though he was prepared to take any job offered, be it choker setter or whatever, it all worked out well, because there wasn't a logger in the Northwest who was willing to assume the responsibility of being boss over Whitey.

It was mid-morning on a sunny Saturday, almost three weeks after he arrived. Whitey was sitting on a log, surrounded by some of his crew, taking a coffee break. A young cat skinner, named Milo, spoke up: "Hosking's coming. I'd know the sound of his rig anywhere."

Hearing this, all the rest ceased their chatter and cocked their ears and listened. Sure enough, a white company pickup pulled in near the landing at the bottom of the hill. The driver got out and walked over to where the donkey puncher was taking his break, and spoke to him.

Whitey watched the unfolding scene. Hoskings was dressed like a woods superintendent, all right: Red Wing boots, blue jeans, plaid shirt, and brown fedora hat. The donkey puncher pointed his finger up the hill toward Whitey and the rest.

"Well, ladies," said Milo, "my pussy's a waitin' for me. I'm gonna go make her purr."

Saying this, he got up, stretched, and headed for his cat. All the others followed suit and quickly went to their respective jobs.

Whitey knew Hoskings to be the woodlands superintendent for Carr and to have a no-nonsense kind of reputation. His was a big responsibility for a corporation of this size. But he knew his stuff and answered directly to Bob Carr himself, and it was rumored that he was second to Carr among the revolving hierarchy.

Right now, Hoskings was making a hurried beeline straight for Whitey, but it was a long, steep hill, scattered with logging debris. Whitey kept his seat for a few moments and watched him come. It was easy to see that the man was in a hurry and was making a labored go at it. He paused now and then, looked up the hill at Whitey, wheezing while he caught his breath, then put his head down and started climbing again.

Whitey sloshed out the remainder of his coffee, picked up his axe, and stood up on the log. Hoskings stopped, wiped his sweating forehead with his sleeve, while puffing, and looked toward him again. His hat shaded his eyes, but Whitey could see him smile. Finally, about twenty feet away, gulping air, he halted and stared hard at Whitey. After a moment, he spoke up: "Jesus a'mighty, Whitey, it *is* you! I couldn't believe it! I still can't believe it!

There was something familiar about the man, but Whitey couldn't quite place what it was. Whoever the man was, he knew who Whitey was, and he was plenty excited. Then Hoskings removed his hat. He was a slight man, balding, with sandy hair and blue eyes. The eyes . . . Whitey knew the eyes. They were the eyes of the boy this man had once been. The years had changed him—he shouldn't look as old as he did. He was still on the skinny side. He spoke: "Don't you remem . . ." But Whitey knew what he was going to say and cut him off short.

Grinning widely, Whitey said: "I remember you, Punkie. How could I forget? Just took me a moment, because you had a little more hair back then, and you were skinnier, and the last thing you could do was jump a loitering crew of loggers back to work."

Whitey stepped off the log and walked toward his old friend. Hoskings was still winded some from the climb, so stood and waited.

Whitey stopped an arm's length away and said: "No one needs to tell me you don't go by Punkie any more. What's this Hoskings business?"

But Hoskings didn't answer. He returned into the past for a moment, and the little punk stepped ahead, spread his arms, and embraced Whitey. He buried his face in the cup of Whitey's shoulder, and Whitey could feel his side heave as he sobbed his tears away. The donkey squealed, the cats purred, the choker setters choked logs, the hook tender tended hook, the catskinner skinned his cat. But each and every eye was on the strange scene, taking place among the strewn logs at the upper edge of the unit. Only the falling crew, who had moved off into the deep woods to fall the next show, did not see; but that evening, it was the first thing they heard when they stepped off their crummy. It was the only time in the history of the big woods that a tough woodlands superintendent gained the undying respect of the logging crews by crying out loud and unashamedly on the job.

None had known that these two men knew one another. The talk, rumor, and speculation in this regard were going to be endless.

Whitey held him tightly with one hand upon his back; the other cupped the back of his head. After a while, Hoskings stepped back, and with his hand, wiped tears away from his eyes and cheeks.

"Want a rag?" asked Whitey.

Hoskings nodded, so Whitey pulled his big red bandanna from his hip pocket and handed it to him. Hoskings wiped his face with it.

"Go ahead and blow your nose if you want," said Whitey.

So Hoskings did. He gave it a couple of big snorts into the rag then wadded it up and offered it back to Whitey, smiling sheepishly

"Keep it," said Whitey. "Now what's this Hoskings handle all about?

"Slim married my ma, Whitey, didn't you hear?"

"I heard that he married a Bandon lady, but I never knew who she was."

"Remember the day Slim gave you and me a ride to Bandon and you left for parts unknown?"

"Yes."

"Well that's the day they met. Got married two months later. Slim adopted me and gave me his name."

"I'll be damned. Wouldn't that be just like ol' Slim." Whitey shook his head and smiled. "Damned good name to get."

"Yep, sure was. I became his boy, and he taught me everything he knew about the woods. Sent me off to school, and I got me a forestry degree. Now, here I am."

Whitey looked into Hosking's eyes and imagined he could see some of Slim in there. Perhaps it was only the deep blue he saw that made him think back to that first morning, amongst the sweet perfume of pancakes and bacon and sausage and gravy and wool and greased boots and tobacco in the grub house in the little camp somewhere on the other side of Remote, when he looked into the serious blue eyes of Slim for the first time. That long-ago time, when Slim was pretending to be a whole lot madder than he really was, because he was pretending to be mad at someone whom he had come to love. Whitey's heart grew heavy, and he said: "Sorry to hear about your dad, Punkie."

"It's been almost eight years," said Hoskings.

"Eight years isn't very long at all, Punkie." Whitey stepped back and looked him up and down. "But I can't go on calling you Punkie, now can I? Maybe it should be . . . sir." he said with a kidding smile.

"Bullshit on the sir. Call me any thing you want to call me. Call me Punkie if that suits you."

Whitey put his arm over Hoskings' shoulders and Hoskings put his around Whitey's waist. With Whitey holding his axe and Hoskings holding his felt hat at his side, the two men walked back to the log where Whitey had been standing. Like bosom buddies, together they re-dreamed the olden days. They talked of Slim. Hoskings told Whitey how Slim had worked for five more years after his marriage and then retired from the gyppo business, hung up his climbing spurs, settled in for a good long while and then died one afternoon, while mowing the lawn.

And they spoke about Hack, who had a chance to take over Slim's operations but declined. A few years later, he mysteriously vanished from sight and never returned. Among those sylvan sleuths who tackle the mysteries of this kind, one sad story says that for some reason Hack completely changed—seemed to come apart. He grew heavy-hearted and ill-tempered. Then he took to the bottle and to whoring in a big way, even for him. Occasionally he paid a whore good money to strip him down, curse him, and beat him bloody with a tree limb. He was a brawler. The authorities ran him out of Portland with orders to never return or be shot on sight. "This place ain't big enough for him," said the cops. He left the land and worked on ocean-going tugs and eventually drifted up to British Columbia. He lost his job one night when anchored in Vancouver bay. Seems he spiced his snuff with sailor's oregano and then got all drunked up and started brawling with somebody and ended up throwing the entire crew overboard. Then he swam to shore and hit the streets. They say he died a long slow death from syphilis, among the opium dens and shanties, and now lies under a blanket of lime in a pauper's pit, down deep in the old section of Vancouver's China Town

However the tall tale tellers dismissed this version as mere rumor, entirely too serious and downbeat a story for such a non-serious and upbeat sort as Hack. They said: "We know exactly what happened to ol' Hack." So they reached down and plucked him out of the pit and placed him up there with the sun. Their version goes this way: "One long dark night durin' the last short days of a deep cold winter, ol' Hack, he said to a bunch of jacks in the bunkhouse: 'Boys, the timber's not so tall an' close together as it used to be, an' somethin' in my gut is chewin' at me; I'm ahankerin' for some sport. It's like I got me a hinder, an' I can't stretch my legs 'cause my bunk's too short. The big woods ain't no longer big enough for my specifics. There's somethin' that sorta makes me wonder, makes me wanna set out to wander. I don't mean to moan an' groan, but it seems to me I went an' lost my home. I just looked around and it was gone. Guess I gotta go find another. Time to say so long.' So he blew up his balloon an' headed for the wide blue Pacific.

"Hack joined the merchant marine and sailed the bounding main, haulin' logs across the ocean's deeps. He made himself quite a name, by pulling hard-stuck ships free from the bars and tropical reefs.

"Then one dark and stormy night, with waves so high they went clean outa sight, there was a fire in the hold and the fuel tanks blew clear to the moon. All the crew cowered in fear and hid under their bunks and said their prayers to King Neptune.

"But ol' Hack was a one-man bucket brigade, took a big piss and soused that fire and then spit on it for good measure. But the engines had blown and the ship was all aflounder. So he looped a cable around his middle, jumped into the sea, and towed that ship, like he was a tug, right into Hong Kong's harbor.

"Said the captain to the crew: 'All hands on deck. Stand by the boat. Don't nobody go down the gangplank. Gotta keep ya on board so's to keep 'er afloat and keep ya all out of the drunk tank.'

"Ol' Hack, he'd always kept the breeze on his stern an' his spar rigged an' taunt an' his sail good an' taut, so's to catch the fair trade winds. The captain couldn't keep Hack off that gangplank. Said Hack: 'Due to me she never sank, an' stickin' around here sounds like a whole lot of work to do. Can me if'n you want, that's up to you. Heck, I don't give a dang.' And he strode down the plank and into the town, alookin' to go get gangbanged.

"Hack hadn't seen it better since he left the timber. He stepped off that boat an' onto the banks of the sweet-flowin' Buttermilk River. He found a sailor's treasure and a dream camp for a wayfaring timber tramp's pleasure. While he was there, he mingled cultures with a whole bunch of them little Hong Kong ladies. Hack was a big man in every way, and loose and free with his sailor's pay, and the gals sought him out both night an' day. 'Hack's in town, time to play,' they'd say. Them gals'd pucker an' squeel with delight, when they glimpsed Hack's . . . Well, let's just say ol' Hack was quite a sight.

"When the ship was fit and sound, ol' Hack was not to be found. So the captain sent out a search crew of Hack's pals. They searched high and low, hittin' each and every bistro, and finally found him all tangled up way down deep in a tossing dusky sea of dark-haired China gals. 'Ol' Hack's down in there, somewhere; he's gotta surface for air, sometime,' someone said. So they erected a crow's-nest and posted a watch, roun' the clock, took turns on duty, non-stop.

"'Thar she blows!' hollered the watch down to the men, and each time they heard it they'd all get ready to heave a line in. But ol' Hack, he'd just sound again. Several days and lots of tossin' and pitchin' and buckin' later: 'He's a comin' up for air!' hollered out a sharp-eyed sailor. And sure enough, up Hack came, a spewin'' off his spout just like ol' Moby Dick. The watch was a clever bloke, knew just what to say, he barbed his words, and heaved his line: 'Hack, sailin' the seas withoutcha is an impossibility. Yer mates are awaitin' on ya, down at the slip. Come on along, 'cause we can't go it alone.' His aim was true and he buried the stick. And so he harpooned Hack with his sense of responsibility, an' yarded him back to the ship.

"But one of them gals sold ol' Hack more than her love-labor. Seems he bought himself a case of the Hong Kong rot. Somewhere south of the Isle of Careanot, Hack's jack wilted, shriveled up, an' dropped clean off. He stood on the deck under a sailor's sky, red in the west—in the east cloudy, looking at where he used to hang his wanger, so proudly. He seemed to be befuddled. He scratched his head and said to the crew: 'Mates, seems I went an' lost my anchor, an' a sailor without an anchor ain't got much for which to hanker, 'cause he can't put in at no port. An' a timberjack without his jack ain't no kinda jack of any sort. If'n I can't be no timberjack, then there ain't no sense in hangin' out around this here camp—time to pack my sack. See ya in the tall timber.'

"Then Hack climbed up on the rail and faced the shining ocean. But before he jumped, he grinned real big, and said: 'Fellers, to leave ya this a way stirs my emotions, but I got me a notion that says I gotta return me to the Sender. But, boy howdy, twas one hell of a shindy! Yes-sir-ree . . . a real hooptedode.' Then he looked at the yellow sun, overhead, got a tear in his eye, and to the sun said: 'Went an' lost my flower, an' now there ain't no place for me, except a place to stop. So here's to ya honeybee, another drop of nectar into yer golden pot.' And with a mighty leap, he cleared the rail and ended this tall tale and buried himself, with honors, in some faraway sea."

That was the tale, or versions of it, the tall tale tellers told in the bunkhouses at night, just before they turned out the light. It made tired hearts sing a song and sugared men's imaginations for the unremembered dreams to come along, take a sweet sip, and pass on through, sloughing off a slight whiff of essence. The tale grew and grew and grew. It still grows. But no one can attest as to whether any of this is true, or simply effervescence. So who knows?

But one thing for certain can be said: Hack's lover was leaving, and he had no intention whatsoever of letting her run off without him.

And so, feeling at ease, as though two pieces of something gone and feared for lost had come back together, the two old friends spoke of all the others they had known. But no mention was made of Abe, until the ruminations were all spit up, chewed, and re-swallowed. Then, Hoskings dropped his eyes, not looking at Whitey and in a halting voice, he stammered: "I . . . I can't even tell you . . . I can't. . . I can't even begin to say, how often I think about . . . about Abe." He put his hat back on to shade his eyes, to hide his tears in the brim shadow, lowered his head, and wiped his cheeks with Whitey's rag. His bottom lip quivered and his head hung as though his neck was broken.

"I know . . . I know," . . . said Whitey, knowing there were no words that could fill this empty feeling and displace it away. *Mother of Jesus, must death need be so damned hard on the living?*

Chapter 20 Boards

It was agreed that Whitey would call Punkie Kevin in public and whatever suited Whitey the rest of the time. Kevin then insisted that Whitey accompany him to his house in Sweet Home for dinner. He said he was married and father of a boy of eight and a girl of seven. Whitey tried to decline, having no real desire for a social excursion to Sweet Home when plenty of good society was available just a short walk from his soogans. But Kevin was persistent and assured him he'd have him back at the camp the very next day. Whitey told the crew to call it quits at six, left Milo in charge, and rode down the hill with Kevin.

Kevin expected that Whitey was living in one of the trailers, but when they walked back into the woods, and he saw the lonely little tent with the ground tarp in front, the awning tarp stretched over the fireplace, and the cups, pots, and pans, all hanging in a row from nails in a tree, an old memory of his first visit to Abe and Whitey returned. He had forgotten what that camp, his refuge during a trying time, had looked like. Here it was again. His eyes grew moist and his sinuses threatened to overflow for the third time in one afternoon. But he only sniffled and refused to cry. Whitey smiled when he offered Kevin a cup of hot chocolate.

The two drank their hot chocolates in complete silence. But in a sense there were three present. Kevin couldn't speak Abe's name and still hold his head up or keep from stammering. It seemed to Whitey that a big black ghost (this ghost would say: "green") possessed Kevin and he was now haunted by his old savior. Seemed strange . . .

Whitey went to the washroom and bathed in the community shower. Then he dressed in his best, shaved close, carefully combed his hair, and headed over the Tombstone Pass and down the hill to Sweet Home with Kevin at the wheel.

The grade off the Tombstone Pass is steep and crooked. Trucks gear down to first and cars wear out their brakes. In times past, the Santiam Wagon Road carved its ruts through this way. At the bottom of the drop sits what was once an old stage coach inn, once a place where bone-jarred bone-tired travelers could sleep over, rest those weary bones and gather strength for the narrow serpentine section between the trees along the river course of the Santiam and on down the hill into the Willamette. It's told that some of those bones gave out and couldn't support their owners any longer and so they were left stranded in this place. The inn keeper made a handsome profit by seeing them through to their demise and keeping the contents of their purses and luggage as a fee for burying the perishables. This tale may not be true. Only the silent forest knows. But many modern-day travelers claim to have seen pale listless people, dressed in old-time clothing (bonnets, shawls, top hats, pantaloons and such), aimlessly strolling through the trees or sitting along the creek bank as if waiting to continue a long journey that never ended and will never begin again. Whatever it once was or might have been, these days it was a hideaway saloon for crews of thirsty loggers.

"There's the Mountain House," said Kevin. "Gotta go in and make a call. Be right back." Kevin was nervous; preparations had to be made. Everything needed to be perfect. After all, a special guest was on his way.

Watching him scamper into the Mountain House made Whitey smile. *Other than older, he hasn't changed a whole lot; he's the same ol' jumpy Punkie.*

Kevin lived in a rambling house with a spacious daylight basement and plenty of rooms. It was situated on a high, overlooking ridge. The daylight basement was complete with pool table, and a bar with stocked liquor shelves—"for entertaining," said Kevin. It had a view over the town from large windows. The yard was neatly trimmed by a landscape service and the garage doors were electrically operated. The furniture was stuffed, the carpet piled, the kitchen tiled, the window glass tinted thermo pane, the paneling cedar, and the entry flooring was done up in parquet.

The house had five bathrooms, three up, one down and one to serve the "home entertainment center." The bath off the master bedroom sported an over-size sunken tub inlaid with swirls of vari-colored ceramics.

Kevin was mighty proud of all of this and enthusiastically pointed everything out, as he gave Whitey the guided tour. "Got it for a song," he said. "Picked it up from the bank, when the previous owner lost his job and left town, during the last lumber slump."

Five bathrooms is an awful lot of having to go, thought Whitey.

Soon, Mrs. Hoskings arrived with a station wagon full of kids and groceries. She was a pretty little woman with light red hair that was professionally done up, a faint sign of freckles, slender figure, light eyes, and petite lips that turned up at the corners into a frozen smile that was the most unreal thing Whitey had ever seen.

Her name was Lorraine, and when she finally met this man, of whom she had heard so much, she couldn't believe her eyes nor hide her disappointment. Although she was careful not to lose her smile and give herself away, she felt almost flabbergasted by what she saw. Here, standing right in front of her in her very own house, was one of those men she saw early in the mornings, waiting in small groups on the street corners for the company crummies to haul them off to wherever it is they go to in the woods. There they stood, lunchboxes in hand, big old dirty boots slung around their necks, pants way to short, with threads hanging down off the leg ends, and held up by big-old ugly suspenders. Old, worn stinky moccasins covered their feet. And those thick wool socks that just had to smell the way they looked.

Late evenings, about dark, she saw them returning, as they filed off the crummies, tired and dirty and obviously sweaty and smelly. They'd be jostling around, poking each other like ruffians. Why, she'd even seen them scratch their crotches. *This is the great man? One of those!* She had never imagined. The only thing this one lacked was one of those silly looking metal hats. He was probably waiting until dinner was served to put it on and embarrass her to tears right in front of the Carrs. Thank heavens he wasn't all sweaty and wearing those big dirty boots. Well, she was committed, so she would give it her best, but this low-class brute had best show proper respect. Kevin would hear about this, later. She put on her biggest smile just the way they taught her to do at the Columbia Charm School in Portland, when she was preparing for her debut. "Lovely to meet you," she said.

"Likewise," said Whitey.

That was all? Not, nice to meet you, Mrs. Hoskings? These are lovely children you have here? None of the proper things a gentleman says when he meets the boss's wife and family? Oh well, how could he know of such things? His vocabulary was undoubtedly quite limited. The children, however, were beautiful. When their father introduced them, Schan held out his hand and said: "It's a pleasure to meet you, sir." Heather curtsied like a lovely little angel and said: "Lovely to meet you, sir."

Of course, the logger said nothing, just grinned. *Goodness gracious,* she wondered, *how could such a rough man create such a big ado?* Why, Kevin had even told her to call and tell Lilly Carr to relate the message to Bob that Whitey, himself, was coming in and to plan on dinner at seven. So she had called, and Lilly had said: "Oh good! Good! We'd heard the rumor and were hoping it was him. Bob's been looking forward to this, and so have I. We're both really quite excited and a little nervous."

Well, do they have a surprise waiting for them! "It really is very lovely to have you here at long last," she said to Whitey. "I've heard so much about you from Kevin. But, if dinner is to be on time, I really must be off to the kitchen. So you two go ahead with your man talk." She started off.

"Did you contact the Carrs?" asked Kevin.

"Oh, yes I did, dear. They'll be here. Do carry in the groceries, dear," she said as she scurried off like a busy bee.

At that time, a squat, big-boned woman arrived. Under each arm, she carried a stuffed paper sack. She walked by on heavy step, took a quick glance towards Whitey, and went through the swinging doors of the kitchen to cook the evening banquet.

It was five-thirty. The Carrs were coming at seven. Whitey sat on an over-stuffed chair and looked out the window at the view. Down below, the narrow strip of the Santiam glistened in the evening sun. Crows perched in the treetops. The children sat on the couch with their hands folded neatly in their laps, as two little angels should. Across the street, a dog barked.

With Whitey in his house and Bob Carr on his way, Kevin couldn't have been more nervous if he were sitting on a cucking stool. He tried to make small talk about the old days, but his words came out sounding stilted; the earlier exuberance and spontaneity had forsaken him. Even the nostalgia had departed.

Kevin's change of mood didn't go unnoticed by Whitey. But he could excuse a man some reserve when the big boss and his wife were coming to dinner. Still, he had the nagging suspicion, barring unforeseen events, that this was going to be one of the longest nights of his life.

While they waited, Kevin told him that he and Lorraine had met at a sorority party when they were in college. She was a Chi Omega Phi he was a Nu Sigma Nu, and it seemed that the members of these two organizations had a traditional affinity for one another, and so they often mated and reproduced. Her father was a prominent Portland steel man who owned his own foundry, specializing in the manufacture of rebar. The coming of progress to the state, its building boom up there in the metro area, with all the new high rises, and the state-wide highway construction projects, "had made him a wealthy man, indeed: a man of no little influence in the city. A good man to get to know, if you get my drift," said Kevin, with a sideways glance at Whitey and a quick wink. "After all, it's not what you know but who you know—you know." Kevin was proud of his trite play on words and grinned.

Spoken like a true toady, thought Whitey.

Kevin said that he was proud of his accomplishments, but regretted the fact that he held no corporate ownership. Things were looking up in this regard, however, because Carr was discussing the possibility of stock as part of the bonus programs, and he was in line for some nice big bonuses. Considering that his bonuses should be substantially larger than anyone else's, this tidy scheme would put him right up there in ownership second only to the top man himself. Of course, there was always the possibility of buying his own mill some day with the money Slim had left him, but this money would not become his until after his mother died. It seemed that Slim had put that stipulation in his will and even Kevin's mother couldn't change it, because it was in the hands of some hotshot Eugene attorney, who didn't know how to listen to reason much less good old solid business sense. Of course, it could all work out just fine, if the money came his way about the time Carr decided to sell out some stock to a few select individuals, and there was no little amount of pressure being expended in this regard.

Whitey could only assume that all this pressure was nothing short of importunity and was being expended by those "few select individuals." But his thoughts did not dwell on stock bonuses, because they were dwelling on lovely pink toilet bowls. All this aimless palaver made him tense and stimulated his urinary tract, which caused him to be in the need of taking a piss such as he had never needed to piss before. And he hated the thought of taking a piss. When an entire mountain chain is where a man is used to urinating, it's a difficult transition to envision standing over a lovely pink, but very tiny, toilet bowl and letting go into it without missing, or at the very least, splattering the hell out of the ceramics—not to mention the gawd-awful noise he was certain it would make.

Kevin, you've come a long way, Whitey said silently, inside his own head, *you have a pretty pot to piss in.* But outside him, on and on it went: "blah, blah, blah," while Whitey, like the kids, sat with hands folded and squirmed and wished he were any place at all but here. *Poor silly little Punkie. He's living one of those lives vaporizing into cloudy dreams—a partly sunny life,* went the train of Whitey's thoughts. He noticed that Kevin avoided eye contact. Whenever their eyes met Kevin immediately dropped his. He was pretty sure he knew why. He'd let events play themselves out and see how right he was.

To make matters worse, Lorraine joined them. Before long, Whitey became completely lost in all the mammon worship. He watched the children restrain their natural tendencies to let off energy and wondered what kind of hellions they were going to be in a few years, when it all went off like an over-heated stick of dynamite from its nitro being packed in too tightly for too long. Then he drifted away from the palaverous sea and entered into a little river of mind-time that flowed inland all the way to Dewey's rain-drenched camp along the Alsea, where he had spent some other long hours many years ago. It struck him as ironically weird how the scene changes but the substance so often doesn't. Punkie was always going to be in need of being saved from someone. But eventually, he had only himself to face, and who was going to save him from his own reflection? *Now there's a real bull of the woods to contend with.*

The Carrs showed up on the dot. They each seemed straightforward enough, with steady eyes that didn't try to hide their dweller. They were early middle-age and dressed plainly with no ostentatious show. Bob Carr greeted Whitey with a firm handshake and a ready smile. He was medium height, balding, and had hazel eyes that paid close attention when someone spoke. He had a quiet manner and saved his words, as though they were worth something. He was impressive and a likeable man.

Men's lives are interconnected like the patterns in a tapestry. The Weaver weaves but the form in the warp is beyond a man's foreseeing. Ominous events were unfolding in Bob Carr's life that would unravel a world, and shatter lives and alter destinies. Whitey had no idea, in this moment, just how tightly he was being woven into an unraveling scheme.

Lilly Carr's hair was as black as raven feathers—a heritage, she said later, from her great grandmother who was Choctaw Indian. It was sheeny under the lights. Her teeth were white as pearls, and her lips were full, with just a touch of pucker. She had high cheekbones that accentuated her soft brown eyes. Her neck was long, her shoulders were narrow, her breasts were small, and her waist was as delicate and sturdy as a flower stem. Her legs were slender, ankles fine.

Whitey had to admit that the Carrs were an impressive-looking couple. However, Lilly Carr, coupled or uncoupled, stood on her own terms. She wore no makeup and probably no perfume, but he could easily smell her across the room. The scent of her filled his nostrils, and he could taste it upon his tongue, and it made his chemicals stir. Her voice was as low and melodious as any owl's, but she chose her words carefully, and when she spoke she demanded attention. For the most part, she stayed in the background where a good wife of her upbringing was taught to stay in matters of men and commerce, but it was easy to see that she hung onto every word that was said. During a pause in the dinner chatter, she asked Whitey where he had come from.

"I came from a farm a long way east of here," said Whitey.

"Why did you leave to come out here?" she asked.

"I ran off when I was a kid," Whitey answered.

"A runaway?" blurted Lorraine. She was ignored.

Whitey and Lilly went back to eating. After a few moments Lilly looked up at Whitey again and said: "Why did you run off?"

"Whitey smiled, and said: "Well, farming didn't seem to suit me and I'd never seen a mountain except for in a magazine picture, so I went looking for mountains and a new kind of life."

None of the others around the table heard this quiet exchange between Lilly and Whitey. They were all too occupied by their own thoughts, trying to think up something to say.

Sensing they were alone, Lilly asked Whitey if he had ever been married.

"No, ma'am," he responded. "I have not."

"Well, then, have you ever considered it?" she asked.

"Yes I have, one time, a long time ago."

"Did you come close?"

"Not nearly close enough; she died," he said and lowered his eyes.

But Lorraine eavesdropped on this last part, and piped in. "In romance second time's a charm." Then she suggested the names of a couple of widow ladies in the town they might mate Whitey up with.

Lilly immediately dropped the subject. Just as well, too, because she wanted her next question to be: had he loved that girl deeply? -- because she only knew of Whitey as a man among men, as big talk in boisterous bars, and idle chatter among the loggers, and the subject of stories and quick poems. But, here in person, was a man not at all Bunyanesque. He seemed reserved and aloof, perhaps even shy. His body was tall and well proportioned, but not huge like in the tales and he carried no challenge in his eye meant to back men down. The tall tales didn't tell about a man who'd loved a girl a long time ago, lost her, and still hurt because of it. Perhaps the tales told too tall or didn't tell nearly tall enough. She thought she knew the answer to her question; plain to see that he couldn't talk about that girl and hold a manly gaze. She didn't mean to pry but she wanted to know for certain. *I'll ask him about this some day in different circumstances, if the opportunity ever presents itself,* she thought.

Whitey glanced Lilly's direction whenever he got the chance, and when it wouldn't appear obvious. More than once, it felt as though he had been lightly touched with a soft finger, and he got the strange sensation that she watched his every move through those subtle brown eyes.

To his surprise, the dinner couldn't have been better: heavy sourdough biscuits, brown gravy smothering mashed potatoes, roasted ham slices, seasoned with the taste of maple and nutmeg and pineapple, and all the rest of the good things that put meat on a working man's bones. He thought he'd died and gone back in time. Visions of ornery old Cookie and some of the other bunkhouse cooks reeled through his head.

Lorraine was hard at work, putting on the airs, but beneath it all she seemed anxious about something and kept looking nervously around the table and dabbling in her food. Finally, she couldn't hide her perturbation behind her fawning, lost her cute smile, glared about the table, and then at Lilly, who was eating heartily, and mumbled something that sounded like: "This is not what I planned. That dumb old . . ." She smiled politely and sang out to the others: "Be back in a jiffy." Using a pinkie, she blotted the corners of her lips with her napkin, rose from the table, and tittupped off toward the kitchen and bolted through the swinging doors.

Some muffled words were heard from the other room. Then a clarion statement pierced the air that Whitey knew could only be the squat, heavy-boned woman he'd seen earlier: "I'm not gonna feed *him* that junk! You want sautéed chicken wings under mushroom sauce? -- then *you* cook 'em!"

Lorraine returned, her face so red her freckles were popping, and dragging her tail in the manner of someone who had just came up on the short end of a ridiculous argument and had their ass chewed on. She sat down in a huff that no amount of charm schooling could hide, and sulked for several minutes. But the food was so delicious that nobody paid her much notice. They all had their faces to their plates and were saying such things as: "ummmm, ahhh, uh huh, yuum," and the like.

After dinner, the little social group retired to the family room and sank down into the over-stuffed furniture. Time for digesting. The squat, heavy-boned woman unobtrusively shuffled back and forth from the kitchen, keeping their coffee cups filled to the brim and finger cakes in the saucers. The children rose as if on cue; Schawn bowed slightly then excused himself, Heather curtsied, and they went to their beds.

At one point, during a pause in the chitchat, Kevin said: "Whitey I just got back from a month's visit to Brazil. You should see it down there."

"What's in Brazil that I should see?" Whitey was sincerely interested.

"Stumpage, Whitey. Lots and lots of stumpage. Remember how it used to be here: trees everywhere just for the taking, punch in a road and throw up a quick camp and work out from there? Remember?"

Nodding his head, Whitey said: "Yes I remember, quite well."

Kevin raised his eyebrows and said: "Well, man, I'm here to tell you this: that's the way it is down there, right now. Except, half the time you don't even need to build the road. You can just do your logging along the river's edge and float them out."

"You mean splash them out," said Whitey.

"Nope, I mean float them out. You cut them down, roll them to the river, push them in, boom them up, and barge them to ships or the sawmill. Those rivers down there flow like thick molasses."

"You're kidding! Simple as all that?"

"Gospel truth, Whitey. And the stumpage is for the taking. Hell's fire, man, the government almost pays to get it logged off. They want the trees out, so's to make more room for settlement. They're trying to attract people away from the coast and into the interior, so they let you have the damned trees. It's absolutely unbelievable! The Southern Gentleman is going after it in a big way. He knows a good thing when he sees it.

"The Southern who?" asked Whitey.

"The Southern Gentleman. You know, that guy who's coming on so strong, buying out all the mills around here.

But Whitey didn't know, and Kevin continued on about Brazil: "Trees, trees, trees, nothing but trees. The big woods all over again—only different."

"It truly is unbelievable," said Whitey. "What kind of trees are they down there?"

"Oh, god, all kinds of exotic types! The list goes on and on. Most of them I can't even pronounce. Weird stuff. But there's big markets being created for it these days, in paneling and specialty items."

"Oh, I see. Being created you say. Are there any mountains down there?"

"Not one damned mountain to slow a man down. Think of it, Whitey, all that stumpage standing there and no grades to fight. Bugs are the only big obstacle down there."

"Bugs?"

The place is alive with them. They lose a big percentage of the felled timber to bugs, because it's so marshy that the bugs get to it before they can man up the power to roll it into the rivers. Makes little difference, though, because there's so much of it, and it's so cheap to get at. They simply calculate in a certain amount of felled timber as going to the bugs before they can get back to it."

Whitey glanced over at Lilly Carr. Bemused, she was trying to avoid Lorraine, who was jabbering on and on about wanting to build an arena and start up an equestrian team. She wanted to discreetly listen in on what was being said by Kevin. This conversation was leading up to something interesting, and she wanted to hear what it was.

Kevin continued: "No damned labor unions, either. Believe me; those workers down there know their place. Why, you can buy the hardest-working labor you ever saw for a handful of pennies. Take it from me, the companies that get in on the ground floor down there are gonna wipe up just like they did up here."

"Wipe up, huh?"

"You got it."

Whitey slowly shook his head. "How do they live?" he asked.

"Real good, man. Like kings. The all-American dollar goes a long way."

"No . . . I mean the people, the workers."

"Hell if I know. They curl up under a tree somewhere or build a thatched-roof hut, I guess. Same as they always have down there."

"The company doesn't feed them?"

"Nope. Don't have to. That's one of the beauties of it."

"What do the people eat?"

"Go kill something out in the jungle or catch it out of the river, I guess. For the most part, they're skinny little buggers and don't need to eat much," said Kevin, with a chuckle and nibble of finger cake.

"What do they do with that little bit of money? I mean, why do they bother to work? Sounds like they don't need money. Do they save it?"

"Mainly, I think they spend it on whiskey," answered Kevin.

"So they're falling the trees where they find their food in order to buy sips . . ." Whitey said this in a subdued tone, but more to himself than the others. He shook his head slightly and thought back to his old friend Carlo, The Fish, and his lost tribe. It seemed to him that the things that *should* change *don't,* and he added: "Well I'll be dammed."

A long silence followed, while Whitey waited to see where this line of talk was leading. Then Kevin glanced at Bob Carr and looked back again toward Whitey, and said: "We're making big plans for that country. Carr Forest Products is interested in getting in on the action down that way, while the getting is good. We figured that somebody with your logging experience and savvy could go down and head up the logging end of that program for us. We're talking big money here. We'll certainly make it worth your while."

"Sounds like a done deal."

"We don't let the moss grow on out butts at Carr."

Whitey leaned back in his chair. He slightly nodded his head, and he puckered his lips and clicked his tongue in disbelief at the words that were just directed at him. These people were offering him an opportunity to go to a place without a single mountain, but full of jungles of some kind of exotic trees that the companies were busily creating a market for. Then he was supposed to use quasi-slaves to fall and buck those trees, expose the logs to worm infestation, compute in a residual, and then float the salvage down muddy rivers full of snakes and alligators. He tried to imagine himself doing all this while wearing a Panama hat and Bermuda pants, but the vision was too much and overloaded his sense of common decency and blew a fuse.

His spirit sagged. *Godamighty, do they think I'm a moron? Have I fallen so low? What a line of crap! No wonder this guy needs five bathrooms.*

Everyone was looking at him. Lorraine was even quiet. She'd quit trying to impress Lilly and was watching Whitey because the others were. Kevin sipped his coffee, smug, obviously proud of his proposal delivery.

Punkie was a punk without the whistle, just an uncapitalized punk. Whitey let out a soft sigh, took a sip of coffee, and nipped a nibble off a finger cake. Looking at Kevin he felt his anger rise and a voice in his head said: *Give them hell.* So, he said: "Look right here, Punk. Look me in the eye. I'd like to see if you can do that and still fib." Saying this, he pointed toward his eyes. Surprised by the words he heard, Kevin's head jerked and he looked directly at Whitey's face but avoided eye contact, as usual. Whitey continued: "Men lording it over others as if they own them. My god, how soon we forget! You, of all people, Punk. Back in the early twenties, I worked with a bunch of hard-pressed horse loggers. Most of them were down and almost out, and there wasn't a man jack among them who didn't treat his horses ten-to-one better than it sounds to me like those workers that you just talked about are treated.

"Punkie, I'm going to tell you something because I think I owe it to you. We had a mutual friend once and he thought you were worth *his* effort. He laid his life on the line for you. Out of respect for him, I think you're worth some effort on *my* part and the least I can do is lay a few words out on the line."

"I had another friend once, one of those horse loggers I mentioned. We called him the Professor. One time he said to me: 'Henry, you're going to meet up with all kinds of blokes offering you alternatives. Hear them out. Someone might come along and offer you heaven. Take it if he has it, but don't bet on that; nothing is that clear cut. Bet on this: he's calling hell heaven. Beware of men *giving* you a choice. Choices are scrambled until you sense both sides at once, in sorta the same way that a smell's not a smell until you smell it through both sides of your nose. A man can't make a choice for another so how can he give him one as if it's the best thing in the world for him? We human beings happen to ourselves but few of us are aware of that. We can happen in heaven or we can happen in hell. Generally we don't know the difference so we happen somewhere in between, lots and lots and lots of places in between. We sniff the air and select our choices. We don't have to be someone else's alternative. But you can turn yourself into that—your choice.'

"Those were his words as near as I remember them. I sure don't claim that I understand it all, but I understand this: that alternative of yours would send me straight to the deeps of hell. Hell no, I won't go to hell for you."

Whitey nibbled a finger cake. There was only silence. Then he shattered the silence, and said: "Now you want to hear something funny, Kevin? That very same old horse-logger friend of mine controlled me with my so-called sense of choice for over six years. He offered me choices but those choices were his, and then he did the choosing. I belonged to him. He was a benevolent tyrant, is what *he* was. I was lucky because a lot of them aren't. I think it was Abe who showed me how that clever scheme works. He never selected a choice for another person in his life. But he did offer alternatives and boy, was he ever good at that."

Whitey looked around the very quiet room. Kevin's face was flushed and his jaw hung as if its hinge was broken. Bob's jaw was set. His lips curved at the corners into a very awkward archaic-style smile. He seemed to be astonished and reeling in thought. Lorraine was blank-faced. It all went way over her head. She got lost in shock way back on the word "Punk." Her lips were busy, forming the word: Punk? Punk? Punk? Punk? Lilly's eyes were sparkling with enchantment. She squeezed her lips together, holding back laughter.

"Now, let *me* proposition *you*," said Whitey. "It seems to me you need a caretaker up at the camp in the winter. It would eliminate the need to send people up there to check things out and keep them maintained the way you do now. He could keep the generator warm and look after any machinery that's left behind, and he could see to it that no lines freeze up and burst. Generally, keep the place winterized. If anybody comes snooping about he could question their intentions. If you see your way clear to create such a position, I'd like to be the man. The price comes right. I'll do it all for nothing, because if you pay me, you may decide to eliminate the job when the price drops on lumber. Just let me use one of the cabins to live in, till the work season starts back up."

Kevin realized his folly, full well. He had only wanted to offer Whitey something, something big, to demonstrate his respect. How stupid he was to think he could offer Whitey something big. It seemed to him as though Whitey had countered by requesting something small and cornered him, leaving him no choice. He didn't even look at Bob Carr for any sign of intent. The alternative was obvious. He looked at Whitey instead, breathed deeply, and said: "The job's yours for as long as you want it."

Later on, after she was excused from her duties by Lorraine, the squat, big-boned lady approached Whitey. Smiling broadly, she introduced herself and said her name was Kathryn. "But they call me Kat," she said. She told him that she, too, had been a timberbeast and had always regretted that their paths had never crossed during those days. "But back then the woods were so terribly big. Not like now," she added. She said she was a cook in the gyppo camps, and it was in a camp where she'd met and married her now deceased husband.

While she spoke, Whitey took her hands in his and looked into her eyes. They were not present eyes. They were of past times and other places. Eyes of a woman alone, husband gone, having long since cast off the drags of a life that worked him too hard for his money, brothers dead in the foreign wars or in the woods from logging accidents, sons laying dead on the blacktop in the wreckage of their logging trucks and hot rods, daughters moved away to better lives. They'd seen countless Pacific storms roar in, set the trees to swaying, and then whisper themselves away. They'd closed down hard at night after long days of toil and gain and loss. And they were hard to open in the morning. They were eyes that had seen life down deep and still saw it that way, even now. Here was a woman with no statement to make: her life was statement enough. They were full but not happy eyes.

The bathroom off the guest bedroom was truly *lovely* with its scented soap and toilet water. The toilet paper was pink with tiny blue flowers, a perfect match for the wallpaper. The picture window in the bedroom framed the town and the hills beyond, and Whitey watched the lights for a while, as he lay upon his first mattress-type bed since those nights at Woody's. He was glad to have this long ordeal come to its end—except for Lilly Carr. She'd shortened it up for him. He sure wasn't glad to see *her* go.

In the distance, down at one of the sawmills, he heard the switching crew revving up their locomotive, as they dropped off some empty cars and pulled out with full ones. Much further away, down toward the big valley, he heard the wail of a train whistle, announcing the coming and the going of a lumber train, trailing a train of boards.

Boards . . . flying down parallel steel tracks, tracks tied together by boards. Riding upon the backs of flat cars, built from boards and bound by steel. Riding through the day and through the night. Boards of every quality: knotty to clear. Random lengths of the fir, cedar, pine, spruce, myrtle, hemlock, alder, oak, and the king of boards, the clear, all-heart redwood. Boards on the car, boards on the semi, boards on the dock, and boards over the transom. Boards going to places where many men want boards but never get to own a board till the day they die, when they are given a few boards from the knotty pine. Boards headed for where a few dead men die their lives away, surrounded by far more boards than a great number of living men could ever need. Boards for the living and boards for the dead, boards for the turret and boards for the belfry, boards for the cradle and boards for the gallows, boards for the hospital and boards for the morgue, boards for the saint and boards for the sinner . . . Boards: slices of flesh from the meat of a tree. Today a million boardfeet of boards, tomorrow a billion boardfeet of boards, and the next day a billion billion boardfeet more. More boards than can ever be counted . . . Boards . . .

But boards were not on Whitey's mind. He didn't go to where boards went. What are boards to a man who's never owned a board in his life? He wanted to be where boards come from, before they become boards. So boards did not interest him. Close in, down the hill, he heard a dog barking monotonously on and on at nothing at all, except the darkness—seemed appropriate. It didn't bother him in the least, because that dog wasn't his and didn't bark for him. And so he simply closed his mind to it. Then his mind conjured up a vision of Lilly Carr, her eyes sparkling over a sly smile, as she suppressed her laughter. And he held it close, as he drifted off to sleep.

In another bedroom, not far away, Lilly lay down next to her husband. She pulled up the quilt and tucked it under her chin and stared toward the ceiling, fighting sleep, dreading the dream to come—wanting more than the dream had to offer—already feeling unfulfilled. She was raised to be proper. She knew she'd carry her thoughts, these nagging visions in her head, into the night where they'd turn into a dream. And it was a forbidden dream, because she was a married woman.

Chapter 21 Crescent Mountain

Daylight to dawn, Monday through Friday, were days given to the company for money. But some Saturdays were cut short, and holidays were never worked, and Sundays were free. When Lilly showed up at his tent on that Sunday morning in mid June it didn't surprise Whitey. He had long since accepted the existence of the variegated color-correlated threads that shoot like beams of light through people and things and weave the matrix of the world. A man attracts his color preference. He took them on faith and with time's passing, more on experience. Abe had been aware of them, had talked about them. They glow with intensity here and dim their luster there, and so the fabric is vari-textured. They're not seen by the eyes, tasted by the tongue, or heard by the ears. But they can be felt, and they can be known, and it is the solitary man, whether in the deep woods or on the city street, who feels them and knows them best. He knows them when they're bright, and when they dim and fade, and he doesn't try to alter them. Why should he? He doesn't know the weave of things. They may weave him into love, or they may weave him into hate, but if he keeps his wit and accepts the woof and warp, they will never weave him wrong. So he keeps on the move and spins the wheel and spools his threads and strings the loom and weaves himself a garment. When time's thread is all used up, if his art came from out of his heart, he will have woven himself a colorful cloak with no seam to stretch and release his heat.

Lilly was wearing dark slacks and a white blouse, and she stepped lightly upon the moss. Whitey saw her approaching through the hoary old trees. At her side shuffled an adolescent boy, around fourteen years old. Lilly held his hand, but the boy pulled free as they neared.

"Hello, Whitey," she said gaily, "I hope you don't mind us barging in on you, but your telephone number is unpublished. We asked at camp, and they said to walk due west."

Lilly's black hair captured the sun's rays and glistened. A smile lit up her face, making her eyes twinkle. *She lights up the woods*, he thought. "You're a good pathfinder," he said.

A mossy-blanketed old windfall edged the camp and threw its soil-clogged roots twenty feet into the air and walled the camp on one side. Whitey used its trunk as a backrest when he reclined with a book, and he also used it like a bench. He motioned toward it and said: "Have a seat and make yourselves at home."

Lilly introduced the boy as Jeremy. Then they small-talked for a few moments about mutual acquaintances and goings on. Jeremy curiously perused the grounds. Lilly said that the Lava Lake camp was their home-away-from-home during the summers, and the family spent many of their weekends there. But this year, Jeremy was going to stay through the week. He'd be spending the entire summer at the camp and Lilly was concerned. She asked Whitey if it would be a bother for him to look in on Jeremy, when it was convenient, just to make certain he hadn't wandered off somewhere and lost himself in the woods.

Lilly was so sincere in her request, it made Whitey wonder if she had the least idea how much she honored him. She went on to say that Jeremy stayed in their cabin but ate most of his meals at the cafe. "Would you please watch and see if he eats regularly, because sometimes his play gets in the way of nutrition," she said. Seeing Jeremy was behind the tent, she whispered: "Just ask Mrs. Roberts, she'll know if he's skipping meals."

And this is how Whitey met Jeremy. It was like his mother had said: he was a young boy with the fathomless energies of the young, and he would play himself sick, if allowed. He was out in the trees, along the trails to the ridge tops, or domesticating the garbage-dump chipmunks. Or he was down in the dry summer lake bottom, along the streams there, or he was playing kick-the-can with the other children during the evening hours. But his greatest joy was those nights he stayed at Whitey's camp.

At first, he came carrying his sleeping bag and asked to "sleep out". Then he stashed his bag in the tent, and his nights at Whitey's soon outnumbered those in the cabin.

The fiber was bright and strong; the thread was longer than time's, and Whitey soon understood that it was as much the boy who brought his mother on that day in June as vice versa. If Jeremy were older and much larger and in a long-ago time from this, the two of them might easily have become partners, walking together along the trails that wove camp to camp.

On occasion, Jeremy came bringing a friend or two through the woods to Whitey's place, and they all had a great old time drinking hot chocolate and telling stories, as the forest resounded to the laughter of children. It was a sound foreign to Whitey's ears, and he soon discovered that the sound of children running free in the woods is remindful of summer songbirds. He lost nothing of his solitude.

A five-mile hike away from the camp, through the old forest, curved a high sweeping ridge named Crescent Mountain. It was a place high in the sky, where Whitey sometimes took his growing troop on weekends. And a merry gang it was, too: the boys from the camp and visitors from town, toting sleeping bags under their arms, fishing rods in their hands, and sandwiches in their pockets. About two-thirds of the way up the mountain's southern slope, the trees abruptly left off and were replaced by krummholz and rock and grassy alpine meadows.

Here was the home and hiding place of mountain marmots. These were almost as big as beavers but looked and behaved like prairie dogs. They froze bolt upright outside their rocky burrows and watched the troop file by. The marmots were polished thieves and no one dared leave a sandwich or a freshly-caught fish lie on a rock unwatched for long, because count on it, it would be gone when they returned

The summit supported a lookout station in bygone years. From way up here, Whitey and his troop could see the summer haze out in the western valleys. To the east, Cascade peaks pierced the blue sky running north to south. It was a good place to watch the vesper star settle. Suspended in the bowl of a moonless August night, they could lie in their bags and count shooting stars streaking its black bottom. Falling asleep was like a falling away, falling away into that night sky.

The ridgeline curved around like a bent elbow that pointed southwest. It sloped off steeply to the northeast in a cascade of boulders and runted wind-blown hemlocks and subalpine firs. A small lake nestled at its base on that side. It was shallow, as most of the high mountain lakes are, and sucked its waters from the mountain through springs gushing from its root. It drained off in a trickling stream that headed east, gorging itself upon more springs, expanding its girth along the way to the Lava Lake basin.

The lake was protected by the mountain from westerly winds and from the dry east wind by a cool forest of old mossybacks. It even managed to harbor some fair-sized brookies and was usually good for a fish or two, if you snuck up quietly.

It was a lonely little lake, left solitary when the frigid high waves of ice bays receded in a far-off eon. When viewed from the mountaintop, sporadic breezes rippled its blue-green surface and scintillated sunlight. Passing clouds cast it in rhythms of shadow and silver gilt. It was remindful of a precious ring, set with tourmaline, worn by a proud giantess, as she slowly turns her pinkie against the light beams, showing off her gem.

This was a place for dreaming dreamers. They'd tell far-fetched stories about Sasquatch and flying saucers and old timberjacks, and such. Or they'd exchange the latest popular jokes, then laugh and tease and often repeat them so the others could commit them to memory. "Tell it again," they'd plead.

One special night, when the stars were especially bright, one of the boys said: "I learned a tall tale. It's called The Hero of the Tillabow. Wanna hear it?"

"A whole tall tale?" said someone.

"Yeah. Wanna hear?" Without waiting for a reply, he was off in the telling. He held his body rigid and stared blank-faced back into his clear youthful memory where he had stored all of the words, neatly in succession, one after another. Firelight flickered off his face and lit his eyes, making them glow like embers. Proudly, he told his tale:

"Let me tell ya the story of when the wind did blow,
set the air on fire an' made the ground glow.
It's the story of a man who we all know.
It's the story of the hero of the Tillabow.
Twas a time long ago when a mean son-of-a-gun,
Called The Great Red Wolf, leaped outa the sun.
His breath was all fire an' his tail was of smoke,
Burnt the skin offa men an' made 'em choke.

He boiled the fishes and scorched poor ol' Earth.
High in the mountains he waited and lurked,
When he leaped he roared for all he was worth,
Men all yelled: 'Where we gonna run to? What'er we gonna do?
It's the end of our days, our lives 'er all through!
Oh, mercy! Forgive us dear Lord if'n our lives weren't true.'
But these scairt men, how were they to know,
That in their midst stood the hero of the Tillabow?
He grabbed 'em all up an' tossed 'em in the cold river,
Sprinkled 'em down with water an' made 'em shiver.
Then, to the wolf he hollered: 'Come here you red rat;
Ya can eat me if'n ya can find where I'm at.'
So, the ol' wolf, he came a sniffin' around.
But the hero, he's alayin' right flat on the ground.
The wolf sees him an' comes arunnin' hell-bent down the hill;
Thinks he's agonna make a real-quick kill.
He digs in his feet, an' he makes a mighty leap,
  an' he shows his teeth—butcha see,
  he didn't' know he was a messin' with the hero of the Tillabow.
The hero, he reached his hand a way up high;
An' he pulled the sun down outa the sky.
He set it on the ground to use as a skillet.
Then he hollered: 'Come on fellas, 'cause I'm a gonna kill it.
I'm agonna bake us some red-wolf pie.
But first, I'm agonna have me a whole lotta fun.'
Then he grabbed that wolf an' rubbed his nose in his dung."

The group of boys threw back their heads and all laughed, uproariously. Fascinated, Whitey joined in with the laughter. Feeling mighty proud, the storyteller ended his little song:

"Then he skinned that wolf right where it lay,
An' all the men shouted: 'Hoo-ray, hoo-ray!
We're a gonna live to sin another day.'"

Whitey was still laughing with the rest—he'd never heard this one. "Who made up that one?" He asked as if he didn't know.

The boy shrugged his shoulders.

"Tell it again," someone said.

So, like a stuck record, the poem played over and over, for a long while. The boys were trying to lock it in their memories, same as their forefathers would have done, because tall tale telling still ran in the blood of the sons. But the words didn't interest Whitey—the visions they conjured up did. He looked into the fire and saw grumbly ol' Bud, turned bottom up, grunting and squirming, his nose in the poop, and chuckled. Then he saw the sun vanish, hell come down, and the sky go up in fire. He heard the booming artillery when trees exploded, splashing of water, and cries of men in despair. He felt the slack in the man with the broken back. But then his eyes looked through the fire into the ashes where he saw another bleak scene, black and dreary and silent. For a brief moment, he stood knee-deep in those ashes; they were cold and dead. It hurt. He shook that scene from his head, raised his eyes, and looked around at the young fire-lit faces, all grinning, straining their ears to hear each word and lock it in, molding raw fear and death and tragedy and heartache into a fanciful hero. A hero who hadn't been nearly so brave and debonair as desperate.

How ironic to be sitting here now, lying and laughing about that terrible fire. We're all sons and daughters of Sorrow, given the gifts of time, mind, and talent to make light of our heavy parentage—time, mind, and talent—quite the gifts. He smiled and slowly shook his head at his thoughts. Then he said: "Boys, let me tell you the story told by an old-time timberjack everybody called The Fish . . ."

So went the year and several more like it. The incessant winter snows came and covered the buildings, and the rains came in late spring and melted the snow away again. The camp was like a living thing that breathed in then out, in again and out, as in came the people and out again they went. It hibernated for a season, when it hardly breathed at all, then sprung back to life and quickened into a flurry of activity, until the season rolled around again to hibernate. Time seemed to be relentlessly repetitive.

Things are never what they seem, change is the thing and serenity is a dream. The Maker of Earth and her worlds never sits still. Like a bubble blower, His creations are not for saving. Not far away, events were coming to a stormy head that would soon completely blow away the time of this woodland world. Things began to slowly change, and then the change quickened, and soon things would never be the same again for Whitey and the camp people and the fragile culture of the big woods.

There was tension in the mountains, and rumors filled the air. Down in the valleys machinations were being conceived, alliances formed, forces rallied, treasuries raided, mercenaries hired, strategies formulated, boundaries drawn, allegiances pledged, and oaths shouted. The lumber barons, like petty warlords, were staging to have another one of their little timber wars.

But, this one wasn't going to be so little. This time, some mighty big heads were going to roll.

Chapter 22 The Baron War

Bob Carr was the youngest of the self-made lumber barons. He'd always fought hard to win, because in his view there were winners, and there were losers. He was a winner. Now, he felt like the old Civil War general who wins the battles, but finally loses the war.

He knew he'd been living in delusion, imagining himself the member of some elitist clique of men—big winners on the world scene—all delusion. They were once a haughty group, living in the plentitude of the times. They were the apples of their own eyes. Times can change, but *they* couldn't because they were too full of *themselves*. The cornucopia was turned upside-down and emptying fast. Now it was a sorry little group, infested by wormy peccants, desperately trying to eat their way out of a poisoned apple. They were among the poorest men in the Northwest who were due to lose their assets in the end.

Finally, Bob saw things and events with new clarity that he had trouble peering into because what he saw was troubling. It seemed downright silly that all those people whose esteem had meant so much to him had only esteemed him out of ignorance—theirs and his. The reality was: he'd been a member of a clique of fat hungry grubs, all gnawing on the same green leaf and due to meet at the center, sooner or later. They arrived sooner rather than later. Here they were: all together, eye to eye and tooth to tooth—it was all over. The leaf was gone and all the gorging had come to nothing. Licking their chops, they eyed one another.

So, now, here he was, in the moment that every person finally lives for: the only moment, before the first and after the last. In this moment, he saw where he hadn't seen before. But it came with a high price, this sudden expansion of perception, and there was no haggling with the distributor.

Expansion is a good thing. This, Bob was always the first to admit. There's diversification in it. But in this particular case, he was drained of his capital and couldn't recapitalize the debt and spread it out over more time, and the staunch banker was calling his note. Caught up in his economic conundrum, he'd grown desperate and compounded error on error. Some people say that error and sin are one and the same. If this is true, then he was a first-rate sinner.

Bob didn't know it, but his banker was not the contrary sort that so many of his cohorts made him out to be and with a little more effort would, probably, have listened to a good and reasonable recapture plan.

Alas, Bob should have scheduled in some meetings and come to know him better and put a little more faith in his banker's judgments and suggestions. But toward the end of it all, something like the devil whispered in his mind and told him that it was too late for him to make amends. He listened to it and believed it. This was his last and greatest sin.

The lumber barons had divided the northwestern forests into eleven fiefdoms they referred to as their holdings. Though one would be king of the big woods, if he could, no single one could overcome the others, so in the manner of feudal German states, a corrupt peace had ruled the timberlands. They called their group "the alliance." It was an uneasy alliance, and there was usually a skirmish going on somewhere, but they kept their big guns aimed away from each other and at the U.S. Forest Service. However, this time it was all-out war because a twelfth baron appeared like a scourge from out of the Southeast and claimed the crown and refused to recognize vague boundaries. It was the Southern Gentleman verses all the rest.

In *this* war, money was munitions. Without some unforeseen event, the alliance could not stand united for long in the face of such overwhelming firepower. He was the new kid in the neighborhood, a big bully-boy.

Of the eleven barons in the alliance, Bob Carr was foremost in terms of ability and respect, if not munitions. The times were abundant. Construction growth was rampant all over the country. The timber industry was generous, threw its money around, making ostentatious show. Like a moth to a bright light, it was this glow of opulence that attracted the likes of the Southern Gentleman. He wasn't the only big-money boy attracted to the fiscal orgy, but he was far and above the biggest of the bunch. He was a big-time lumberman from Georgia who made his first fortune in the lumber drying business. Then he was off into other ventures, layering fortune on fortune, merging industries into an empire. In short order, he established himself as a baron in the Northwest by buying out a large number of sawmills and plywood plants. He then took quick profits by sapping the plants and logging operations of quality—but not quantity.

So what had once been neat mills, clean as whistles through pride of ownership by the men who'd built them, now deteriorated into eyesore scrunge and refuse piles. Who said a lumber mill had to be attractive to make lumber? Pretty doesn't pay, lumber does. Never mind that the mills were the focal points of the small valley towns that had sprung up around them. He increased production, and this created the illusion of job security, and it increased the populations, and this made the towns feel like little boom cities—for a short time.

Bob was approached by the Southern Gentleman's top henchman, a man named Ammon Reed. Reed offered him a handsome price for his mills. Bob declined. The ante was upped and declined again. Bob dreamed of the day Jeremy would enter the business at his side. That would mean time spent together—time he'd never had time for. He loved what he did and saw no incentive in selling out for sake of more money. It was an empty dream.

City of roses . . . These days Portland was where *it* was happening, *the* place to *be* for the ambitious Northwesterner looking for his place in the golden money glow. In prior years she was a tidy little city. She was pampered and even a bit spoiled. Squat and close to the ground, tough as a buttercup and every bit as beautiful, a true Northwestern lady. She nestled in the valley between the West Hills and the banks of the inland waterways of the Willamette and the Columbia.

She was influenced by virgins, and she smelled like a virgin, and a man could taste her clean mustiness of virginity upon his tongue. The virgin forests of the Coast Range and the Cascades merged in her and surrounded her, and tall firs snuggled in against her.

In the hot summer, the breezes dropped off the hills and wind whistled through the gorge and picked up moisture off the Columbia and fanned her and kept her cool. When she needed it, the Pacific rolled through in the form of a cloud and gave her a drink. Autumns were sunny and mellow. Winter was never too cold. She bathed in warm spring rains. Roses bloomed freely among the firs of her hills.

Then came big-time commerce, and with it the Southern Gentleman and others of that ilk, following the sensuous smell of money and not virginity nor roses, holding their erections in their minds like dreams, naming them after themselves. The world was hungry for lumber and logs. Portland was expanding, getting fat, literally a real boomtown. She dug out the wild roses, domesticated them into reserves, and replaced them with high-rises. Giant derricks worked the skyline from where that line started to where it ended, realizing those dreams into tall stiff erections that probed the sky and masculinized its line.

The Southern Gentleman showed up, riding in a long white limousine. He wooed Portland like a well-endowed gigolo. He planted his erection in her valley and carved his initials in its head. She rewarded him handsomely with favors. The grateful mayor and his councilmen, virtually every politician in the state, groveled and stroked it with their slick tongues. Ecstatic, it spewed money and mayhem upon the virgin forest, raping her and defiling her as if she were a harlot. These were spasmodic times and spasms was all that there was to them, the same old empty no-gain thing; *nothing* came of it, no sense of relief, no laying back to savor the passing moment. It was the climax of an era – the era of the big woods could only contract from here. Those same rivers that had once run through so sweet, now, bottoms reamed by dredges, ever-larger ships discharging their holds, re-gorging and throwing up bilge, flowed away foul.

But Portland did well, indeed. She grew up and went into business. She sold her virgin daughters to the foreign sailors and her virgin forests to their captains. In the fifties and for some time thereafter, Portland was *the* place to *be* for any prospective timberjackoff king.

It seems to be the nature of men to think that when things are good they can never go to bad or when things are down and out they can never rise to the good again. It's an age-old lullaby that lulls fat cats to sleep and drives skinny ones to the brink of despair and beyond.

The economic surge ended as fast as it had started and became a severe slump. The wisest of the barons had over-extended his capital. The fat cats awoke with a start. Being die-hard capitalists, one and all, they were now, to a man, over capitalized and hard against the wall—all except one, and he would be king. The barons had weathered rough seas before. However, a good ship can weather any storm, unless it has been sabotaged, and many an old wreck lies sleeping in its rot on the ocean bed from this cause.

Timberlands are claimed under the ownership, not stewardship, of the federal government. It cannot manifest a single thing, yet it coerces men to agree that it owns the trees. Then it lays claim to the forest, and God-like, reserves the right to do with it as it pleases. Of course, anything owned can be sold, and it sells the stumpage to timber interests by issuing parcels, large and small, for monetary bid. These are called "timber sales" and "stumpage auctions," and it all amounts to timber for the present generation and stumps for the next.

When the region was civilized and the wild natives were finally exterminated, the civilized men who settled and tamed it were not interested in the trees. Trees deserved no place in their world. Being natives themselves, and wild, trees were simply considered obstacles to also be exterminated. In the valley bottoms, the newcomers burned vast stands to the ground or cut them down and left them to compost and then burned off the slash. The forests were felled, torched, sawed, split, torched again, rolled into heaps, torched again, and the nutritious ashes between the charred piles were farmed. The ash made rich compost and farmers called it "black gold." So, land that once said, Douglas fir, red cedar, big leaf maple, spruce, hemlock, alder, ash, grand fir, oak, yew, and madrone, among others, was made to limit its vocabulary to beans and spuds. The wild land had been domesticated. The pioneers built barns and sheds to contain their produce and these invited in the rats.

An ironic thing: fate. How could any single one of these pioneer men have possibly imagined or conjured up in his most far-fetched dream that approximately one hundred and fifty years in his future his great grandchildren's children would hitch up a subsoiler to two hundred horses, more or less, and spend a day or two ripping up many of the fields that it took him and his all of their working lives to clear of trees -- all this in order to support plantations of *trees*. And so the soil went back to speaking its archaic tongue for the same reason it had been forced to adopt a foreign one: *money*.

Large virgin stands stood tall on the rolling hills that surrounded the valley floors, which were left alone back in the olden days, because the steep land was not farmable. Most of these stands were included in the claims of settlers, and many descendants became wealthy beyond the wildest dreams of their settler forebears. The expanding nation had squandered its eastern woodlands and began to hunger for more lumber for ever more buildings and for ever more logs to export. These Dougfir stands that still stood came to be called "green gold."

Many wars have been waged over yellow gold. Entire empires and civilizations have been rubbed out in a yellow gold frenzy. Now, empires and civilizations were going to be rubbed out in a green gold frenzy. The greater stands, rolling away like inland oceans from off the Pacific beaches, fell into the hands of the federal government. These became the national forests and were called a "resource." So began the bidding contests until the great and natural national forests had gone the way of the great natural dinosaurs, leaving only a few scattered bones as testimonial of their passing. The barons were like scavengers about the leavings. Best of pals at the social club, they waged a discreet gentleman's war at the stumpage auctions. Literally, this is where money talked. This activity was encouraged by the timber holder, because the higher the bid, the more the flow of currency pouring into the coffers of its treasury. The state and its counties were gleeful, for they participated in their share of the take.

The barons could bid up the price of stumpage to extravagant levels, thereby locking out the man of modest means and pass the costs onto the gullible consumer. In this regard, they formed a united front -- their alliance. They were able to control huge blocks of stumpage free from outside threat, except for occasional limited raids by fellow barons. This was their gentleman's agreement: You raid me, and I'll raid you, and no one, but no one, raids *us*. If he tries, we'll join forces and bid him up to a price where he can't afford to log and saw it with a profit in it. It was: "The enemy of my enemy is *our* enemy."

Many outside raiders tried to break into the circle of the agreement; none succeeded. All participating parties were happy: the state because it got its yellow gold, the barons because they got their power, the workers because they got to work, the consumer because he got his boards. It was a system that stood and served its purpose for a time; it was a system founded upon a shifting sandbar. All it took was a brisk breeze from the southeast along with a heavy spring freshet of newly-minted money to undermine it and splash it all away.

The Southern Gentleman upset the logging truck. Here was a raider the alliance hadn't reckoned for. Under the waving pennons of Atlantic Oregon Kilns, his pugnacious onslaughts were ferocious, and the alliance began to retreat from his thrusts and parries. It seemed the Southern Gentleman recognized no gentleman's agreement. The "little" man, wanting in for a piece of the action, was no longer the imagined threat to the barons—Geronimo was dead. This was the Golden Horde, marching from out of the East; the Mongol was in the hinterlands and advancing.

What a lousy idea! Dumb too. It turned out to be the undoing of the old dynasties. It's the kind of idea that desperate economic-men get when their economics turn against them. It was Evan Grace's idea, or at least he was the first to project it.

"Bob," said Evan, on the phone that fateful day, "we've got to get together and talk."

He sounded concerned, and that was unlike him.

"What's on your mind, Evan?" Bob was curious; calls from Evan were rare.

"Oh, not much. If you'll drive in I'll buy you a beer?

"Okay with me if you make it worth my trip and buy me a couple," kidded Bob.

"You're on." Evan paused as in thought, then said: "Let's keep this private. I'm saying that I'm going home. I'll meet you at the Timber Topper."

So Bob told his secretary that he was going home and headed off to the Timber Topper lounge in Eugene. He thought he knew what was on Evan's mind, and his assumptions were well-founded. Coming out of the mid-day summer sun, entering the windowless lounge was like stepping into a dark hole. The place was deserted, except for the bartender and a short-skirted waitress. Evan sat at a corner table, fingering a beer glass. When he saw Bob, he smiled and held up two fingers as a signal for the waitress to bring two more beers.

Bob seated himself across from Evan. The waitress quickly approached, leaned over in a way that proudly flashed her cleavage, and placed the beers on the table.

"On your tab, Mr. Grace?" she said.

Evan nodded. "Bring some more when you see these disappear."

"Yes, sir, will do."

Flashing a friendly smile, full of white teeth, she turned and walked back to the bar. Evan studied her legs. His ruddy face was under-lit by the flickering light of a candle that was concealed in a cheap, translucent red cylinder with a hole in the top. Shadows danced and darted across his features.

"Likes to show off what she's got," said Bob, trying to sound relaxed.

"Hell, this show ain't nothin'. Got it from good sources she's more'n willing to show off all she has. She works as a stripper in the Fallers Inn on Tuesday and Wednesday nights."

"Yeah, I know those good sources, too. I can see one on each side of your nose, right now."

Evan laughed. "No . . . no, not that I wouldn't like to; just can't conjure up a way to go incognito. I'm afraid they might notice a little old guy in dark glasses with a big red nose like mine. Don't wanta spoil my clean image into one of a dirty old man. Demitt told me. Said she could snatch up a nice new five dollar bill with her, shall we say . . . ." He paused and smiled. "Well I guess I already said it."

"Demitt would know if anyone would. He probably lays them on his face for her to snatch at."

"Wouldn't doubt that at all." Evan was still smiling, but the smile quickly faded, and he appeared to frown. He leaned over the table and rested on his elbows, casually cupping his drink with both hands. "Glad you could make it, Bob. Thanks for coming," he said.

Perhaps it was the light, but Evan's face looked haggard and baggy-eyed. *It looks like I feel,* Bob thought. It occurred to him that Evan was probably seeing the same thing in him. They both knew they had a big mutual problem, and that this was a desperate meeting by desperate men. He said: "No big thing, Evan. I need the break. Gets tiring sitting around Sweet Home, counting money all day and trying to find a big enough vault to stash it all. Appreciate the diversion."

Only a flicker of a smile crossed Evan's face, then he said: "All kidding aside, Bob, these high stumpage prices are gonna kill me. With the price of lumber as low as it is, I can't even afford to log the crap, much less saw it." Evan was one of the more powerful barons so he felt comfortable saying what he did, because he knew that Bob had to be facing the same set of conditions. "I can do for a while longer by loggin' off the cheaper stuff, but I can't honor those goddamned contracts we got bid up so high on. Without a big jump in lumber prices or contract relief by the government, I'm in deep shit just a little ways down the line." His tone was one of disgust. He took a big swig of beer, sloshed it around in his mouth, and gulped it down.

"Yeah, know whatcha mean," said Bob, "I'm in the same kind of stew. I figure I got me a year's breathing room, but if this market doesn't pick up a lot, and I mean a lot, well hell . . . I don't have to tell you what's gonna hit the fan."

"Hell, man, *we're* the *little* guys now! You realize that? That one son-of-a-bitch is forcing us out of the markets! He's bidding up the price of stumpage to where we won't be able to log our own blasted trees 'cause the market won't pay it. Shit-o-dear, Bob, there ain't no way lumber's gonna sell for those kind of prices any time soon. Not without at least three points off the prime. The damned fed's moving the goddamned thing up! People ain't buying, and the Japs sure's to hell won't buy the logs; they'll go to Canada or even Russia first."

Evan was saying the obvious. He was beating around the bush, waiting for Bob to say what he wanted to hear. Much too coy to come out with it himself, he sipped his beer hoping Bob would take the bait – and the lead. And this is exactly what Bob did—and to his everlasting regrets, because the whole fiasco that was about to unfold was going to be blamed on him by his fellow plotters. He carried the guilt of it to his grave. He took a deep breath and said: "We both know what it is that needs to be done. We gotta quit this bidding one another up and face off against this bastard."

Evan pretended to ponder these words he was searching for, then nodded and said: "What yer saying we gotta do is all get together and agree to not allow him to bid us up no more, if I follow you right, and I think I agree. Seems there's no other way to keep him out."

"For Christ's sake, Evan, that's a foregone conclusion! Keeping him out isn't even the issue any more: keeping us *in* the game is the name of the game these days."

"Yeah, I know. There at first, I figured he'd overextend himself, like all the others before, but the bastard just kept right on comin' at us. Jesus, I couldn't believe it! Still can't, I guess. Where the hell does he get all his money? Can you tell me that?" Evan slowly shook his head and looked into his beer, and mumbled: "You're sayin' just what needs to be done. The only way to keep us in is to drive these stumpage prices down."

Bob took a deep breath and sighed in sympathy with Evan's mood. "Evan, my man," he said, "the long and the short of it is this: if we keep piling up one high-priced stumpage contract after another, we're all dead-broke down the line, if we're not already, and that sucker knows it."

"Well, you just hit the nail on the head, but we gotta keep on bidding just to get the stumpage to keep our mills arunning. Ain't none of us got enough private first-cut stuff to see us through, not even Demitt."

"He doesn't have one single section of his old-family timber left standing. He's gotta start in bidding for first-cut because he's got no choice," said Bob. His own words pricked something in himself. Maybe it was his conscience, or maybe it was his fear, or maybe it was the beer. Maybe it was something else, something he couldn't come to terms with. Whatever it was, it was irritating him more often these days. "Evan," he said, "there's something sticking in my craw, but it doesn't have much to do with what we're talking about. I wonder what you think."

"Well then, spit it out where I can examine its contents."

"Once we weather this storm, what are we gonna do on down the line? We're running out of good stumpage. Surely you can see that. We're going farther out to get what we need to feed the saws and there's more players coming into the field all the time. Everybody's fighting for what's left and there's less of it each year. I think what we're seeing, right now, might be the boil coming to a head."

"Sustained yield," said Evan.

"Sustained yield? Oh, come on, Evan, you don't buy into that line of bull, do you? That's just a catchword invented by the Forest Service to sooth their critics. This ain't corn we're fallin'."

A slight smile lifted the corners of Evan's lips, but his eyes weren't smiling. He said: "I'm hard on the heals of very old age. On down the line, you say . . . The end of the line isn't down there very far for me. The woods will outlast me.

"You don't have children, do you?

Evan dropped his eyes and slowly shook his head. He fingered his beer glass for a moment. "You know," he said, "I came out of the woods. I didn't come to here from somewhere. I was born in a shack in downtown Sweet Home in eighteen eighty eight." He wriggled his eyebrows and said: "Betcha didn't know that, did ya?" But he didn't expect an answer. He continued: "Only place to go was the woods. I started out as a skid-greaser kid on the skidroads in niney eight. Ran my short legs off to keep ahead of them bulls, swabbin' grease on the skids with a broom. Know what they made that grease from?" Bob shook his head. "Rendered-down fat, rotten butter, dogfish oil, dead fish, pulverized slugs," said Even, "anything that would be slimy, slick and oily. Think they even mighta thrown in some people shit. Often as not it was more'n a month old. When I puked I just puked in the bucket 'cause that stuff's slick too an' didn't dare break stride. Those bulls were steel-shod, ya know. So were the bull whackers. A kid didn't want to fall down under the feet of either one. Finally worked myself all the way up to choker setter, before I started up that dinky sawmill over in Cascadia. I worked day an' night, an' all the times in between making a go of it with that mill. Anything but the skid roads. Never regretted a minute of it – maybe till now. So, Bob, I know what you're sayin'. I know it don't appear like it, but I love these damn trees. I never had any idea it would come to this. It's all happened so gawddamned fast I still can't believe it." Evan took a big swig of beer, sloshed it around in his mouth, and swallowed hard. He lowered his eyes and mumbled: "The forest was my home, where I was born." He raised his eyes and the two men looked into one another's faces for a long moment.

"Well . . . yeah . . . Let's get back to business," said Bob, trying to escape this dark mood.

Evan leaned back in his chair and sighed. "What do you suggest? How do we go about getting this bastard off our backs?"

"What I suggest is that we contact the others and agree to not bid against each other for a while. Make the bastard buy cheap. As we know, it lets him in more than he already is, but there's no getting him out. He's entrenched."

"You know what I think, Bob? I think that's exactly what we gotta do. You know what else I think?" Evan paused and sipped his beer, looking over the rim of the glass at Bob.

Bob said nothing, just waited for Evan to come out with it.

"I think . . . I think maybe it's just what the bastard is ahopin' and aprayin' we'll do. It's in all our best interests to get this stumpage cost down. He's got mills to run too, ya know. Maybe it's time to accept him as one of us, and he'll start to play by the rules."

"Maybe . . . That could be the case," said Bob. But he didn't think so; this situation wasn't that simple. There was a whole lot more going on here than The Southern Gentleman just wanting to be one of the boys. He had a hunch, just a hunch, that beyond the seeming face of events, there was something else at work, something that didn't give a whit about stumpage, or markets, or profit, or loss, or mills, or forests, or anything else, any more than all these things together plus a whole lot more, add up into something like power or control—or something . . . It seemed to him as though the Southern Gentleman had some sort of guardian angel that led him through the maze of pitfalls along the economic highroad. He had a hunch that there wasn't an alliance in the world that could win this war. No truce, no ceasefire—all-out surrender was the name of this game. Bob's hunch came closer to the truth than he'd ever know.

Bob looked across the table at Evan, who seemed refreshed now that the dye was cast, and sat over there, sipping his beer, with visions of sugar plums in his short future. He left him alone in his fantasies. As he watched Evan, an old ancient Egyptian lamentation, recorded in the days of the Pharaohs, came into Bob's mind. He'd read it in a *National Geographic* or some such publication. In it, a man cried about the fallen mighty and the rich who had become poor and destitute: "Time of desolation! Time of devastation! I was once high; now I am low! I am food for the crocodile."

Bob was not a poetic man. Metaphor was barely a concept for him; he'd worked in other fields. However, he wasn't so poetically ignorant as to think that the lamentation concerned profit and loss in terms of money. But now, something slipped neatly together and the occasion fit. Here he sat, sipping his beer, *looking* at a mighty worried lumber baron across the table, who was willing to blatantly break the anti-trust laws and risk prison just to protect his niche. But Bob was *thinking* about an old Egyptian who lived four thousand years ago. It occurred to him that he was *seeing* himself across the table, and he wondered if things had really changed in four thousand years and if this modern mechanized America was really any different from that old Egypt and if anything *new* ever actually happens. The train of his thought surprised him, and he looked across the table at a lamentable old Egyptian. *Maybe we're all food for the crocodile,* he thought.

Chapter 23 The *Real* Impresario

To anyone whom Bob knew, the Southern Gentleman was simply a designation for a man whose real name was rumored to be George Presco. It was suspected by some that the Southern Gentleman didn't exist and that he was only a facade for eastern money men. It was like confronting a phantom. There were those who claimed to have met him, but he never made any public appearances, and all his dealings were conducted through high-rolling but very effective henchmen—one in particular. His major-domo was Ammon Reed. Reed had such an uncanny knack for anticipating the whims of the market it was almost as though he were manipulating it. Nobody knew where he came from. His competitors agreed he came from hell.

Reed was a corporate man's corporate man. His business suits were tailored pin stripes; his pants never showed a wrinkle; his shoes were black and polished up as shiny as a royal doorknob; his collars were stiff and starched. Silver cufflinks flashed from his wrists. A solid gold watch chain ran from one pocket of his vest to the other, and attached to its center-most link dangled a glowing ruby. His tie tack was a perfect pearl. A large diamond ring on the pinkie finger of his right hand shimmered when it caught the light. His copper-hued hair lay neatly in its place. His big round eyes were blacker than a Moor's. Like the midnight sky, sans stars and moon, there was no way to measure their depth or to even know if they contained depth. Like a shark's, those eyes never blinked, and they glared right into a man as if they were searching his soul for something to eat. They made steadfast men fidget.

Reed didn't say much; mainly he listened, but when he spoke, he chose his words carefully. One word followed another in precise order, quick and sharp, striking the ear like tossed darts, rarely pausing for thought. His favorite word was "efficiency;" his favorite phrase was "team player." The best and brightest team players were promoted and rewarded handsomely. He held no respect for poetic beauty. It was as if language were a nuisance. So where he could, he reduced the language to acronyms. He referred to his executive staff as his "T.Ps"—for team players. Underlings took to calling it the "teepee society," its members "mahogany Indians," its interoffice memos "talking leaves," its executive meetings "powwows." If a T.P. lost his temper, he was on the "warpath." If he got canned, he lost his "scalp."

To maintain their T.P. status the T.P.s had to put on the panache and ape Reed's ruthless efficiency. Of course, one's efficiency was measured against one's ability to carry out Reed's desires. Most T.P.s got scalped. Like a master corporate gardener, he weeded and thinned his managerial crop and selected only those men who were most imaginative to be his top T.P.s. These men he called his T.L.s (for team leaders) and he sucked on those bright imaginations like a bloodless leach.

People who had business dealings with Reed said he was somewhat detached in his manners, and never attended business lunches or had cocktails or dropped in at happy hour or took time out for the office parties or went on vacation. He kept to his schedules and expected others to do the same. They said his office was always cold, and he worked like a demon. He mystified them. To Reed, such tête-à-tête and body comforts were aggravating peccadilloes, distractions from business.

He was called many things. His T.P.s called him: "Mr. Reed" to his face, "Chief" among themselves. Some in the rank and file often referred to him as "the impresario;" others in that group called him "the ultimate entrepreneur." To the more imaginative of his competitors, he was "the goddamned devil," and they claimed that the Southern Gentleman had traded his divine soul to Satan for economic power, and that Reed had flown straight up out of the deeps of hell to go to work at fulfilling his master's end of the bargain. To the less imaginative of his competition, he was simply "that hard-eyed son of a bitch." They all respected him as much as they feared him.

Whatever or whomever he was, one thing was for certain: like a cheap whore to a petty pimp, Ammon Reed didn't give a whit for the integrity of Earth. Her things were his to use and abuse.

The egg that Bob and Evan laid in the Timber Topper lounge was hatched during the following months. It was an ugly ducking, indeed, that pecked its way out. The owner of the stumpage experienced a sudden decrease in the bid prices at the federal stumpage sales—much too sudden. There was something rotten in timberland, and it smelled like anti-trust. Obviously, an agreement had been struck, and it was far too immediate to have jelled within the non-verbal grapevine. At this rate, billions in projected revenues and tax incomes were going to be lost, and the government was incensed. It rallied its lawyers.

The Southern Gentleman raided his treasury and mustered his troops, and the stumpage owner massed his bureaucrats and these two allied against the alliance. Charges of price fixing were levied against the once great lumber barons, and the full weight of the anti-trust laws came down upon their heads. They knew their roots were shallow and their asses stood bare to the legal axe, because the charges were absolutely true. Of course, at any time in the past twenty years the charges would have been true, just harder to prove. But nobody with the power to do anything about it had ever much cared, before this, because anybody with that kind of power was in on the take.

Evan couldn't have been more mistaken when he thought the barons could sign a truce and recruit The Southern Gentleman into their alliance. Their nemesis had absolutely no intentions of quitting the war and joining the old boys club—not Evan's little club, at any rate. The trap was baited, and the barons all filed in, like eleven blind mice, to take a nibble. Then it sprung shut with no way out, and all they could do was chew on stumpage – high-cost wood in a low-price lumber market. They had no choice; it was fall it and saw it at a loss, or lose it altogether.

For a time, jail appeared certain, but their lawyers negotiated them out of doing jail time. After all, the economy of the region couldn't stand the sudden jailing of eleven of its biggest tycoons. Even The Southern Gentleman couldn't possibly take up the slack fast enough, so the lawyers bought the barons some time with outrageous fees. With the threat of jail behind them, their biggest threat now was those high-priced stumpage contracts The Southern Gentleman bid up so high. In actuality, it wasn't The Southern Gentleman who drove up the stumpage prices. The Southern Gentleman learned his bidding techniques from them, and they were simply experiencing the echoes of their own past deceits. As Evan said to Bob that fateful day in the Timber Topper: they were stuck "in deep shit." The Southern Gentleman held the shovel. In a matter of time the government was going to demand payment on the stumpage contracts. The money had better be in the bank, or it planned to pursue the holders for damages following contract default.

The price of lumber was up, then down, up again, and down again. There was no rhyme or reason to it. Cheap lumber pouring across from Canada was devastating. Each time the price of lumber inched up, the flow from the north increased driving it back down again. There was no end in sight to this vicious cycle.

The barons made desperate appeals to the communal sense of nationalism to speak up and demand tariffs, duties, legislation, anything to protect them from this foreign "dumping." They rallied their employees and urged them to gather petitions containing thousands of signatures. These they mailed to senators, governors, the president, congressmen, anybody important. Everybody who was anybody made a speech or two. Newspapers took up the cause. Displaced workers, wearing long faces and towing their sad-eyed children, paraded publicly for media appeal. It all came to nothing. Obviously, there was something rotten in Washington, and to the barons, it smelled like payola.

The Southern Gentleman sat like a vulture on a limb, waiting for his poison to work.

Finally came the time when the baron's inertia was exhausted. The politicians were indifferent. The dreaded time was at hand: time for outright begging, beseeching, bribing, or whatever it took. At any rate, supplication was in order.

As some weary farmer, during a drought, crops all shriveled, fields turning to dust, his hat in his hand, and his tail tucked between his legs goes to beg money from his hard-nosed lender, so went Bob Carr. He was going to the place where the hot wind blows and the bullshit flows, and he would rather be going to everlasting hell. He was on his way for a meeting with the little senator.

Bob didn't know if he had been selected as group spokesman because he was most respected as a man or as a beggar. It didn't much matter. Holding his hat but not much hope, he went alone. But that was another time.

A spirit is graced to be born into life and doomed to die out of it. A man is an alchemist stirring events in the flesh pot of his world, hoping to stir up some sublime gold to keep because the gross is discarded at the end. He needs the gold to buy off the merciful musical Angel of Memory – the more gold the better. She plucks the mystical cords of memory for the sake of harmony and dies away from discord and the price for all this mercy isn't cheap: the poorest of dead men never lived for a moment. And so, in this final and single moment, Bob's memory of the little senator was fading fast. It was one of those memories a man wants to die away from, and now Bob Carr was a dead man, haunted to his grave by the relentless demon of guilt. Dying was probably the sanest thing he'd done since that sweet night he lay with Lilly and fathered Jeremy. Perhaps the world he left behind would go lightly on a distraught widow with a young son. He could only hope so.

His wife and his son—oh, these were memories he would try his best to hold. But the memory of the unctuous little senator, he could feel that one slipping fast, as though something was purging it with warm oily water, as bile not worth storage. He watched it as it floated off as if sucked away, leaving in an enema. *Good God! . . . What a God-awful vision! Save me, merciful eternal Lord, from such ghosts.*

Fading memories: With the exception of his bankroll, there was nothing, absolutely nothing, *big* about the senator. He was a titman in every respect, inside and out—except for his wanger. It was rumored he was well-hung and loved to screw. "He'll screw anything," said the rumor. "He holds the Bible in one hand and his cock in the other. Why, he'll screw a snake if somebody'll hold its head down." It's also rumored that he himself started the "well-hung" part of the rumor.

"Rumor, rumor," replied the senator. "Not a word of it is true." He told the truth, sorta; he wasn't a Bible reader – just claimed to be.

The senator perceived only one world, and it was an outside world, and that world was for the taking. If there was an inner world to the senator and a man in there to reflect upon it, that man viewed a very small world. He'd kissed a million asses and only a few of those were baby-bottoms. His short stature had a positive aspect: his lips were constantly at ass level.

The dreaded event had arrived: here comes the senator, sporting a phony smile, his glad-handing hand at the ready.

Good God! He struts! The mercenary little jerk actually goose steps! Bob forced a smile out through his thoughts.

Fresh out from the inner circles of Washington, D.C., the senator looked every bit the part. His was the ensemble of the in-man, connoisseur of fashion and the con arts. Today he was dressed in pleated baggy pants that tapered toward the ankle and were held up by narrow black suspenders of woven leather. His shoes were two-toned white and black with perforated toes. They were his way of saying he never had to walk in the rain or mud. His shirt was white with frilly cuffs that stuck out under the sleeves of his tweed sport coat, and he capped it all off with a red bowtie.

But the senator had a slight dilemma: he was a city slicker from a rural state. This fact nagged his insecurities, come election time. But he was tricky. This was the same character Bob saw running for office a year before, wearing denim pants and a plaid shirt and making a big to-do about them in one of his television adds. There he stood, bigger than life, flashing his teeth through a wheedling smile and saying: "Yessir, folks, reelect me and put a bigger bulge in your jeans pocket." Then he patted himself on the ass, where people who actually work in denim carry their thin wallets.

The senator didn't hold a whit of reverence for the land about him, or even for his fellow man. He'd signed his soul over to political expediency, and he measured success in this world only in terms of his own ambitions and counted it in units called votes. The way he figured it, one vote for him in the ballet box equaled twenty dollars in the bank.

Bob was well aware that he met with a man that only an elitist group in the capital knew. This was not the condescending little supplicant out begging for votes. This was a vulpine cuttlefish, able to change colors on a whim and blend himself clean away and right on out of sight. If you tried to out talk him you'd only end up where you started, because he'd lead you in a circle every time.

So like the good hunter, you had to know his hiding places, and this little sybarite hid among vague words that seemed to shift their hues from one sentence to the next and sly double-ended innuendoes that, like worms, doubled up on their tails and turned back on their trails. He was a first-rate practitioner of the fine art of speaking between the lines. He wrapped himself in his elevated station like a grub in a cocoon and bought his station back every four years. Fed only a diet of word games, spiced with sly implications, his substance was wasting away into spiritual marasmus.

His constituents made considerable inquiry concerning his millions of dollars of campaign contributions. Where all that money came from, no one knew. This money had not come from the population who elected him, and when questioned about it, he always attributed it to out-of-state sources in tune with his "noble stands on lofty issues of national and international prominence."

He also claimed that a good deal of his money was gifted to him by women admirers from all over the country, though it was plain to see that he was his own greatest admirer.

He had scalded his humanity and sterilized his soul. In his value system, he was counted a great success. But success didn't come cheaply for him. An important impotent man, he paid the price with his soul's balls when he entered the domain of royal eunuchs, who cater to the kingship of public whimsy at the expense of their own spiritual procreation.

But no man lives without some gain, somewhere, no matter how slight. The little senator's gain was in learning a particular kind of delicate patience, for he had developed an ability to straddle the fulcrum of any issue and remain as still as a vulture on a limb. When he felt the weight shift, he knew which way to jump and swoop, and it was always on the side of weight. This talent gained him the envy of his peers. Of course, it was not a talent unique to himself. It was one he learned from mentors among the gelded functionaries, and he practiced it with utmost finesse, maintained his sinecure and grew his whiskers.

However, he had to be given his due credit, because he was one hell of an actor, and an actor always acts. This meant, to arrive at the spoken truth, you couldn't believe a word he spoke. You had to find him – hunt him down. In this case, to be a good hunter meant you had to sneak into those little spaces between words and silently crouch there and wait and try to figure out where he was headed, because the crafty fox was hiding in what was *not* said. And like the fox, he was strong on cunning but weak on courage.

"Mr. Carr, nice to finally meet you." The senator shook Bob's hand as though campaigning for a vote.

"Likewise, Senator, be assured," said Bob, through a big smile that was as fake as the one he was looking at.

Then there followed a few empty moments, gorged full of idle palaver about the weather out here vis-à-vis back there, the state of the union, prospects of war and peace. It's a type of civil protocol. It buys some time for men to size one another up through use of timeworn mundane verbosity. It's like a poker game: raise the ante, bluff, and counterbluff.

The game was underway:

The senator said: "I've long admired your accomplishments and have looked forward to meeting such a distinguished lumberman as yourself. It takes some real doing and lots of guts to go off into the sticks and build yourself an empire." Now, these were his words, but what was *said* was: "I know very well who you are, and I know you have lots of money."

"This state's been good to me and mine, Senator." (Me and the others I represent have a great deal of money, and we can be good to you in return.)

The senator raised his eyebrows, ever so slightly, smiled slyly, and said: "Yes, it's been good to me also, Mr. Carr. I guess we have a lot in common and much to be thankful for. Yes, sir, I'm proud to represent this fine state." Then he smiled broadly, leaned back in his swivel chair, and placed his feet on the corner of his desk, crossing one foot over the other. Bob sat in his stiff-backed, uncushioned wood chair, eye level with those pathetic sissy shoes, holding his hat in his lap. (See these shoes you stix-hick? These establish our relationship to one another. Do they look like calk boots? Cram this good-old-boy bullshit, because I ain't no good old boy. Time to get down to business.)

What an effortless dexterity! -- Almost admirable. Bob's thoughts irritated him because here he was once again, in the presence of his disgust. He knew this breed well and it was bred to be irritating. It's a man-made breed of man, developed with quite a bit of input from stud devil. Its bloodlines go way down.

It has even developed its own convoluted way of expressing itself—been bred in. In much the same way that a high-bred stock dog line is bred to be fast on their feet and quick to switch directions, this lineage was bred to be fast and quick with their tongues and so they're born with split tongues that can switch and turn on a flip. He knew their double-ended language as "sleazespeak" and it takes a sleazespeaker to communicate with one of them. It's called "forked tonguistics" by some straight-tongued people, who can interpret it but refuse to split their tongues. It's a defensive-based communication that says two things simultaneously: the *words* and the *said*. If cornered, sleazespeakers can always claim they didn't really say what they are accused of insinuating, and the record will prove their argument every time because only the words can be read back. "Words do not lie," they will say, "only interpretations do."

It's very clever, this forked tonguistics, and entire races have been overwhelmed by it, before they wised up. It borders on poetic genius of the diabolical kind, being entirely mercenary in application. It also requires the reading of various unwritten rules of protocol. Many of these rules are subtle and are expressed through the use of certain repetitious physical gestures and body stances, remindful of the way herd animals interact, as when bulls puff themselves up just before they start to bellow. Bob had become somewhat skilled in this obscure, language-within-a-language semantics through his years in high-level business dealings, lobbying, and court appearances in lawsuits and the such. But here, in front of him, sat one of the foremost artists in the practice – definitely *low* bred.

Bob tried hard to psyche himself up for this meeting. Much was riding on it. His life's work, all that he had fought for, all his accomplishments, his corporation, his family's standard of living—everything he identified with was at stake here. This inurbane twerp, homely as a dog turd, and who claimed that much of his campaign contributions came to him through his charm, clutched him by his balls, and Bob felt the squeeze of cold icy fingers. He silently cursed himself for having worked so damned hard to obtain to the awkward position in life where some squirt of a ball squeezer could get a hold on his. He tried to look relaxed, casual, and cocksure, and still express unmistakable humility.

"Well, Senator, as you know, if you have problems on the federal level you best go as high as you can go to solve them." (You're my last ditch effort. I've tried everything else. If you can't help us, no one can.)

"Well then, Mr. Carr, you've come to the right place." (I know I'm your one great hope. Also note the last name basis.)

"You're aware, Senator, of the severe problems we face meeting those recent stumpage contracts we bid on. We bid on those contracts in good faith. The economy of the time warranted the bids and they were encouraged by the government. But now, due to economic conditions beyond anyone's control— you know, high interest rates, the rising dollar and all that—we're in a real bind. We've spent a great deal of money combating these problems. If we don't get relief on those contracts, well, I hate to consider the consequences on the economy of this state." (Are you with us or against us? Once again take note of the suggestion that we are willing to spend plenty of money to get the feds off our backs.)   .

The senator shuffled his feet and leaned back some more in his chair. He looked off into the corner of the room and rubbed his chin between his thumb and index finger, the way deep thinkers are supposed to do. Then he said: "Yeah, you have a real problem there, all right. But I can't say that I agree that the federal government encouraged you to bid those contracts up so damned high. This is a capitalist society, you know. The government has to try to make a profit, too. When the bids are going sky high, all the more stumpage is released to bid on. Back in the Midwest I think they call it making hay while the sun shines—or maybe its corn," he said, through a sly smile. "Out here, it's called making stumpage available while the rates are up. Sounds to me like you lumbermen were chasing those prices while they were going up. You should have known better." (I'm not with you, buddy. I'm not even discussing the issue here. Notice how I veered off into whimsy. We could jabber on all day about these things, couldn't we?)

"Oh, believe me, Senator, I didn't mean to insinuate the government was at fault. I realize it has expenses to meet, same as we all do. No, to be frank, our real problem is a company called Atlantic Oregon Kilns, which is bidding up the price on these sales. On down the line, this tactic will be sure to create severe economic problems in this state. (The cards are dealt. The players are named. Who are you playing footsie with under the table?)

The senator smiled at the mention of Atlantic Oregon Kilns. "Oh yes, George Presco, the so-called Southern Gentleman. I talked to him just the other day. Have you ever had the pleasure of meeting him?" (Presco got to me before your group. The game is high-stake's poker here and he dealt the first hand.)

Bob swallowed back his cotton and tried not to show his dejection. "No, I have to admit that I have not," he said.

"Not a bad sort, ol' George. I think his mercenary qualities may be a tad bit over exaggerated." (Note the first name basis. You think you are familiar with bidding wars? Big bidder, huh? How high can you bid?)

Those words were the big bombs dropping, and Bob knew the baron war had just ended. Anything he said from here on was only a retrenchment process, preparing to be sued for peace—surrender. But the silly poker game would continue, because this game player was addicted to the sport.

"As you are aware, Senator, Mr. Presco is in the same boat with the rest of us. There aren't any of us who can afford to honor those stumpage contracts at current prices. Did you discuss this with him?" (Did you and Presco make a deal?)

The senator cocked his head and slyly smiled. "Oh, I don't know that he's in the same boat as the rest of you or not. From what he tells me, he owns his own boat. In fact he owns a fleet of them, and if one of them springs a leak, he simply ties it on and buoys it up with the others." (How many boats do you and your bunch own? I know you just own one, and it's tied to me, isn't it?) The Senator shuffled his feet again. He tilted back his head and raised his eyes, going though his deep-thinking process for a moment. Then, feigning a serious air: "Mr. Carr, it's like you said, this is all federal level stuff; no stix-hicks back there. These things we're discussing are not decided out here. I'm in total agreement with you when you say contract relief needs to be addressed, but time is against us. If you boys default on those contracts, the government will come after you for damages. It would take an act of Congress to change that. I'm far from being the final say in this sad affair, as you can plainly see." (This is an affair that will be settled in a place where you and yours don't mean diddles, by people who think big and what they think is money. Any money that comes my way will be distributed, so there best be a lot to distribute, and I know for a fact that there's no way there's that much money out here in the sticks.)

Bob drew one more card, but it was the same old deuce he'd been drawing all along. He said: "I don't think any of us should make the mistake of short changing the economic consequences this is likely to have on this region. People are getting upset." (Do you want to face the voters in a down economy? People have a way of voting their pocketbooks, you know?)

The senator slightly shook his head, while he maintained that same sly poker-playing smile. "Believe me, I'll do my best to make certain that the owner of these contracts gets relief when the time comes. It pains me to think that good hard-working people might lose their jobs." (You dare to threaten me, so I counter with one of my own, and it ain't bluff, buddy. I know you're out of it, but I have a pocket full of time. Help will come when I time it, but it will come to whoever owns those contracts at that time. By the way, notice the singular in my use of 'owner'?)

That was it . . . The poker game was over. It ended on a condescending note from a cocky winner, just the way Bob suspected it would. It's a foolish game. You can't win at poker when the dealer owns the cards and all you're dealt is deuces. Now, all said and done but the *scenario*. Bob knew exactly how the scenario was going to play itself out: the only way the barons can save their hides will be to sell out at the buyer's price. The alternative is bankruptcy and perhaps even prison. There is going to be only one player left in the game, and he is called The Southern Gentleman. Atlantic Oregon Kilns will own the whole damned shebang. Then, just at the right time, which will coincide nicely with the senator's reelection campaign, the increasingly understanding and compassionate political leaders will suddenly come to their senses and wake up to the needs of the working population, threatened by plant closures. The owner of the contracts will receive concessions by way of price rollbacks to levels supportable by the current lumber prices. Then the Canadians will be throttled by tariffs, or threats of tariffs, and many billions will be made in one giant windfall. Everyone will be happy. Saved in the nick of time, the workers will feel secure. The price of lumber will go up, and the state will get its gold through an increase in tax flow. The Southern Gentleman will be king, and money will be distributed to the key players who orchestrated this entire damned scenario. The little senator will look like a hero. The old barons will all retire into lives around the country clubs and racetracks and disappear from the realms of power. *And that's the way she's going to go. Same old timeworn line of crap. It wouldn't be so damned disgusting if it weren't so damned predictable.*

Bob didn't see it, but his mental scenario prophesied the ending of the world of the big woods; and so he was a blind foreteller. But how could he've seen such a thing? Bob was a little woods sort of a guy.

The senator casually removed his feet from the desk. He opened a fancy cigarette holder, leaned over, and offered Bob a smoke. Bob declined.

"Mind . . ?

The man was as tasteless as egg white. Not waiting for a reply, the senator struck his lighter, touched the flame to his cigarette, inhaled deeply, and let out a long slow drag, as if he'd just had good sex. This was true in a sense, because Bob knew for sure he'd just been screwed; he felt thoroughly reamed.

At least Bob knew exactly who he was up against. He knew this was its spokesman sitting across from him, sardonically blowing smoke out of his nose. Yes, the game was over. Only the shouting remained. Bob felt like a dyspeptic peering into his own excrement, seeing what he was looking for: worms.

"I hear George is in town today," said the senator, sounding very relaxed and casual. "I was serious when I said he's not so terrible as rumored. You know how rumors follow a man who knows his numbers. You really should take this opportunity to get to know him. You might even take to liking ol' George. (Time to start negotiating and be sure to sharpen your pencil.)

Those words ended the forked tonguistics. There was no more that needed to be said, but Bob had one more thing that he wanted to say. It was very literal, containing no sleazespeak, and the feel of saying it would be a big relief—sorta like taking a shit when constipated. He knew that he shouldn't say it. It countered all his better business judgments, and it certainly didn't make for good negotiations in the forthcoming stock sellouts. But right now, he seriously wondered if there really was such a thing as *good* and *right* business judgment any more. The words lay there and simmered like hot coals on his tongue. So he spit them out, through a sly smile: "When you next see good ol' likeable George, tell him I said to stuff his head up your butt—his money, too." *Take that, you little piss ant.* Now he felt a whole lot better.

Bob held out his hand and the speechless senator, slack-jawed, mouth flopped open, held out his own in a programmed reflex that sees every out-thrust hand as a thing for shaking.

And the senator faded, faded, faded. Farther away he went, getting even smaller, fading into nothingness. *Save me, merciful eternal Lord, from such ghosts.* Bob's final prayer was answered.

Bob didn't meet with the Southern Gentleman. He knew the senator's remark, about the man being in town, was a mock. He probably wasn't any place near Portland. But Bob knew who would be there, waiting for him with a firm handshake, a fake grin and cold black eyes. Reed would surely be there, and he knew Reed; he'd had dealings with Reed. That slick bastard could out sleasespeak the little senator, and he sure as hell didn't need any more of that kind of game today. He drove straight to Eugene, met with Evan, recapped his meeting, and sent poor Evan spiraling down into a whirlpool of depression.

Several weeks had passed since his visit with the senator. This was a brand new morning. As usual, Bob was the first to arrive at the office complex. He nosed his car into the carport and entered his office through the back entrance. His private phone was ringing. This was strange: there was no receptionist present to be putting through calls. She must have left the lines open when she left yesterday. *Who could be calling so early?*

Bob picks up the phone. *Hello.*

Hello, Bob Carr. This is your banker. I'm calling to offer you relief from your woes.

Oh, yes . . . yes, I'm glad you called. I've been meaning to contact you to discuss an extension on my loan.

My good man, you do not understand, you're a day late and a dollar short. You're in default, and I'm calling your note, time to examine your collateral.

Bob felt a sharp jolt, as if all of his nerve ends suddenly made contact and shocked him. He gasped for breath. Again the agonizing jolt. This couldn't be happening! After all the hard work, the risk taking and sacrifices to the future – to come up short and so utterly unfinished . . . He felt his body grow numb. His world collapsed in an instant. The last words Bob heard on the phone were as fleeting words, words that he both saw and heard—electric words that seemed to drift in from somewhere far away, enter his ear through the telephone line, hang before his eyes for a moment, and drift off again into that place where darkness merges with the light and consumes it: *Say goodbye to Bob Carr. There are those that claimed to know him who said he died in disgrace. It's true that he never balanced his black-white marbles, and his ledgers were all amiss, and this was accounted in his life. But don't mark him off as a bankrupt quite yet, because there were fine people who loved him and will love him. He went the way of rare courage, to where few dare to venture, and risked his stock in a dire and risky business, and according to the world's accountants, he came out a failure. But they could not cipher those dimensions in him where their numbers fell short, and this he glimpsed in the final statement. So he gained some profit at last. Invest it wisely, Bob Carr.* So said the banker.

End of memory making . . .

That same morning, Lilly was leaving to take Jeremy to school. It was cool. The sky in the east was glowing red and yellow, same as the leaves. She went out to start her car and turn on the heater to pre-warm it. Bob's car was still parked in the garage. Strange . . . he had left for work three hours before . . . And so she found him, slumped over the steering wheel—dead for three hours. His fingers had turned the key to on but the motor never started.

There was no little excitement in lumber land. Some say it is fated, that every man must die at least once, and Bob Carr, the great lumber baron, was dead. Sawed on by stress, he was felled by a single stroke in the early hours of the morning. The news hit the big woods like a windstorm.

The word reached Whitey's ears at the end of the day, when he stepped off the crummy. The personnel director was waiting at the camp and broke the news to the loggers. It was the company's aim to keep rumors cold-decked and cooled down, and he was there to sprinkle soothing words on them.

Whitey considered Bob to be a fair man, and he was deeply saddened by the news. He was aware of all the rumors and innuendos that were lurking about, always ready to jump out of some dark hiding place and scare a person and steal their self respect, and he knew Bob had been the subject of these cowardly whispering thieves. The barons and others involved were putting out lies that it was Bob's independent actions that had sucked them all into the whole anti-trust fiasco. But Bob Carr's world was not his, and thieves couldn't jump the gap between the two, and so Whitey was safe from such deceit. He gave it no mind. Still, it seemed to him that forty-six was just too young to die of a stroke brought on by the crush of your own life's mounting tides.

Not more than a month before, Bob had toured the logging operations and made it a special point to look him up and thank him again for the time and attention he had given to Jeremy. Bob said that it was the kind of time that he wished he had gleaned from his life. "But I've always been a man rich in commitments and poor in leisure," he said. Whitey got the impression that Bob did not, in the least, consider himself to be a wealthy and powerful man. But he certainly didn't appear to be a man on the brink of death—somewhat haggard maybe, but not dying.

Whitey's thoughts went out to Jeremy and Lilly, and he felt his heart give. He knew that theirs was a family that harbored big love, and so Bob Carr was considerably wealthier than he had counted himself to be. This death was certain to be difficult on the two of them, but they were both strong and would weather the storm. Still, the tragedy of it struck him deeply.

"Christ's sake, Whitey, what do ya think about all this?"

"Yeah, whatcha think, Whitey?"

The words jolted Whitey out of his thoughts. It was tall, blonde, good-looking Milo with his constant sidekick, short, dark, homely Shorty. They approached him, looking shocked and anxious.

"I can't say. But I sure hate to hear it," said Whitey.

"Any idea what might become of it?" asked Shorty.

"No, I don't. I haven't had enough time to mull it over, and there's no need to add grist to the rumor mill. But I guess life goes on for the rest of us. No need to get all in a tither." Whitey saw need to make light of this situation. He knew there would be no end to speculation and exaggerated fears. Thoughts of working conditions and job security lay heavy on a logger's mind. What else can a logger do but log?

"Ya gonna stay on if those bullshit artists at Atlantic Oregon move in and take over?" said Shorty.

This was the very kind of speculation that concerned Whitey, and he didn't want the men on his crew to go sour on him. "Well, Shorty, someone has to take it over," he said.

"Mr. Carr was a good man, wasn't he?" said Milo.

"Yes, I think he was. At least, what I knew of him was."

Whitey saw Shorty's bottom lip quiver, as he quickly turned and walked off toward his trailer house. One of the bright red Diamond T's rolled by loaded with logs, kicking up cinders and spreading red lava dust. The woodsy smell of fresh cut trees hung in the evening air.

Milo, watching Shorty walk away, said: "Jeesus, he's snarly lately." Then he looked at Whitey, and said: "This is serious, ya know." This was an interesting statement, coming like it did from this far-from-serious young man.

"What is it about it that makes it so serious, Milo? No man lives forever."

"Way most of us see it, Carr was about the only decent one left to work for. What now?"

"Well, a man's not a tree. If he doesn't like it where he is, he can always move onto some place else."

"I liked it the way it was." Milo glanced again at Shorty walking away, then back at Whitey. "Something stinks. The men can smell it. This is gonna drive a lot of 'em out, 'cause that fast-talking bunch will take over fer sure." Then he smiled, and said: "But what the hell, huh? Like ya say, life goes on. Wanna have a beer with me an' Shorty, later on?"

"I'll look for you when I come in to shower," said Whitey. As he walked through the trees to his camp, he realized that Milo's question was a good one, and his answer fell short. Milo was surely one of those green people Abe had spoken about—Shorty too. His heart went out to them even more than it had to Bob Carr and his family. This was not an easy world for green people.

Perhaps green people are fools, on the go, with nowhere left to go to. So maybe they have to let go . . . Where can green people go from here? Where? Whitey sighed and headed for his tent.

The funeral was a large one, for Sweet Home, and was well attended by Bob's employees and close personal friends. But there were none of those so-called *important* people present who had come to play such a dominant role in his life during the past several years, after he had chanced into wealth and status. In the end, he'd fallen from power and status and respect, and not a single lumber baron showed up to pay his final respects, not even Evan Grace. They feigned the pretext of noninvolvement in his life's affairs. On this same day, some of them sullied the name of a dead man with tainted lies, given out to newspapers, in a vain attempt to cover their own dirty rears.

It seemed Evan Grace soiled even his soul and couldn't stand the stench of it. One year later to the day, he was found hanging by his neck from one of the laminated redwood beams that spanned the length of the vaulted ceilings in his living room. He'd taken a shower and put on a bathrobe. Then he climbed up on a stool, noosed his neck with a rope, and kicked the stool away. There he hung, draped by his robe, his eyes staring away into nothing, his feet dangling above droppings of his excrement. He left a note. It read: "Please do not bury me in the forest."

Lilly Carr glanced in Whitey's direction. Even here, in a funeral parlor, even shrouded in dark sorrow, her bearing pulled at him, and in him something slipped off center. Thoughts, out of order in a funeral procession, filed through his head. She nodded a subtle salute. He acknowledged with his own slight nod. Then she walked slowly up to him. "Hello, Whitey," she quietly said, "thank you for coming. Bobby would have liked that." Her eyes suddenly misted over with tears at the mention of her husband's name. I'm sorry. I . . . I, didn't come over here to cry in front of you." She wiped her tears with her hankie.

Whitey felt an overwhelming urge to reach out and hold her close. He wanted to say something to console her, but got lost in his awe instead and clumsily stumbled through his thoughts, searching for words. Some awkward moments passed, until he managed to say: "I'm sorry too, Lilly." His words felt and sounded stilted and stoic. He wanted, more than anything, to sound warm, and compassionate.

She regained her composure and looked at him. Their eyes met, and the corners of her lips formed a slight smile. So, as it turned out, she soothed him and melted the frigidity from his nerves, and he added: "He was a fine man, Lilly, and he will be missed by some good people."

She looked him directly in the eye and didn't shirk a bit when she said: "Do you think so? Do you really? There are a lot of people about who have been saying that he wasn't. You know all about that, don't you?"

Fact was, Whitey knew little about it. He knew only enough to know there were character thieves, sneaking about. Her easy courage touched his heart and he could only stand and gawk in respectful amazement. Then he said: "Lilly, do you know that old story about throwing the first stone?"

"Yes, I know it well enough," she answered.

"Well, that all happened in a different world from this one. These days, there are just all too many people who would have been more than willing to throw that first stone, as well as the last one. Except, now, stones are words and gossip is the rock pile. That girl wouldn't have stood a chance, here."

Hearing this, Lilly relaxed and squared her shoulders. Whitey knew he'd helped her and he felt more comfortable; still, her sorrow saddened him and he suddenly felt warm and gushy. His eyes misted over, and he reached for his back pocket but his hand came back empty; he'd left his rag at home. Quickly, Lilly offered him her own damp hankie. Again, he thought he saw the beginnings of a smile. As he wiped his tears, feeling her moisture in that hankie was almost more than he could bear. She stepped forward and put her arms about him and embraced him. Her hair brushed his cheeks. That sweet natural redolence that only fine women exude entered his nostrils and sugared his brain. This *was* more than he could bear. The congregation instantly faded away, along with the room where they stood, along with their separate worlds, along with pretensions and societal baloney. They stood together, the logger and the lady, embracing in solitude.

Lilly spoke. Her words seemed to fall like soft tears: "Oh, Whitey," she said, "always be my friend. Never forget me."

"I could sooner forget myself," he said.

She said: "I've lived a thousand years in this last single year. I'm afraid this next year isn't going to be any different. Will you forget me in another thousand years? I'm afraid you will."

"Not in a thousand lifetimes, Lilly.

"Whitey" . . . Lilly paused. "Are you . . . are you going back to the camp or staying over?"

"Staying over. Headed back tomorrow with Milo."

"Where?"

"Santiam Motel" . . . Now, Whitey paused, wondering about his next words: "Room nine."

The funeral processed.

It's quiet in early autumn: summer's gusts have died away; winter's winds remain unborn; songbirds are flying away; air's crispy dry; leaves are wrinkling up and falling onto the sluggish river then patchworking into a colorful but cold quilt and then folding up in the eddies. Night comes early and stays later—plenty of time for moon shadows.

Night is falling in. A short distance from here, just beyond the Coast Range, out over the Pacific, the sun and the loons are settling into their water bed. The sun closes his sleepy red eye, and the loons fold their wings and rest their heads upon the downy pillows of their backs. Seems the sun has diddled the moon: she can't sleep at night, rises and wanders around in the dark, pregnant, carrying the seed of her lover in her big round belly. And the drifting loons sleep upon their silvery sheet and cast tiny moon shadows, thousands and thousands of tiny moon shadows.

There's no time in death. The way Lilly figured it, Bob was as cold right now as he'd ever be. How could he possibly give a damn? And if *he* didn't, what the hell did it matter who might? She wasn't headed for heaven or to hell based upon the opinions of other people. And now, other than Jeremy and Whitey, other people was all there was for her.

I'm not married any longer. I'm no man's wife, now. So be faithful . . ? To whom? To what? To death? To futureless memories? Or to desire—desire for touch, for life, for love? She'd heard it said that desire unfulfilled is desire that must be filled, sooner or later. They say it's a cosmic law. *Better sooner, then. Sooner, because I can't stand to wait until later, law or no law. Besides, later may be too late.*

The thoughts in Lilly's head were haunting, like the dark moon shadows that fell upon the road, moving in and out, first here then gone again -- shadows of the moon, shadows of the mind, too dark, too scary to peer into. She tried to ignore them. She couldn't say which bothered her most, the light or the shadows. She wished the moon would slip behind a cloud and the fleeting shadows disappear once and for all, and she'd be hidden in the dark.

Her darkest thought was like the deepest shadow, hardest to face, to approach, to step into: she'd held this desire long before Bob died. She'd gone to bed with it every night and woke up with it every morning since the dinner at the Hosking's. Desire had filled her dreams, but the dreams were empty and couldn't fill desire.

Yes, unfulfilled desires must be filled. Is it a cosmic law? -- Or maybe the devil's curse . . .

Lilly pulled the car to the curb and parked under some maples. She stepped out into moon shadows. A shadow amongst shadows, in her widow's black, she walked briskly toward the motel, went to room number nine, paused, knocked. Her heart was beating in her throat. Whitey opened the door. Both felt awkward. Whitey avoided eye contact; his mind searched for words, but Lilly spoke: "I don't want to be consumed by another person's death. I don't want to die before my life is over. I'm afraid you'll forget me, Whitey. I can't leave here and live with that fear, without going insane."

"I could never . . ."

"Please don't . . . don't talk. I'm not here to talk. I've come to make a new memory, something to hold onto—to see me though for a while—for a thousand years or more."

"I'm not the talking kind, Lilly."

And Whitey said not another word this night, because he knew what Lilly knew: there's plenty of time for words, so little time for touch. He reached over and turned off the light. Lilly stepped in and closed the door. Moonlight poured through the window and etched the walls with moon shadows.

Moon shadows touching the wall, embracing, making love upon the wall, loving in the second dimension. Night rhythms flow and the shadows rock to and fro, up and down they go, parting, coming together, and with no other dimension to separate them, merge.

The air was cold in the late night hours. The nip felt good. Lilly lay awake, listening to Whitey's soft breathing. The tireless restless timberjack was tired and resting. His head lay upon her breasts. His warm breath upon her cold nipples made them pucker and stand erect.

She smiled. Quite a successful strategy this turned out to be. Her desire was filled to overflowing. Now she had something to bank on. The fear of dying while still living was gone. Only living remained—money in the bank—ahh, sweet security. There was only her duty to do, and by God, she could see it though, like a good executive, and not be haunted by moon shadows. She had a new memory, a fresh full memory, pregnant as tonight's full moon and just as bright, to fill her dreams. There's no moon shadows on the moon. She'd displaced her desire with a long-term, high-interest bond and bought some time to boot, and all it had cost her was some love. Love—she was the manufacturer and the buyer and the seller of that commodity. What a wheeler-dealer! Whitey couldn't forget her now, even if he wanted to. Some love, of which she had plenty in her treasury, and a little bit of touch thrown in to clinch the deal, in exchange for time and for Whitey—what a sweet deal! Talk about bargains . . . She'd recapitalized and renewed her interest in life. Her equity was compounding, building in her soul, living and growing, a living trust, and security for her future. Was she one hell of entrepreneur, or what! A *real* impresario. Ahhh, security.

She closed her eyes. Outside, a cloud drifted in and covered the moon and everything else with peaceful darkness.

And so, Whitey and Lilly touched tonight and merged, like two moon shadows in a passing moment, and came together as a man and a woman and mixed memories for eternity—but not their worlds. Worlds move slowly. Unlike shadows, worlds need time's dimension. He was still the logger with one last job to do and she was still the lady, widow of a lumber baron with a child to wean and a lumber empire to dispose of. A lady has commitments. And it takes a mourning widow lady a long time to bury her complicated world. It's a deep grave to dig.

The sleepy moon settles into bed with her lover. He opens his eye, rolls over and rises. The loons wake up, spread their wings in a stretch, and go looking for fish. Whitey and Lilly part. Lilly heads for Portland, where she will loosen her knots and tie up all of Bob's loose ends. She needs to contemplate upon her life and eventually free herself from the pressures of the past, so that she can live unencumbered in the present. For the time being, she'll hold her new memory close and dream of the future. She'll wait till she knows the time is right—what time? Time for what? Who knows? She has her intuitions and her inclinations and she's got her timing down pat; she'll let time work for her like an employee should. Whitey goes back to the woods. His world is nearing its end; he has to see it through. Like a good captain, a man shouldn't jump a sinking world.

It might seem to the casual observer that Whitey and Lilly had put miles and even cultures between them, but to one who sees the invisible threads, they hadn't parted by an inch. One or the other or both together often reeled in a certain fine thread, and so they met from time to time, both day and night, in the land of fancy.

Things are language. They speak and they can not lie. An apple says: look at my hue and study my shape, is it not a fine fit for your hand, enticing to your eye and your tongue? Now look *and* see: I abide in my silent core. All else, every single bit, is simply my texture, so juicy sweet and transient; the same sun that feeds the green tree that grows me burns it all into a shrivel – if I but hang out there on my limb . . . So take a bite my man, and keep right on eating, devour core and all; but don't swallow the rest and spit *me* out. And when the purging urge comes, brace your back against the trunk of my tree, then bend your knees so's to lower your ass and and spread your bung. Strain a little and pass me through back down to the ground so that I will forever over and over be here for you. My dear man, we are not so different, you and me...

In the ancient days, back in the time when Pan was sovereign and when the wind and the forest were lovers, the forest greeted the sweet wind in the spring when he arrived and sighed when he touched her. He slid softly in through her limbs and caressed her, and he licked her with his wet tongue, and her limbs trembled and her leaves quivered. His moisture swelled her cones and opened their slits, and she oozed and spewed her seeds. The wind carried the seeds near and far and then lay them gently down in cool damp places. But *that* time was not *this* time.

All that changed when the wind lost his lover. In this time, trees are thinned and vast stands cut away, leaving little resistance to the sharp-clawed storms of winter. Now, the melting snow loosens the soil, and a stiff wind funnels through a river canyon and the canyon rolls it up into the form of a spear, pointed at the forest's heart. Once, the forest could stand against these wind shears because it was thick with trees that formed a solid wall of wood and was secure within a towering defense that dwarfed The Great Wall of China. It stood over two hundred feet high and over a hundred miles thick and many hundreds of miles in length. Only the timeworn defenders succumbed and fell out of the ranks and gave up their juices to the ground. Others quickly closed the line.

But now, the spear is thrown from the canyon by the advancing storm and the ancient phalanx is fragmented. It can be breached in countless places. One spear comes and then another and then another (for there are many canyons, and storms are ceaseless), and each spear spreads and forms a shear, and the forest is raked with many sharp points. The forest's defenses fall back and crash down upon their limbs and spread their roots to the sky and lay in long columns of blow-down and splintered spikes raking at the sky, and these are called "salvage" by commerce. The soft green floor that was carpeted with moss and grew fiddle fern and twinflower and nettle becomes a litter of dead and rotting limbs and "unsalvageable" carcass.

The litter is called "slash" and burned away in clouds of black smoke. The shade-loving salamander and the moist earthworm give way to beetles, and the ground grows hard and brittle under the wind and sun. The beetles do what *beetle* does and crawl among and upon the dead and into the living, and burrow down under the bark into the cambium and lay their eggs upon tender fresh meat. And the grubs hatch from the eggs and grubs do what *grub* does and feed on the meat and suck away the juices and reemerge as more beetles. And the trees grow sick and weak. The ants come, and ants do what *ant* does and enter in through the beetle burrows and scurry about the grub tunnels and chew their way into the marrow. Green turns to yellow and then to red and then to brindle brown, and the needles fall away, and the living trees die, standing.

In time, even the dead fall into Lucifer's fire, until only empty air stands there in that place that was once filled and overflowed. The emptiness can be peered into, like a polished mirror, shimmering and clear, reflecting the poverty of mass ignorance. Few individuals dare to look because to peer into the depths of the ignorance and the poverty means to see one's self—and nothing else.

The Forest Service sends in crews of men and machinery to saw down the dead and dying and then heap them up and burn them, because they say these trees are "diseased" and that the forest has been invaded by insects. The bugs are to blame. Chemicals are dumped to rid the forest of its invaders. And the thunderheads form, and the thunder rolls and booms, and the big raindrops fall and leach the insecticides, along with the topsoil and the nutrients of long lost eons, into gullies, and the gullies carry it to the streams, and it mixes with the streams and flows into the rivers and mixes with the rivers and travels with the rivers to the ocean.

A beginning and an end—a history—short tall tale—a sliver of time whittled out like a woodchip, falls away into selective memory—an era. Like a timberjack knifed in a barroom brawl, a mighty era ends in a trite *scenario*:

The alliance sues for peace on the winter solstice—darkest day of the year. The Southern Gentleman is now king of the woodlands. To the victor goes the stumpage. To the loser goes the slash. The baron's surrender unconditionally. No terms. Sign on the dotted line, please – or else.

The dictates: the name Carr Timber Products will be retained for two years as a commemorative to its founder and builder, and to pacify the employees. After this, the new owner's identity will be ceremoniously and officially adopted. There will, however, be a gradual blending, as one name is phased out and the other name is implemented. With certain variations, but in similar fashion, the rest of the barons surrender their fiefdoms.

Most of the barons will remain on the payrolls and receive bloated wages in the form of *consulting* fees. Of course, it's all a ruse calculated by the tax accountants for corporate and personal capital gains and the rest of the tax gimmickry. In effect, they are stripped of power and hold figurehead positions.

The elimination of the many old names and tying it all into one new name is referred to in the corporate syntax as "the consolidation." This new consolidated entity grows like a bark fungus and The Southern Gentleman stretches his corporate belly, as he gorges on trees and culture. He digests the forest and shits his eastern privies full of money. Near the end of his tenure, he's informed by the justice department that he may, just possibly, be in violation of some vague anti-trust laws that state that it's, somehow, unfair for one thing to own all of everything, whether directly or indirectly, and in effect brook no competition in a system that is supposed to encourage competitors. All sorts of high-level legal mumbo jumbo get mumbled about. Rumors swarm like starlings. Eventually the consolidated corporation *regrettably* agrees to do the *proper* thing and whittle itself down so that others can get in on a piece of the action. The Southern Gentleman is advised by the regulators to break off chunks of his holdings and sell them. This he does, and reaps incredible long-term capital gains. The selling off of equity chunks is referred to as "the dissolution," and good ol' George Presco vis-à-vis The Southern Gentleman or whoever or whatever'n the hell that was, finally, supposedly, goes his merry way, leaving the once great forest enervated beyond redemption—ancient no longer. It was every bit and all rape and run. Left in the Southern Gentleman's swath, a dozen or more corporate clones jockey for position. There are spoils to reap. End of *scenario.*

The ground that a man stands upon grounds him. The place where people live tells a true tale if they will listen. It defines them, telling them where they came from and what they are and what they can become. It's the *what they are* part that is most immediate, therefore of most concern, because this part of the equation tells them what they *have* become and in this, the case of the woodsy folk: deaf people who should've listened to their place. Because, as is the case with so many tales, tall or true, this one ended with woe. The only real loser in all this warfare and peace-making was the unique culture of the Pacific Northwest. The woodsy folk felled their Lebensraum. The era of the big woods has fallen away with the giant trees. Only tears remain to fall—time for Diaspora.

The board of directors of Atlantic Oregon Kilns Inc., joined together around the oaken board table, merged minds, divined the corporate psyche, and manifested their logo. Atlantic Oregon Kilns Inc., they reasoned, was too big of a mouthful, and to simply refer to it as "the company" lacked proper respect. It was decided that henceforth it would be referred to as AOK. Besides easy to remember, there's a mollifying ring to it; the hoi polloi takes official statement and the written word as truth. Their appeal was to the literal sense. This is the only sense comprehendible to this particular mindset, because it thinks its core is empty. So, they stated and they published.

The company's public name became its initials, and in the name of aesthetics the vertical line of the letter K was extended upward and spread into an abstraction of a tree. In such manner, Atlantic Oregon Kilns Inc. managed to revamp and upgrade its image without actually changing its name—or much of anything else. However, there were more than a few people who transcended the literal sense. They remained unimpressed and said with some humor that the abstract tree in the K looked like it had a propped-up hard-on and was out to put a screwing to everything.

Golden-yellow, trimmed in green, was adopted as the company colors and applied to its banners. All buildings, vehicles, hats, jackets, and the like would be colored in golden-yellow and branded with the green AOK logo. There could be no mistake about property rights. Then, dipping into its endless sea of yellow gold and green paper money, AOK started painting the entire region golden-yellow, trimmed with green.

In this manner the woodsy folk were presented with their golden calf molded into the form of *progress*. A multitude danced and orgied about it. They flocked to their churches every Sunday morning where they begged the vicars to bring them good economy and prayed to their lords for more of the same – as if God could be converted into a good company man. There was no Moses in their mountains to descend from the highest peak and save them from their folly. He lives, now, in the hearts of men—some men—and men such as these chose to stay upon the mountain and let the frenzy proceed. These men remained above the fray and preserved their clay tablets.

After the baron war, things settled down, as though into an efficiently sustained schedule, and life in the Lava Lake camp took on a monotonous beat, much like that of a well-oiled machine. The old light-hearted pizzazz that once filled the atmosphere seemed to be blown away by some heavy air of ennui.

But, things were popping on the corporate scene. The price of stumpage was falling as fast as the timber. The newspapers typed up the mantra of the times: all the much-ado about the overbid contracts and how the bidders, those poor old ex-barons, could not possibly have foreseen the economic repercussions, and how they were forlorn victims of a quirk in circumstances beyond their control. The papers begged for pity on behalf of the *present-innocent* contract holders and their *at-risk* employees, and like ancient prophets foretold of economic catastrophe—short of contract relief. Of course, there were many contract holders, but only one owner.

When they were in charge, the old barons couldn't afford to close down plants, even in the face of losses, because the mills were all they had—to shut a plant down meant to run the risk of never being able to start it back up again. But the Southern Gentleman can shut them down. The king has a new weapon in his arsenal called "plant shutdown." Shut down an antiquated plant here and another there and then blame it on the high stumpage contracts. Threaten the economy with disaster, prick security, and whip up hysteria. Yell it loud. Publish it: "The castle is falling! The castle is falling!" Now scare the bejesus out of lawmakers with loss of votes. They'll sell their soul for another term. Buy it at a bargain. Rally the workers for the hundredth time and parade the streets with hoopla; line up the sad-eyed kids; blow the air horns. Tie ribbons around your antenna and fly your colors. Write your congressman a dozen times and cry tear spots onto the stationary. Keep going to church; be persistent.

Behold! Praying must pay off . . . The mood in the capital city is miraculously changing. Congressmen are counting signatures on petitions, reading their letters, hearing the pleas, and their ears are now opened to compassion. The great senators have reappeared. Animated again, they wield their mighty power, power garnered by long-standing membership among the political elite, committee-chairmanship-kind-of-power that no newly-elected newcomer could possibly hope to command, power enough to convince the federal government to forgive the old contracts and roll them back. "Contract relief" is the political catchword of the day.

AOK is granted substantial rollbacks on every one of its contracts, those same contracts bid up so high by the old barons. Relief is as thick as fall fogs. The workers of the woodlands sure are happy and grateful; the corporation is going to survive and *grow*. Hallelujah! Hallelujah! God *is* merciful to those who *believe*.

Heady times are back again. Interest rates fall as fast as the timber. Canadian lumber imports are stopped dead in their ports, with tariffs. A building boom explodes. Lumber prices skyrocket straight up to over the highest tree top, and along with them goes AOK's stock for a high ride. (Eastern money-men must know how to pray, too.) The consumer's appetite for wood products is insatiable. People are encouraged to measure themselves, not by the space *they* displace, but by the space that houses them, and so happy homeowners stretch their tape first this way then that way, times the one against the other, and add up their square feet. Clear all-heart of any kind is the trend of the times. Crummies depart town earlier and return latter while logging crews work overtime in all weather. Mills spin their circle saws around the clock. Day shift, night shift, graveyard shift, shift and merge, as mill workers double up their hours. No matter how hard they work to gear up for the unleashed demand, the logging companies can't fall the trees or saw the logs fast enough to feed it.

Manufactures of logging machinery can't weld and rivet their iron together fast enough. Black-bottomed Asian ships, lined up at the ports, waiting for logs, can't get in and out fast enough. Lumberyards stack it higher and expand their stacking space. It's like wood eaters in a feeding frenzy. Oh happy days! Progress has returned to the Northwest. The AOK products development labs are kept busy conniving new uses for wood products. Legions of salesmen plan advertising blitzes and create new trends in such things as chipboard siding, paneling, and throw-away paper diapers.

Whitey stayed on the mountain side where the view is better. In his view it was all and every bit searching after effect and hiding from fear of failure. It was nothing but dissipation, shriveling on the tree limb, so *nothing* was what it amounted to and so failure was certain. Those paper diapers held more substance. It seemed to him as if people meant nothing to *themselves* these days – transient texture with empty cores. Seemed they'd *re*-grounded themselves into their seedless corporation. They wanted the *corporation* to transcend its numbers, diversify, profit and grow. For all it came to they'd do just as well to go out into the woods and devour the toxic fruit of devil's club.

Finally, at long last, he figured he'd mastered *"nothing."* The Professor's last lesson for him was that he had *"nothing to learn."* As usual with the Professor's lessons, this one went over his head at the time, but now he clearly saw the meaning reflected right back at him. Woody told him that the machine was going to take over. He'd understood that at the time, sorta, but disregarded it because he didn't like the sound of it, and the way it made him feel. He'd preferred to ignore his mood, and so had forgotten the weight of Woody's words, till now. Abe walked away from a world he loved rather than deny the truth of its impending destruction, and participate in it. So, the Professor taught him in his teachings, Woody told him in his tellings, and Abe showed him by example and still he chose to disbelieve the truth of it. Well, so much for belief, one way or the other. Now he understood that *nothing* is the seat of the devil because there's no power in it. The devil loves powerless people. He can easily gather them and lead them. He's a liar without shame. He says: "Follow me and you'll have *nothing* to fear." This is the only truth he's ever told.

Powerful people find what they're searching for even if they have to make it up.

Chapter 25   The Beer-Bellied Man

There was once a sublime presence in the Cascades. It sang under the stars and cast long shadows that loped between the dark trees, and it melted into the wood with the crepuscular mists. Rodents were its tidbits; the blacktail was its supper. It was called the Cascade Wolf. It had lived in these mountains since their fiery beginning. And it ran free. But it ran across the path of some men, and they called it an interloper. It only took those few men a few years to poison away the Cascade Wolf. And so, the Cascades lost their wolf...

AOK couldn't abide the thought of anything, man or animal, running free and wolf-like upon its timberlands. Gates of metal I-beams at the road heads kept the public out of the *tree farms*. The U.S. Forest Service served: thinned the grazing herds and ran the clever little black bear—who strips the bark to lick the sap—down with hounds and exterminated him, as if he were a black rat.

Open season, all year long, was declared on poor, slow little porky. "Kill the porky out of the pine," was the slogan. Along the forest trails and roads, signs were posted that said: "Please Shoot Porcupines". Porky curled himself up and thought he was safe, but quills are little protection against hot lead.

Virtually all critters were considered enemies of the same trees that had harbored and nurtured them for millenniums. But AOK was the friend of the tree, for after all, wasn't it planting some shoots? Why, that takes an expenditure of capital! The forest was in its debt.

Chemical warfare was declared, and the wretched *barren* war began in earnest. The planter sprayed the mountains with chemical defoliants from aircraft in order to keep out "unwanted growth" such as: rhododendron, viny maple, salal berry, kinnikinnick, huckleberry, and other broadleaves that shade the ground and keep it moist. Gotta make room for the seedlings to grow their thickets. Good-bye bright-eyed dogwood, alder groves, shaggy-headed beargrass, delicate Indian pipes and pearly everlasting. Good-bye to the tangy Oregon grape, till another time, perhaps. Hello corporate plantings.

Those mandibled enemies, those hoppers and crawlers, complete with wing and armor, would live to rue their timeless challenge with a whiff of pesticide.

The forest was "fertilized" with the same aircraft that poisoned it. So, instead of bees, the forest shook to the drone of aircraft, spraying white pellets, and was left looking like an out-of-season hail storm just passed through. The mess festered for several days until the elements did their job of decomposing it all into leaf and soil. The delusion is that the new forest doesn't need the old and can grow without its humus—as though a human could grow minus the humus of human history and the genetics of creative thought.

Innocence was dead. Any native logger with at least one good eye and an open mind could see the devastation going on in the woodlands. This was the age of hard steel verses soft wood, and of money and greed verses intelligence and sympathy. Free-flowing streams that had flowed through millenniums were destroyed in a single day, watersheds laid bare, entire mountainsides denuded by powersaws and dozed open by cat tracks.

What didn't make the *grade* was stamped with "reject" and discarded. Reject trees, not worth hauling to the mill, lay scattered about with discarded logs, or in heaps like jackstraws, that were torched and went up in flames, scorching the soil. Earth died, bit, by bit, by bit. A pall of smoke blackened the blue eye of heaven.

The old abundance was fast qiving way to nonexistence. Endless networks of graveled logging road, stretching and twisting like hardened veins, connected pockmarks; like smallpox these spread at their edges and merged. Dust was kept down with a coating of petroleum residues. Of course every mile of this road was necessary, went the argument of the day, in order to prevent forest fire. This made it sound like the forest was being done a favor by cutting it down to save it from burning down. The red wolf was not only fought – he was *banned*.

One summer day, while having lunch, Whitey looked down at his side and saw a bumblebee resting in a mountain aster. A closer look revealed that the bee was dead. He'd seen this scene before. Looking at that bee, he felt awed by the last act of that bumblebee. When it was his time to go, the bee sought out beauty to die in. It was the same beauty that had supported that bee when he lived. It fed him. Now he would feed it. His thought often returned to the vision of the dead bee in the flower. What a noble vision that was—to die in beauty. It seemed as though the world of men was upside-down: the bee was as busy as ever, but the flower was dying. A busy bee in a dead flower makes no sense at all.

Whitey was witnessing the apex of a dire mistake. It all started a long time before in the form of a misconception. In the olden days the woodsy folk said they wanted to "open up the woods and let the light shine in." Cut out a place for a man to live and spread, where children would grow tall. They didn't know better. The way they saw it, there was plenty of forest and scant light. But the forest doesn't grow *in* light. It grows *toward* the light. That was before they knew that the Pacific yew will die in bright light and even the hardy hemlock has a hard time living there. That was when the big woods seemed endless. That was then and not these days. These days, men knew better—but they were doing it regardless, because there's a market for *quality* in Japan, and the Italians don't want knots in their window frames. Clear lumber requires clear wood, and clear wood requires limbless logs, and logs of such pure quality can be cut only from tall trees. At this rate their replacements will never grow tall.

Where the wind once blew cool and whispered through high evergreens, and where seedlings had sprouted in the damp shade, now it was blowing hot and unimpeded through acre upon empty acre of stumps and tangled cables, wasting away, rotting and rusting among the ground-hogging blackberry vines.

Whitey stayed at the camp and held his job as side boss. Kevin made the corporate transition, in good form. He was promoted to the title of Vice President of Timberlands and moved to Portland into the erection.

Poor, pathetic little Punkie . . . He happened to be in the area and dropped by to see Whitey. It was a sunny summer day with a stiff wind rocking the treetops. Kevin was introducing a newly-hired executive to all the side bosses, orienting him to his new position, a big-footed, ruddy-faced man named Claude. Claude seemed disinterested in talking to Whitey, so went walking all around, looking things over, busily taking down notes on a pad. Kevin and Whitey stood alongside the spanking-new, golden-yellow pickup.

Kevin was in a talking mood, but he didn't discuss old times. Old times, it seemed, were too old for a modern-type man. It was plain to see that he was shackled by golden handcuffs. Whitey's heart sank at the sight of his fettered friend. Kevin was suffering from a bad case of light-headed stupors, brought on from gulping too much corporate moonshine. This causes severe memory loss, and so he had forgotten all the hard-learned lessons. He boasted of his recent promotion and then lowered his voice, almost to a whisper, saying: "I made a killing on the sale of my house in Sweet Home." Whitey could only assume that Claude had been killed. Then Kevin boasted of his new house: "One of the finest in Portland's West Hills." He said that Lorraine was absolutely giddy with the developments. Whitey said: "That's lovely." Kevin went on to say that the new company was "very generous," and he was allowed to buy in "on ground floor level" and that he was going to "get rich" through stock options. Whitey said: "That's lovely, too."

And so Kevin went on, babbling trivia but acting somewhat nervous all the while. Whitey was well aware that Kevin fidgeted the entire time and looked first this way then that, then up, then down, but never, not once, did Kevin look him in the eye. Kevin's last words before departing were: "Lorraine wants to have you up for dinner again, real soon." He fibbed. Then Kevin called Claude back over and they climbed into the golden-yellow pickup, with the logo of a tree with a propped-up hard-on, and Kevin disappeared in a cloud of red cinder dust.

Whitey knew all was pipe dreams pouring out as fibs and self-delusion from the end of Kevin's wordy pipeline. Watching him drive away he felt his heart harden towards the venal man. Time can do *for* or do *to*. Kevin was done *in*. This same man was once that forlorn little punk, who wanted only some friends he could trust. Godamighty, one would think he'd never found them!

Looking into the dust-trail of the disappearing pickup, he drawled out a slow low tone that he hadn't heard for a long time. It was mellow as though pulled from a deep well, and felt to the ear like cool flowing butter; the words were soothing upon his tongue: "He ain't worth savin' this time, my ol' frien'. Hell, ain't nobody'd want to." But the tone was not his own to keep and he spoke only to the wistful wind.

Like an insecure executive, the Lava Lake camp changed its personality with the changing of logo. Whitey felt uneasy in the presence of these new folks. They were too much the company men and had lost something of themselves in a poorly struck bargain. They seemed to have lost a degree of love, reciprocal love, requited love, a certain kind of ineffable intensity. It seemed theirs was a one-way love, and it centered around exploitation only. He couldn't say they didn't love these mountains and trees and forests. Surely, Kevin did. With his roots, he had to love them. But they needed an excuse to be there; plain love wasn't enough for them. They needed to say they represented the company, so they could say they were there for business; any other reason was beneath them.

This new thing Whitey saw, like a growing cancer, made him feel more and more uneasy and even began to pique his conscience. This was all take and no asking and no giving back—there was no expending of the man into it. These men couldn't see the tree. They saw only so much wood, measured into board feet, converted into section yield, then into growth cycles. It was all measure by scale, and sadly, it seemed, they didn't even measure men much differently. It was far from them to see into the core. In days past, a man with a sharp saw or quick axe in his hand could feel the core. He could say he had a reason. He could say to Tree, herself: "I am taking you so that I can come to know you better," suspecting that the *knowing* was reciprocal.

These new men didn't believe that a tree could have a heart with a beat. How to measure heart? Where measuring stopped, they stopped. They couldn't transcend their simple math. To such men as this, the sight of logs piled up in the mill's cold decks, sprinkled down with water from the stagnant millpond, was more sublime than the standing forest from which those logs had come.

But strangely, the thing that piqued Whitey's conscience the most was the corporation's insistence on referring to its holdings as "plantations" and "tree farms" and claiming they were harvesting crops. This "crop" didn't feed the family; it was gobbled up by mill machinery. This viewpoint made him a farm laborer, something he'd run away from a long time ago. Was he lost in the woods? Had he run full circle—gone nowhere? One thing was for sure: the free-wheeling logger had gone down the road of time like some runaway.

Goddamned . . . Goddamned! Am I a reluctant farmer, growing food for a damned machine? Then he asked himself: *What the hell does that make me?* The answer was unsettling: *A machine's machine.*

Now, just like once before, he determined to run away from farmers and hard-headed plow mules and become a timberjack. And so he honed his double-headed axe.

They were new to the mountains. Whitey saw the tree planters, with their heavy hoedags and their canvas bags, filled to overflowing with fir seedlings, strapped about their waists. Before the daylight, they gathered along the logging roads and filed off toward the scalped hillsides.

This morning, he sat on a stump, taking a break from work. A thick mist was gathering on his hat, water drops hung off its rim. The whistle was beeping out electronic signals from the choker setters to the yarder operator. The yarder was straining and roaring, and the cables in the highlead were swinging through the rigging. The guy lines were as tight as fiddle strings. The spar tree stood firm against the pressure. He'd rigged it well. Off through the mist on the hillside the other side of the canyon, some planters were hard at work. He wasn't listening to the whistles or to the singing of the cables or even to the roar of the yarder. He was listening to his vision.

The scene was silent, almost ghostly. It was late autumn in the mountains. The logged-off hillside across the way was hued in browns and blacks and russets. The planters were clothed in wool, same colors as the hillside; some wore metal hats but most had on brown or navy blue watch caps. The mist absorbed the sounds of their movements. They stood shoulder to shoulder in long thin lines across the steep grade, their backs stooped, their heads down, their faces to the ground. Up went the hoedags over their shoulders to above their backs, up into the air, and there they paused, then down arced the hoedags to strike the ground, digging holes between stumps for the roots of clones that had done nothing to deserve this honor, made no effort, took no risk, never flew in the wind.

Whitey had made the acquaintance of one of those men over there. He was a congenial fellow with the big belly and sallow skin of a heavy drinker. The dark circles around his eyes sagged, and his nose was red and puffy, and the corners of his mouth drooped. As it turned out, his beer belly is why he was up here in these mountains. He and three others were living in a dreary rain-soaked tent camp, alongside the logging road where it sliced a clearcut. A few days prior, headed home after the day's work, Whitey told the crummy driver to let him off at that little camp. He was curious about all these men, suddenly showing up with their hoedags and seedling sacks.

The only person present was the beer-bellied man. He said the others had worked out their time, so they went back to the city. "But plenty more are on their way up. They won't let me get *too* lonely, might drive me to drink." Saying this, he smiled; but only his mouth smiled. Then he said: "I got one more week's work left until I serve my time."

Whitey didn't understand. "What do you mean by that?" he asked.

"Till I work off my sentence," said the man.

Still, Whitey didn't quite get his drift. "What sentence?"

"It's either here or the tank for me."

Whitey suddenly understood. He looked closer at the man, into his eyes. He saw a cold man, who was physically and mentally miserable. The poor man spoke with downcast eyes, as a man with a downtrodden spirit will do. He was as out of place in these high cold mountains as a camel. Yet he had nowhere else to go, except to a cement cell.

For God's sake, what kind of value system is this? Something's bass-ackward here, Whitey said to himself.

Some men are loggers, some are truck drivers, others are mill workers, painters, bankers, lawyers, doctors, priests, or whatever—all comes to the same thing: doings. This man was a conscript. And Whitey felt the grating irony of it all, as if it were a dull-toothed misery harp, sawing away a piece of his heart. He and others like him made good wages falling the trees—bold men, men for myths and tall tales. And this poor bedraggled beer belly was replanting them, one seedling at a time, to keep from going to the drunk tank. It seemed to Whitey they were a couple of unwilling cosmic clowns on a comic's stage, where a man could completely lose his sense of humor—where a man had no choice but to laugh or go straight to morbid hell. He stared into the man's vacuous eyes and felt his own vigor and the vestige of his youth and his sightless ignorance sucked away by those eyes.

How the hell does a person laugh in the face of this vision?

The man was glad to have the company, so Whitey dallied for a good while. As they talked, a heavy mist blew in and settled in the draws. Occasionally, the wailing call of a pileated woodpecker drifted out from somewhere deep in the old woods, resonated with their chatter, and echoed itself away against the canyon sides.

Chapter 26 The Company Man

"For safety," they said. "Bright colors are better seen in the woods." So was the word from above, and it sounded reasonable. There was always an unarguable rationality to what the company dictated, as though everything was thought out, hashed over, changes made, more thinking, more hashing, and then submitted over to a committee and sifted, sent back with recommendations, more changes made, and the final result implemented. Thought makes perfect. Then they would say: "Okay, hand it down." And the edict would be posted.

Who can argue against *safety*? Only a fool would try, but a man can sure bitch. Right now, bitching was precisely what the crew was doing, while gawking at their brand new golden-yellow company-issue plastic hats. They were big bulky things and complete with that corny logo on each side that ended with that stupid K in the form of a horny tree with the propped-up boner.

The personnel manager made a special trip up the mountain from Sweet Home in the early morning hours, and sat a large cardboard box in each crummy as it loaded up. "Here ya go, boys. They'll keep your noggins safe. Compliments of AOK," he said. Then he walked Whitey off to the side and quietly said: "I'm supposed to tell you to tell them that any man who refuses to wear one of these is to be fired. Sorry to lay that on you." Then he took off in a hurry, headed back to Sweet Home and the safety of his office—he knew loggers.

Someone opened the box and peeked in, then hollered out: "Oh, holy shit, won'tcha lookie here at these gawdawful beanies!" and it had been sour grapes ever since.

No more of the silvered metal doughboy-type were to be allowed. If safety meant being colorful then they were going to be plenty safe enough, no denying that.

Whitey held his own new hat in hand, watching the crew all standing about beneath the trees, in the cool early morning light. Each man was clumsily fumbling with the adjusting straps, trying to get a fit, and complaining to hell itself. It was a comical scene. Some of the hats were too big and flopped down over ears, while others balanced like big apples on the tops of heads. It sounded like a grumbler's convention as they fiddled with adjusting straps and tried to get used to the feel of their new headgear.

Funny thing how a person can become attached to an old hat. If it lasts him long and sees him through hard times as well as good, it can take on the aura of a talisman, and to part with it is akin to leaving something exposed that should be covered. A good hat melts into a man after a while, and he doesn't even know it's there until it's gone. Then he misses it, as if he lost a sweetie who dovetailed in very nicely with him. A person's old hat will often say something about them. There wasn't a man in the bunch who couldn't look at his hat, during quiet moments, and see bits and pieces of his past: the dent when it absorbed the fall he took that time when he jumped from a log in a hurry to get clear of the whipping chokers and fell on his head, and the permanent smudge mark from the glancing blow it received from that swinging limb two years back, and . . . But these new space-age-material plastic hats were just more of the company cloning, and each man knew it. They had no personality to them and never could have. Why, they couldn't dent or even smudge. And they were branded with that dumb-looking logo . . .

Some were growing bold in word, if not deed, except for intrepid little Shorty, whose deeds most often rose to his boasts.

Said Shorty, "Over my dead body, I'll wear a gawddamn apple on my head!"

Grinning wide, Milo said: "He's afraid a bird'l land on it lookin' for a worm and pluck his brain out."

Milo's words helped to lighten the mood. Still, all were exclaiming that they wouldn't wear these "gawddamned cornball hats."

But Shorty was feeling snarly these days. Milo's words didn't humor him. "Then the birds can have the damned thing! At least I'll save my brain!" he yelled and cocked his arm and threw his hat as hard as he could let go.

Whitey watched it fly away. It was pretty up there, sailing through the morning sunlight, catching the rays, tumbling and flashing. It flew way off down the hillside, then dropped and hit square on the top of a stump, bounced like a football off to the right and on down the hill, hit another stump, bounced to the left and then hit the ground square in the thickest part of a thorny blackberry thicket.

Whitey chuckled at the ridiculous scene. He removed his own doughboy hat, that old hat that had survived so many a bump, shed countless raindrops, and reflected away the burning sun and even the hot breath of the Great Red Wolf and several lesser wolves, to boot. He hung it on a tree limb, where he could retrieve it later. Then he walked toward the job site with all the grumblers in tow. All except Shorty, whose boast exceeded his intentions. He was down the hill on his hands and knees with his butt in the air, crawling around in the berry vines, mad as a riled bantam rooster, busily looking for his new hat.

Whitey had to admit those bright, shiny golden-yellow hats, abobbing up and down along the unit edge with the sun-glow lighting them up, certainly made a colorful picture. No argument about it, they were easy to see.

The crew walked through a thicket of knee-high bearberry bushes interspersed with huckleberries. Unseen by them, an entire forest lay just to the side of their trail. On a green leaf, about three feet from the ground, lay every forest that's ever been and every forest that will ever be—all the forests of the ages. A tiny seed lay, still and quiet, upon one of the huckleberry leaves. A leg brushed the bush, but the seed held fast.

It was only a seed—just a seed. Such a tiny thing, a seed, no bigger than a mote in a man's eye, but innate within, it harbors Tree herself. She holds down the flesh of these thin-skinned mountains that face the winds and driven rains. With her to shield them, the mountains live almost forever.

In the pitch dark of the previous night, a sudden breeze shook a limb and rattled a pregnant cone. In the cool wind, a winged seed departed and flew away, flying further than all the others—countless numbers of others. It landed and tumbled its way down through blackberry and huckleberry, wanting the cool dampness of their shade, seeking soil. It settled on a huckleberry leaf and mixed with the dust film. The sun rose bright and red. This is a dangerous place for a tiny seed. Up here against this dark leaf, away from the shade, the sun is deadly.

But danger is not the sun's intent. It warms the bosom of Earth and warms the morning air. Following age-old laws the air expands and rises—up and up and up it rises. Way up high it cools and then condenses and grows heavy and moist and falls and falls and falls. Falling, it warms and dries and slows and then heats and expands and lightens and starts to rise again. The sun moves ever higher, grows hotter, air heats from warm to hot, rising ever faster. Going upward in a rush, the air rubs against itself still coming down. The cold seeks the warm, the warm seeks the cold, and the two create inertia but contain it within their spinning circle. Trapped within itself, inertia takes on the form of a towering cumulus cloud. Up and up and up, goes the cloud, for twenty thousand, thirty thousand, forty thousand feet and more, to the high places where rivers of wind flow eastward. Swift streams clutch at its shaggy head and comb it out, swirling into a flying anvil.

Rising to heaven and falling back down, the cloud tumbles over and over, faster and faster, splintering and mixing, rubbing belly to belly, rumbling amorously, generating friction heat that throws off sparks and glows within its black womb. Finally, growing out of itself it transcends *cloud*, is reborn into an electric cumulonimbus, and radiates a silver nimbus. Its power becomes far too great for a mere cloud to hold. Craving release, it splits open and gives birth to lightning. Heaven grows ominous and dark and streaked by spears of electric fire. (And all of this for a single newborn seed dying upon a leaf.)

Far below, near the ground, the broad leaf warms. Too hot, dehydrated, the tiny seed nears the end—oh, but the flight had been grand! No regrets. Suddenly, a flash of light shatters the gloom! **"Craaak!"** goes the sky; power shatters the air. A resounding boom shakes the ground and rattles the leaf. Another flash: **"Craaak!"** goes the sky again. The seed feels the flash, like heat, but this heat isn't hot. The boom and the rumble, then another boom and another deep rumble; lightning heat stirs the seed.

A water droplet, smaller than the seed, hovered in the wind that morning, where it was clutched by the swirling air and carried around and around and higher and higher and joined with others of its kind, mingled, mixed, and grew. Still higher it flew, ever upward into the cold to where it froze into a pearly stone, large as a hen's egg. Heaved this way and that, rolled and bumped along, rubbing against others through a swirling sea of icy stones, filling with light-power and glowing like a gem, up and up to where a wind river snatched it and carried it away through thunder. Outward, it drifted, swirling in eddies, rolling and bumping and tumbling and finally carried into a shallow bay of the anvil where the currents couldn't support the heavy weights and cast them out one by one by countless millions.

The ice stones fall and fall. For thirty thousand feet or more they fall. Warming, melting into water, they leave off liquid parts of their selves and divide into countless numbers. The once tiny droplet has become a clear shiny drop, round and wet. The drop lands upon the broadleaf and hits it with a force that splatters and streaks the dust and cocks it downward on its springy stem. The stem tenses like a trigger with a cocked hammer, then it releases and springs off and shoots away the seed. Up flies the seed, for maybe an inch or so. Down it tumbles through dripping broadleaves. It hits first one leaf, then another, but doesn't settle this time. Washed away with the dust, it follows the persistent waterfall to the cool black soil beneath, and there it snuggles in. It has found a home. If it is strong and can dig in and stand and grow against heat and ice, mandible, beak and tooth, and the raging winds, perhaps, just perhaps—it is one chance in a million millions—it will give birth to a tree.

High in the sky, the mighty thunderhead, dying, passes away.

When they reached the logging site, Whitey looked up through the spar rigging. The sky was as blue as a deep lake. It was going to get mighty warm this afternoon, for sure. *Good day for thunderhead build-ups. Glad I brought my slicker.*

TIME IS MONEY. Green words against a golden background—words to stir the muse—make a thinking man think up ever more thoughts, inspire the lazy one into action. **CLAUDE EDGER.** Black words against a white background, not as pretty as green on gold, but the name looked damned good snuggled in its prop on the shiny oak desktop, sitting right alongside **TIME IS MONEY**. Usually, the words pacified his whims and urged Claude to dig into his ledgers and set about turning time into money on paper, but today Claude was restless and felt like stretching his legs. Sunbeams streamed through the Venetian blinds of his office window. Outside, there wasn't a cloud in the sky. Scents hung heavy in the air, and the musty smell of the millpond wafted through the half-open window. He was bored with pushing numbers, trying to juggle them, make them balance, justify his projections and secure his position. He pushed away the ledgers and quota reports, walked along the always freshly-waxed hard-wood floor between the looming walls of knotty pine, then right on past the receptionist. "Be gone for the day; headed for the lake," he said back over his shoulder. Then, more to himself: "gonna look things over."

He stepped down the brick steps and walked around the side of the two-story cedar office building to the V.I.P. parking area. He went to his reserved parking space. There he paused and looked out over the twenty acres of cold-decked logs, nested neatly, like a package of giant toothpicks, to a height of forty feet or so.

The water sprinklers were doing their duty and spraying the logs with water from the log pond.

His golden-yellow company pickup was nosed into a neatly printed sign that read "Claude Edgar -- Regional Timberlands Chief"—black on white. Like he always did, he eyed the sign as he opened the door. He turned the key and started the motor, and then pulled out of the mill yard. The pickup turned east at the highway, destined for the Lava Lake operations.

This was a great day. Claude felt invigorated, almost like he was still a kid back in the marines, when he was an up-and-comer in the ranks and on the boxing team. Boy, did he ever kick some ass in those days! -- flattened a few faces, to boot. As he drove, he thought about how he missed the service. He would have died of old age there if they'd have let him, but he was pensioned and once pensioned there's no staying. Then the go-getter goes to work on getting his second pension. Most of the officers went into the bureaucracies, because they're easy. But he didn't want *easy*; he was in the mood for wild and wooly, so he chose the logging industry. He submitted his request, and his contacts came through in fine order and plucked him a prime job with one of the up-and-coming companies in the country. In another ten years he'd still be young, and he'd be in fat city. With two pensions going for him, and if he could get in on the stock incentive programs, how the hell could he go wrong?

Logs were *pouring* into the mill these days, so he was up to quota already and felt like the cock-of-the-walk, like beating his chest and crowing out cock-a-doodle-doo. But what he really wanted to do was to beat the hell out of those quotas. With the price of lumber sky-high like it was, extra production would look mighty good to the big boys upstairs, and the Lava Lake operations were his biggest producer. There were only two months to go up at Lava Lake before the snow put an end to the logging—time is money. So he'd squeeze time like a sponge and get a little more value out of it. Those loggers needed jacking up and thinking *production*. And, he was just the man to do the jacking and make them think—by Jesus if he wasn't! AOK doesn't hire wimps for management.

His biggest fear was that the snows would start too early and cost him lost time and production and this would get Hoskings on his ass. That cold-eyed bastard wasn't anybody a man wanted on his ass. But he had an in with Hoskings. Hadn't he bought his house in Sweet Home? Didn't even haggle over the price. So if it took a little bit of kicking ass today to cover his own bottom with some insurance, well . . . he'd simply do some ass kicking. Have a little bit of fun, maybe.

On the way, along the winding asphalt, paralleling the South Santiam, Claude met a vari-colored river of logging trucks flowing down the hill, floating their logs upon their bunks between hard banks of steel stakes and cheese blocks. One rushed by at least every minute on its way to the mill sites down in the valley.

If Claude could look *and* see he'd know that the caddis flies are emerging from out of the water, in the full bloom of an endless circle, faithfully fulfilling their destiny. The big slow-flying bugs are everywhere, especially along the surface of the Santiam. Some are hatching, others are laying eggs down there on the pools, taking their chances against the birds and fish. For them it comes down to beget before you die; time is prodigy. Most will hatch, breed, and die on the same day.

Vine maples are beginning to blush a bit of pink, and the river dribbles along at this time, shrunk up to a series of riffles that cascade into turquoise pools, where it rests for a quiet moment or two before the next riffle. The riffles run and sparkle in the slanting September sunbeams.

Swallows are gorging on the hatch. They're diving, darting, swooping, and skimming the surfaces of the pools, sipping up emerging hatchlings, cripples and vulnerable egg layers. Their olive-hued backs are almost invisible against the pools but a quick eye can catch their movements, if it tries. They dimple the river's wet skin then bank away and speed upward through the air, catch the sun, and expose their bellies in silver flashes against the dark firs. In the river the olive-backed, silver-bellied cutthroats and rainbows are doing exactly the same thing in reverse, in their own space. Two feeding frenzies are going on, coming and going, meeting at the water's surface. There's one world above and another world below, separated only by the fathomless, depthless, two-dimensional world of a water skipper.

Claude couldn't consider that—even in the same moment the scene was changing—that in the next moment's time, it will be old. So how could he know that if he didn't see it he lost it forever? The swallows are fattening up for their long flight to far-away southern places. The caddis flies will power them there. These mountain breeds won't even slow down at Capistrano, coming or going— nothing less than the high Andes will appeal to them. For the trout, it's time to go to work. Those mighty little fish are out of their summer lethargy, stocking up some energy, getting prepared for the floods of winter and spring, when this lazy trickle they live in today is going to turn into a menacing torrent of silt and debris, threatening at every curve in its path to jump the high banks and challenge the timeworn courses of eons. The trout challenge the river.

All this is cast in a revolving kaleidoscope, held up against the light of the sun, and it's here today right in front of his eyes for Claude to look *and* see -- and for Claude only. His are the eyes that this moment's *being* is *being* created for; his are the senses it wants to feed and food is power. Poor Claude, doesn't know power when it's right in front of his eyes. So, Claude's busy at wasting it away into vanity.

Claude's not where he is. Why, he won't even see the swallows, much less the fish. But he'll look. So, he looked at the logs on the trucks as they streaked by. Red trucks, blue trucks, green trucks, trucks of all the primary colors and their various mixes. Some were two-toned, some had stripes and there were others with swirls and patterns of polka dots and each and every one was loaded with *production*.

The westbound truck drivers had the sun to their back, so they saw the caddis flies as fluttering flashes, tinged bright orange and brown. Claude was traveling east into the sun, and for him their gossamer wings flashed in silver-hued light streaks just before they splattered guts all over his windshield. An occasional dragonfly, with its wings afire and breathing out smoke, cut a swath through the caddis flies, and lucent swallows swooped through. Salsify seeds floated along on the slightest breeze and caught the morning glow, too. Air was visible and moving everywhere; there was no space out there that wasn't alive.

Claude didn't see any of this because Claude refused to see. Claude was as blind as a one-eyed mole. He was a looker only and his looking stayed in its groove, so he selected the logs flying by to do his looking at. He also looked at the late summer shower of gooey gut-drop splattering in front of his eyes. Perturbed, he pushed the switch on the wiper control that put pressure to the windshield washers. A stream of water soaked the window surface. Then, he turned on the wipers and smeared bug juice all over the glass. This spurred his mood and he mumbled: "Damned blasted bug shit!" He continued to wash the window surface, till the wipers did their job and cleared a looking space.

But to say Claude couldn't *see* is hyperbolae, of sorts. What Claude *saw* was that sign back at the Sweet Home parking lot, transported from there and neatly tacked to a concrete wall of the Portland executive parking mall. He saw himself, pulling in off the busy city avenue, entering the dim basement of the new skyscraper that towered over all the others, and driving by rows on rows of parking spaces with numbers but not names. He came to that special row, nearest the elevator, where all the neatly printed signs (green on gold) were hanging in an evenly spaced row. And there it was: his name, his title—green on gold. And wonders of wonders, in the journey from Sweet Home to Portland the sign had miraculously transformed itself! As he pulled into his private space he read it out loud to himself, just like he always did. The sign proudly said: Claude Edgar: Vice President of Timberlands. Those words belonged to Hoskings at this time, but the rumor was out that Hoskings was headed places—big places—up and out of the V.P. slot. It was a corporate light-year, from being a timberlands chief in Sweet Home to being a V.P. in Portland, but . . . just possibly . . . Hoskings made that jump.

Somebody new was going to own that title. Hoskings would name the man, and he was on Hosking's good side, no doubt about it. During his last visit to the Sweet Home plant, didn't Hoskings say: "Claude, you're one hell of a company man. Glad to have you on board." Yep, those were his exact words. Quite a compliment, too, coming from a man who wasn't known for compliments. Hoskings was known for just the opposite. He'd rather chew a man's ass, just to sharpen his teeth.

Claude's mood improved. He even smiled.

The vision suddenly faded along with the smile, and Claude was peering through bug guts again. But he wasn't worried; the vision would come back. It always did. It was a projection that took Claude away from where he was at and refocused him someplace where he'd never been and was never to be, and so there was no *being* to it. But, he chewed at it anyway, and then chewed some more, swallowed, spit it back up, and went to re-chewing, day and night, all the time. Claude was a *hopeless* ruminant, re-chewing his bone soup, fleshing up for his worms.

It was noon when Claude pulled up to the logging site. Everything was quiet. An empty log truck, bright golden-yellow sat in a pullout, waiting for its load. He looked all around. *Why'n the hell's that blasted truck parked there? Where's the damned driver?* The yarder was shut down. No one was in sight. This was agitating as hell! "Where'n the shit is everybody?" he mumbled.

He stepped up on a stump to get a better view. The unit covered two hillsides that rose in opposite directions from a small creek that was lined with cedars and sliced the clearcut in half. The road skirted the timber along the bottom edge of the hillside, where it crossed the creek over a culvert and continued about a hundred yards though the clearcut to the landing.

They were highlead logging over here but using the cats on the other side of the creek. The cat tracks came down through the unit over there, all the way to the road, and then turned up it and continued to the log deck. This meant they were taking the long way around to get those logs to the landing. "Dumb shits," he said. Plain to see that they could skid those logs through the creek higher up and eliminate the dogleg. This would cut the number of turns by at least a tenth and save money. Claude was a numbers man and the numbers say that saving money is making money down there on the bottom line where turning green to black is the name of the game—and numbers don't lie. But first they'd need to get those worthless cedars along the creek out of the way, and it was obvious these damned loggers on this show were just too blasted lazy to put forth the effort. The illiterate bums would rather do what came easy, even if it took longer and wasted company time. Anybody who can read knows that time is money!

Claude always carried a pad and pen when overseeing the operations. The marine officer in him needed a swagger stick. Then he pretended like he was taking notes. He silently looked around not saying much, while he scribbled nonsense in his pad. Fact was: Claude was city born, city raised, and he earned his accounting degree from an Ohio college. He was a good example of the military taking care of its own. He got his present position because he came out the revolving door just when AOK needed to hire a body who would keep them in solid on their military contracts. They hired at least one of these a year and then put them some place where they couldn't do any real harm. Everyone in the woods knew this, and so did Claude. His problem was that he wouldn't own up to it and kept it neatly tucked away in a part of his head where it couldn't bother him.

True to his nature, his managerial technique involved appearing to others as imposing as he possibly could, thus dominating through intimidation. The way he figured it, he might not know much about what he was doing, but he knew stupidity when he saw it, and this was just pure, plain stupidity that he was looking at right now. There was no reason in the world to be doglegging around with those cats when they could be cutting a straight line.

He spotted the bunch he was looking for. They were lounging around way down there by the creek, sitting under the cedars. That's probably why they left the cedars standing; gave them a place to hide out. Then he heard an old familiar companion of his: *"Dumb shits! What're they still sitting there for? Didn't they see you drive in? Time to kick some ass, damned if it ain't!"* It was his very own personal tyrant speaking. Claude sorta liked the tyrant, so he figured this was a good opportunity to give him some exercise, a little sport, maybe even get in a hell-of-a-good butt kicking. *I could use a good workout.* Claude gripped his paper swagger stick and headed in a huff in the crew's direction.

Chapter 27 Leave Those Cedars Astanding

The redcedar is the most feminine tree in the woods. It's said that the forest queen selected it for her clothing because it's the deepest shade of green, it's soft, has lacy foliage, and just like her, it loves to stand near running water. The cedar tree smells so sweet because that's her perfume...

Shorty was getting along better with his new hardhat: he was using it for a bucket. The huckleberry bushes were in fruit, and when the crew sat down for lunch, he showed up with his hat full of plump berries. He'd been grabbing at the bushes while he worked and stuffing his mouth full of berries all morning.

"Yer gonna be shitin' huckleberry-blue for a week," said Milo.

Shorty shrugged. "Blue shit, green shit, pink shit, purple shit—shit's shit so who the shit gives a shit," said Shorty.

"Bet they're wormy," said the log truck driver. "Too much rain too late, this year."

"Yeah, Shorty, how 'bout that. You checked those things for worms?" said Milo.

"Christamighty, ya think I couldn't taste worms?" said Shorty, munching on a mouthful of berries.

"Not if all they been eatin' is what yer eatin'," said Milo. "Check 'em."

So Shorty broke open a berry, squeezed it, and out squirmed a worm; then another berry and another worm. Every berry he tested produced the same results. His eyes grew ever wider with disbelief. He felt his gut turn over there seemed to be a lot of wiggling going on in there. He urped. All eyes were upon him. He saw the grins and heard Milo chuckle.

There's no going back, no backpedalin', no retreat, gotta hold yer ground. So whatever you do, don't puke. If they win this one there'll be no end to takin' shit about it. They'll razz the hell outa ya all day long an' you'll get no peace on the crummy, said Shorty's thoughts. So he just shrugged and said: "Well, what the hell. It's not like the li'll squirmers've been dug outa dung. Like ya said, Milo, all they been a eatin' is berries." Then he scooped a handful from his hat, shoveled them into his mouth, chewed them just a little bit, and swallowed as hard he could and then forced out a satisfied looking grin. It was the crew's turn to urp.

Shorty won the day. After this incident, word went about that he could eat glass if he should get a mind to do so. And nobody gave him any shit.

"There comes Bigfoot," said the trucker, looking up toward the area where the road crossed the creek.

"Milo looked up the hill and, spotting Edgar, said: "Gawdamighty yer right. Bigfoot does exist just like they say: he's big, dumb, hairy, an' ugly. There goes my appetite."

"Not mine," said Shorty, as he tossed a berry up and caught it with his tongue.

A boy with wavy red hair and freckles, one of the choker setters, said:

"Wonder if'n he'll be carryin' his toilet paper pad."

Shorty said: "Prob'ly is. I think he needs a lot of paper, considerin' he's plumb full o' bullshit."

"It's his pacifier," said Milo.

Everybody had a good laugh as they casually went about their lunch.

The stream in this spot was about six feet wide and very clear, despite the logging going on up the hill. Pebbles peppered its bottom. Salmon were consumed in their spawning ritual in many of the other streams, but not here. This one was spring fed and flowed into Lava Lake. It also fed thirsty taproots and the strong perfume off the cedars spilled over in the cool, shaded air. The men came here every day for lunch and sat on the moss with their backs against some windfalls. Like an oasis to a thirsty nomad, this was one of those special places that a hard-worked logger looks forward to.

"Two bits says ol' Claude don't make it down here without fallin' flat on his face," said Milo.

"Yer on," said Shorty, who couldn't pass up a bet. "First time I ever hoped you win a wager." Some more laughter rattled the air. But, to the disappointment of everyone, Claude made it all the way down, without so much as a stumble. They sat and watched him come.

"Gimme two bits," said Shorty.

Claude heard the gaiety and suspected that it was, somehow, at his expense. This thought piqued his already fouled mood. *Dumb loggers! By God, I'll show 'em! -- Teach them a little respect.*

Whitey screwed the cap onto his thermos and rose to meet Claude. All the others kept their seats and watched him approach. Whitey smiled as Claude walked up and held out his hand. The two men shook, but Claude's grip was cold. His countenance was stern, and his eyes mocked as he loudly said: "Sure hate to disturb your lazy-butted reverie down here in the shade trees."

In this moment a roll of thunder rumbled through. Both Whitey and Claude looked up. A cumulonimbus cloud towered over their heads. High winds swept its anvil to a long way out in front of it.

Whitey had his back to the men but he felt them stir at Claude's caustic remark. He'd hold his tongue and let Claude take the lead.

"How're we doing around here?" Claude was asking. "I'd say not very damned much." He was also answering.

Whitey saw that Claude was trying to get his goat. He knew the breed: they'll do anything under the sun to look high and mighty to other men.

Whitey smiled. "Right on target," he said.

A thunderclap split the air, followed by low rumbling. Neither man looked up; their eyes were on each other.

"Whose *target*, yours?" asked Claude. "I'd say nobody's *target*," he answered. "Man, I'm not *shooting* at targets. You can miss a target, and I don't aim to miss what I'm shooting for. I'm not shooting at schedules, either, already hit them,

I'm aiming to *beat* them. So how's our aim pointing in *that* respect?"

Play along with this bullshit, thought Whitey. "Well Claude," he said, "it's like I said, your schedule is my target, and we've already hit the bull's-eye. That means we've both hit it *and* beat it -- best of two worlds. How's that for good aiming?"

Whitey was imposing even to an ex-marine boxer, and Claude could tell he hadn't backed him down by an inch. Though Whitey hadn't changed expressions and even sported a slight smile, it seemed to Claude that those pale eyes were slicing him up like a scimitar. He'd only met Whitey once before and that was briefly. Hoskings was in a hurry that day when he introduced him to the various side bosses up here in the Lava Lake operations. He'd been back several times since, but as chance would have it, Whitey was gone each time. He was usually off rigging spars for the next show, because he was the company's highclimber and rigged all the spar trees.

On the day they were introduced, Claude paid little attention, because his mind was boggled by all the new input Hoskings was running through it. Right now, he wished he'd been more alert, because he sure as to hell didn't remember this man as being this formidable. And for a brief moment he hesitated, taking time to consider just what he might be getting into here. His mind hung on its hinges and swayed: *Should I step ahead or should I step back? Ahead or back? Oh, which way to go . . .* But Claude had that tyrant in his soul. The tyrant was mean and tough and proud and dumb—a wannabe bull of the woods who didn't know bulls and didn't know woods. He likes to run the show, and so he was only too glad to surface into Claude's mind and fill it completely up with his sense of self and take control of the situation. And he didn't take no shit of any kind. He could handle any big bastard of a thick-headed uneducated logger.

Claude was a bully who carried a lot of beef, but he sure as to hell weren't no bull. What the tyrant didn't know was that this particular logger had known the real bulls of the woods—bulls of the big woods, locked horns with them. What could some pretentious tyrant possibly mean to such a man?

Ahead or back? Ahead or . . . Claude oscillated. But not the tyrant; that part of Claude saw his opening and up he charged in a rush. He threw his shoulder against the door of Claude's mind and barged right on in, and to Claude said: *"You're the boss, by goddammit! The power belongs to you! Use it or lose it!"* The way Claude's tyrant figured it, with four little words he controlled the woods in this region: *pick up your check.*

A sudden bright flash and a thunderclap. Some intermittent raindrops started to splatter—big ones.

Through Claude, to Whitey, the tyrant said: *"What the hell do you think you're doing, turning the cats out around the ends of the unit and running up the road, the way you are? Jesus, man, don't you understand that time is money?"*

Whitey knew Claude didn't know much, no matter how hard he tried not to show it, and figured a short explanation might set him at ease: "Well, Claude, we'd need to cross the creek otherwise, and the cedars are in the way there. Besides that, the cats would bog down in the creek, because it's soft in the bottom. We'd have to lay down a culvert to save the creek. Then you're talking about bringing in more rock, and so on. Whatever way we do it, time's probably a trade off and so are dollars."

Through Claude to Whitey said the tyrant, using his most condescending tone: *"Whitey, then take the blasted cedars out and drag them out of the way, or better yet, lay them along the creek bottom and run the cats over them. That way you'll keep the tracks out of the bogs. If they start to sink in, simply pile in more cedars or move to another spot. Think, guy. Think."*

Rumbling, like a growl, high in the sky, low, then lowering on down to way down deep, pausing, then rising and then to low again.

Whitey said nothing for a long moment. Such arrogant stupidity as this almost boggled his mind. He was astonished to the point of speechlessness by such effrontery. He couldn't believe what he had just heard. He needed to collect his thoughts. *Doze out the cedars in order to save a little bit of time? Denude the creek? Pile the draw full of the felled cedars? Run over them with the cats? Desecrate the creek . . . for nothing. Good grief, even Dewey wouldn't have tried anything that pathetic!*

It was now that Claude made one of the biggest mistakes of his life. He interpreted Whitey's silent astonishment as silent acquiescence. A viscous temerity surged through his veins, overflowed his heart and made his head throb with the excitement of his old fighting days. The tyrant smirked. It was kicking-ass time! Claude looked past Whitey, to the crew, and to Claude his tyrant said: *"You jokers can't get the blasted job done, sitting around on your round bottoms. Get 'em up and move 'em."* And poor ol' thick-headed Claude parroted them.

More cumulonimbus clouds rolled in shoulder to shoulder, forming a long squall line. Constant rumbling resounded between the ridges. Leaves shook. Sky turned gray-black. Air flickered and vibrated with static.

There were only stark and silent stares as each and every man sat frozen in bewilderment. Even Milo was speechless. They all thought with the same mind: *Did this ignoramus have any idea who he was talking to, over there? Could he possibly be serious, for God's sake?* Two or three of the men snapped out of their stupors and started to rise. Whitey heard them and without looking back held out his hand to his side with the palm down, as an order to remain seated. They instantly sat down, and not a man moved an eyelash.

When he saw this, Claude's blood rose and flushed his face bright red. Outraged, the tyrant almost burst out of his hardened husk. Claude felt the blood veins in his head swell. The tyrant started to yell at the men and tell them to move their asses or, better yet, say: *pick up your checks,* but Whitey throttled him with these words: "Cut down the cedars, you say. Pile them in the draw and run over them. Scour the hell out of this creek. I gotta beg your damn pardon, Claude. If I heard you correctly, and if that's what you really said, you're going to have to do it yourself. And we're all going to sit right here and watch you, because I'm not going to do anything of the sort. Neither are any of these men, if they ever want to work for me again."

The light gloomed. Air instantly cooled, as though the sun had just set without sinking. Static electricity sizzled in the trees and through the men's body hairs.

Claude was beside himself with rage. He bristled and stood stiffly, glaring at Whitey. He stretched his neck, curled up his upper lip, and started huffing and puffing like some helpless old bull. He was so furious he lost his composure, started shaking and sprayed spittle as he blurted out: "Pick up your check!" Of course he was just saying what his tyrant told him to say. Then, to the crew: "As of this minute, all you men are working directly for me, because I just fired this man!" But no one moved or made a single sound. "Well, get up and get going, goddammit!" he yelled again.

Once again, two or three of the men started to slowly rise, not really knowing how to react.

"Sit down," said Whitey quietly but firmly. The men instantly plopped back down, more than glad to remain under the cedar.

Claude dropped his eyebrows and his eyes formed into long slits. For a moment his tyrant was struck dumb. His lips moving, feeling for words that wouldn't come, he glared out at Whitey. Finally: "What the hell's going on?" he growled—no answer.

A quick flash of light cut the gloom like a stainless steel blade. Another thunderclap, close in, shook the air. Raindrops the size of marbles bounced off the two men's hardhats. Whitey wore a slicker. Claude was getting soaked.

Whitey looked Claude directly in his eye, and said: "Only man in this world who can fire me is the one who was in charge when they hired me, and his name is Hoskings." At the mention of the name Hoskings, Whitey saw Claude's body jerk and a spasm run through it, as if he had just received a shock from the lightening.

Claude didn't know how to react in the face of such steadfastness; he'd never been trained for this. Trepidation displaced temerity. The tyrant shirked. Claude tried to hold his *intimidating* glare and cast it like a spear, but couldn't. As an excuse to drop his eyes, he automatically raised his pad and started to write but was wishing he hadn't done so, because his shaking hands belied his ruse of self-control. He was in one hell of a fix: he couldn't write, but to lower the pad again in the presence of all these men would signal a loss of nerve. To make matters worse, rain was splattering against the pad, soaking the paper. He felt ridiculous.

"It's real simple," said Whitey, and then he started to slowly spell words to Claude: "g-e-t, h-o-s-k-i-n-g-s, t-o, c-a-n, w-h-i-t-e-y. Be sure you capitalize the h and the w. One more thing: when you give him the message, make it a point to tell him that I said that he has to do it himself. He's going to have to come up here and look me square in the eye, and say: Whitey you're canned. If he does that, I guarantee you, I'll be out of here within the hour. In the eye; don't forget the in the eye part."

Claude could see the men all sitting in the background, grinning. His entire body felt numb-stricken, and he was suddenly light-headed, starting to spin. He was a large man, for whom physical size related to dominance. When threatened, he always puffed himself up to his full stature and sucked in wind for more. This was his fighter's stance, which had served him well. It was, of course, full of hot air. But, now, he had no choice; it was all he had left. His tyrant was being strangely silent. He'd never felt so all-alone. So Claude sucked in wind and puffed himself up, like a silly puffer fish, which made his face grow red and taut and made his lips turn blue and get all thin and rigid. His head felt so light he couldn't even feel his feet. Meekly, he said: "Anybody can be a big man when they're carrying an axe and the other man has a pad of paper."

Eerie light hung among the trees and across the clearcut. It wasn't the kind of light that creates shadows. It glowed through the eyes of the men and turned their faces phosphoric. A bolt of lightening ripped through, zigging and zagging immediately overhead, and cracked the air like a blacksnake. It popped Claude's over-inflated bravado balloon.

To Claude's consuming horror, Whitey took a step toward him moving the arm that held the axe. Hiding in Claude now, the tyrant squealed: *I'm outa here!* And Claude would have turned to flee, too, had not all his adrenalin surged at once, tying his muscles into one big knot and freezing him to the spot where he stood. His light-heartedness of this morning was completely gone; he felt like one big clumsy foot, stuck in the ground. A fatal black cloud covered his eyes. In the cloud, coming from out of it, like a bolt of lightning, silver-edged and streaking red, he saw the axe's blade cut though the air and sever his head like a stew-pot chicken's. Decapitated, he went charging all through the unit, running in blind circles, tripping over every stick in his path. Blood and mud were flying everywhere. His head was lying on the ground watching his death dance and listening to the men, laughing, howling, cheering. It was as if the entire blasted world was laughing. Then: rumbling, low rumbling, as coming from the sky, or gathering in the recesses of his mind, coming closer—what? -- his death rattle, maybe—no . . . He listened—*shhhh*. His head was dead but hearing words, far-off words, coming closer, stacking up against one another like stormy clouds, drifting in, slowly saying: "I don't need the damned axe, Claude, because I'm not the one planning to fall the cedars. Here, you take it and keep the pad to boot." As if in a slow-motion dream, Whitey held out the axe and offered it. Fear of dying gave way to fear of living, and so, Claude was utterly defeated.

Trained to give and follow orders blindly, and receiving a direct order, Claude responded, like some dimwitted myrmidon, and took the axe. Then Whitey stepped back, and Claude could see him brace himself. Pathetic Claude, it was as if his mind was trapped in a stammer, and he was incapable of rational thought. He gripped the long smooth handle and was amazed that it consumed his attention. The weight and heft of the axe felt good in his hands, as though it gave him something solid to hold onto and keep him grounded. The handle was smooth and it felt soft to his touch, not hard like he would've thought. The heads mesmerized him. They flushed in this weird light, seemed to throb—two heads—staring off in opposite directions—seeing the same thoughts—two, seeing for one—one head—choosing between them--like a pathetically-beautiful naked Siamese twin. Then he heard Whitey say: "You go ahead and come at me with that axe, Claude. But when I'm finished with you, you'll be wearing her like a monkey wears his tail. The handle will be the part in the daylight. I've seen that done, and so I can do it, too."

But Claude wasn't considering anything of the sort; he wasn't considering anything at all. Coherence had completely left him, replaced by numbness and a feeling of empty hopelessness. He had no intention of charging on Whitey; he had no intentions whatsoever. Even his wizened perceptions could see that this would be akin to a primped poodle charging on a timberwolf. So there he stood, not knowing what to do next, and trying to avoid the toothy grins of the crew. With what little will he had left, he tried to come back to himself.

When a man is down and out, help can come from unforeseen quarters, and it was Whitey who came to Claude's aid.

Speaking easy, Whitey said: "The way I see it, Claude, you have three choices. You can try to use that axe on me, or you can fall these cedars with it, or you can lay it aside and get on with your business, because we all know you're a busy man with important business to do. Then we can get back to our business. The choices are yours, but I'd like to suggest the last one, if you don't mind. So what's it going to be, Claude?"

Thunder was a slow constant rumbling, receding into the distance.

The sound of his name hit Claude right between the eyes. The lightening couldn't have delivered a sharper blow. He felt a surge of painful relief. Whitey was letting him off the hook, giving him a way to back out of here. *Go with it.* "Oh . . . oh, uh, yeah . . . You're right, I have business to do. I gotta get about it." He gently leaned the axe, handle up, against one of the cedars and turned to leave. He took a few steps and racked his brain for something to say, because he was the boss, and bosses always get the last say. It's tradition. He stopped and turned again to face Whitey, and said: "I'll take the issue of these cedars up with the powers that be. You'll see." Even as he was saying these words Claude was regretting them, because even to him, they came out sounding void of any authority and sounded more like a nasal whine.

The clouds separated in several places, and sunbeams speared through and filled the air with an amber hue.

Whitey's face remained expressionless, but Claude saw the men in the background, looking at one another and making mocking gestures in his direction. Then he heard a chuckle go up, when Whitey replied.

Said Whitey, softly: "Claude, you do just that, if you ever climb so high."

The cumulonimbus that was directly over their heads rolled its anvil away from the sun, and suddenly it was bright daylight again. The sun warmed the dark ground and it began to steam.

Claude was only dimly aware that he had blundered out of his tidy civilized world of prepared orders and debits and credits, schedules and production quotas, to enter a different one: a wild and wooly one; one where borders are not nearly so well defined and fought over; one he couldn't possibly know. He came here today to smite some heads, but now, stripped of his hierarchical thicket, where he'd hid for most of his life, he headed for the pickup with the devil in his mind nipping at his heals. As if things weren't bad enough, he caught a toe on the branch of a fallen tree and awkwardly stumbled forward. Fortunately, he managed to keep his feet, though he dropped his pad and his hat fell off and his pen fell out of his shirt pocket. He stooped forward, scanning the ground, and didn't immediately see the pen so left it and picked up the pad and his hat. He didn't even bother to put the hat on and carried it at his side. His hair was mussed, so he combed it over with his fingers. He heard some loud laughing behind him. "Two bits! Two bits! Gimme back my two bits!" he heard someone holler. "Aww shit!" said somebody else.

It was bright and sunny, as though the thunderstorm never happened, except the ground was damp and cool. Vapors rose and disappeared into the air like ghostly apparitions.

It was at this moment that Claude's world imploded and filled his head with mind-feathers. Everything he'd ever imagined himself to be, everything he dreamed he might some day become, was sucked away and drifted off, thousands of tiny feathers, floating in the vapors, leaving a seeing, breathing, hearing, smelling, unthinking man. The golden-yellow pickup was like a huge sunflower up there against the hillside. The September sun made him sweat. Sweat trickled into his brows and down his ribs and through the crease of his buns. He wiped his wet face with his sleeve. The damp air brought out the smells of soil and cedar and these blended with the aroma of fresh-cut firs. It swirled in the breeze and mixed together and filled the canyon until it flowed over the rim. The melodious sound of the men talking in the distance was fading away. Bees were humming in the brush, knowing they were working against time, because the snows were close at hand; he felt an old kinship with those bees. He heard some birds: they weren't singing, more like calling to one another through the trees and across the unit. They sounded anxious. Perhaps they had some place to go and were running late. Another truck rolled in, breaking against compression. Rumbling, it eased its way down the hill. The road was drying fast, and the truck trailed a low cloud of heavy red dust that hung softly in the still air and scattered the sunlight.

The ridge parted up ahead and rose high up and swept away on either side and disappeared behind him, like ebony wings feathered with trees, flying away, leaving him behind. His heart felt as heavy and cold as a waterlogged sinker log, bumping along the bottom of a river. Time itself took on a strange, translucent hue: the walk down the hill took five minutes; the walk back up took forever. His legs felt like they were rooted stumps.

Finally, he was at the pickup. He reached out and touched it. It was warm and the new layer of dust, laid down by the passing truck, felt gritty. On the door, fancy lettering, green on gold: **AOK**. He opened the door and sat down. But, the keys were not in the ignition! He looked in the ashtray. *Oh, good God, not there either!* Claude returned to himself through a swelling sense of panic. He thrust his hand into his right-side pocket. *Not there!* A horrifying vision of losing his keys flooded his mind. He envisioned himself scrounging around on the ground, like some idiot, as he searched for them in plain sight of the crew, retracing his steps, all hunched over, and looking in the brush. Maybe he'd stumble again. Then, horrors of horrors!: should he fail to find them, he'd have to wait around and ride the crummy to camp with the loggers! In desperation, he thrust his hand into another pocket, almost tearing it. And there they were! His relief was overwhelming. *Oh, thank You, God! Oh, thank You!* said a silent inner prayer. He thought he might cry from relief. Tears welled. He chocked them back.

He observed his hand insert the key and heard the motor crank to a start. He observed his foot on the clutch and the shift to low gear. He observed the red-cinder logging road, coming up to meet him. He felt the pickup strain, as it pulled the hillside. The sky shone bright blue at this altitude. He was leaving the clutter of the unit behind. His eyes were glued to dead ahead and not looking in the mirror or he would have seen that all the men had walked out from under the cedars to watch his departure.

So he couldn't observe what he was well aware of—that they all had big grins on their faces. That is, all except the one who was saying: "Come on, fellas, you're not getting paid to stand around and gawk. Get back to it. We got a target to hit, you know." As they grabbed up their nosebags, he added: "By the way, I don't want to see any of these cedars getting fell or run over. The company says to keep clear of the creek bottom and leave those cedars astanding."

Whitey was wrong when he said that Claude had important business to do; he headed straight home. He never took his case to the higher-ups, and he sure as hell never asked Hoskings to can Whitey. Going back down the highway, he met many of the same trucks returning empty for their next load of the day that he'd met going in loaded that morning. The caddis flies were still trying to lay their eggs in the shiny asphalt, and flew this way and that through the sunbeams and spattered his windshield. The swallows swooped and banked, and the invisible little trout down in the river did the same. Dragons flew, salsify sailed, and skippers skipped. The river trickled and pooled, then trickled and pooled again. And it has been pretty much this way: rivers and bugs and birds and fish and . . . for further back than most men can dream. Even the nearest-sighted seer can see *this*. But Claude didn't see; Claude was a *looker* of the first degree; Claude would never see, and this time he had no excuse, because there wasn't a single thing in his mind to clutter it. This time he didn't even *look*, and when he got to his house in Sweet Home that perched in the hills and viewed over the little town and all its commerce, he didn't remember a single mile of his trip home. It was as if a blank slate had driven down that road and dumped off a blind man. So he lost another seventy miles out of his life, no sweet memories to dream back up, to ruminate on later in life or in existence or perhaps in being, no *soul-cud* to work on during leisure, re-chew into even finer stuff that'll digest well and add some substance to a spirit's body. Now, *there's* cud worth the chewing.

Claude wasn't a drinking man, but he poured himself a few shots, and soaked his self-contempt in pickling juice, as he sat on his sofa and dreaded the thought of going to work in the morning.

Claude didn't know much about logging or loggers, but he knew enough to know that he'd shot his wad in this game. The next day he called Hoskings and resigned. He dumped the house on the market and one week later was out of town—gone to where? Nobody much cared.

News travels fast through the media of the woods. Carried by the crummies on the way to town, then through the strings of ribald bars and honky-tonks, it covers the town in a flash, and then jumps the gaps to the others. The news turns into gossip and the gossip turns into boast and the boast into outright lies. The more it's crowed the more it grows. By the time it reached Astoria, it had Whitey turning Claude bottomside-up over his knee and spanking his bare ass with the broadside of his axe, as the pathetic man hollered and squealed to high heaven.

In the mountains north of Lava Lake, these days the ancient forests are all but gone. Somewhere south of the South Pyramid, not far from the headwaters of Park Creek, there remains a place where the little creek still tumbles cool and clear through its narrow evergreen stand of sheltering cedars.

Chapter 28 The Raven and The Wolf

A new notice was posted on the camp's bulletin board:

To all of our Lava Lake employees, greetings.

I would like to announce the most recent decision of the board of directors of AOK, concerning its plans for the Lava lake camp. There will be one more work season, following the present one, after which the camp is to be dismantled. I realize that there has been some speculation in this regard, and now that the decision is final, we can all get on with our plans. This decision will save the company considerable sums of money. Everybody should understand this and applaud the decision, because a company that makes money is a secure company and those fortunate enough to be in its employ are secure in their jobs. So rest assured folks, it's all being done with our employee's welfare in mind.

Kevin Hoskings, President of AOK

The board had spoken: the camp was coming down. Bob Carr was dead for over three years, and they reasoned there was no need to maintain pretenses any longer and feed a dinosaur for nostalgia's sake. And they were right, to a certain degree. The camp had grown into a dinosaur that had outgrown its ability to support its own weight, and so, had set the stage for its own destruction. The crummies could serve the area from Sweet Home with a fraction of the present cost, because the crummies were no longer crummy. They were high-speed, comfortable busses. And loggers weren't paid for travel time -- sometimes time isn't money – for some people.

It was finally decreed: the whole shebang would come down the following November -- 1960. The last sentence in the last chapter in a tragic story was being written. All it needed was a period. Whitey was fated to dot it. None could possibly understand how large and final that dot was going to be.

The entire population of the camp was dejected. The camp was the only real home that many of them had known because they were transients and this was the only place where they had ever felt at home. There was no mention in the decree of job security—only corporate security—only those who could melt their identities into that of the corporation could feel secure.

The deal he struck with Kevin that night after dinner several years prior was as good a bargain as Whitey had ever made. These days, he often congratulated his business sense and patted himself on the back for the clever way he traded common position for divine leisure. Winters in the Coast Range had been full of work, under gray clouds that were soaked with rain, or waiting out the winter storms in a lonely rain-drenched camp. These years, the months of December through April were slaves to his whims.

When the snows shut down the operations and all the snowbirds flew away Whitey stayed on. He laid claim to the Carr's cabin as his winter quarters, because it was the newest of the bunch, being the least used, and contained the lingering scent of Lilly. He performed his duties and kept the camp's machinery and its buildings free from snow damage and its parameters free from the intruders who never came. But winter hikers came on skis and snowshoes, and exchanged greetings through their breath vapors.

The flimsy-roofed trailer houses couldn't bear the weight of the snow. So they were sitting out the winter down in the valleys and out on the sagebrush plains. The only buildings that wintered here were the cabins, the washroom and the cafe, and Carr hadn't employed fools for builders. These were built by men who knew the mountains. They were stout with timbers and beams and steep-roofed and shed the snow in the same manner as a silver fir. So all Whitey had to do was to ambulate the camp's boundaries, if there had been a heavy snow, and give it a quick looking-over. The water lines were drained, and the machinery winterized, and the generator was not needed, because he used an oil lamp and a woodstove—easy living.

He loved to walk on top of the deep snow and spent most of his days hiking first to this place and then that. Sometimes, he hiked down to the frozen lake bottom; other times, back into the deep old forest or down the road to the creek. It didn't matter where he went because the scene about him constantly changed. Here in these winter snows, silence was like a living breathing crystal, changing with each breath, and he breathed within its heart and its heart beat in cadence with the rising and the setting of the sun.

And he had visitors who came only to be with him. Milo and Shorty came up almost every weekend. On their way back out, Whitey usually gave them a list of things he needed from town, thus keeping his stocks up and them coming back. They were more than glad to oblige.

During these days of hermitage, eternity presented him with a train of pure moments. Time became his constant friend, and the two vagabonds jumped the boxes and went riding on that momentary train together, each determined to make the best of it, before the caboose passed by.

Evenings were devoted to reading. As in the old days back in the Rockies, study became his nightly passion. His library grew and filled the shelves and he heated tea on the stove. More and more often, as he sat reading in his rocker, or at the muse, a sense of deja vu lingered through the air, like perfume, which smelled somewhat of pipe tobacco blended with oriental teas. He leaned back and looked up into the beams and imagined smoke rings dissipating against the ceiling. Suddenly, present again in his mind, there was the Professor, jabbering on and on about whores, the meaning of life, his Percherons, and the philosophies of the Upanishads. But the Professor couldn't haunt him any more; the Professor was a ghost he could kick. And Lilly; Lilly came, too; Lilly visited often; Lilly was the perfume he loved the most.

Down the steep slopes and away from here, the world at large chugged along its common-carrier tracks, trailing its line of cars, overloaded with machinations of every size, shape, and color all pulled along by loco motives. Sometimes it went slow and sometimes fast, and other times it went too fast for its narrow-gauge tracks and it jumped them at the first sharp turn, with considerable clamor and clangor. Then there'd be all kinds of shouting, finger pointing, blame fixing, hot heads, cool heads, empty heads, hard heads, smart heads, and all the heads in between, until they reorganized and strung it back out and got it to moving down the tracks once more. Then they'd call a party and celebrate their success. But what was that to him, who had never rode those boxes? Whitey was barely aware of the whole shindig.

Sooner or later the shindy was bound to come even to this high place: the word was official, and Whitey was as disappointed as all the rest of the camp's population. In another year, this place would be just a piece of another clearcut. In a few years, a passerby could not know, by looking, that people had lived here, men had died here, and that women gave birth here when the baby was in a bigger hurry than the mothers were and left no time for the trip down the hill to the nearest hospital. Nobody would know that children once played tag games in the unit in the dying light of the day and that chipmunks tasted domestication and that couples loved and copulated and quarreled and split up and came back together and split up again and generally lived the lives of itinerant logger couples and that bachelors got drunk in the night and then sobered up just in time for work.

That passerby wouldn't see the place come to life and light up before the sun, when groups of men in knee-high calk boots and stagged pants and wool jackets and hardhats and carrying lunchboxes headed off through the dim shadows, going to the crummies parked along side the road. They'd never hear the roar of twenty bright-red Diamond Ts, waking up one by one and spewing hot breath, warming up their cold lungs in the thin mountain air, getting them ready for the long slow pull up the hill.

Who can say what those future passersby will see? But there are certain to be some, just a few, hopefully at least one, who will pause here, and won't know why, and will cock an ear and listen, and won't know what for, and will hear murmuring, and feel a brisk activity brush against his skin, and will know it's not just the wind.

This was the first day of February. Snow fell hard for the past three days and nights, and the storm blanketed the mountain with new snow. Whitey restricted his outside activities to checking the structures and keeping the cabin's entrance clear. But this morning, the storm abruptly ended, and the sun rose into a nacreous sky, as though a reckless lady of the night broke a necklace string in her revelry and sent her pearls flying in all directions. They rolled along and turned from pink to pearly white.

After breakfast, Whitey strapped on his snowshoes and walked down the road to a nearby section of old forest. Over three feet of new snow had fallen during the night and landed on ten feet more. After a storm, the snow underfoot is not as deep in the old forest as it is elsewhere; it's overhead. It gathers and piles up in the crown, turning the old mantle sheeny silver in the new sunlight. Later, the sun warms it or a breeze blows against it and shakes the boughs and causes it to slide off in big fat flakes and hit the ground with loud-sounding "whoofs."

And that is why he came here today: because here the second snowfall can be heard as well as seen. The air was cold and clear and frozen and swarmed with tiny ice crystals that sparkled and glittered in the sunbeams.

Whitey wasn't alone. A mysterious presence always lurked close by. A solitary mountain raven also wintered in these mountains. He had dark black eyes and a Roman nose, and he lurked like a necromancer amongst the trees. When heard, he could not be seen. When seen, he made no sound. Most often, he was seen as a swift black shadow among the dark firs, first here, then there, then in the flash of an eyelash he was gone, like some foreboding omen.

He was big and old, and his deep raspy voice seemed more ancient, even, than the forest—yet it was a part of the forest and sounded as though it were created from wood and bark and pine cones. The hooting of the owls had flown away, and the song of the Forest Service's mountain canaries that pastured in the summertime lake meadow, had flown away with the owls, and the songbirds were long gone. The crickets were in the ground, clustered in eggs, and the tree frogs slept in the hearts of trees, and the squirrels curled up on their cache of nuts and seeds and covered their chirps with their bushy tails. But on rare moments, the raven called out from somewhere in the deeps of this silence, as though it were calling a world to be born or reborn, and the sound cut through the hard air like an old misery harp and then resounded away into the trees and the snow.

The raven and Whitey eyed one another through the frozen winter months. Like Whitey, the old bird could have left these high cold mountains for a lower and warmer climate, for the easy pickings in the valleys, and where, perhaps, even a warm-feathered breast waited in a nest for him to snuggle up next to. But he stayed here.

Whitey considered him an equal, dropped the "the" and called him by his name. Here was a kinship between a man and a bird, as though they were of the same tribe, Whitey and "Raven", a tribe of two, a true mountain tribe. He often left scraps of food, along his walks, as if carelessly dropped. But he never knew what became of them. They disappeared, but he figured Raven was independent of his charity.

On this day, Whitey had the old forest all to himself. He dallied awhile, listening to the snow "woofs." Then, he returned to his cabin. He ate lunch and drank some tea to warm his gut and then headed down to the lakeshore. Down the trail he went, past where the garbage dump was humped with snow, on down to Lava Lake.

Streams drain the slopes, flow in from the north and west, then settle into a large shallow bowl that sits between the timber and the lava beds. Here they merge and form a pool that grows deeper in the spring when the snow melts. In May, it's a wide lake and storms beat its surface and make waves that could sink a small boat. Ducks and geese, migrating through, land upon it, hunker in, and wait out the storms. But it sits on ground that's torn and shattered and contains fissures that drain away the water, and in July it's a meadow of waist-high grass, cottonwood seed, willows, and wild flowers.

In summer, the wise old bucks come here along with their pretty does to lay back and wait for the rutting season. The beaver are busy. Otter pups play in the streams. Some of the ducks and geese drop out of the northbound migration and summer in the beaver ponds and in shallow pools that the lake leaves behind when it retreats underground. They raise their broods among the willows.

Autumn comes and the grass grows red and the breeze begins to puff and stir as it whiffles through the willows. The leaves begin to fly and the willows shed off, and then tangle their bare limbs. The geese lift off and fly away, laughing, and the otters hole up, and the beaver retire to their lodges. And then come the snows and cover it all, again. The place never sits still for long, and it leaves the sun guessing in his rising about where it's going to be tomorrow.

The path gradually descended to a point on a rise above the lake bottom, then broke off into a short but steeper drop where water ruts carved through rock. Foremost on the point, right at the edge of the lake bottom, stands a huge cottonwood tree. There are others of her kind, circling the high waterline, but this one stands solitary. For some strange reason, Whitey loved this tree. He came here often, in all seasons, and stood under her or sat and leaned his back against her and mused upon the present scene, sharpened his perceptions and whittled some time away.

She's an ancient old hag of the woods. She loves deep snow and quiet running water and thrusts her tongue way out under the lake bottom, where she sips her fill of its juices. She has a body, in composition, more like that of a man, being comprised mostly of water. The winter snows, along with the lake, had come and gone many times in her lifespan. In the winter, she's silent and stately nude, but in the summer, she spreads her seed like flakey snow, over the dry lake bottom, where it gathers and piles in the hollows of deer tracks. She whispers into the warm breezes with a thousand silver-green tongues. To Whitey, it was as though she said: "Shh, shhh, be patient, be patient, and listen, listen." Being a schoolmarm, she divides her boles close to the ground and appears to be two-fold with common roots. Her soggy wood, rendering no utility to commerce, renders her a secure future.

Today, Whitey stood on the snow under the cottonwood for a few moments and looked out over the lake bed at the lava beds on the other side. In the summer, the lava beds rise like tall splinters of black glass and cut the sky to pieces. It's a hot viscid flow, frozen in place by time to form a timeless inland sea of heaved and tortured slag. It possesses harmonious beauty that sings an old song about forces at war, long ago. It's forever stormy, choppy stubby waves build up into waves as high as buildings and crest as sharp as knives. It offers no hospitality to a man or a beast. Only the nimble-footed can transverse it, and even these do so at great risk. Like the baneberry, its beauty is for beholding only. It's a good place to stay out of.

But in the winter, the lava beds express a mellowed tone. The hollows between the crests are filled with snow and the waves appear like giant hummocks, soft to the touch. To Whitey's imagination, this was what a cloudy spring sky would look like if viewed from above the clouds. To walk up there on top of the clouds seemed like an honor reserved for the Greek gods. He'd been waiting for a day just like this one, and now it was here. This one was a perfect day for cloud walking—so it seemed.

He headed out over the snow-covered plains of the lake bottom, going southeasterly. The peaks of the lava fields loomed ahead much like the Rocky Mountains did, when he first saw them as a runaway kid. But unlike the Rockies, these mountains didn't have a ready-made road he could follow in. He skirted them, looking for a good place to ascend. It would not be easy in this deep snow. He discovered a long trough that sloped in from opposite sides and formed a pass, inclining to the south. Here, he left the lake bottom behind and began his climb into his new fanciful sky world, complete with layers of strata and rising cumulus and cumulonimbus with windblown anvils. He headed up. The only sound was the squeaking of snow under his snowshoes.

Whitey reached the top of one of the cumulonimbus and stood upon its anvil. He looked all about. Under his feet, the lava tossed and crashed and flowed away in rolling waves and deep troughs and floated its foam of snow. Looking out over it, there was no shadow in the troughs, so the sense of depth was misleading. The sun was barely visible through a thick haze, and the sky was the color of mother-of-pearl. If not for the dim sun and the trees in the distance, a man might lose his feel for down from up, standing here, and fall in either direction. To shatter the silence and reinforce his sense of reality, he said: "Zeus, you never had it so good." His voice sounded like the clanging of a harsh bell, and he laughed at his own words. His laughter echoed back to him.

Unknown to Whitey, a wolf was creeping through the trees, gathering his strength for the fatal leap. Silent as the dark he loves, and as invisible as a night shadow, he crouched in the snow and hid between the hummocks and slunk, staying low on his belly, waiting for the sun to set. He hunts mainly at night. His canines are as sabers with edges as sharp as razors. He's so fleet he can be everywhere at once. When he leaps, he grips and stabs, and then he won't let go. His victim is unable to move. He gnaws and sucks and licks away the life from its bone.

The air was starting to bite. Whitey pulled his collar up and his hat down and headed out over his clouds. He walked for a mile or more, across the hummocks and though the troughs, listening to the squeaking of snow. The going was slow, and he took his time. Suddenly, something like a cold breath brushed against his neck causing goose bumps to tickle his skin. A heavy feeling swelled up in the midst of his euphoria, displacing it, and he began to feel ill at ease. The silence had a weighty feel to it, and the air seemed to be getting murky. He looked at the sun, again. It was lowering in the sky and butted against a looming cloudbank that was the color of lead. A hazy dun-colored halo, cast by the sun, arched to the east.

Wispy high clouds, with burnished edges, rose up and spread out high overhead, as though stirred around by the dipping sun. Thick light poured through the air like chilled honey. Whitey imagined that if he had wings like a fly he might get gooed up and stuck in this light. It was as though the world was suddenly voided of contrast and took on the bland texture and expression of cream of rice. There was a mysterious oppression in this blandness.

Though he didn't feel cold, a shudder ran down his back. A man could get lost out here without the sun to steer by, and darkness, mixed with falling snow, would present an impossible situation. To die in this place would mean to never be found, not that not being found would matter. It was certainly a fit place for a man of the mountains to be buried—that is, if he's *ready* to be buried. It seemed strange to Whitey that his fanciful mood of just a short while before had vanished so suddenly, plunging him into this new one that bordered on anxious despair. Why? He wasn't lost and there was plenty of time to walk back out. So he passed it off as an over-active imagination that was growing gloomy with the sky. This was a mistake, for as the wise old cottonwood said: "A man shouldn't hurry; he should say 'shhhh' and then listen." If Whitey were listening, he'd hear a silent voice saying something like this: *Surfaces will surprise you; it's black down in the snow. Don't nibble on the root of the creamy-colored camas. Consumed by the trance of naked beauty, men may not perceive it dark root as being deadly. Farthest from their minds is the thought they might die in it, be killed by it. A swallowed diamond can cut like a knife before it's passed. Best not to sip at the surface, but if you drink deeply keep a wary eye open, for it could be that death lurks in the depths, and like the black snapping turtle suck you down and hold you, hold you . . . hold you . . .*

Whitey listened to the snow squeak.

He spotted a hummock, higher than all the rest, dead ahead. This was going to be his last winter here, and wanting one final good look at his sky-world, he headed for its summit. He reached the top and stood for a moment. The sun was behind the overcast and all the sky was leaden. The snow was stark white. Everything appeared two-dimensional. And, the wolf crept ever closer. . .

Then it leapt! He experienced a sudden surge; in an instant heaven fell away and he fell for hell! In total silence his feet disappeared from sight and then his torso. His heart leaped up and beat on the walls of his throat like a frantic drummer and so even the silence was gone. All he had left was solitude. He couldn't know how far this fall was going to go, but he knew he had to do something or his head would be the last to disappear. He threw his arms out wide and heaved his weight backward. He gulped in some air, threw his head back, and closed his eyes and mouth. Cold snow washed over his face. He had a gut-wrenching feeling of being swallowed down the throat of something huge. Suddenly, all movement stopped. Only blind white silence remained where he had just been standing.

There are trees among the lava beds: poor runted things, trying to make ends meet in a world that doesn't appreciate them. Some huddle in copses, others cling tenaciously to whatever little patch of poor dirt their seed could find. Such a one it was that stood its solitary ground here for its brief lifetime. It grew to the grand height of twenty-five feet or so, and may have gone even higher. But in its greed to reach for heaven, it overreached its ability to hold its sparse ground. Then, in November, a gust of wind, hard from the south, overwhelmed its resistance and down it fell. With a muffled crash, it bridged the gap between the apexes of two rocky crests, and then, its needles intact, the incessant winter snow commenced falling. Storm followed storm. The driving winds drove fresh fallen snow to fill the gaps between the outer branches, but its limbs formed a bulwark against the wind, and the snow piled up layer on layer around it and buried the dying tree. This created a large graceful hummock, so apparently easy for a curious cloud climber to ascend, which was deadly hollow in its middle.

The hummock contained a black hole of about fifteen feet in diameter. Brittle rotting limbs, groaning under increasing layers of weight, were supporting all they could bear. Then the most recent storm blew in, and new snow fell, stressing the limbs to their limits. Whitey's added weight on just the right spot was enough to bring the whole system down like water through a funnel. The black hole was sucking up everything that surrounded it.

A fallen sky-walking god hung suspended between heaven above and hell below. He'd call upon the lowly Greeks for help if he could, but there was no one to hear him. Men don't hear gods in distress.

Mustn't panic. Keep calm and think.

Slowly, he moved his hand to his face and brushed away the snow. For a moment, the sky flashed into his vision, but sliding snow quickly covered his face. He cupped his hand over his mouth and nose, cleared an air space, and breathed in. He remained as still as the silence, pondering his situation.

To drown in a snow bank seemed more than absurd. He'd crossed hard-rushing rivers, thousands of times, with a stuffed sack on his back and nothing but his feet to ferry him, bending his knees against the surge, hanging onto the water-worn stones with his toes. And he'd lost his footing more than once, coming close to losing more than just his footing and the sack on his back. But he always made it. He always found a way to reach the other bank. But this time, drowning was not his enemy. He would welcome drowning with open arms, rather than succumb to the predator he faced.

The sky was darkening, color of pure lead, pregnant with snow clouds. Dusk was early. Soon the night would be coming down hard. Then the wolf would dig in his teeth, biting like hot needles, going for the bone and the heart.

Whitey knew the wolf, but he'd never feared him. He'd heard him at night, from the safety of his cabin, howling in the wind. He'd seen his breath gathering upon the windows, as the beast peered through, wanting entry. During early morning he sometimes saw ravaged, winter-killed deer, shriveled up and tossed in a heap along the trails. Their skin looked like scorched toast. Their eyes were sucked dry and sank into the eye sockets. He'd wondered if they had felt pain. He's a hungry wolf and knows no pity. He knows only the feel of his hunger. He even devours what he begets and sips up the snow and licks away ice, leaving only hollows in the ground, where water once was.

Whitey's mind was racing. To move might mean to fall farther into the hole and drown, but not to move would mean to become bait for the wolf. Again, he pushed the snow away from his face, this time using both hands in a swimming motion. This cleared his vision, and he used his arms and hands to pack the snow away from his head. Through the port of the funnel, a circular piece of sky was in view. Fluffy snowflakes were beginning to fall, coming in flashes and blurs, straight toward his eyes. It was the beginning of the storm he'd seen looming in the west. The snow was gathering on the side of this funnel he was in; soon it would start to slide downward like thick oil. He was plugging up the spout. It wouldn't take much to cover his head. Until then, all he could do was use his hands to keep his face clear and keep packing the snow to the side, but this just seemed like buying time to trade for the moment of death. He had to do more. *But, what to do? What to do?*

Slowly, ever so gently, he tried to move his legs, but the snowshoes attached to his feet prevented movement, and he didn't dare to bend forward to reach for the shoes. Such an action would likely cause the entire thing to crash down, gulping him deeper. Then, there would be no hope. While he could see the sky, he could hope.

He thrust his hands into the snow on all sides, feeling for rock, or limbs, or anything solid that he might grasp for support. But there was nothing to feel, except the creeping cold. He lay very still for a long while, conserving strength, wiping snow from his face, and gasping for air. The sky was almost black. The light was the color of chestnut, and his thoughts grew as numb as his hands and legs. Hope was fading. Desperately, he lunged backward and to his horror, felt a sinking sensation and braced himself for the plunge. But it held, and he didn't fall. His head was still free. He wiped his face. There was no feeling in his hands, arms, feet, or legs; blood was retreating from the parameters, pulling back to the center to protect the heart.

Unseen by Whitey, a winged crescent moon sat low in the southeastern sky, perching on a treetop. Its light was enough to make the snow glow and the falling flakes sparkle. But it was a short-lived moon. It wouldn't fly tonight. Darkness, thick and black, descended in a heavy cloud and the moon was swallowed, and the moonlight faded away into that lightlessness most loved by bats. The snow-glow vanished like a ghost, and the silent invisible snowflakes fell.

Once more, he swung his arms and pushed away the snow. He felt for himself. He couldn't feel anything of his body. He felt only the heaviness of exhaustion. He laid back his head and faced the sky and breathed in a long breath. He opened his eyes and saw the blackness descending. Then it was dark—hopelessly dark. Time passed and there was no counting it.

Drowsy . . . drowsy . . . heavy, heavy. Time now for sleep, wrapped in the oldest blanket on Earth. Tonight, sleeping, he would sublimate with the ice. Far off, he heard a howling sound. It was low and then high, like a lullaby, lulling. Like a chip caught in an eddy, he felt a swirling away into darkness. He took a long deep breath, and the beautiful snow fell upon his chin and covered his lips and upon his lids and filled in the hollows of his eyes and upon his nose, forming a tiny hummock. And in an instant it was spring. He stood in a mountain meadow full of flowers and fescue and he lay down and rested his head upon a patch of pale white camas. And in this moment, he knew those deer had felt no pain. Memories . . . Sleep . . . Dreams . . . He breathed out.

"CRARARUCK! CRAAAAK! TOK! TOK! TOK! CRARARUCK!" Sharp flashes of jagged light, silvery and searing, pierced his slumber and burnt through his very soul. He felt a rumbling and his body shook. Again, closer, much louder: **"CRRAACK! TOK! TOK! CRAAAAK!"** This light contained sound, harsh and primeval. The sound came omni-directional. It was painful and grated on his serenity like a raspy file. He heard something in it he recognized: it was the first attempt of a brand-new babe, and it was the rattle from the throat of a timberjack, being crushed by a slow-rolling log. It was the first sound on Earth and it will be the last. He felt as though he were falling, falling, falling, and then he hit and shattered into countless painful pieces.

The sound held substance. He pushed against it and tried to push it away. Again, it split his senses: **"CRARARUCK! TOK! PRUUUCK! TOK! TOK!"** He felt each sharp note of the sound. Its resonance raked him through his heart, cutting, sawing—back and forth it went, miserable. His nerves were seared with pain. Again, streaking through, the eerie light pierced his brain like a Clovis point. He knew this light. *But, from where? From where?*

The falling sensation ceased. He felt buoyed in a vast void by this substantial thing in the dark. Then, he realized it was the darkness he felt, and the darkness was the substance, and he was of the darkness, inseparable. He became the dark and the darkness grew heavier than he could bear, and like a womb turning inside out, escaping from the pressure of its own weight, he started to rise up though himself. It seemed as if he were mounted upon powerful black wings. He glimpsed a glow of light apart from the other, much different, more like a star or a planet, mellow, tinged with green. It appeared to be reflecting from, or suspended in, a fathomless black eye. Mesmerized, he peered into the eye and there within its deeps floated a green mote, small as a seed, ever so slight, so delicate and iridescent. Suddenly the flight upward stopped, and the mote receded into the mist as the eye closed in upon itself, and he shed his wings and hung suspended in the cold snow.

Electric shocks convulsed though him wracking his body and his mind. Each shock split his brain with light, and seared his skull. He felt his body jerking in vibrant spasms. Thick blood surged through veins like rivers of molten lava, setting him on fire. Sharp teeth all over his body were gnawing, gnawing, biting deeper. He agonized.

"CRARUCK! CAARUUCK! TOK! TOK! PRUUUCK!" Again came the call, but this time, no mistake, it came from without and above. It came from a nearby tree. It tore the fabric of silence of this cold world and ripped it at its poles. Then he heard it once more, growing fainter, as though flying away and disappearing out over the lake, going north into the trees. And then there was only the silence.

He raised his arms over his head, into the darkness, and flailed at the empty air. He shook his head to clear his face of snow and gave voice to loud screams: "AWWWWWWWWWWW! AWWWWWWWWWW! UH, UH, AWWWWWWWWWWWW!" Again and again, he took deep breaths and screamed alone and unheard into his own resounding echo.

He paused for a moment to take a breath, and it was in this moment when a voice came through the darkness, as clear as wind chimes and like streaks of light, a voice heard *and* seen, one he'd never forget if he lived forever. Said the voice: "High upon the cold mountain, the great man dies, while in the warm valley, the newborn baby cries." And the voice paused. Whitey knew there was more. Breathing hard, gasping, he lay back his head and spread out his arms to rest against the snow, and with all the power of his will, he listened. His body was numb; blackness engulfed his eyes; the scentless odor of snow filled his nostrils. Fear of death was forgotten; listening was life; he was pure listening. He heard the sound of his breath: in and out, in and out. "Return, return, don't stop, return, don't stop, stay," he pleaded.

And then: "His perceptions will milk the teat. To his senses all things will be meat. As seeds flying in the wind, we will light and begin again. And he and I, the two shall tie: one tight knot."

Whitey didn't know exactly what this voice was, whether life in death or death in life; he didn't know where he was. But he knew this: whichever, he'd brought the two together in him and now he understood that one doesn't end where the other starts and that from here on out, he could live with the power of his death— if he lived at all, or died from here. Like working a double-headed axe, it's an art that takes skill—and practice. Whitey, seeing his choices of life or death or both chose both and to the voice said: "I have always carried a double-headed axe and I always shall."

The voice replied: "Keep the blades sharp and out of the dirt and it will forever serve you well."

And so, he was fated to tramp the crossover world.

Thick silence flowed in as viscous as cold oil. These precise words were not his to keep. Already they were as cosmic comets receding back into unknowable depths. But never would he forget the voice or the crux in what he'd just witnessed, because those were left upon the surface and, therefore, accessible.

Here he was again, suspended between the downside deep and the high black sky, wondering what the hell to do next. He felt a sensation of something running warm and wet, stinging his cheeks and stinging his legs, and he realized it was tears and urine. His screams had cleared his throat and warmed his lungs and opened his eyes and cleaned out his bladder.

Escape was certain. He'd gone into the unknown voids and climbed back out; he would do the same with this black hole. *But how? What to do?* He still dangled like a dingle berry on a hair. That part hadn't changed. What had changed was fear. He felt neither fear of death nor fear of life. But he still felt fear, because fear is a reality, and like hate or love, it is a powerful motivator. What he feared was not rising to the challenge, but more than that, he feared not recognizing the true challenge and being only the man challenging fleeting moon shadows. Like a tree, a woodsman must grow up out of himself, challenging the elements that would stunt him, so that when he's felled Truth falls with him and shakes Earth.

But the challenge at hand was obvious: to escape from this cold hole. He had a job to do. He had to carry his own saw. There'd be no sleeping on this job.

He wiped snow from his face, buying time to think, and then felt an impulse of power surge through his body. He leaned forward as far as possible and with all his strength he shoved his hands down into the snow, in desperate hopes of forcing his body upwards. It was caution aside. Then he felt something solid, protruding up from below. He pushed against it and clutched the round shape of a stout limb. His hopes sprouted wings. If he jerked on it, it might pull him deeper, but there was no other choice. He had to have it. He jerked—nothing. He jerked again and felt it break free from the tree. He pulled it from the snow and tried to look at it, but the darkness was too thick. He felt it best he could with his numb hands, and figured it to be an inch in diameter and five or six feet long. Now, he had a tool. It was only a limb with broken off protrusions, but at least it was more than nothing.

Now, what to do with it? What to do. . ?

Exhausted he leaned back against the snow, and again he used his hands and arms to pack it in around him. If he could only get a knee up . . . Suddenly, in a flash of insight, he knew what the limb was for. Using both hands, he thrust it into the snow in front of him, clear down as far as its length allowed. Then he began to work it back up, trying to snag a snowshoe on the way and pull it up free of the snow. But it didn't work; the limb came up clean. He thrust it back into the snow and tried again and again until the limb pulled against resistance.

The pain in his hands made him want to scream, but that was good; pain is good; pain means life; his hands were still alive. *Oh, God, don't let it break!* Ever so slowly, hand over hand, he pulled on the fragile limb, praying it wouldn't break, knowing his life was hanging from a rotten stick. He humped his shoulders and buried his face in the snow for leverage. He was gaining, walking his hands down the shaft. He threw his head back and tried to rock backwards. As he pulled, he felt his back putting pressure against the snow behind him, and then his knee came free of the snow. He was certain it had. He felt for it, and sure enough, there it was, right in front of him. Just a little more and he could reach the snowshoe. He pulled harder, and to his horror, he heard the stick snap and the pressure against his arms and shoulders slacken. *Oh, no! God, no! So close! So close!* Blindly, he groped for the stick and found a piece protruding out of the snow. Spasms of relief shot through his body. He gripped the stick and pulled. It was still hung up on the snowshoe. He pulled for all he was worth and felt his foot rise and the shoe break through the surface of the snow. Hope surged. A gush of warmth shot through his body. He bent forward and tried to feel for the shoe. His hands hit something solid and large.

"Oh, good God; thank God," he said. The sound of his voice was as sweet as sugar, and it gave him strength.

Now, if the tree held up under him just enough longer for him to get a hold on that shoe he could escape. He struggled to reach the bindings. With both hands, he groped for the thongs that secured the shoe. There were no feelings in his hands. He had only the knowledge in his head of how the leather thongs were secured. He saw them in his mind, so in his mind he moved his hand to the ties and watched as his fingers studied the laces. Painfully he worked the thongs with his fingers. Finally, he felt the shoe come loose from his boot. He clutched the shoe and pulled it toward him, and held it against his breast for a moment.

He grasped the shoe by both ends and laid it to his side, parallel with his hip, and pressed down on it, compacting the snow, making a hollow. Then he did the same on the other side. He used the shoe like a scoop shovel, reaching out with it as far as he dared, and scooped snow down from the sides of the funnel next to his body into the hollows and compacted it. If he could displace enough of the air under him with the snow that was over him then perhaps, just perhaps, he'd build a base down there to support his weight. Doing this over and over was exhausting work, but the labor hurried his blood flow, thinning it and warming his veins. First one side then the other: scooping and campacting and scooping and compacting; pushing against the compaction with all his strength building a base, praying that it would hold. When snow under the weight of the shoe began to give he held his breath. But it never gave far and seemed to settle and gain body. Finally, he lay over on his belly on top of the shoe and pulled his other leg free of the snow. Then he squirmed around till he could lie upon his back on top of the snowshoe.

His energy swelled like a rained-on mushroom and he felt his cheeks flush with new life. He couldn't see the snowflakes that floated down like soft feathers, but he could slightly feel them now, as they came gently to rest against his cheeks. Soft tiny snowflakes, so slight, so delicate—so deadly.

He needed only to keep his strength, and he was free. He bent his knee toward his chest, and using the same mental technique as before, he removed the second snowshoe. Using one shoe as a platform to lie upon and scooping and compacting snow with the other, he started to dig a trough out of the funnel. The going was slow, painful, and tedious. Inch by inch, he gained ground. It was hump and scoop and hump and scoop and then compact and lay the shoe down and flop forward upon it. Then, reach back, pull ahead the other shoe, and compact and scoop some more.

Sometime toward the first light of morning, like a weary half-dead inchworm, he crawled out of his hole. He lay on his back and secured the snowshoes to his feet, and with all the will he could summon, he stood. Strangely, it felt little different from when he was suspended in the pit. His mind was as numb as his body. Thoughts wouldn't come. He was completely disoriented. "Which way to go? Which way to go?" He asked. He listened.

The way Raven went . . . Go the way Raven went. He heard.

With blind eyes and unfeeling body, he took his first step. It was the only step he would remember. Some all-seeing instinct took control of his steps, and he slept a dreamless sleep. Off in the distance, to the southwest, something wailed, trailing away into silence. Probably a gust of wind whistling through the v of a branch.

Just another dead night on the gut. Sweet Home was not where things were happening on this night, most other nights neither. As he thought on it, Milo realized that things never happened in Sweet Home; the action was always some place else. He looked across the seat of the old pickup truck at Shorty, who was nursing on a bottle of Lucky Lager. At the moment, Shorty was occupied deep in thoughtlessness, gazing off down the half-empty gut. He felt Milo's eyes, looked his way, and shrugged his shoulders.

"Dead, ain't it?" said Milo.

"Uh huh. Ever'body lit out for Lebanon. That's where the hell they went," said Shorty.

"Yeah, prob'ly."

"Ya know, Milo, we always end up where it's dead. If we go to Lebanon, all the action turns out to be here or if we go to Albany it's back in Lebanon, or somewhere else. Ever notice that?"

"Yeah . . . maybe it's dead ever'where where we are. Ever thought of that?"

"Yeah, I thought of that. I think our timin's off. That's our problem. I think it's sorta like fishin'. You know how the fish are always bitin' yesterday, or if yer at one lake they're bitin' over at another one? Ever notice that?" Shorty swigged the last of his beer, placed the bottle in the empty slot in the sixpack carton between his feet, pulled out another one, and opened it. "Last one left. Want it?" he said.

"Naa, go ahead," said Milo with a quick shrug of his shoulders. "Yeah, know whatcha mean about the fishin'. It's always the guys over in the other lake that get lucky."

"With us, it's the guys in the other *boat*," said Shorty. "Christamighty, remember last time we went to Suttle Lake, when them guys in that boat were catchin' fish hand over fist and we couldn't get one damned nibble? Remember that?"

"Hell yes, I remember."

"Hell, I can't even catch suckers no more!" said Shorty.

"Be careful with them suckers—full o' bones," said Milo, smiling.

"Closer t' the bone, the sweeter the meat," said Shorty. He was silent in his thoughts for a moment, then he said: "That's what I need, something bony and sweet. Perferably a sucker." He looked disgustingly through the windshield, watching the approaching car lights reflect off the wet asphalt. His own words were giving rise to his lust. "Jeesus, man, I'm hot as a fresh-fucked fox in a forest fire!" he said and took a deep swig of beer.

"Well, just pour some of that beer down yer britches. That'll cool ya off."

Thinking about his hornyness perturbed Shorty. "Like I said, it's the last bottle," he grumbled.

"By gawd, how about Melody Lane?" said Milo, as though he'd just had an inspiration.

"Hell's fire, Milo, we went there last Friday. Don'tcha remember? It was dead then, an' I bet it's dead now.

"Our problem is we always piddle around too long, Shorty. When we finally get around to arrivin' somewhere, all the gals are taken up."

"What's the time right now?" asked Shorty.

"Just a minute," said Milo. They passed under a streetlight and he glanced at his watch. "Eleven forty-five."

Shorty rolled his eyes, swigged on the beer bottle, and then said: "For shit's sake, Milo, it'll be midnight before we get there, an' you know well as I do that all the good lookin' gals will be taken."

"We're out of beer, anyway. Besides it's as good a place as any," said Milo. "C'mon, let's go."

"Yer drivin'," said Shorty. Then he mumbled: "Like the man says, it's as good a place as any, when yer horny with no place to go."

Milo pointed the hood ornament of the pickup toward the west and the ten miles to the little roadside honky-tonk bar. It wasn't much of a place, but it had a dance floor and a band that played until half past midnight.

"Ain't very many cars," said Milo, as he nosed in under the glare of the neon sign that lured good-timers in off the highway. "We can pick up a six-pack an' head to Cottonwood."

"Go right ahead, but I ain't goin' to no gawldang Cottonwood," said Shorty. "Hell, that's another half-hour from here. We'd get there just as the band's quittin'."

"Just a suggestion," said Milo.

Inside the honky-tonk, a couple stood on the dance floor tangled up in each other's arms, weaving side to side to a slow-moving song. The girl wrapped her arms around the boy's neck, while he fondled the ample cheeks of her buttocks. Instead of counting cadence, the three-man band counted time and appeared bored. The lead singer pressed his lips against the mike and swooned: "Hello walls, how'd things go for you today?"

Milo and Shorty headed straight for the bar.

"Hi, Milo, you too, Shorty. How's it goin," sang out a happy greeting.

"Steady by jerks, Betty Lou, steady by jerks," said a cheerful Milo to the young woman standing behind the bar. He sat down on one of the red vinyl swivel stools that lined up in a long uniform row.

Shorty dallied, watching the dancers. Then he took the stool next to Milo, and said: "Where the hell is ever'body at?"

"Ever'body's gone," said Betty Lou.

"I can see that fer Jesus sake. Wher'd they go?"

"Dang if I know. It was hoppin' lively for a while, but the place cleared out about an hour ago."

Betty Lou was as cute as a pixy. She was about five feet tall, had peroxide hair that was frizzled, firm rounded nates, little-girl hips, green eyes, and a ready smile that covered her face and showed off her perfect teeth. Now, she grinned out at them from behind the same bar where she had spent the past six years of her life.

"See? Knew we were comin'," said Shorty, looking disgustingly at Milo. "Missed the good fishin' again."

"Hell's fire, cheer up, boys. You always got me," said Betty Lou, obviously glad to see them. What'll it be?"

"Beer an' a hot sausage," said Milo.

"Same thing here. Only gimme two of them sausages," said Shorty.

Betty Lou poured two beers from the tap.

"Ya think ever'body headed off to Cottonwood?" asked Milo.

"Maybe, but who should care?" said Betty Lou.

"I ain't goin' to no Cottonwood," mumbled Shorty.

The band ended their song and stood around on the stage talking for a minute. Then the singer put his lips next to the mike again and swooned out: "Hello walls, how'd things go for you today?"

Shorty frowned and looked back over his shoulder at the singer. Then he said: "They're singing the same song again."

"Dancers keep requesting it," said Betty Lou. "Guess it's their song or somethin'."

"Yer kiddin'! Over an' over?" said Shorty.

Betty Lou nodded at Shorty. "Over an' over," she said.

"Oh, for gad sake! I don't even like that dumb song," said Shorty. "Talkin' to walls; how dumb can ya get?"

Betty Lou chuckled. "What's eatin' him?" she said to Milo.

"Pay him no mind. He's just horny. Says he's hotter'n a fresh-fucked fox in a forest fire, except he's not as lucky as the fox," said Milo, with a big grin.

Betty Lou laughed.

Shorty's mouth flopped open and his faced flushed bright red, redder than the swivel chairs. "Gawddamned it, Milo! Didn't say no such thing!"

"See what I mean?" said Milo. "He's grouchedy as a rooster without a hen. Any ideas where he can go get lucky?"

"He's full o' bullshit," grumbled Shorty. Unable to bear the grin and flashing eyes of Betty Lou, he glared at Milo, then turned the swivel chair toward the dance floor and pretended to watch the dancers. At that moment, the band quit playing and started putting away their instruments. Cheek to cheek and hip to hip, the dancers walked out the door.

"He did so say it," whispered Milo to Betty Lou, loud enough for Shorty to hear.

Changing the subject to one she liked better, Betty Lou said: "Where you been keepin' yerself, Milo? Ain't seen you around here since last Friday night, when ya hightailed it outa here soon as the music stopped. Hang around sometime an' you an' me chat a while."

"Been logging for AOK up along the Quartzville."

"Still cat skinnin'?"

"Yep, still a playin' with them big ol' yellow pussies."

"Shorty, too?"

"Yep, Shorty, too. Ain't that right, Shorty?"

Shorty only nodded. Milo and Betty Lou watched the back of his head bob up and down. He was washing down his sausage with a gulp of beer, watching the band pack up.

"It's good to have winter jobs, ain't it? Lots of guys ain't workin', these days."

"Yeah. Them unemployment checks get kinda skinny, don't they, Shorty?"

Shorty turned his stool to face the bar. "S'pecially when they quit comin'," he said.

"Here, have a couple on me," said Betty Lou. She quickly poured them some fresh beers. "AOK's good outfit to get on with, ain't they?" she said.

"Ain't worth a plug nickel. Ain't that right, Shorty?"

Shorty had a mouth full of sausage, so he readily agreed by nodding his head.

"But they keep ya busy," said Betty Lou.

Neither Milo nor Shorty could deny that. They kept Betty Lou company until she turned out the lights. Then they bought a six-pack and some more sausages to go and climbed into the pickup.

"She likes ya, Milo," said Shorty, as Milo cranked the engine to a long start.

"The hell she does!"

"She does, man. She wanted to take you home with 'er this very night."

"You really think so?"

"Don't think so; know so."

"Aww, bullshit. How can ya tell?"

Shorty slowly shook his head. "Well, just look at her look atcha. She oozes."

The engine was still cranking.

"Oh, bull. She's got guys ahittin' on her all the time, workin' behind the bar the way she does."

"Nope," said Shorty, matter-of-factly, "that ain't the case, because they all think that very same dumb thing. She's real good lookin', an' so they reckon she's hit on a lot, an' so they leave her alone. She don't encourage 'em neither, but she hits on you. Yer just too dumb to know it."

"Reckon so?" said Milo, interested.

Shorty grinned and slowly shook his head. "Know so. Ain't got no doubt about *that*," he said.

About this time, the engine sputtered to a start.

"Where we goin'?" asked Shorty. But he knew the answer.

"Lava Lake," came the reply.

And they were on their way, drinking their beer and blowing beer-sausage farts. Through the headlight glare, weathered teasel and cattails lined the ditches and sped quickly by. Feeling good now, Shorty started singing a song that kept running through his head: "Hello walls, how'd things go for you today?"

They didn't even slow down at Sweet Home. Up and into the mountains they went, just like they did around this time every Friday night. The mountains were their hangout and the forest queen was their lady love. They didn't want to find any gals. When they saw gals coming their way, they'd hide. Gals wanted attention and this put demands on a man's time. This would mean hanging out around town, and town was the last place they wanted to spend their weekends. They worked in the woods and they played in the woods. They would live in the woods, if they could. But they were modern loggers, and modern loggers didn't live in the woods.

And so, this weekend was a replay of all the others. Horny but happy, they headed into the hills that led into the mountains. The mountains didn't put demands upon a man, on his energies maybe but not on the man. Sometimes, the wind through the trees makes them whisper and lull him and sing him to sleep. The breeze plays with his hair. Showers kiss his cheeks. The forest queen has ladies-in-waiting and so the woods are full of amorous little nymphs, waiting and ready for the lucky young man who's loved by the forest.

But these were two boys with a lot of living ahead of them and hadn't learned what Whitey knew: the mountains are colder than they could imagine, and the dreams that trees lull in can test a soul beyond its limits.

At the Mountain House, Milo pulled over and parked the pickup in the parking lot. They cracked the windows and slept for three hours, until the cafe opened. They ate some breakfast, bought another six-pack, and at the crack of dawn, they hit the road that wound its way up and over the summit of the pass.

The sky spread overhead like a tranquil mountain lake. They left the rig in the turn-out along the highway, strapped on their snowshoes, and hiked the mile into the camp.

"Heey, Whitey. Yooo, Whitey," they yelled, announcing their arrival, like they always did. No answer this time.

The forest is full of dark mystery that surpasses the conceptualizations of a couple of Sweet Home logger boys. How were they to know that the same ol' Whitey they had known was forever gone from here?

"Christamighty, Shorty, hurry up with that fire! There, burn those." Milo pointed at the bookcase. He was leaning over Whitey. Whitey was laying on the floor with some blankets pulled over him.

Shorty scurried about, frantically trying to get a fire going.

Whitey was indestructible in their view, and to see him laid low and helpless was inconceivable until just a few moments ago. All of a sudden, he seemed so mortal—too mortal. The view set their teeth on edge, and they were beside themselves as to what to do.

"Gawddamn, Milo, is he at all conscious?"

"Don't know. He opened his eyes then squinched them shut again. I think he's barely alive."

"What the hell ya think happened?"

"Doesn't make no sense to me. Guess he must o' got caught outside in the storm an' froze, but made it back, somehow."

"We got to either get a doctor up here, or we got to get him to a hospital, damned fast!" said Shorty.

"Hell, we can't take him out of here! Heat's what he needs. How we goin' to sled him over the snow?"

"We can't. We got to get some help up here."

"Then you stay here with Whitey an' get that fire agoin'. I'll hightail it to the Mountain House an' call a hospital."

"Take my snowshoes, in case the doc needs 'em," said Shorty.

Milo headed off in a rush across the deep snow. He was puffing through his breath vapors. The air sparkled. The going seemed unbearably slow, and he thought he was never going to reach the road.

What if that damned ol' truck won't start in this cold air? Damn, damn, damn! Milo's thoughts were not kind and they cursed him for being so careless and neglecting the maintenance on his pickup. But to his overwhelming relief, it started up on the first turn of the crankshaft. He beat it back over the hill and down to the Mountain House as fast as the icy roads would allow.

Some time later, Whitey opened his eyes upon the four sterilized walls of a hospital room.

Whitey recuperated in a boarding house in Sweet Home. The nights were long this time of year but getting shorter. However, the long nights suited him fine, because he slept a lot. Sleep was what the doctor ordered. He was a wise doctor, because sleep was silent, and Whitey needed silence. He lived in silence. From the silence, he heard much commotion during the day: visitors stopping by with lots of chitchat and the ruckus of birds and dogs and children outside. The visitors meant well, and most of the time, he extended them his courtesies. Other times, he pretended to be asleep – doctors orders, after all.

The ruckus started early. A large murder of crows squadroned in a stand of firs, across the way. At the crack of dawn each day, he lay and listened as they stirred about and started their obnoxious motors—*sputter, sputter, squeak, squawk, squawk*—until they were all running at the same time. Then, in dark exquadrills, they fanned out like marauders, looking for trouble and plunder. But he didn't hold it against them. They're truthful. A crow acts out from the silence. A crow is a crow and a crow will be true to its nature. But it seemed to Whitey that those innocent crows set a bad example for some people, who then tried to act more like crows than men.

Today, the sun was breaking through the rain clouds. The apple tree outside his window was beginning to show some buds. Plump chickadees and juncos hopped about in the branches. Spider strings hung from its bony limbs and whipped in the breeze, catching the light, changing hues along their length. But Whitey wouldn't see this tree bear fruit. Perhaps one of the ladies of the valley would pick some and bring them up to the camp, when she came up on a weekend visit, and offer him a taste. And, so, the valley comes to the mountains.

Sweet Home was as good a town as any, but there were too many weeping willows down here. It was hard to understand why the valley dwellers planted such a tree to adorn their yards instead of the grand fir—they'll grow here, too. But the noble fir grows in the mountains. He lay in his bed and longed for mountains.

The Lava Lake camp was already back in operation. But they were working in snow, and it was still cold up there. The doctor said he had a few weeks to wait before his recuperation was complete. At least he'd see the apple tree bloom.

Chapter 30 The Ancient

It's told that there is not a god that Manu is not, therefore a god or goddess is but a part of a company in what Manu Is. But this is not *so* with the sons and daughters of Manu. The birth of mankind broke the ancient mold because this birth was something *new* under the sun: the first contradiction—a soul born whole, so humanly alone and forever unfinished. On that day *each* and *everything* under the sun was brand-new – the *sun* was new. The gods are old and these newborn children of Manu called them *"The Ancient."* They are what they are and what they are is all that they will ever be; old gods have no choice in the matter because they can't die away from Manu. In effect, they have no future. But a child is like an evergreen tree, growing up from humus, and will grow tall and wide and fill up space and will cast her seeds and will add on growth rings forever.

The ancient is beyond the reach of conceptualization, but not beyond that of realization because the ancient is what is original in the human being and whispers secrets through the inner ear of those who choose to hear. Mankind wasn't born yesterday…

Whitey had to move his campsite. He'd been gone too long and without him to support them the gargoyles weren't nearly ferocious enough to keep the machine at bay. The walls were breached and the sanctum was desecrated. The section of old trees where he located his camp, on that day he arrived, was gone. He'd lived there for eight years; it had stood there for over eight thousand years; it took eight days to cat-log it off. A plain of slash, cut by cat roads, disappeared over the hill in the direction of Crescent Mountain.

He relocated to the strip of trees that buffered Lava Lake from the unit. The trees were smaller and more varied and there was more light so more brush. From here, he could hear the sucking sounds the lake made, as it sipped itself away through the lava fissures. The ducks and geese flew in, took up house in the shallow pools and jabbered. Redwings and yellow heads and tanagers warbled in the reeds. Camp robbers flew in and hopped about in the trees, talking to one another (probably planning their heist) while furtively eyeing the camp grounds, looking for valuable tidbits and waiting for their opportunity. He let them rob him by allowing them to keep his crumb tossings cleaned up. As always, he kept a neat camp, so the robbers couldn't get to his vitals. Chipmunks were his dinner guests. They showed up neatly dressed in striped suits. Later, in midsummer, the Forest Service turned some of their mountain canaries into the grass in the dry lake bottom. It was a busy noisy place, far different from the quiet old trees.

The Sunday air was crispy as a fresh cracker. The sun was rising, and the coffee was hot. He heard some trucks pull in up the hill and stop at the truck shop, but thought nothing of this; truck noise was common. Then a racket, like a herd of beasts stomping on steel, shattered his reverie. It was a sound that he once knew well but had forgotten. It was a foreign sound to these mountains: the sound of the grassy plains—cattle. He heard the hoops and yahoos of the drovers and felt the ground shake. He stood and walked to the trail that went to the lake bottom and arrived there just as the cattle showed up. The ones in back were pushing the ones in front and the wranglers were pushing the ones in back. All kinds of bawling and whooping were going on. Nothing much surprised him any more, but he had to admit, this was somewhat shocking.

Down the trail they stampeded, past the wise old cottonwood, shaking the ground, making her leaves vibrate. If Whitey was surprised, she had to be astonished. The ride in had been a long one with no water to drink. They stampeded out onto the dry lake bottom, crashing through the willows and scattering the goslings, in their rush to the pools to satisfy pent-up thirst. They crowded knee-deep into the pools, turning the shorelines to muck, and then headed on a heavy-footed run into the meadow. The mountain canaries, wide-eyed with wonder, came running up to meet these strange creatures who'd come to steal the grass.

Two weeks later, the willows were beat down and disappearing, reeds and rushes were stomped into muck, and the once waist-high grass of the meadow was all a mess and turning to stubble. The bucks led their does off to higher meadows. The clangor of cow's bells quickly displaced the songs of the geese and blackbirds and tanagers. Whitey missed the singing birds, but he understood that those cowbells came from the same silence as the songs of birds. Difference was: unlike the songs, the cowbells didn't know their proper place.

More people walked down to the pools and the meadow creek this summer than in past years, because the camp was no longer fit for human habitation. The trees to the west of the camp were completely gone. Instead of the view out into the green sea of firs and flowing shadows, the camp looked out into a littered swamp of stumps, burnt slash, hot air and flowing heat waves. In the old days, the sun set behind the trees by two o'clock. These days, the same sun beat the camp to blazes with its pounding rays all day long.

The trailer's inhabitants baked like sugared apples in their tin ovens, and the kingpins in the cabins started clamoring for air conditioners. Of course, they got them. Now, the constant whir of electric motors turning fans, sucking up pure mountain air to condition, mixed with the persistent drone of the electricity generator. Whitey rarely went to the camp any more, but everyone was quick to clear out of there and beat their steps to the woods where it was cool and still smelled sweet. They walked farther every day and had to search harder to find those sweet cool places.

On a Sunday morning in late summer, just as the sun was rising, Whitey awoke to something like a calling—a voice in the breeze. Or was it a felt feeling? Or perhaps it was the echoes of a fading dream. Whatever, it seemed to be coming from the direction of Crescent Mountain. Why, he hadn't climbed that mountain since Jeremy left. At first, the calling came in his sleeping dreams, but when he awoke, dreams merged and it was still calling. He knew not to ignore such invitations, so he headed north, through the sleeping camp and crossed the black desert of slash and into the woods and up through the high meadows and climbed the mountain all the way to its summit. Mountain marmots whistled greetings as he walked by.

Upon the summit, he stood in the exact spot where he used to sleep-out with his troop of boys. He looked all about. The lake still glittered below, but the logging was encroaching from the east and the poor little pool was soon to lose its border of trees and then the hot east wind will blow against its water. As he thought on this, he felt an old familiar squirming in his gut that he thought he had purged long ago. *That damned longing worm is back,* he thought. Suddenly, he realized the worm never left; it just got settled-in and comfortable. It had found itself a home and all it wanted in its complacency. But here it was again, scenting longing, feeling hunger, squirming, and wanting food. *Insecure bastard! What a gorger! Well, by blazes if I'm going to feed it any longer! Not in my gut! Time to starve that squirmer out.* The thoughts made him chuckle. The irony of it all was downright comic. The fates must never cease laughing. Seems that a man on the go with a universe to do his going in would be content enough to sink his root into the soil and faithfully thrust his green sprout into the heavens—a tree of wood or an indifferent man, maybe - if there is such a one—but not a man who's searching for the evergreen man. The evergreen man is a full-orbed self-serving eidolon, who's so full of his *self* he overflows, into ever more rings. Perhaps he's the only *free* man on Earth.

As with a rainbow, he's always on the go and always there for all the other colors. There are more colors than green in a rainbow, but it's the anchor color. Other colors must move inward to find it; all it takes is a little bit of grit; those that move merge and mix and blend their edges; the more they move the greener they get. But colors were of no concern to Whitey because color merely symbolizes potential; they're there to be seen by those who see.

He'd been a loyal servant, came when called, never doubted his trail master, kept to the trail, stepped forward even when backsliding, and negotiated all of the switch-backs right up to where it ended at the treeless meadows – beyond the green. There, he was presented with his manumission. And so, now he saw the colors between black and white. He understood that the rainbow, itself, is colorblind. A man sees its colors for it and reflects them into each and every proper place, if he's true—if not they clash. And it's as though an old paradox is finally answered, and the answer comes from through the ear of his heart. He listens; a door opens and he hears. And so, at long last he knows his hue, and he sees that there is no end to seeing color.

Whatever else the evergreen man might be, he was here to be found and once a man has found him—been found—he becomes a pure green devotee and he finds his mentor everywhere. His soul is iridescent green.

For sure, that old evergreen man is hard to find and harder yet to catch. Like the rainbow, he aims for the sky and touches the world lightly; move toward him and he seems to move away. Just when you think you got him – *poof* . . . There's no restful nest for the high-flying bird that searches for him. Green is but a mote in his dark eye. He's a loner who can blend with other colors without loosing his integrity.

Oh, that evergreen man! Follow him if you can, and he'll take you by the hand and lead you to the land along the misty banks of the swift-flowing Alahkazan. And once you've arrived you may actually find that you've been there all the time. But it takes a ton of time to make the trip—indeed, it may take all of it— even that may prove insufficient. But he's a faithful servant to the man who seeks him—banish slavery and service is always reciprocal.

Here stood Whitey on this fine day, upon a high ridge, exploring his senses. From far away came a sound of joyous laughter and singing, getting closer, drifting down from overhead, shaking the silence like thunder. He bent his neck and looked up. Way up there, high in the sky, black motes in the blue, a flock of Canadian honkers flew, chanting back and forth in rhyming antiphony.

"What's their message to a man?" he asked. He listened . . .

"They represent fleeting felicity. Grab at them and they're gone," was the answer. *"Reach for them; stretch it, don't clutch, don't hold on. Let words fly away."*

The honkers sailed beneath the full bright-orange moon, dimming in the morning light. It was too soon in the season for migrating honkers. This was curious. Whitey reached, stretched his reach, took to wing, and soared as if awake in a sleeping dream. He fell in line and sang with them.

"What's your hurry so early?" he sang.

The one flying immediately in front of him cocked its head, eyed him, and said: "We're given wings along with lots of sky and air, so's to fly way out to there."

Whitey looked about and saw only the mountains below, with creeks and lakes laced by trees—and the open sky and the round moon above. "To where?" he said.

Another one, off to his right, and a little farther back in the wedge, said: "Through there; through the window. The moon is a window, you must surely know."

And the gaggle sang out: "Window, you know; window, you know. Through the window; though the window."

Yet another, somewhere behind him, sang out: "'Tis time for us to go."

All the others, in unison, sang out: "Time to go; time to go."

Whitey looked up at the moon.

Then the leader, flying at the cutting edge of the formation sang out: "And we shan't go slow. We gotta hit it at its perigee if we are to winter along the Sea Of Tranquility."

All the others picked up the last three words and chorused them.

Another sang: "Are you coming with us, too?"

Whitey said: "Yes, soon, but first I have one last job to do."

Hearing this, they all laughed with resounding glee; laughter filled the air and mixed with the sky—flying through waves of laughter, blue-tinged laughter, laughing to the moon. "Job to do; job to do; job to do . . ."

If he flew through the window of the moon, perhaps he'd never return, and with one last job left to do he let this choice fly away with the geese. So, Whitey wished them a good journey, dropped his left wing, and banked off to the east, circled once or twice, and then returned to where he stood.

Standing there on Crescent Mountain, he took one last good look around. The moon was slightly saffron-hued, chalky in its rind. The geese were gone but their chorus remained, like winged thoughts, singing in his mind: *Maybe I'll cut a wide circle and come back through here some day, after the fires have burned themselves out, after the oceans have rolled in and then receded again, after the ice flows have surged and melted away. I'll look about and then toss a seed to test the wind, see how she blows. I'll step off the mountain and go to wandering to and fro, tramping another line in time, to see how tall the Tree grows.*

He bent his steps for camp.

Chapter 31 Kevin Picks His Eye

There was once a yew tree just north and little bit east of Lava Lake. He wasn't tall but he was thick and tough, and old -- must've been pushing a thousand years. For all of those years he lived in the shade. During those thousand years, a million birds or more flew down and hopped around in his branches and sang and built nests and nibbled at his fruit and flew away again, spreading his seeds in their droppings. But the old boy died before his time was up; he refused to live in a clearcut...

The camp was all abuzz. The big president himself was somewhere about. Why, he hadn't been around here more than two or three times since Carr died. What on Earth would an important man like that be doing here? What did he come to say? Rumors flew buzzed about like mosquitoes:

"He's come to say they're not closing down the camp, after all," said one.

"He's come to say they're closing it down immediately, and we gotta clear out," said another.

"He's come to say they're taking it all apart and moving the whole shebang to over on the westside. Gonna put her on the M-line out north of the Mountain House," said yet another.

"Nope, puttin' 'er up aroun' Britenbush."

"Sheep Creek," someone said.

"Big honcho like that ain't here fer no reason. Big things are abrewin', that's fer sure," said someone else.

Truth was, the big honcho had come to see Whitey and was at his camp this very minute, and blubbering like a baby.

It was cool, almost cold, in the first glow of morning, when Kevin pulled up in front of the truck shop. The glow laid upon the big clearcut to the west. The view cut into his anxieties like a rusty file. He felt half sick. *Oh for God sake! Damn the blasted luck!* He remembered the day—that happy-sad day of their reunion—when he and Whitey walked over that same ground, through the old growth, to Whitey's camp. *Damn! Damn! Damn! Christamighty, I should've stopped that in its tracks—had I only come up here from time to time—I just didn't know.* His gut swallowed his heart; now he dreaded more than ever what he had to do. But he couldn't turn tail for Portland because he'd made Lilly a promise, and besides: this was something he had to do for himself more than for her—or go completely insane. So he bit his lower lip, cursed his ineptitude, and like a good corporate executive, tried to ignore his feelings and put his mind to the task at hand. But a tear started to form and so he bit down harder.

He loved this place. He'd always felt renewed, like he was young again and full of the magic of living, whenever he came here. Next to Slim's long-gone camp on the Rogue, it was his favorite place on Earth. He remembered this camp as it was, as Bob Carr had kept it, nestled in among the old growth, shaded and happy and peaceful and special.

The massive clearcut that defaced the area cut into more than his anxieties; it defaced a part of his heritage. What he saw now is what he was doomed to remember. *I had the power to have preserved this little place—but I didn't do so. But I hadn't known. But I should've known. But I was preoccupied with other business. But I'm always preoccupied by business. Hell, I'm enslaved to business. I'm owned.* As if Lorraine weren't enough, he felt hen-pecked by his own thoughts.

Looking through the windshield, his eyes scanned the camp's buildings. *Good grief! The place looks like a blister on a scar.* He wished he'd never laid eyes on this. But he had to come here today. He came for two reasons: Lilly Carr had asked him to, and he had to face Whitey before it was too late. Two compelling reasons, or so he'd thought. Now, he knew there was a third reason: he had to see this desecration. *Serves me right. It's all a reflection of my worthless life.*

No camp, no Whitey. No doubt about that. Whitey was no mere employee of AOK, praying for resettlement. Yes, that's what he had to do today, he had to face Whitey. He had to stand up and look him in the eye and express his feelings to him without blubbering. He'd rather get run over by a D-8.

He'd worked like a damned demon to get to where he was. He'd stared down many big egos, and he'd even looked Ammon Reed in the eye without blinking or backing off. But that was just looking. In the eye of Whitey, he melted like a butterball in a hot skillet. How in the hell do you look into eyes that don't look, that see right through you? But he had to look into those eyes and hold onto himself or forever feel like a just a whistle punk, lowest on the totem pole in the old-time big woods. He felt grateful to Lilly for giving him an excuse to come, but knowing he needed an excuse made him feel trite.

He pulled his car around to the far side of the shop, where it couldn't be seen from the camp. He was going incognito today. This wouldn't be a good place for the president of AOK to be trapped in a torrent of questions. There was only one worker on duty. He felt relieved. The grease monkey was busy under a truck. Kevin hung onto the truck's frame, squatted, and peeked under. The boy was backside-down on a creeper pushing it along with his feet, aiming his grease gun at a cert on the drive line. He looked at the boy in his greasy coveralls, big grease smudge across his forehead, concentrating on his job. The boy was about the same age as his own boy, who was smudged with the filth of greasy habits.

"How ya doing there," said Kevin.

The words surprised the young man out of his concentrations, and the gun missed the cert.

"Mighty good," came the simple reply.

"I'm sure you are," said Kevin. "Can you tell me where I might find Whitey's camp?"

The grease monkey was an insightful lad and hard to fool. He detected the sound of sadness in the voice he heard—or maybe it was loneliness. But he didn't suspect that the man squatting on his hams, talking to him, was one of the most powerful men in the Northwest, icon of the lumber industry, mover and shaker on the corporate scene, pillar of society. He thought the man was simply a visitor, needing directions to his friend's camp. "Down the trail to the lake," he said. "Pass the garbage dump. Keep going to where the grade drops off, you'll see a smaller trail that Y's to the right. Go about a hundred steps or so an' you'll be there."

So far so good, thought Kevin. But when he walked out the door, who would be entering but Orville Vanderfeen, the head mechanic. Orville had worked here for years and knew who he was. They came face to face, and Orville's mouth flopped open. Kevin only said: "Hi, Orville," and he went on his way. Orville was speechless. But he knew Orville. Orville loved news. He knew full well that Orville had spun on his heels and beat a dash to the sleeping camp, faster than Paul Revere could ride, waking it up with cries of: *"The president is here! The president is here! Hoskings is in camp."* In his mind, he could hear Orville, right now.

Blast it all! Almost pulled it off. This means I'm going to have to run the gauntlet getting back out of here.

Whitey wasn't at all surprised to see Kevin walk into his camp that morning. He was expecting him. He even had the water boiling and the hot chocolate ready. Kevin's pathetic appearance didn't surprise him, either. Kevin was pallid, old too early in life and on the downhill side of his time. This was decay of the kind when a tree is rotting inside and it shows outside: its bark gets brittle, needles grow sparse, and shelf fungi wrinkle its surface. In many ways, body language is more expressive than the wordy one. It's truthful, too; animals don't lie. Kevin was trying hard to put some spring into his step, look chipper and in charge. His effort was obvious.

"Hello Kevin," said Whitey, smiling gladly. "It's early. Come for some hot chocolate?"

As always, Kevin was amazed when he saw Whitey: *How can a man not age?* He'd have been more than just amazed had he known how old Whitey was and how young. But this sort of knowing was way beyond Kevin. There he sat, dressed in his stagged-off pants, black suspenders, gray and white striped shirt, wool socks, and moccasins, serene as Brahman. His thick white hair was neatly combed. In his mind's eye, Kevin remembered him on another day in an old scene he'd never forget, not if he lived forever. In that scene the past becomes present: a storm has the crew holed up inside. Alone, sitting on a produce box, he's cowering in the corner of Dewey's dingy grub shack, as far away from Dewey as he can get. The door unexpectedly swings open and Whitey steps in followed by Abe. Whitey's wearing a blue wool watch cap, Abe a brown one. Each is draped by a black shiny slicker, dripping water, and carrying his blood-red axe. Unsmiling, their eyes study the surroundings. Godamighty, they look like Titans! They remove their slickers and ask for coffee. Whitey doesn't notice him, but Abe's looking right at him. Their eyes meet and lock on. And the world changed.

"Watch out: it's hot."

For the thousandth time, the timeworn scene receded back into it's own time and place. Abe's eyes were suddenly Whitey's. Vapors rising, the cup of hot chocolate was suspended by Whitey's hand above the little fire. He instantly dropped his eyes to the cup and held them there as he reached for it. "Yes, I can see that. Good and hot – just the way I like it. Hot chocolate's exactly what I came for," he said, feigning light-heartedness.

This camp wasn't in an old growth, and it didn't have a mossy windfall to lean against, so Whitey had set some chairs. He was sitting in one of these, and Kevin sat down opposite the small campfire from him.

"Awww, this never tastes so good as here," said Kevin, taking a sip.

"How's business?" said Whitey.

"Couldn't be better."

"And the family?"

But Kevin didn't answer. He changed the subject and said: "Lilly Car came to my office the other day and gave me this to give to you." He handed Whitey an envelope, then said: "Go ahead, read it if you'd like. I'll just sit here and enjoy my chocolate and listen to the birds."

"Thank you, Kevin," said Whitey as he slipped the letter from the envelope. He caught a subtle scent: sorta like wild lilac in the woods. He hoped his excitement wasn't too obvious; here was Lilly after all this time.

"Dearest Whitey:

My thousand years in Purgatory, apart from you, are over if you wish it. You promised me that you would not forget me. I have held you in my heart since we were last together and now I intend to hold you to your promise. Bob's affairs are filed away and I am finally finished with all of that. Jeremy is on his own and gainfully employed. I am done with being a busy widow and ready to jump that camp. I want to become a timberbeast and go to tramping from here to there, if not in the big woods then in the big world. I hear that the mountains are tall in New Zealand and the treelines grow high; that the rivers are wide in Europe and the forests are thick in Madagascar. Will you be my partner at the saw? Ours will be a happy harp. Please say that you will. I will remain right here in Portland until I hear from you.

I carry my Love of you.

Lilly"

He held the letter for a moment just to feel it. He saw her creamy skin glisten in the moonlight. He tasted her: thick and wet and sweet and tart. Her warm breathing was like a zephyr in his ear. He felt her touch; her soft voice. His memories stirred his chemicals. He hadn't felt this warm in a long while and it wasn't the hot chocolate either: hot chocolate's not that hot—nor that sweet. He remembered when he told her about his times running as a timberbeast in a big woods filled with misery harps and bulls of the woods and her keen interest in all of that. It was on one of those days that she came to the camp to check on Jeremy, and now he knew, to see him. She surprised him that day when she asked him if he'd truly loved that girl he'd wanted to marry. He said that he loved her then and loved her now. "It takes more than time and distance to kill love," he'd said. Lilly had smiled and said: "I thought you would say something like that. Not many men ever love a woman. They want one; they want to have a woman; but they don't want to give her real love, because her *real* love is not what they really want in return. Real love is something that you carry around with you."

Kevin peeked as Whitey replaced the letter into the envelope. He saw Whitey smile and he, too, smiled. He said: "She's the finest woman I've ever met."

"What did she say to you?" Whitey wanted to get as much of Lilly as he could garner on this day.

"She wanted to know everything I knew about you these days. I told her that we'd lost touch." Kevin paused, wondering ahead about her next words: "She said that wasn't very smart of me." He paused again, stared into his cup, and said: "I told her that was because I'm not a very smart man."

"And she said?"

"She said that she thought I was smart enough but not the least bit wise." Whitey chuckled. Kevin pretended not to hear and continued: "But it's like I said, she wanted to talk about you, not about me. She asked me when I'd be seeing you again, and I told her that I didn't know. She then asked me if I'd do her a favor and take some time from my important schedule and look you up and deliver her letter. She said I should do it for old-time's sake, if for no other reason. And then she told me to do it right away. That was yesterday."

Kevin paused and sipped his chocolate.

Whitey hadn't expected this kind of conversation. He figured Kevin had come to do some blubbering. It was overdue. So he just watched Kevin sip his chocolate, waiting for him to get on with it.

Kevin was leaning forward, resting his elbows against his legs, and holding his cup with both hands between his spread-out knees. Whitey watched him sink like a pitchy old log in a mill pond. His entire body seemed to shrink and his shoulders sloped. He stared at his boots. Whitey knew severe self-depreciation when saw it. Good God, the guy was in danger of shrinking clean away right here in front of him.

Mumbled Kevin: "They've gone all to hell."

Well, here we go . . . To hell with this penny-ante crap! Whitey thought. "For God's sake, Kevin, look in my direction when you talk to me so I can hear what you have to say and then say it like you mean it."

Whitey's bluntness and the tone in his voice shocked Kevin. His head jerked up like he'd just been slugged on the chin. He spoke up: "I don't know what the hell they're into any more. Worse yet I don't know what the hell they're putting into themselves," he said, avoiding eye contact.

Whitey knew what Kevin meant. It figured. Those children of Kevin's were only reflecting his own values right back to him. They were only looking for substance and had been all their lives. There wasn't any to be had in their home. But now, it seemed, they'd finally found some substitute substance. He said: "Well, what did you expect. They couldn't be little angels on a string, forever. We all have some of the devil in us, you know. We should allow him to ooze out nice and easy-like. Better to take your time with him so you can get to know him and keep him in control than to watch him burst the chains of hell and drag you in, because that's probably just what will happen if you don't have someone who loves you give you some help." *No pity, by God! I'm going to feed you to yourself, Punk and see if the taste of it makes you throw up.*

Whitey was going to pull Kevin out of himself today, even if it pulled the twerp in two. He knew what Kevin's problem was. Every time Kevin looked at him, he also saw Abe, and he couldn't bear up under the image. That's why he avoided eye contact. He saw *Abe's* eyes peering out at him, and he knew full well he couldn't measure up to the standards of those eyes. They made him feel one inch tall. Well, it was time he dropped his petty illusions and took the measure of himself.

"And how's Lorraine?"

"She can go to hell."

Well, listen to that. This character may be starting to come around, thought Whitey.

Kevin sniffled, retreating into Punkie. Whitey loved the little punk and would be nice to him now and save him from his woes. He waited for the offer of a rag, but none was forthcoming. He wished he'd brought his own, but he'd forgotten it. *That was stupid.* He couldn't get around Whitey for very long without blubbering. He could plot out corporate maneuverings five years in advance and strut like a rooster when he faced the board of directors with his high-falutin' schemes. High-seated judges sought favor with *him. B*ut he couldn't remember to bring a snot rag when he had to face Whitey, knowing full well he'd end up bawling like a hungry calf. So now here he sat, as slumpy and droopy as a fiddle fern in the rain.

Let him use his sleeve, thought Whitey. And that is just what Kevin did. *Put him on the hook. Hold him up to the light, where he can look inward and see the worms.* "I'm curious about a few things and you're the big president of AOK. If you can't satisfy my curiosity then nobody can," he said

"What do you want to know?"

"We don't log these trees the same way we used to. Why not?"

"What exactly do you mean?" Sniffle.

"You know what I mean, Kevin. You could see it driving in here, if those are eyes next to your nose. We used to leave a lot of trees standing. We left large sections just the way they always had been. We cut out the units in blocks. We didn't clearcut the entire mountain chain. The idea was that the forest could rejuvenate itself, from itself. Now, we're going back and taking out the uncut sections. We're even taking the seed trees out of the old units, for God's sake! How the hell is that going to work? Is there some reasoning here that escapes me?"

Kevin wiped his nose with his sleeve. "Reforestation," he said.

"Oh, I see. Reforestation, you say. A one-word solution to my mental dilemma. How could I be so dim? Reforest with what?"

"With trees. Seedlings," said Kevin. "We plant a bunch for every one we fall."

"All trees?"

"What do you mean, all trees?"

"Good godamighty, Kevin! Have you ever gone into the woods? I thought you were born and raised there. Do you replant them *all?*" Whitey shook his head as though disgusted and started naming the trees: "There's: Grand Fir, Douglas Fir, Noble Fir, Silver Fir, Red Cedar, Western Hemlock, Mountain Hemlock, Ponderosa Pine, Sugar Pine, Pacific Yew . . ." He was ready to go on like this and name every tree he knew, evergreen and deciduous, but Kevin saw what he was doing and interrupted:

"Dougfir."

"Dougfir . . . Dougfir. That's it? Dougfir?"

Kevin nodded.

"Well, that's short but sweet. Also easy."

"It's the crop tree," said Kevin. The ugliness of his words registered, and he hung his head again and looked at his boots. "They're called 'supertrees,'" he mumbled.

Kevin's words were damned near as funny as they were ugly. Whitey chuckled, and said: "You mean they'll be able to fly and jump over buildings?"

"They're genetically improved. They're supposed to grow faster," mumbled Kevin.

"Thickets . . . You're planting thickets of pulp wood, Kevin. Kinda like corn," said Whitey, sadly. "I sure as hell hope they have good deep root systems to support all their beef. The blasted things are going to burn down before they grow big enough to be felled. Earth, herself, will burn them down trying to make room for what's right. You want to see an example of what you're talking about? Walk down into the lake meadow. You'll see a herd of cattle, but you won't see any blacktails. Cattle ate and trampled the willows away, and so the geese lost their broods and flew off. They won't be coming back until it's all set right again." He peered at Kevin. Kevin wasn't looking at Whitey, but he could feel Whitey's gaze. Whitey slowly shook his head, and said: "Monoculture . . . Pretty sounding word for such an ugly concept." He paused for emphasis and to see if Kevin wanted to speak, but Kevin remained silent.

Some moments passed while Whitey sipped his chocolate. Overhead, a bullbat ripped the sky apart, then another. Instinctively, he looked up. The trees blocked his view and hid the fast-flying bullbats, but not a fleeting vision in his past: long rough sack dragging the ground, a young boy's fingers blistered and cut from picking, back sore from stooping. He said: "Ever farmed cotton?"

Kevin shook his head.

"Well I have. It doesn't come to much, just a lot of monoculture."

"Silvaculture," mumbled Kevin. "It's called silvaculture."

"Silvaculture? Sil-va-cul-ture," said Whitey, playing with the word, letting it roll off his tongue. "Why I'll be damned, that's even a prettier word than the other one. Reforestation I think it was. Downright poetic. I must admit, that corporate syntax of yours does have a knack for prettying up ugliness with fancy words." And he chuckled at the ironic absurdity of it all.

"It's Reed that's doing it," Kevin blurted. "The guy has no heart—cold-eyed bastard can stare down the devil. He gets anything he wants from anybody he wants. He owns the politicians and a whole lot of other big shots, and I'm not kidding. He literally *owns* them. It's unbelievable! It's like a man who owns an obedient dog and he tells that dog what to do, and the stupid damned dog sticks out its tongue and wags its tail and does it mindlessly. Only this guy owns lots of dogs."

Manculture. Goddamned manculture. The words in his thoughts stung his mind like nettle pricks and stimulated his blood flow. For the first time today, Whitey's heart went out to Kevin. It was plain to see that Kevin identified with that dog he spoke of, sitting there all droopy-eyed, tail between his legs, chained to the company like a mutt to a stake, the stake being the only thing left that the poor little dog can identify with in the world. Quietly, almost under his breath, Whitey said: "Then he tosses that dog a bone." Then: "Who the hell is this Reed?"

Kevin glanced at Whitey, surprised by the words he heard. In his world, the whole universe knew who Ammon Reed was. But Whitey had never even heard of Reed, and Whitey was the most intelligent man he knew. Whitey stood so far above Reed that Reed didn't even exist for him. Reed didn't deserve his attention. But here *he* sat, just a punk, in a place where Reed would never dare come. He respected Whitey more than ever and he suddenly felt honored. "The CEO," answered Kevin.

"Well, that's tidy for you, isn't it? If it's *his* doing, then it's *your* non-doing. Can you come to terms with what I mean?"

Kevin was silent for a few moments. Then he shook his head and said: "No."

"Well then, let me put it into perspective for you." Whitey pulled his voice down deep and mellow, and drawled out: "I know it ain't right what's about to happen to that punk, but it be Dewey's doin'—not mine. Think I'll find me a cedar tree an' sit on my ass an' drink hot chocolate till the Chinooks blow over."

Whitey watched Kevin squirm. Then he said: "Do you think this mono . . . excuse me, I mean silvaculture scheme is going to work?"

"No," said Kevin, shaking his head.

"It's cut and run, isn't it?"

Kevin, nodding, said: "For the most part."

"How long is it going to take before she's all gone?"

"Between twenty and thirty years, most all the first cut timber will be down to pretty much nothing. AOK intends to sell itself off into pieces and hightail it before then. After that, she might be good for two, maybe three more cuttings of real low quality stuff before it all plays out." Kevin shrugged his shoulders. Then, in a subdued voice, he said: "I don't know exactly how many more cuttings she's good for. In lots of places probably only one, if any. You know, steeper hillsides up in higher elevations—places like that."

"Twenty to thirty years of the old stuff . . ." Whitey took a deep breath, looked away, and sighed it back out. "Sweet Jesus forgive us because we didn't know what in hell we were doing." Looking back at Kevin, he added: "That means falling at several times the rate it's being felled now."

"AOK's not the only player in the field, Whitey; gets more crowded all the time. Competition's fierce."

"Oh, that's right. I forgot. You're busy doing your non-doing and collecting your stock bonuses. It's the other guy who's doing it. Don't hand me that corporate mish mash. And don't lay supply and demand economics on me, either. I'm not interested in gibberish. I'm trying to get to what's *right* here. Are you interested in what's right? If you're not, say so, and I'll shut up and drink my chocolate before it gets cold."

"Nothing's right. The world's going all to hell, Whitey."

"If the world's going to hell, you're going to hell. It's your world. Do you expect to survive it?"

Kevin shook his head.

"Then, go to hell, Kevin. Don't be so damned spooked by it. Confront it. Hell can be one hell of a happening."

Kevin nodded his head.

Whitey was tired of looking at the top of Kevin's head. "Damn it, Kevin, look me in the eye!"

"I can't," mumbled Kevin, almost ready to cry, again.

"Is that because, when you look at me, you see Abe looking back at you? Is that it?"

Kevin nodded. "Something like that," he mumbled.

How sad that Kevin had turned Abe into a haunting ghost. "Well, Kevin, you're going to have to face him some time. How else are you going to know how to do the right thing?" Whitey paused for a moment in thought, grinned, chuckled to himself, and said: "Looks like you're going to have to kick your ghost and pick your eye, doesn't it?"

"What do you mean?"

"I mean, look at it this way: it's Abe's eye or Ammon's. Which is it going to be? Pick one."

Hearing this, Kevin squared his shoulders and pulled himself out of his slump.

He quit blubbering and looked Whitey directly in the eye. He tried, but he couldn't quite hold on to it. Lowering his head he said: "I'm on the wrong side. I know I should've done everything differently. Too late now."

"Time has nothing to do with it and the same man whose eye you're afraid of taught me that *should'ves* are just plain chicken shit. There was a time in my life when should've was my favorite word, too. What does it matter what side you're on? Just try to do the right thing while you're there. Be where you're at. You're a woodsman, Kevin, so sharpen your axe, and keep it out of the dirt. Hone both heads and simply be aware of your direction. Put a handle on yourself. Be prepared to use that axe. Swing it in the right direction and it'll hit the mark every time. If they kill you . . . well, that was the mark you hit. At least you'll die right, and your last word won't be *should've*."

Kevin wiped his nose with his sleeve, then looked up and smiled into Abe's eyes again and he didn't drop his eyes ever again.

When he walked away, Kevin heard Whitey say: "Good-bye, Kevin. You take care, and keep your axe sharp." He didn't say: So long for now, or, See you later. It was a firm and final good-bye.

As he walked up the trail, past the garbage dump, Kevin saw the camp's population milling about and knew they waited for him. It occurred to him that he didn't have the slightest idea what he was going to do next, but for the first time in a long while, he didn't give a damn. Finally he felt free. When Whitey conjured up the eye of Abe and forced him into it, it was as if he'd fallen into that deep dark eye-of-a-place. In there, like the rumor of death, his life flashed by in a moment. He'd felt his ending, so final and certain. It was an empty feeling -- no gain . . . *Holy Jesus . . . How blind can a man get? If someone like Abe can end, what in the hell makes me behave as if my life is going to last forever?* Thinking this, he decided right here in this step, mid-stride, that he was going to live for death, because he knew that he had some answering to do, somewhere along the line, most likely at its end. He wanted to have the right ones, *real* answers. His life's line had been real; what happened had happened, all right. And the powerful people who'd shared their lives with him: Abe, Whitey, Slim, his mother, The Little Willy, Hack and even Dewey were real because they were unforgettable. Their effect certainly had been and now they each were a part of what he was. But the adding it all up into a lump sum and then pretending, acting as if he was a big man because they were in him, was a big mistake. He had to shoulder his own saw. It was time to detach, to finally begin to grow into what he was—whatever that is. He'd let his *should'ves* wither on the tree as something unnatural right along with *should be*, and all the rest of the damned shoulds. *That all comes to nothing but grafting – manculture,* he thought.

He left the garbage dump behind, stepped over the sewage trickle and walked in among the people who were waiting there. He'd call a meeting this same day and promise equivalent jobs elsewhere in the company's operations to the ones being lost here. It was the least he could do, no *should* to it, being the only *right* choice in the matter. He didn't have even the slightest idea what was going to happen after that, but that was okay because he had one hell of an axe to swing.

Good god, I've been nothing more than a corporate catamite to a bull-of-nothing who keeps young men and screws their brains out and perhaps even their souls – till he's done with them – till they're thoroughly reamed and all used up, and ashamed of themselves! This time, I'm going to do my own saving, gonna save myself from my own stupidity and expose George Presco to be the dirty-money pimp that he is. He may be from the South but he's sure's to hell no gentleman. And if that son-of-a-hell-whore, Reed, doesn't like what I'm going to tell these people today, he can shove it up his hogo. Once the word's out, there won't be a thing he can do about it, short of losing face. He'll most likely do what's not right and tie the can to my ass. Just let the bastard try. I'd be a hard man to replace, and I can make him regret it, with what I know. I have one hell of a whistle to blow and know how to blow it; I'm an old whistle punk, after all. I can dispatch that son of Satan right into the hell of Alcatraz, with his tail tucked between his legs. Like a good powder monkey, I have access to some damn hot stuff that would blow the wigs clean off of a whole bunch of bigwigs, if I were to stick a fuse in it with phone calls to the right people and strike a match with some well-timed documents for certain newspaper reporters. The face of a particular sawed-off stump of a senator filled his vision. *Elections are coming up real soon -- good timing. Could mean some jail time for me as well as him, but what the hell . . . we both like big houses with lots of rooms. This might even be fun . . .* He smiled at the novelty of the drift of his thoughts.

The people pressed in. "Howdy folks. Got some good news for all of you," he said. The words sounded as good to him as they did to them.

Whitey heard the cheering coming from the camp and he knew that Kevin was using his new axe. Sounded as if he'd just felled the punk with one well-aimed swing. Abe would be proud of him. He reached into his pocket and removed the letter. He read it again and then to the letter said: "Lilly, my love, I'd get up this very moment and come running to you if only I could, but I've got one last job to do before I'm free. And then . . . well, I guess we'll just have to wait and see. But of this I am sure: I'll shoulder your love wherever I go, regardless of what comes of me."

Chapter 32   The Last Spar Tree

She wasn't always ancient. She was once the newborn daughter of the sun god and the goddess of pure water--cradled by light, swaddled in rain, and rocked by the wind. Though she took many forms she would only *be* what she was. They called her "Truth" in heaven. She thrived, grew tall upon Earth, took root in Adam, and when he came and saw *Truth* in her he was amazed and exclaimed: "So that there should be no confusion, on Earth I will name you *Tree*." She wed Earth and they gave birth to the woods and to all of the woodsy spirits and creatures and to woodsy folk; in early times these included Druids. Druids were born old and wide-eyed and so were great seers. Of all the races of that time, Druids were her most devoted and beloved. They honored her above all gods and saw that she was like a queen of all things growing and green and that the tree was her finest expression and they paid her homage, calling her "Queen Sooth." From *her* they drew their powers. Her high priests were called *"Seers of* Sooth" by some, *"Soothsayers"* by others. It's fabled that the greatest sayer of all of the Soothsayers foretold the coming in and the going out of the timberjack race, and a tall foretelling it was, too. With the passing away of the Druids so, too, passed her title, but her name remained. All of that was way back then, when she was young. She waited long, long, long for the coming of her timberjacks. When they finally came they were born young and blind and powerful; from *themselves* they drew their powers, standing and adding up their rings from the inside out. She cherished them as children and mothered them with service right up to the last of their kind. Archaic now, she craved to be free from her marital yoke. But how? The way she figured it, the great god Pan had found a way out of the weariness of his obligations, having been dispatched by the hand of a lover who loved him with her *whole* heart. Then, alone as alone can be, she'd stabbed herself in both of her eyes with a raptor talon, rather than see him sunder.

The only way out of the rings of time is to die out because only survivors may live within the orbits of Earth. She longed to go out along the *way* of Adam, her first lover, to wherever it is that way leads because this is the way of all things on Earth including, eventually, Earth. Fought over, sectioned off, divided up like spoils, beauty scarred, deserted, disgraced in so many foul ways, the passive primordial queen of Hammas, Druids, and Dryads all but died away during these trying times. But worldly tyrants lack the power to kill a queen such as this, and to simply pack up and leave on her own would be like committing suicide and as with men so with gods: suicide is sin. Such can only be slain by a Soothsayer. In these times, in the case of Tree, this means a Sooth-seeing timberjack - - a witness. Who else can possibly know? As with the Druids, there can't be timberjacks without a forest queen; so this timberjack is doomed to be the last of his race. This that he must do will be this last timberjack's last job...

Spar trees were being replaced with steel towers, called metal spars. "Metal spars are the latest thing," said the logger of the times. "Why hell m' man, just you look at the money those things will save. An' ever'body worth their salt knows that time is money." But, it was more of the same old thing: replacing men with heavy metal, tradition with technology, skill with machinery, a living tree with a dead steel tower mounted on a platform of wheels, another poor logger bogged down further into the bottomless red pit of debt just to pay for the expensive thing with his time and money. And so, the spar owned him.

But a timberjack's a timbertramp and a timbertramp has a job to do—always another job; and that job is forever some place else on up the line.

Up there on a ridge stood the spar tree, waiting for him to come and do what he had to do. No one else was going to top this tree; there was no one who could. Whitey and this tree were foretold. It had been quite a relationship between these spars and the men who climbed them and challenged them. It was a man and a tree pitted against one another as in a duel and there were survivors and diers, but there were no winners or losers.

"Whitey, I gotta admit, that's really somethin': that company bigwig comin' in an' tellin' the folks they don't have nothin' to worry about, ain't it? Said he personally would see us all through it. Ever'body feels a whole lot better."

Whitey glanced at Milo, who sat behind the steering wheel of his old pickup, negotiating the curves of the cinder clad logging road.

"That's really something, all right."

"Doesn't save the camp, but it saves a bunch o' nerves. Lots of them people didn't know what to do." Milo pondered his own words for a moment. Then he said: "Ya know, maybe this AOK outfit ain't so rotten after all."

Whitey smiled and said: "I think it just got better."

"I gotta tell that bull-head, Shorty, about this. He hates 'em, ya know. Maybe he'll come back when he hears this."

"What's Shorty doing these days?"

"Sellin' cars out there in Springfield. Ye gawd! Can ya imagine standin' aroun' on the pavement all day long, tryin' to bullshit a bunch of shiny-faced city slickers into buyin' some damned ol' shiny cars?"

"He's trying to sort things out," said Whitey. "He's managed to convince himself that he's doing what he wants to do. He'll figure out his mistake when he discovers that his tree can't grow where's he's taken it. Then he'll be off to somewhere that suits him better, maybe even back to here. Who knows? It's not *easy* being a woodsy boy these days." Whitey paused, thinking for a moment, then added: "An old timberjack once told me, back when I first came to these woods, that *easy* isn't in a timberjack's syntax."

"Yeah," said Milo, "tell me about it. I could sure use some *easy*, and ol' Shorty don't help none. I just wish he didn't have to go an' get so damned bull-headed about it all."

Said Whitey: "He's sad and without knowing why, and so he can't put any reason to it. That's why he's snarly so much of the time; he works too hard in his mind, trying to dig up reasons; he can't dig up the root of his moods. He knows it's there; it's just grown in too damned deep. I've known other men a whole lot like him."

Whitey eyed Milo through his peripheral. He looked sad and lonely and maybe even a bit confused right now. He'd lost his buddy and partner to the changing times. Whitey sympathized with his mood better than Milo could possibly know because, like Shorty, Milo was sad and didn't know why. In this respect the only difference between those two was that Milo was the better liar and probably a bit lazier in his mind. Milo was going to be okay; Shorty too. Though they were forest dwellers in a shrinking forest each was due to find his proper niche in the big woods. This is guaranteed for green people; they'll always go to where their tree can grow. Their resistance to their worm will see to that.

When they approached the area slated to be logged, Whitey told Milo to pull over and let him out at a place where a high ridge paralleled the road.

As Milo feathered the breaks, slowing to pull over, the engine died. He coasted into the pull-out, stopped, and said: "Well the hell, guess that's that: sucker won't run." Guess I'll just have to go up on that ridge with ya an' help ya mark that spar tree."

Whitey chuckled and said: "You get this engine started and go on back to camp and drink a cold beer for me. "Tell the crummy driver to be looking right here for me in the morning."

Milo started to protest, but Whitey stepped out, tossed his soogan over his shoulder, and took up a canvas bag stuffed with clothes and food. He headed up the ridge, leaving Milo bent over the fender of his pickup with his head down and his butt in the air, tinkering around with something under the hood. Before long, he heard the hood slam shut and the motor turn over about fifty times and finally start with a roar. Then the pickup went to clanking and rattling its way back down the road. He listened until it vanished from his hearing.

It was just another ridge in the mountains, but it was a high one that crested and dropped off from the hogback before it lost itself in the folds of other ridges. If it were in the Willamette Valley, instead of these mountains, it would most likely be named after some long-dead man of local history or politics. But, in the mountains, it's a nameless ridge among many nameless ridges and this ridge was slated for logging.

Up there on the summit, a tree waited for Whitey where it had been waiting for a long time, marking its rings. All around about, swirling within this living wood are the countless rings of eons, the jewelry of a queen. In there somewhere was the ring for the year Columbus sailed, another for the year they cracked the bell, and one for the Great Red Wolf. Nineteen rings were for Peppa, fourty four for Abe. The Professor's rings included the six they spent in one another's company; the same with a sliver off of Woody's final one. Lilly was there, as yet untotaled, and Kevin; sixty circled for himself. They were all in there together, and because they were with him he knew that his outer-most ring would be more than his first. To him *that* was of utmost importance. And there's a ring circling all the others for the end of the big woods—one last ring. Soon, there it'll all be, lit by the light of day, for any mortal man or woman to come along and to take a look and see themselves numbered there, if they're so inclined, recorded in the fading rings of a stump.

The going was steep but easy, walking on a soft carpet of moss. A dusky grouse jumped and roared off in a flurry, shot like a bullet straight down the hillside. Douglas squirrels jumped between the trees and trotted along the branches; like petty property owners they scolded his trespass. An innocuous brown creeper, tiny and barely visible against his tree, spiraled in short hops up the side of an old fir. About thirty feet from the ground, it fluttered off back down to the base of another fir and continued its endless routine. It's a good friend to these giants, constantly grooming, pecking, and digging into the grooves of their bark for its dinner, keeping them de-bugged. As the big trees go so goes the unsuspecting little creeper.

He found her waiting on the ridge top right where he *knew* she'd be. He reclined and used her bole for a backrest. The air was nippy and growing colder, but he felt the warmth of this royal tree and the beat of her heart against his back. From here he looked out to the east at Three-Fingered Jack and his friends. Northward, his glaciers streaming, stood tall Jefferson high into the sky. South of Jack gathered The Three Sisters. Poor old Jack has lost his timber along with some of his fingers and has nothing to show for it but rock and rubble. Long ago he was full and proud and reaching for the sky, but now he's backslid into a nubbin of his old self. Seems he didn't build a solid foundation and so time's trials found him wanting, took their toll, and now there he is: short, broken, old-looking, and craggy. Not a single one of those Sisters would give him even the slightest come-on, especially not with tall silver-headed Jefferson standing right over there. Now there's one-hell-of-a mountain.

A dirge, as though in sympathy with Jack and anxious for the cloak of night to hide his sorry view, floated in from off of one of the other ridges: "HOOOO, hooo, hoooo." Whitey ended his musings, pulled his soogan over his legs, closed his eyes, and drifted away into sleep, snuggled up against the tree. The two hearts beat together partnered up and like two ol' timberbeasts dreamed a mutual dream. Up the trail they went, towing their pal Time along—for entertainment. Now there's the biggest tall tale teller of them all. What a polished fibber; he doesn't originate them or add in a single rhyme. He just keeps them.

Time, what's money to Time? Unlike money -- or a man -- Time doesn't need *more* of himself; Time is indifferent. He better be; he's prayed *for* and cussed *at* more than anything else on Earth -- and all in vain. Like the leaves of a deciduous tree that finally know they're leaves when they detach and leave, leavings are all that he sees of himself; it's easy to be indifferent when you're complete. As with thought, he's an always-old, bass-ackward apparition that passes away each and every moment. In his passing, seeds turn into seedlings, seedlings into Sequoias, Sequoias into coal, coal into crystal, crystal into diamonds, and diamonds into desire. Man the mythmaker lives every moment suspended in the moment, scripting hieroglyphs upon the walls of Time's tomb. Tomb plunderers gawk in amazement as their fingers search the spoils; scholars search the libraries with their minds for the key that opens a closed door to ancient knowledge and to fame; poets seek to decipher the symbols with their vision; historians claim they own the Rosetta Stone that interprets the cryptography and so knowledge is theirs to hold and store in their manuscripts.

Somewhere, a seed is flying, and a thunderstorm is busily creating a raindrop, which may or may not quench a seed. Oh, to be indifferent like a seed—merciful, primordial indifference. Only through indifference can a crazy man maintain his sanity—or regain it—or give it up as lost and unredeemable without giving a damn. The spring-born fawn loses his footing and the glacier-fed stream sweeps him away, with indifference. The heavy-hearted doe crosses and walks away into the woods, with indifference. Perhaps only indifference is sane and wise.

Tree left behind her symbol in her vestige and so *she* no longer counts her rings; symbols don't grow, they tell tales; *life* grows, like an evergreen tree, rising up out of humus, reaching for the sun where she'll sprout her cones and throw her seeds out into the future. Now it's up to the sons and daughters of Humankind to fill the vestige with their own fertile lives and make it grow, or leave it empty and watch it wither on the limb, seed and all. If they can fill it full, then Tree will be in on the Omega just as she was at the Alpha—with one big exception: she will be taller, with tales to tell and songs to sing, because, besides the times of the clock and the mind there is another time altogether. Her song is her vision and her vision is a chorus. She sings of when Earth was young and pregnant, when Humankind was yet the unborn of Manu. She sings of timberbeasts and timberjacks and forests without edges. Her notes are the tall symmetrical Redwood and the squat lopsided Yew. The notes remain. The refrain is there for the person who can listen through the beat of the heart.

In the woods, each and every trail is fated to branch. Before the break of dawn, Whitey used his axe and branded a large X into the bark of the tree right down to her sheeny skin, so the fallers would know to leave this one -- for him. Then he descended the ridge to where the crummy waited.

A few days later, the crummy full of sleepy-eyed loggers bounced along a logging road. It made a sharp turn onto a new spar road. The driver geared down and the crummy pulled the ridge where the last spar tree stood. The timber fallers had been busy, opening up the sky. Soon the sun was going to rise and the light shine in. Whitey saw the tree ahead rising up and out of the glare of headlights. The naked X glowed in the light beam.

"Thar's our baby!" exclaimed Milo when he saw the branded tree.

The crew let out a whoop. They unloaded from the crummy, and stood about in the glare. They were sipping coffee, chatting at the base of the tree.

Last night saw rain, but now the stars were shining overhead. Whitey pulled in a deep breath and held it. There is no place on Earth so sweet as the high Cascade forests on the morning of the first day after a summer night's rain. Tiny, thirsty resinous needles, thick with the scents of the woods, had sucked in the warm water and bloated themselves in the cool of the night. Now, they were feeling the warmth of the morning and expanding and releasing their essence to keep from bursting. The smell of lava cinder mingled into the musty scent of virgin Earth. Water was in the air, suspended there, invisible Cascade water. Water so pure it contains no taste, no aroma. Cool as moss, like crystal, it fills the atmosphere and magnifies the elements.

These young loggers lapped it in with every flick of their jocular tongues and sniffed it up with each breath they took. The elixir made them giddy. They were wide awake, fixed, laughing and having a great time.

Milo was standing next to the tree. He patted it like it was a friendly dog, looked over at Whitey, and said: "This one's gonna test ya." Then he sidled up to Whitey, looked him in the eye, and quietly said: "All kiddin' aside, is it *big* enough?"

Whitey didn't answer. Milo wasn't waiting for one: "Too damned big, Whitey. What were you thinking about? Why this one? It's likely full of heart rot." Milo was concerned because he knew what the others didn't. He was a natural and in a previous time he would've been a highclimber himself. The bigger and older a spar tree is, the more likely it will split and spread when the top falls free, especially if rot's set in. "Why this particular one?" he insisted.

"I didn't have any choice in the matter," said Whitey. He walked around the tree, sizing it up for the job at hand. *Let the men dawdle for a while. This job is not to be rushed,* he thought. Then, wanting to set Milo at ease: "Thanks for your concern, Milo. Believe me when I say that I can assure you that she doesn't have a single rotten fiber in her heart; she never outgrew it."

Milo studied Whitey's face for a long moment, then grinning real big, said: "*She* doesn't, does *she? She* didn't, did *she.* What the hell, anyway. Who am *I* to debate with *you?* I'm not the highclimber."

Said Whitey: "Don't sell yourself short, Milo."

Milo turned and walked off. But he was an intuitive logger, and he sensed something that didn't set right, unsettled him. How was he to know that he was feeling finality? He couldn't just turn and walk away like this. Something in it just seemed too damned certain. So he looked back over his shoulder and said: "I still don't like the smell of this . . . I just hope you climb back down from there."

"So do I, Milo . . . So do I."

Milo went on his way.

Whitey returned to the crummy, picked up his climbing gear, and walked out to a stump and sat down on it, facing east. The sky was starting to glow. The same mountains that he had to peek through the trees to see just a few days before this were in clear view because all those trees were felled. There they lay, nice and neat, in long strung-out vertical lines, not one crossing the other. Those fallers knew their art. The mountains were dark against the pink horizon, protruding like canines out of a wolf's jaw. Even old Three-Fingered Jack looked distinguished in this light—shadow hid the rubble at his base.

Whitey poured a cup of coffee. He waved Milo over and said: "Set the crew to it. You're in charge. I've got me a tree to top."

Milo put aside his concerns of a moment ago, jumped upon the stump, and hollered: "Okay, girls, off your plump bottoms." Then he sprang from the truck and headed for his cat. The men snapped to and busied about their duties. They fired up their machines, and the forest roared with echoes. Then they started stringing out the cables and laying out the block and tackle.

Whitey sipped his coffee and smiled. Milo was going to make one hell of a side boss.

The approaching sun pushed against the horizon, making it bow. The sky glowed bright red, trimmed with yellow. Lucifer sat burning in the east. Whitey kicked off his moccasins and laced up his corks. He rolled down his red wool socks into a neat tuft at the boot tops. As always, on the day he topped a tree, he was dressed in his best: corks were freshly greased, stagged-off jeans were unsoiled and supported with wide red suspenders, hickory shirt was neatly pressed, and his red and black checkered jacket held off the chill. On this day he was the undisputed king of the woods, therefore subject to no rules but his own and so he wore his old metal dough-boy hat. The hat glowed silver, tinged with pink. He poured another cup of coffee and took his time sipping at it because it takes Time and the patience of a tree to practice indifference. After all, this was going to be his last climb and perhaps, just maybe, the end of his personal time, because departing gods and goddesses don't like to leave their mortal lovers behind.

Soon as he saw the first sliver of the wide eye of the sun he took his axe in hand and said: "Well now, sister of Ruby, are *you* ready for this?" Then he stood and walked over to the spar tree. He buckled up his climbing belt, strapped on the leggings and tested his spurs. He looped the tree with the rope. Then, flicking up the rope and stepping up the spurs and trailing his axe on a tether, he climbed the tree. The eye of the sun grew wider with the men's. Old Sol was as red as blood, and Lucifer was blazing himself away into nothing. From east to west the sky was one huge rainbow, color pressing against color, merging slightly at the pressure points. With his old double-lipped axe, he cut the face. Then, using the cord, he pulled up his harp, kept his cadence smooth and timely, and cut into the cheeks of the face from the other side of the tree -- no hurry, no rush – steady and deliberate. And the sun rose higher in the sky. Finally, feeling it give, he dropped down a few feet and dug in the spurs, leaned against the line, and waited for whatever was to come.

The old tree queen lost her crown with a groan and a shriek. It fell to the ground and set the spar to swaying. Round and round and to and fro it went, moaning and quivering. The sky spun about overhead and he felt the pressure strain against the rope. And then she settled down and relaxed and his spurs were still digging and the rope was still holding and the bole was still whole, and his heart still beat – a thousand times a minute. After she settled and while she quivered he bent his knees and scurried to the top and sat there silently, like he always did when he honored the dead. The world opened up from here. The sun was bright yellow, bulging. Lucifer was a burnt cinder. As always, today's sun rose on a brand new day. The end of an age—more than an age—a world had set with yesterday's. Today's sun is yesterday's but today's is always new and this day's rose on the end of an age—more than an age—a world had set with yesterday's sun. A song was over, a theme was done, but the fiddle still plays. And Whitey was glad. He hadn't known whether he was to remain or be taken out on this climb. But that was because he'd woven himself in a little too tightly with his jack, and who is a mere timberjack to question the will of his queen? But a queen is wise -- that's why she's a queen -- and so she knew that he was far more than just a timberjack. He was a man who had another lover whom he loved even more than he loved her and who loved him right back. And besides that, she held no choice in the matter: who is a mere goddess to counter the will of a woman?

This tree was the last spar tree, and Whitey was the last highclimber. This day finalized the era of the big woods and the people of the big woods and their mythical timberjacks. As dry autumn leaves swept away by the wind, the big woods vanished from the sight of men. The man who looks for them will find them only in linier history and broad myth and in old grainy photographs, showing giant trees and weary-faced men shouldering their harps and determined women standing alongside their grimy children, fading away with time in the pages of books written by dead men.

Then, it was as though the hamadryad of the tree, departing the severed heart, entered in through his bung, his eyes, his ears, his nostrils, his mouth, and the pores of his skin, flooding his soul for a brief moment, to where it overflowed its timeworn banks. His knees were limber and his legs felt like branches that wanted to sway in the wind and he moved his legs up and down and he shook his feet like leaves. It was as if he filled with sappy hydraulics that went surging through flesh and bones and flushed his long-held fear of heights. He unbuckled his rigging and bent his knees. He lifted his feet, removed his spurs, and then pulled his legs under him with an easy motion and squatted on his hands and feet high up on the pinnacle of the spar. And there he crouched, for a frozen moment, as still and silent as some old stone gargoyle, staring eastward beyond the peaks. Magic fluid, like some heavy logger ale, seeped his mind, turning him light-headed. And it was as if a subtle will, not his own and yet not foreign, unbent his knees and stood him straight up. He'd never stood so tall. Far below, the men paused in their labor, laid their heads against their backs, stretched their throats and pointed their Adam's apples at the sky and gawked in disbelief. He lifted a foot and wiggled it, and then lifted the other. His legs felt springy and his feet felt as light as feathers. There was a strange little tickle in his toes. It seemed the queen wanted one last dance. He thought he heard music starting up from somewhere far away, and he cocked his ear. In a sudden flash, the forest life below his feet took to flight. A chorus of dryads was singing and sylphs were dancing to an old classical score. A soft breeze drifted in, zephyrs whispered through the limbs, and the trees gently swayed back and forth. To Whitey's ears it sounded like the tune of a familiar old timberjack gig. The fiddle was playing:

> *"Welll, nowww, grab up yer axe 'n go t' choppin'.*
> *Then, head for the halls an' go t' rompin'.*
> *An' kick up yer calks an' go t' stompin'.*
> *Yes 'n dance yer life away lad."*

He raised his hands into the air, as if saluting the sun and a new day. Then, to the orchestration of the dryads, he cut a rug to the lively step of the music he heard: *"Yes'n, play yer life away lad; Play yer life awayyy . . ."* And he threw back his head and laughed. Then the old timberjack: logger, king of the highclimbers, living legend of the big woods, like a loyal subject should, died away with his queen, leaving a man dancing on that spar, simply a man—the old woodsman—food for slugs. He danced and he laughed and he danced and he laughed.

Before long, the last of the old timberbeast tall tale tellers departed Earth, making room for other great things to appear. But they weren't forgotten, and now woodsy folk emulate them through their wordy talk in the bistros and the honky-tonks and around the campfires. But having never shouldered their own saw the emulators are not nearly so polished. They have a feel for what they want to tell; they just don't know how to put a certain woeful but easy-going cadence to their rhyme. Except for imitation, emulation holds nothing to lose, to leave behind, and so there is no tone of sorrow in their song. Ambitious to surpass, they try to sing too high and so their tellings are too tall for the foundation. The tale went about that Whitey spread his arms and sprouted wings like a red tailed hawk and flew off that spar and disappeared going westbound. According to the men who were present this was just a lot of farfetched tall tale telling. "He didn't fly away till later," they said. They told that Whitey topped the tree and rigged it, but he didn't utter another word. When the job was finally finished, he was the last one on the crummy and the first to step off. He didn't show up to catch the crummy the next morning, and they waited. After some time, Milo went down to his camp, but it was gone, and the ashes were cold in the firepit. They rode along with heavy hearts that day, because they all knew they'd never see him again.

When they arrived at the logging site, they were astonished to see the old ruby-headed, double-lipped axe kissing the spar tree where the crosses of the X-mark came together. Each man took his turn at trying to pull it free. None could budge it. When the show was finished and its job was done, they fell the spar and bucked it with the axe still stuck in it. Last they saw, it was riding high upon the topside of the log of a one-log-loaded log truck, headed for the mill. Where it went to from there, who can tell? One thing's for sure: no one ever pulled it out. Or so the telling goes. But who knows?

Still, even to this day, some tall tale tellers tell that Whitey flew away free with the spirit of the tree. And the literalists stick to their claim that this is far-fetched exaggeration, but they're hard-pressed to explain how he vanished so completely.

Rhyming Little Willy was still tramping along life's trail at this time. Not long before he bent his last step, he told the last one of his many little tales, about Whitey. These are some of the words:

"From these woods, they say ol' Whitey has gone away.
To where he went, no man knows, though some say,
to where the free forest grows, he still goes.
He climbed over the summits of the mind,
to far from here, higher than time.
If you care t' find him, search if you dare.
Bend yer knees and go up there,
to where the forest queen reigns:
along the high crests,
deep in the tall trees,
where the timberjack rests,
where the timberwolf sings."

About the Author

Dean Barton grew up in the woods of western Oregon in a large clan of loggers and log truckers. He spent much of his childhood in the Lava Lake logging camp that is described in Book Two. He worked in the shop, and drove a water wagon and log trucks. Dean farms in western Oregon where he grows commercial trees, raises livestock on managed pastures, and stewards wildlife habitat. He lives with his family—Elena, Max, and Lily. Darcy is all grown and lives in California with her husband.